ABOUT MAGGIE LE PAGE

Maggie lives in Christchurch, New Zealand with her partner and two children. By day she juggles motherhood, part-time work, and general household drudgery. By night she turns feral until everyone leaves her in peace to write—usually around midnight. She is ably assisted at the keyboard by her ultra-fluffy, ultra-talkative cat who is quick to 'assume the position' (on Maggie's lap, tail draped over keys).

Maggie's favourite pastime is escaping to a café to people-watch and catch snippets of conversation, extrapolating wildly to invent new characters. Maggie loves travel, reading, and lazy hazy beach days, preferably presented to her as a tropical island holiday combo. (She lives in hope.)

For more information:

Visit Maggie's website www.maggielepage.com
or
Find Maggie on Facebook www.facebook.com/maggielepage

A
Heat of the Moment Thing

Maggie Le Page

A Heat Of The Moment Thing is a work of fiction. Names, characters, places and incidents in this novel are either the product of the author's imagination or used fictitiously. Any resemblance to actual people, either living or dead, to events, businesses, or locales is entirely coincidental.

ISBN: 978-0-473-24046-2

FOR EV

For believing in me, even when I didn't.
For putting up with the lonely evenings and crazy hours and wild mood swings.
For reminding me to sleep every now and then.
For being you.

ACKNOWLEDGEMENTS

Writing a novel sounded like a nice diversion when I first embarked on it; a fun thing to do in my spare time. Spare time? Ha! I thought I knew what it involved. Another ha!

Now, though, I do know what it involves. I also know that without the help of a whole bunch of people, this novel would not be what it is today—and nor would I.

Firstly, my family. You've been an incredible support in this crazy journey of mine. I only hope I can do the same for each of you in your own life journeys. My heart is full to bursting with love for you all.

My critique partners, Bronwen Evans and Gracie O'Neil. Thank you, girls, for everything. Your friendship, talent, feedback, advice, inspiration . . . everything. You're both a special part of my life, and you always take my writing to the next level.

My cyber-home: the BI50D loop. We may live in different islands—countries, even—but you're always there for me. Without the camaraderie, drive, focus and expertise of our loop I'd be bereft. I love you all.

Catherine Robertson and Toni Kenyon. You really went the extra mile for me. Thank you. Your comments helped me gain distance and perspective when I needed it most.

Harriet Allan (Random House) for your detailed and honest feedback. It was exactly the butt-kick I needed and I hope we have the opportunity to work together in the future.

Eve Boyce (now sadly departed) and Sue Yorke. What an amazing mother-daughter team! I squirm when I think of that incredibly 'green' first draft you both critiqued. It was so very, very early in my writing career and you treated me with the kid gloves I needed. Without your input, I doubt I would have reached this point in my writing.

Ian Bieniowski (of Lothian Buses Plc), for brainstorming bus accidents with me and not assuming I was a complete nutter; also for the Edinburgh bus route specifics.

Jen, for the emergency room flavour. Suran, for the Brodrick Road setting. Janet, LaVerne, and Nicki for the cerebral palsy insights.

Jules, Mands, Nick, Rach, Sonja, Steph and Trish, for beta-reading Becky so willingly.

Finally: Carla Munro, Charitha Fernando, Heather Smyth, and Peter Walker; local writing buddies who became dear, dear friends. I'm sure you all ended up sick to the back teeth of Becky, but Becky thanks you! Those fortnightly slatings improved my writing, and this novel, immensely.

CHAPTER ONE

Feathers of anxiety fluttered in my gut as I took in the busy swimming lanes. Why did I keep putting myself through this? "Liz, I don't think—"

"No thinking allowed. Forty laps, then coffee. Right?" Her smile sweetened her words but she had that don't-muck-with-me look in her eyes and, best friend or not, she wasn't letting me off the hook.

The feathers moved up, nasty tickles of nerves making straight for my throat. "Um . . ."

Liz frowned, cocked her head to one side. "You okay, Becs?"

"I—it's busy. You know I hate crowded pools."

She glanced at my lane. "Six swimmers. That's not bad."

Only six? I squinted down at the blurry blobs, doing my own head-count. Three swimmers coming at me each lap. It could be worse.

It could be a lot better, too. I always wore my contacts under my goggles. Why, oh why, had I forgotten them? Even with twenty-twenty vision, lane-swimming wasn't my idea of fun. But short-sighted?

"I'll come back this evening," I said.

"Hey." She squeezed my hand. "You'll be fine. You've been doing this for months now."

"Yeah, but today I'm half-blind."

She sighed. "Becs. You can't back out now. We made a *commitment*."

Sheesh, we were swimming for fitness, not the Olympics.

I cast around for a better excuse as I drew my hair—miraculously straight, thanks to my genius hairdresser—into a ponytail. "I didn't bring a swimming cap. What if my hair turns green? Or goes back to halo-frizz?" Then, "If I start my new job looking like a freak I'll blame you."

"Come on." Liz made for the fast lane as usual and dived in.

Damn. I faced my blurry, congested lane.

It wasn't like I really *needed* to see, right? If I could feel my way through London's infamous fogs, I could make it down a swimming lane. I plopped into the water, adjusted my goggles, waved a swimmer on. Okay—now. With a nervous glance at the next swimmer I pushed off, doing something approximating freestyle.

Next New Year's there would be *no* resolutions, *no* good intentions, and if I had to drink soda water all night to avoid Liz's pinkie promises, then so be it. Seriously—swimming? What the hell kind of New Year's resolution was that?

Warning bubbles fizzed past my cheeks. I lifted my head and stared as some lane-hogging idiot approached in a mess of arms and churned-up water. What was he doing? Oh, for goodness sake . . . *butterfly?* I held my breath, thought thin and scraped past, earning a poke in the ribs and a clipped ankle.

I switched to backstroke, plunging my annoyance into my strokes.

Get fit, to hell with men, have a life. It had sounded good at the time, but the fitness thing? Big mistake. Even so, lose that resolution and I'd still be winning. Fancy new haircut, fancy new job, and as for asshole Mickey—Mickey who?

Butterfly guy's next attack was an arm-*thunk* to the head that knocked my goggles askew and turned my in-breath into an in-water. I floundered, spluttering. No time to rest, though: behind me approached another swimmer, then another. I did a one-handed goggle adjustment and reverted to freestyle, but I'd lost my rhythm. Each breath became a gasp. My legs sank, my arms slowed. Come *on*. I forced my head down, counting the strokes, kicking faster, regulating my breathing.

Poker-hot pain exploded in my head. I gasped, taking in a mouthful of water that burned a fiery route straight down to my lungs. I choked.

Air! I clawed for oxygen. Surfaced. Floundered.

Pain. Pain everywhere.

Lazy swirls of red blended with the water. My world kaleidoscoped then shattered into dizzy blackness. Thunder in my head. Rocks in my limbs. Inferno in my lungs.

Everything decelerated. White noise pressed in, closer and closer. Fear mutated into raw panic. Please don't let me die. Not now. Not ready. Too young.

My heart pumped louder and faster, louder and faster. Shite. Maybe thirty-one wasn't too young.

2

Louder and faster, louder and faster, louder and faster, until the din obliterated everything . . . obliterated me.

* * *

Flying, floating, swirling with the current.

Where was I? Somewhere dark. Black hole dark.

Icy knowledge inched up my spine. I'd died. I'd really gone and died.

Regret and anger washed over me, and on their heels, confusion.

Why? What had happened?

The floaty sensation stopped with a jolt. This was it, then. The Heaven/Hell decision. A *way* bigger deal than sitting my A-levels, and look how badly I'd screwed them up. This wasn't going to end well.

Then, like dawn infiltrating the night sky, I realised I could feel. Poolside tiles, cool and rough against my skin. Pain—the same shrieking pain I'd felt earlier. And my heartbeat, fast and erratic, sweet certain proof I wasn't dead at all.

Which should have been a relief, but I had other things to deal with. Like breathing. And—oh, dear God—something was wrong. Where was the air? My eyes bulged in panic. Dying once was bad enough, but twice in one day?

Strong arms manhandled me into the recovery position. I coughed and retched and brought up half a swimming pool of water, my head bouncing off the tiles. Agony rippled through me. I groaned.

"Try to relax. Just breathe. Focus in, and breathe." A chocolate-y voice seeped through my senses. Rich, smooth, compelling.

Oh, the effort of breathing.

"That's it." I felt a warm hand on my back. "You're doing really well."

Idiot. I didn't feel even remotely well.

And would everyone just shut up? What was their problem? Shouting, screams, people dashing this and that. "So much blood!"; "Get help!"; "Bloody hell! What happened to her?"; and even "She's dead!", to which the chocolate voice, near my head, replied, "No, she's not."

Crap. Was this cacophony about me?

"Don't try to sit," said Chocolate. "Take it easy. You'll be fine." Then louder, "We need a lifeguard. And an ambulance. Someone call 999." And to me, "Good girl. Keep breathing. An ambulance is on its way." He stroked my back.

I began to shiver, and even that hurt. I whimpered. My head felt as if someone had picked me up and used me as a battering ram.

Chocolate arranged a towel over me and, somehow, his comforting touch soothed the hurt in my head. In the distance a siren wailed. What had happened? Swimming, that's right. The swimmer's arm had come down on me, but then what? Pain in my head. I must've swum into something. Another swimmer? The wall?

I attempted to prop myself upright. Made it painstakingly to all fours and willed my body not to collapse.

"Careful there," Chocolate warned.

I waited for the dizziness to clear. It didn't.

"Sorry," I whispered, falling back against him.

"No bother." He shifted into a sitting position behind me, his legs and arms enveloping me. "The ambulance will be here soon."

Gently, rhythmically, he stroked my arms and I relaxed into him. Eventually, quietly, steadily, his hands moved up to my head. I stiffened.

"Don't forget to breathe," he said. "I'll try not to hurt you."

His fingers sifted through my matted hair and I winced as he found the spot, on top of my head, where I'd obviously connected with whatever-it-was.

"I think," he murmured in my ear, so close I could feel his heartbeat against my back, "you'll need a few stitches, but you're going to be fine."

"Okay, folks. Give us some space, please." A gruff voice took control. "The lady needs air."

This must be the paramedics, then. I tried to sit up straighter.

"Take your time," Chocolate told me, staying exactly where he was. "No need to rush."

Indeed not; not when I had him at my back. It was an Arctic blast when he gently squeezed my shoulders, removed his hands, and stood.

The paramedics took over, briskly checking my wound before flashing an interrogation-strength light in my eyes. I flinched. They watched intently.

The dark, weedy one spoke up. "What's your name, Love?"

I closed my eyes against the light. "Rebecca Jordan. Becky."

4

"And what day is it, Becky?"

Clearly he was checking I still had all my faculties. I did. Every last one hurt. "Saturday. Fifteenth July."

"Excellent." He inspected first one, then the other, eye. "Hmm."

'Hmm' what? But I never found out because, at that moment, Liz appeared.

"Becky!" she shrieked, pushing her way to the front of the oglers.

"You're bleeding!" She sank to her knees, all but elbowing the medic out of the way. "What happened?"

Good question.

"She hit the end of the pool," said Chocolate. "I was in the next lane."

Oh no! Shame ripped through my body. How could I be so stupid?

Liz touched my arm. "You what? Why?"

I looked at her, shrugged an I-don't-know. My lip trembled.

"Hey, it doesn't matter," she said, then grimaced. "Sorry, Becs. Headache. I was off taking painkillers."

She backed off as the second paramedic, a chubby fresh-faced kid, brought over a stretcher.

Excited murmurs from the crowd. Horror from me. Stretchers were for half-dead rugby heroes, not me.

I wiped my eyes, took a shaky breath. "I'm okay now, thanks." A barefaced lie, but I didn't want to make any more of a spectacle of myself than I already had, half-naked and all.

I eased myself to all fours. Standing would be a challenge. Even breathing wasn't high on my list of favourites.

The staring masses reminded me of beady-eyed seagulls, creeping ever closer. I wanted to yell at them, wave my arms, scare them off, but I had to make do with closing my eyes.

"Becky, we're taking you to A&E," said Chubby Kid, displaying an unexpected assertive streak. "You need stitches, and you may have concussion."

Nice.

They manoeuvred me onto the stretcher and I felt like a six-year-old who'd just wet her pants in front of the whole class.

Liz hovered at my shoulder, a sympathetic hand on my arm. "I'll go get our gear," she said, and disappeared.

Where was Chocolate? I missed him. Everything seemed easier when he was near. I opened my eyes and scanned the crowd.

Ah, there. He stood at a discreet distance, just in front of the onlookers. My blurred vision definitely didn't do him justice—he looked sort-of blended and abstract—but I could see he was tall and tanned, with swimmer's shoulders tapering down to slim hips. Mmm.

I smiled. Saw a flash of teeth as he smiled back.

"I think my swim's over," he said and tugged off his black swimming cap.

Ooh! Tanned *and* blond: my favourite Man Combo.

Liz reappeared at my side, packhorse-ish with all our gear, as the paramedics trundled me out of the leisure centre.

Hang on a minute! That man—Chocolate—had just saved my *life*. Blond, tanned, fantastic hands, and a hero to boot. I needed to at least thank him.

"Stop," I commanded my stretcher-bearers. "Just for a second," I pleaded. "I need to thank my rescuer."

They paused, but didn't lower the stretcher. *Make it quick, lady*—the message was clear.

I lifted my head. Chocolate had turned to go.

"Excuse me," I croaked.

Oh no. He hadn't heard.

"Hey, Mister!" The weedy one called out. "Lady got somethin' to say."

Chocolate stopped, looked back at us, then walked over to my stretcher.

"Thanks," I said. "You saved my life." I lifted a hand towards him. "I . . . Well, thanks. Thanks so much."

He smiled at me and, even without my lenses in, I felt warmed. Then he squeezed my hand. My limbs turned weak and this time I couldn't blame it on drowning.

"Glad I could help," he said in that chocolate voice, then turned and headed to the changing rooms.

"Hold on a—hey! Stop! Please! Let me buy you a . . ."

Too late. Chocolate had just walked out of my life as quickly as he had walked—or, rather, swam—into it.

CHAPTER TWO

"Did you get his number?"

Liz frowned at me as if I'd just asked her to run naked through the hospital. "No. Was I meant to?"

"Of course you were. How can I ring him if I don't have his number? Ouch!" I glanced down at the offending needle, then up at my nurse. "I think you've drained me now."

She gave me a sympathetic smile. "Not much longer," she said, but I'd already turned back to Liz. "Tell me you at least know his name."

"Becs, I barely saw him. I was getting in the ambulance with you, remember?"

"All done," murmured the nurse.

"So," I said. "No name and no number. Some friend you turned out to be."

Liz arched an eyebrow. "Hey, I'm not psychic. Anyway, I thought you said you weren't dating anymore."

"I'm not."

The nurse briskly taped some cotton-wool to my arm, then secured a blood pressure cuff to the other arm.

"It's just typical," I grumbled, "that when a decent man finally turns up in my life I'm in no fit state to do anything about it." *Pump, pump, pump.* The pressure built in my arm. "Do you think he's married?"

"No idea."

"I think he's single."

"You would." Liz's tone was parchment-dry.

Phsssht. The pressure slowly released.

I glared at her. "You're making fun of me!"

She laughed.

"Liz, I know you think I'm a sap, but I really felt a connection with him. I'm sure he felt it, too."

"Of course you felt a freaking connection. He was saving your life."

"Gosh," the nurse murmured as she noted my blood pressure. Then, more loudly, "I think we'd better take another reading. Are you relaxing, Rebecca?"

Warm, considerate, strong, determined, good-looking, great hands . . . How often did I meet a guy with a near-perfect score?

I leaned forward, my voice urgent. "Liz, I have to find him again. Be a pal. Dash back to the pool and get his name and number."

"He'll be long gone."

"Someone will know him. Go!"

"I'm not leaving you here on your own."

The nurse huffed and puffed. "I'll take it again later, then." She whipped the blood pressure cuff off with bad grace. "Rebecca. Please. No more talking. Just for a few minutes. I'm going to dress the wound and I need you to be still."

"Oh, okay." I widened my eyes at Liz and jerked my head toward the door.

Liz responded with a loud "No" and folded her arms.

I shot her a mutinous look. She looked away. The nurse hummed as she applied the dressing to my scalp, securing it with a stupendous bandage that looped under my chin. I eventually recognised the tune: *Just My Imagination*. Great. Even the nurse was picking on me.

"Right," Nursie concluded, "that'll do until Doctor Palmer can do your stitches."

My stomach clenched with raw fear. Stitches?

With a forced smile she departed, her sensible shoes squeak-squeaking on the linoleum.

I shot Liz a panicked look.

She grimaced.

We were silent a few moments.

"Thanks for staying," I muttered.

"Oh, Becs." She bridged the gap between us and gave me a much-needed but ever-so-gentle hug. "You don't need to thank me."

All hints of teasing gone, she perched on the edge of the bed and looked at me, her face etched with worry. "I should never have pushed you into swimming."

"Rubbish. It's good for me."

Her chin trembled. She sucked in her lips, breathed deep. "I thought you were dead."

"Hardly." I reached out and nudged her arm. "I was whining too much."

"All I could see was blood. Your blood." She shuddered, closed her eyes.

"Everywhere," she added in a whisper.

Oh dear. I squeezed her hand, then tugged at my bandage with a forced a grin. "Do I look as stupid as I feel?"

She took in my headgear and her lips moved in a faint echo of a smile. "Yes."

"Oh no!" My heart skipped a beat before hurrying to catch up. "What about my new job? I'll still be able to start on Monday, won't I?"

Liz hesitated. "You'd better ask the doctor. Does it matter?"

I wiped clammy palms down my wafer-thin blanket. "Of course it matters. First impressions are everything."

"It's not as if you've just got a cold. I'm sure they'll understand."

"Yeah, that they've employed an idiot."

"They don't need to know the kamikaze-into-the-wall bit. Just say you've been in hospital."

"But they'll think 'hypochondriac' and demand details, and it'll slip out." I picked at the blanket. "You *know* I'm a terrible liar."

"So go with the truth, Becs."

"Uh-nuh. No way. It's too embarrassing."

I chewed on a fingernail. It started to bleed. "Blast."

"Grief, Becs." Liz shifted on the bed. "What is it with you and blood today?"

I sucked my finger. We fell silent. Liz stood and paced. I day-dreamed about my delicious rescuer. Maybe I should lift my dating ban.

"I've never had a hero before," I said.

"Becs . . ." Liz shot me a warning look.

"What? It's true."

She groaned. "I know you. You're about to turn this into another man-fantasy. He was Johnny On The Spot, that's all."

"Liz. Trust me. I'm over men. Forever."

"If only."

9

I avoided her eyes. Then looked up with a *mea culpa* grin. She saw right through me and we both knew it. "He is gorgeous, though."

"How would you know? You were half-blind. And he was wearing a swimming cap. *Nobody* looks good like that."

"I can see past a mere swimming cap," I declared, then immediately made a liar of myself, "Do you think he's got curly hair or straight? Long or short? He's blond. I think. He looked blond, anyway. And you know what I'm like with blond men."

"Becs, you're an idiot." Liz gave me an affectionate smile. "But fantasize away; you won't be doing anything else for a day or two."

I planned to do just that.

* * *

Jim, my un-heroic house-mate, knew something had happened as soon as Liz and I walked through the door. Not that it was exactly rocket science.

Observation One: We had just arrived home, swimming gear in tow, seven hours after leaving. We don't swim marathons. Especially on Saturdays.

Observation Two: I was sporting a bald patch and stitches, looking very much the worse for wear. Admittedly, I often look the worse for wear, but I don't often do the other two.

Observation Three: Liz's over-attentiveness was faintly reminiscent of eighteenth-century courtship rituals, and I wasn't even questioning it. We're close, but not that close.

Jim's face took on a horrified wish-I'd-never-come-out-of-my-room expression. He edged towards the stairs.

I hobbled into the lounge and eased myself into the nearest chair.

Liz hung back to give Jim an abrupt Reader's Digest version of events.

"She's fragile . . .", ". . . probably concussed . . .", and ". . . needs watching . . ."

"I'm not deaf," I called out.

They came through and Jim hovered in the doorway with a deer-in-the-headlights expression.

Liz carefully positioned a cushion behind my back. "Comfy?"

"As I'll ever be," I muttered.

"Okay." She paused, brought a hand to her head, then refocused on me. "So. You've got painkillers. And you should probably eat." She ticked off her fingers. "Then get to bed. And sleep. Soon. Okay?"

"Yes, Mum."

"Right. Well, if you think you're okay . . ."

"I'm fine."

"Great. I'll go and sleep off this headache, then."

"Sure. Jim's here."

She made a moue as she walked to the door. "That's what I'm worried about."

With a warning glare for Jim and an "I'll ring you" for me, Liz left.

"Thanks," I called after her.

Jim ventured further into the lounge and stood, watching me guardedly. Jules, my battle-scarred cat, took the polar-opposite approach and jumped into my lap. He lifted a leg and started licking his nether regions. Lovely.

When Jim didn't leap in with one of his usual bad-taste comments I knew he must be really worried.

I looked up at him. "Hey, you don't have to take her quite so literally." Gave a small smile, "I'll let you know if I feel any worse, I promise."

"O-kaaay," he said, eyeballing me as if I were about to expire. "How about a cup of tea?"

I pulled a face. "How about a Bourbon, more like. Something a bit more appealing than a cup of bloody tea."

"Er, I don't think so." He scratched at his five-day blue-black stubble. George Clooney wears it a lot better than Jim. "Not for me, and definitely not for you."

"Why not? After the day I've had?" Irritation stirred in me. "I can tell you, right now I'm in need of some Jim and we both know I don't mean you."

His silence ricocheted off the walls.

"You think one small drink's going to make me fall down the stairs and rip all my stitches?" I flared.

"No-o," he said, clearly meaning yes.

He glanced longingly towards the door, and I felt guilty for snapping.

Hell, it wasn't *his* fault I'd ended up with stitches. Or that the med. student who'd applied them had felt compelled, in spite of my vanity protest, to shave a patch of my blood-soaked hair.

I sighed. As much for me as for Jim.

"Sorry, Jim. I know you're just worried about me. But"—I fluttered my eyelashes at him—"it's only one little Bourbon."

He frowned. "Don't do that eye thing with me," he said, uncharacteristically stuffy. "It won't work. It's tea or nothing."

"Fine," I snarled. "I'll have nothing."

I tossed a yowling Jules off me, creaked to my feet and, wishing I had the energy to slam the door, hauled myself upstairs.

Bloody Jim. Since when had he turned into Hitler? I crawled into bed. Yanked the duvet up. What was his problem? I eased my throbbing head into a more comfortable position. A lump rose in my throat, resentment threatening to mutate into self-pitying tears. Why had I lumbered myself with such an insensitive ass of a house-mate? And for how many years? I did the sums. Heavens, *nine*, no less. Time for a change.

Yuk. Chlorine. I swallowed, but the taste lingered. Ditto the band of fire in my chest. I tried to keep my breathing shallow but it didn't help. A tear escaped. How long until my next dose of paracetamol?

Eventually, calmer—but no less sore—I stopped hating Jim. I even, grudgingly, allowed that perhaps he hadn't been acting out of insensitivity so much as—well, the opposite. I shouldn't be annoyed with him at all: I should be *glad* to see he cared. And it did prove that, despite all evidence to the contrary, he had at least a smattering of decency in him.

Chocolate. What was his real name? I stared up at the ceiling with its flaking paint. Rob? Declan? If only I knew his address. Not that I'd stalk him or anything. But it would be nice to . . . chat. Thank him. Get to know him. Music, sports, hobbies, whatever. Meet the man inside the hero.

And there I went again.

I closed my eyes. Forget it, Becs. He'd been there when I needed help, that's all. Dig deeper and he'd be like every other jerk I'd wasted a second thought on.

My new job, on the other hand—*that* was worth thinking about.

Imagine! Me, a travel lecturer. I wiggled my toes with anticipation, or maybe nerves. Travel agent to lecturer was quite some change. A whole new career, really.

And two days before it began I'd gone and splattered my head open. Typical.

Still, with paracetamol on board I should be able to start on Monday. I fingered a crunchy curl. A scarf should do it.

I limped to the mirror and—oh God. Make that a paper bag.

Where was my beautiful hundred-plus-pound, starting-a-new-job haircut? The blood-clotted dreads were a right mess, but the med. student's shearing skills had really topped it off.

It could only happen to me.

Ooh! The Riviera! *They'd* tell me Chocolate's name and then I could ring him. Tonight, even.

Pulse tripping with excitement, I shuffled to the phone and dialled the swimming pool.

"We cannot take your call at present. Our hours are . . ."

Stupid bloody digital voice. Served me right. Ridiculous love quests did not lead to happiness. Fantastic careers did. And the sooner I remembered that the better.

CHAPTER THREE

My scarf's reflection bounced off the elevator doors, and Jim's Belisha Beacon comment taunted me. Cripes. He was right. I looked ridiculous.

The doors opened, 'Gillingas Tertiary College – Tourism and Travel Division' greeted me in proud gold lettering, and it was too late to bail out. I took a bracing breath and approached reception.

"Hi. I'm Jebecca Rordan—" I blushed. "I mean, Rebecca Jordan. I'm here to see Gary Silverton."

Perfect. Now they'd think I was dyslexic as well.

The receptionist choked back a laugh. "You're the new lecturer, right? I'll page Gary for you." She glanced at me, all innocence. "Jebecca, was it?"

Just as she said 'Jebecca', a suited, senior manager-ish looking man emerged behind her. His eyebrow shot up. My cheeks flamed Belisha Beacon-bright.

The receptionist turned to him with a smile. "Speak of the devil. Gary, this is—"

She paused.

I cringed.

She shot me a doe-eyed look. "—Rebecca Jordan."

I sagged with relief.

"Ah. Becky." Gary came around her desk and shook my hand. "Welcome to Gillingas Tertiary College."

"Thanks." I fingered my new headscarf. Was it slipping? I had a Worzel Gummidge horror hidden under there.

"How are you feeling?" Gary's eyes fixated on the headscarf. "Sounds like you had a close call."

"Much better, thanks." I dropped my hand back to my side. "Sorry I couldn't—"

14

I gasped, feeling serious scarf slippage, and grabbed at my head.

Gary, with a stricken look, tried to help. It only made things worse. The headscarf, hooked on my finger, shifted floorward, then skyward, before collapsing with ballerina grace in my hands.

I stared in dismay at the mess of fabric.

"Oh dear," said Gary. "Here, let me help you."

No. I scrambled for my headscarf, curse the sodding thing, and wheeled away, consumed by full-body flaming shame. "If you could just show me to the ladies' . . ."

The receptionist leapt out of her chair. "I'll take you. Would you like some pins?" She fossicked around in a drawer and produced a handful.

"Thanks."

Curse this rotten scarf. Curse the med. student who'd left me with a bald patch. And curse me for swimming into the end of the freaking pool.

When I returned, headscarf secured to hurricane-proof standards, Gary took me on the grand tour of Tourism and Travel.

Nerves fluttered in my belly, only partly due to the scarf. I'd taken a huge gamble with this job. Could I make it work?

Gary stopped and opened a door with a flourish. "Here's your office."

My office. Nice. I'd only ever worked in open plan offices, where you couldn't even yawn in private. I walked over to the window. Lush lines of oak trees and a green expanse of park stared back up at me. Pleasure swelled in my chest. As far as London views went, this was pretty damn good.

"I love it," I said.

"Sal can help you out if there's anything else you need."

Like pins, presumably. My fingers strayed yet again to my headscarf.

Gary turned and led me in the other direction. "Down here you'll find the coffee dispenser. It's everyone's first stop in the morning so"— he winked at me—"the earlier you get here, the better your chances of a decent coffee."

"Thanks for the tip."

We reached the kitchenette. "Some people, of course, live at the coffee machine. Matthew Frobisher, for instance." He indicated the man in front of us. "This guy's intake is nothing short of hazardous."

The addict in question straightened and, coffee in hand, turned our way. He checked as he saw me, then smiled.

Wow. I took in the tall, toned body, the broad shoulders, the mess of blond hair with a couldn't-care-less fringe flopping over one eye. *Hot.*

"Becky," said Gary, "meet Matt, London's biggest caffeine junkie and your course supervisor."

Matt's eyes locked with mine. Deep, chocolate-brown, come-to-bed eyes. Under the fluorescent lights they looked almost black.

He shook my hand. "Well, hello again."

My stomach did an elevator-swoop down to my toes and back. Oh God. That voice. Rich, compelling, *familiar.*

Chocolate.

Every droplet of moisture on my tongue dried up, rendering it a useless blob of flesh.

"I know you, right?" he prompted, still holding my hand.

I watched his lips as he spoke, my mind replaying for the zillionth time those unforgettable minutes after I'd regained consciousness; leaning back against his chest, cocooned by his hard muscular strength, his arms holding me close, his heartbeat strong at my back, the warmth and gentle power of his hands, his deep chocolate-y voice a caress in my ear, tempting me, enticing me, seducing me . . . and stop! This had to stop! Right now!

I dragged some air into my lungs and it fuelled the fire in my cheeks. A few more degrees and I'd spontaneously combust.

Which, all things considered, might not be a bad option.

I withdrew my hand and licked my lips. "Um, no, I don't think we've met; no." *Liar, liar.*

I moved to inspect the coffee machine, every hair on my head aware of his gaze. Why had I just said that? What good could it possibly do?

"Oh. I could have sworn . . . Hmm. Sorry, my mistake." Matt cleared his throat. "It's good to have you on board, Becky. I'll catch up with you later, once you've had a chance to settle in."

He paused. "Nice scarf, by the way."

"Thanks," I mumbled.

I couldn't turn around. I daren't turn around. He'd read the truth all over my face.

Gary cleared his throat. "Right, then. Let's go and meet the rest of the team."

* * *

"How can this be happening to me?" I wailed, hugging a pillow. "It's *so* not fair."

"On the plus side," said Liz, "at least you've tracked down your rescuer."

"There's no plus side. He's my boss. And he's seen me half-naked, concussed, and looking like an idiot."

She gave me a sly glance. "You begged me to hunt him down after he saw you like that."

"I was concussed."

"Off on another man-fantasy, more like."

I waved a no-no-no finger at her. "Only for a moment. Then I woke up, straightened my halo, and—"

"Went for a brain transplant?" She shot me an affectionate smile.

"Ha ha, very funny. But there's no transplant needed. It's my New Year's resolution at stake. No more dates, no more disasters. That's it. Just me and my stellar career." Even as I said it, I knew I'd failed on the enthusiasm front.

"You make it sound like a life sentence."

Yeah, that's how it felt. I sighed.

"Becs, it's only a New Year's resolution. If this guy's really got you hooked, go get him. Just . . . don't make him into something he's not."

"No." I leapt up and stabbed a finger at the note taped to the mirror of my dresser. "Look. See? *Thou shalt not ever, under any circumstances, date SSW's.*"

"SSW's?"

"Seriously Shaggable Workmates. I think we can safely say he's an SSW."

"Let me see that." Liz came and looked over my shoulder. She took in my signature, the scrawled date. "Ah. Post-Mickey-itis."

Then, gently, "Becs, there won't be another Mickey."

"Here's hoping." I pinched my eyes closed. "What am I going to do?"

"What do you want to do?"

"Turn back time." I paced the room, then flung myself on the bed. "I don't know. Own up to recognising him, I suppose."

"Why did you lie about that?"

"I have no idea." I sat up and chewed on a fingernail. "I guess I knee-jerked. Saw him, thought 'hot boss', leapfrogged to Mickey, and the words were out before I'd even decided what to say."

I stood. Started pacing again. "Damn Mickey! And damn Matt!"

Liz watched me in silence. Then, "You really like him, don't you?"

I looked at her, bit my lip, nodded. Returned to my bed and slumped against the headboard. "But this is the job of a lifetime. I can't screw it up."

"What's to screw up? I know loads of couples who met through work."

I sighed. "Yeah, but none of them had my track record."

"You've just had bad luck."

"In large doses. There's too much at stake this time. I can't go there. He's off-limits." Then, wistfully, "What a waste."

She came and sat on the edge of the bed. "Look, Mickey was an asshole. That g-string on the noticeboard stunt was unforgiveable. But, hon, you weren't to know."

What—that for all he was funny and witty and fantastic company, he was also a complete prick? One who thought nothing of trashing someone's reputation and career for the sake of fifty quid? Humiliation rippled through me all over again.

"Hey," she said, "everyone makes the odd mistake."

"Not as many as me, though. And look! I want to do it again." I buried my face in the pillow. "I should be sent to a nunnery. Or locked up. Right now. Forever."

"He's probably nothing like Mickey."

I looked up at her. "He's my new boss. End of story."

CHAPTER FOUR

"Isn't this what we all dream of?" the interviewer gushed, her American twang dragging like fingers down a blackboard. "The fairy-tale ending?"

"Yes!" the studio audience cheered.

"I know." Coy and proud, I smiled at Matt, by my side. Then turned back to our interviewer. "I always hoped, of course, but I never thought it would happen to me."

"Does *this* feel like it's happening to you?" Matt murmured in my ear, his hand roving over my breasts.

Did it ever. I turned, my lips meeting his, my breathing shallow. He stood and, ignoring the marauding cameras, pulled me to him, his erection intense against my belly. His tongue plundered my mouth and desire stormed through me. My knees buckled. He held me tighter, moulding me to his length. Passion took over and my last traces of modesty slid away. We dispensed with clothes, foregoing the bed at stage-left—when had that appeared?—for a convenient shag-pile carpet just feet away from the audience whose presence was, truth be told, a huge turn-on. In fact—gosh—I was only seconds away from ecstasy . . .

Matt's body continued to play mine as, with sensational skill, he took me to the brink and back, to the brink and back. I was a dam of liquid sensation, his every plunge increasing the pressure within like a burgeoning tidal wave. Our bodies a perfect fit, our minds in perfect harmony, our pairing the perfect outcome.

His mouth burned a hot trail from my lips to my ear and I gasped as the tidal wave loomed, colossal, above us.

He gave my earlobe an erotic nibble and murmured, "Take this. It's hot."

The tidal wave crashed down, consuming me, consuming him, consuming us.

"Hey! Careful, you'll spill it."

A slight pressure on my wrist rapidly morphed into searing heat and pain. I whipped my hand back and opened my eyes to see my house-mate's face only inches from mine, looking more than a little demonic as he held a coffee mug aloft.

I screamed and flung myself to the far side of the bed. "Are you crazy?"

Stupid question.

Jim cackled. "Drip by drip or all at once?"

"Bloody idiot! You could've given me third degree burns."

"Nothing more than you deserve if you won't shift your lazy butt and take a hold of the cup."

"I was *asleep.*"

He sat on the edge of the bed. "I do the decent thing and wake my house-mate with a cup of real, hand-ground coffee . . ."

I took in his filthy paws and hoped his hands hadn't done the grinding.

". . . and all she does is whine. I don't know why I bother."

"Me neither." My adrenalin rush subsided and, yawning, I slid back to the warm patch I'd just vacated.

He handed me the mug and I placed it with exaggerated care on the bedside table.

"Thanks. Next time, try waking me first."

With an energetic leap, he Fosbury-flopped onto the bed and lay full-length beside me, hands behind his head. "Hey, it's not my fault you sleep like the dead."

He turned on his side and waggled his eyebrows at me. They looked like synchronised black caterpillars. "Or maybe they took you to the Mother-ship for experiments."

I wished I could be back in my dream.

Jim fixed me with a stare. The caterpillars met in the middle. "Are you Becky or a stand-in? What's your sister's favourite food?"

"Oh *please.*" I pulled the covers over my head. "Let me wake up in peace."

Jules, my battle-scarred cat, gave a warning *mrowl* and leapt up onto me with his usual hurled-brick finesse. Clearly it was the boys versus Becky this morning. I gave up on peace and re-emerged.

Jules settled high on my chest, lifted a leg and started licking his privates. Nice. I shoved him off me. He glared. I glared back.

"Do I get to drown him?" Jim asked, propping himself up against the headboard.

I transferred my glare to Jim.

He slurped a mouthful of coffee. My coffee. "You've got bad breath, black eyes, and dried-up dribble on your chin."

"Whatever." I scowled at his unkempt black mop and tried to think of a clever response. Nothing sprang to mind. I surreptitiously rubbed at my chin to remove the dribble; the rest would have to wait.

"Coffee?" He proffered my mug.

"Not anymore." The cheek of him. First he chose some ungodly hour of the morning to wake me from the most delicious dream, then he offered me coffee and drank it himself.

I caught a whiff of the coffee beans and thought of Matt. At-Work Matt, not Horny-Dream Matt.

Trouble was, give or take a garment or two, they were pretty close to identical. Even I could see that might be problematic.

Could I really do this? Have erotic dreamtime encounters with my boss all night then go into work and make like he was nothing special?

Well, I just had to. Either that or quit my fantabulous new job.

Jim slurped at the coffee, gave an audible *ahhh*. I scowled at him.

Could I talk to Jim about my Matt/boss quandary? Maybe. He'd seen me at my lowest, after Mickey destroyed my world. He'd been a great support then.

"This has to be my best brew yet," said Jim. "Try it."

I gritted my teeth. "No." God only knew what diseases he harboured.

He swung himself up off the bed. "Pity."

With a flourish he flung back the curtains and launched into song. Whatever song it was, though, he was destroying it.

"Shut *up*." No, deep and meaningfuls wouldn't work today. There was no telling how he'd respond.

"Look," I said, "it's six-fifteen in the morning. I'm still in *bed*, dammit. This is really social and all, but what exactly are you doing in here?"

"Just making sure you don't sleep in," he chirped. "Can't be late for Day Two."

21

Day Two. It felt like a death sentence.

"What's on the agenda today, then? Press conference? Spank a few students?" He executed a couple of lewd hip-thrusts. "Blow-job for the boss, eh, *BJ*?" He emphasised the nickname.

Sudden anger ripped through me. "Get stuffed."

I hauled myself out of bed and stomped to the door. If he wouldn't leave, I would. "Asshole."

He chuckled. "You're too easy to wind up, BJ."

"So don't bother. And don't call me that. I have a name."

"Cute PJs. Are you really *Purr-fect In Bed*, BJ?" His fingers scribed quotation marks.

I shot him a withering look, and yanked my robe off the hook. Yanked harder when it resisted. Heard it rip.

"Typical. You know what? I don't have time for this," I stalked off to the bathroom, trying to hold the robe and my dignity together.

Jim wolf whistled after me. I sacrificed dignity and flipped him the bird.

When I eventually went downstairs, far more presentable and a muzzle on my mood, Jim sloped in and hovered as I buttered my toast.

I looked up, annoyed. "What?"

"Well." He leaned against the fridge. "I just realised, you haven't said squat about the new job."

I returned my attention to the toast.

He waited. "Well? How was it? Your first day?"

"Okay."

"What, your ultimate job and it was only okay?"

I turned toast-buttering into an art form. "It's hard to tell on the first day."

His eyes screwed up as he read my words, my posture, my mood. Dammit, he knew me too well. He seemed about to speak, then changed his mind. I bit into my artwork.

"That's bullshit, Becky," he finally said.

He'd stopped using my initials, and just as well. The butter-knife would've been messy but it would've been worth it.

"What's bullshit?"

"You must have some idea whether you'll like the job."

"Well, I don't, okay?" I looked longingly at the knife.

He cracked open a can of coke, took an impossibly long drink, and burped.

"Then I'd say," he concluded, "you've got a problem."

Yeah, and no easy solution. What a bloody, bloody mess.

* * *

The mess felt even messier once I was ensconced behind my desk at work. On the one hand, I was thrilled to be here. Applying for this position had been ambitious, and I'd never really expected to get an interview, let alone a job offer. This move was everything I needed: a fresh direction, new challenges and, hopefully, a long-tailed career arc.

On the other hand, I was terrified. What if I wasn't cut out to be a lecturer? What if I was, but then threw it all away over my too-hot-to-handle boss? What if I screwed up so badly my students complained?

Stop it, Becs.

Concentrate.

I looked down at my notes and took a deep breath. It skittered out in a flurry of nerves. I glanced at the clock. In less than twenty-four hours I had to deliver my first lecture. Not some off-the-cuff ten-minute chat to a cosy group of friends: a two-hour, professional presentation to a hundred-odd students. My chest constricted. I needed to nail that lecture.

Out in the corridor I could hear Matt talking a student through something they hadn't understood in class. He had such an easy manner with everyone. I liked that.

They laughed at some comment or other, and Matt's baritone rumble reminded me once again of our poolside encounter.

Lecture, Becs.

I blocked out his voice and flicked through the course outline. Re-read last year's assessments, making notes in the margins. Waited for a moment of creative genius to hit me.

It didn't.

Rats. I'd have to rely on hard graft to get me through.

Not that I was bothered by hard graft; I loved the satisfaction of a job well done. I just wished I had something—anything—to offer that would stack up against my predecessor's impressive track record.

Something better than a gaudy headscarf for Matt to remember me by.

And there I went again.

I groaned. Banged my forehead on the desk once, twice, three times. This was not about Matt. Or any other man, for that matter. This was about me and my career. And if I wanted to concentrate on my career—which finally seemed to be on track—then Matt was a no-go zone. That way lay mortal danger.

"Becky. Hi. How's it going?"

I looked up, startled, and dropped the folder, scattering papers all over the floor.

"Hi." I scrabbled to pick them up. Great. Now he thought I was a dim-witted hypochondriac with head-banging tendencies.

Matt put down the box he was carrying. "Here, let me help."

He reached for some pages. Our hands brushed as we went for the same piece. *Zing!* An electric bolt shot up my fingers, echoing in my girlie bits. I snatched my hand back. This was crazy. I wasn't sixteen anymore.

He picked up a couple more pages and handed them to me with a friendly smile.

"Cheers," I said, avoiding his touch and feeling foolish for it. I retreated back behind my workstation.

He deposited the box on the desk between us.

"Sharon's bequest to you," he said, sitting in a chair opposite. He raked his too-long fringe up off his face, and I watched, entranced. How did it manage to balance there?

I blinked, looked away. Work. Focus on work.

"Thanks."

I opened the box and pulled out the top file. It was full of documents, all colour-coded and labelled to the enth degree.

"Wow." I flicked through the folder, relief surging through me. "This will save me so much time."

He leaned back, tilting the chair on two legs at a gravity-defying angle. I pretended to peruse the documents, watching as he hooked a casual thumb through the belt-loop of his anti-management jeans. He wore them well.

SSW. SSW.

I dragged myself back to Sharon's notes, breathing out long and slow, trying to deflate my libido as well as my lungs.

"Knowing Sharon," he said, doing that fringe thing again, "she'll have left everything you need, and more. She's incredibly organised."

I put the file back in the box and smiled at him. "I really appreciate this. If you're talking to her please pass on my thanks."

He stretched, his arms reaching high, and I pretended not to notice the strain of pecs against fabric.

SSW. SSW.

"Sure." He stood. "Well, I'll leave you to it. You've got plenty to do."

Yeah, like get ready for my lecturing debut. Nausea clawed at my gut. "My first lecture's tomorrow, right?"

"That's right. Only the first-years, though. The others have independent study this week."

Clearly I looked as scared as I felt because he grinned. "Hey, you'll be fine. Look, I lectured this course a few years ago, so if you've got any questions just yell. I can help with anything you need."

He probably could, too . . . and the less I thought about that the better.

* * *

I sorted through Sharon's box of goodies with increasing panic. Instructions, lecture notes, assessments, student records, suggestions for future course developments, budgetary stuff; all there, faultlessly organised. Anxiety swamped me. What had I been thinking? This job was a massive step up. Too massive. I'd felt totally confident in my safe little job at my safe little travel agency. Did I really want to swap that for a swanky career I knew nothing about?

Of course I did. I was a big girl now, and I wasn't afraid of hard work.

My messy workstation stared back at me. Okay, maybe a little afraid. But I could do this. I could. Think positive.

"Ready for that lecture?" Matt loitered in my doorway yet again.

Wasn't he checking up on me just a bit too often? Maybe he thought I wasn't up to the job.

I'd just have to prove him wrong. "Yes. All sorted."

"Excellent. Can I take a look? Make sure you're on track?"

"I, ah . . ." I fidgeted with some papers. "Can I bring you a copy later?"

"No need. I'll just check it on-screen." He walked round to my side of the desk.

"No!" I switched off the monitor, feeling like I'd been caught downloading porn.

His eyebrows shot up.

I pinched the bridge of my nose between thumb and forefinger. Sighed and looked up at him. "Okay, maybe it's not quite sorted. But it will be. I promise."

He gave a lopsided smile. "I'm not the lecture police."

He was my boss, wasn't he? And wanted to see my work? That sounded fairly police-ish to me.

"Relax," he said. "It's just first-lecture jitters."

He leaned closer to turn the monitor back on and I breathed in a heady mix of aftershave and musky masculinity.

Whoa. I held my breath, not trusting myself.

"Come on, talk me through it. I'll be your sounding-board." He tap-tapped the top of the monitor as he retreated to the other side of the desk and sat down. "Got a topic in mind?"

I released my breath as naturally as possible, then looked at him across the desk. He gave me a lazy smile and my heart-rate kicked up. Stop it, Becs. This was work. This was *not* a lesson in seduction.

But my body wasn't listening. Golden heat shimmered in my belly, radiating through my body and leaving me breathless. Matt's gaze flickered down to my lips and back up to my eyes with unmistakeable meaning, and for a moment I felt exposed, hunted—and downright sexy. I ran my tongue over suddenly-dry lips. Then saw his eyes darken and realised what I'd done. Bad move. I picked up a pen to keep my hands busy. Closed my eyes to put some distance between us.

What had he asked? Oh, yeah. Did I have a lecture topic? "Not really. That's half the problem."

He didn't respond. Eventually, unable to stand the suspense, I opened my eyes.

"And the rest of the problem?" he prompted.

I looked out the window, avoiding his gaze. "Nothing, really." You. Sharon. Everything.

"Hey." He leaned forward and *donk*ed his hand flat on the desk. Waited until I returned his gaze. "You'll be fine. You're not"—*donk*— "Sharon"—*donk*—"so don't try to be. Be yourself."

Hell, was I that easy to read? Best I work on my confidence fast, or the students would slaughter me.

He stood up. "Your first lecture's with a group of new students. They have no preconceived ideas. Don't try and achieve miracles; just introduce yourself and the course." At the door he turned, adding, "Play to your strengths."

Strengths? My strengths?

He took in my expression and chuckled. "I'll come and pick up your bones afterwards."

* * *

I peeked in through the small rectangle of glass. The room beyond was crowded, people squeezing themselves in any old how, climbing over and around each other, jostling for better positions. Exuberant noise seeped through the door: students chatting, papers being shuffled, bags being rifled through, mobile phones ringing, seats banging up and down as people arranged and rearranged themselves Musical-Chairs-style.

An old wooden lectern stood to attention at the front, flanked by a good-sized bench. Soon I would be standing there.

So many faces! One hundred? No, more. Feck—*more*. Sheer terror rocketed through my limbs, stilling me, chilling me. If this failed, my credibility would be shot to pieces. Could I pull it off?

I'd practised on Liz. I'd practised on Jim. I'd practised over the phone to my kid sister, Dani. I'd practised in front of the bedroom mirror at two in the morning until even Jules, poor long-suffering beast that he was, had retreated under the stairs for some peace and quiet. I'd been living, eating, breathing this lecture for the last twenty-four hours solid, and now here I was, and there they were, and all I had to do was walk through the door.

A student pushed past me into the lecture theatre and the moment passed, my body and brain in sync once more. I braced myself and followed him in.

As I began my long, long walk towards the lectern a hush dominoed around. I was the person they'd been waiting for, and now the whole theatre focused their attention on me.

After a few moments of stunned silence, the murmurs began. They'd clearly noticed my clothes. Hardly standard lecturer garb: Hawaiian shirt stuffed with a pillow (*voila!* Instant beer gut), glaringly-white Bermuda shorts, straw hat, sunglasses, walking sandals, false moustache.

Terrified though I was, I had decided to take the bull by the horns today. If I won, the rest would be easy with these first-years. And hopefully the grapevine would do its thing and make my life easier with the second-years as well. If I lost . . .

Well. Best I didn't think about that.

I reached the lectern and confirmed with a glance that my props were behind the bench. Then I placed a picnic basket containing lecture notes on top.

For the next few minutes, though, I didn't need notes. I had this part of the lecture committed to memory.

I pulled out a sun umbrella, unfolded it, steadied it in its weighted base, then snapped up a deck chair in its shadow. Stepped back and nodded at the effect. Gave my audience a lopsided smile, then sat on the deck chair and rested my feet on the bench. Stopped. Stood again and went to the picnic basket. Pulled out a bottle of *Becks*. Sat down again, feet up, and opened the beer.

I tilted the bottle towards the tiered seats. "Cheers."

I took a swig, the reactions by now audible. Murmurings, the odd whistle, a few claps of approval. I let it continue and feigned sleep, using the time to get my breathing under control. Then I stood, stretched lazily and, beer in hand, man-swaggered over to the lectern. Turned on the microphone and looked around the theatre.

My stomach flipped. So many *people*.

I hid my trembling hand in my pocket.

"Travel," I said. My voice boomed out larger than life and I leapt back from the microphone. Sipped another mouthful of beer to steady myself, then continued. "Imagine getting paid to drink beer and chill on the beach all day."

A few comments floated down from the tiered seats.

"Paid to take holiday after glorious holiday. All in exotic destinations.

Just one big Full Moon party after another."

Laughter rippled around the theatre.

"And that's why you're all here, right? The parties!"

A few raucous whoops and cat-calls rang out over the growing noise.

"Yep," I said. "Life's a beach when you're in the travel industry. Sex, drugs and rock'n'roll."

The theatre erupted.

I felt euphoric. My memory hadn't failed me, my body hadn't betrayed me, and my props hadn't fallen to pieces. The introduction had gone without a hitch. I smiled around the theatre—my theatre—and my terror faded to a pinprick of distant memory. I could do this job. Maybe not the way Sharon would've, but it was my cat, now, and I'd skin it the way I chose.

I retrieved my lecture notes and stood at the lectern. A slight movement at the edge of my vision caught my attention and I glanced towards the door. It was open a few inches. Someone had been watching the entire performance.

A blond fringe.

My breath caught. My heart raced.

Matt.

CHAPTER FIVE

Hands on hips, I watched as my house-mate, thirty-three going on twelve, completed his silly little trick.

"You call that skill?" I said. "Here, give me one of those."

Jim, still sprawled in his bean-bag, handed a maltezer up to me. I lobbed it in the air then lurched around beneath it with an open mouth. Cursed as the chocolate ball bounced off my nose and hit the floor.

He snorted and handed me another maltezer. "You need practice."

I tried again. Failed.

"See? Skill. It'll be an Olympic sport soon. Here, let the master show you how it's done."

"Stand up and do it." Maybe it was his posture.

He stood, tossed a maltezer in the air and waited for it to plop cleanly into his mouth. Shot me a smug look. Passed me another maltezer. "Best of three."

I needed to keep my body still; that was it. Ever so gently I lobbed another one towards my waiting mouth. The doorbell ding-donged. I started. The maltezer rolled down my cheek.

"Fail," said Jim.

"I was distracted. Give me another go."

The bell pealed again.

Jim threw three maltezers in the air and caught them all in his mouth like a famished baby bird. "Distractions are irrelevant. Skill takes focus."

He flopped back into the bean-bag and picked up the remote, studiously ignoring the bell.

I prodded him with my toe. "Fine. I'll get the door, since you're so busy training for the Olympics."

Dani stood there in the gathering dusk. A tear slipped down her cheek. "Can I come in?"

I threw off the long-suffering act and hauled her inside, whipping into big-sister protection mode. "Dan, what's wrong?"

Her chin trembled. "Nothing," she said, and broke down in shuddering sobs.

Oh dear. Another love crisis, I bet. Her break-ups were always spectacular, and she always did them like a Shakespearean tragedy. Luckily I knew her. She'd be fine in a week or two, once she found the next guy.

I hugged her, unable to repress a wince as she clung to me.

She noticed and stepped back, gulping back her tears. "Sorry. Did I hurt you?" She honed in on my bald patch. "Oh my God! You've got *stitches!* What happened? Becs!" Her tears went on hold. "You should've rung!"

I walked through to the kitchen and put the kettle on. "I did. Twice."

"Oh. Sorry." Her voice lowered to a mumble. "I haven't been thinking straight. I've had . . . stuff going on."

She's always got stuff going on. But Dani is Dani, take her or leave her. She'll always be the star of the show. I love her to bits, of course.

"Another break-up?" I prompted.

She closed her eyes, sighed heavily. Her face crumpled and she dashed away more tears.

"The worst," she said, her voice ragged.

I switched off the kettle—more serious measures required—and guided her through to the living room. We sat at the table and I poured a dollop of brandy into a glass for her.

"Men are such bastards." She stared down at the formica.

Jim shifted in his bean-bag. The TV volume rose.

I pushed the glass closer. Dani took it without looking up.

"Bastards," she repeated, then tipped her head back and downed the brandy.

I blinked at the empty glass. Refilled it. "Want to tell me about it?"

She gulped more brandy but didn't drain the glass this time, thank goodness.

"How *could* he?" she whimpered. Then, with vicious fury, "Bastard."

"Who?" I asked. Not that it mattered. I'd long since stopped trying to remember their names. There were just so many. She reeled them in and tossed them back so fast it was a miracle even *she* remembered their

31

names.

Jim held a dramatic hand to his forehead. "How could he?" he mimicked in falsetto. "Those Kenny Rogers CDs were my life."

Dani shot him a scathing look. He pretended not to see, but I knew he saw everything where she was concerned. He fancied my sister rotten. Not that I blamed him. Enviably slim, with long, sleek blonde hair and olive skin (both only slightly enhanced), Dani was nothing short of stunning. My frizzy auburn halo and parchment-pale skin, though cute in a just-like-your-grandmother kind of way, didn't have quite the same impact. At five-foot-eight she was just an inch or so taller than me, but somehow that inch lent her a poise and slenderness I envied. Beside her I felt like an ugly duckling who never quite made it to swan status.

Dani dabbed at her eyes with a tissue, all vulnerability and exotic beauty. Honestly, Jim didn't stand a chance.

She looked at me. Focused. Frowned. "Becs, your hair is hideous."

"Gee, thanks."

"What happened?"

I'd wondered how long it would take her to show some interest. Even so, now I finally had her attention I hesitated to admit the clumsy truth.

"It was the most random thing," I said. "I was walking up the street, minding my own business, when a crazed madman wielding a baseball bat"—her eyes widened—"jumped out in front of me and—"

Jim piped up. "Hardly. She swam into the end of the swimming pool."

"What?" Dani swung from me to him and back again. "Really?"

I shrugged. "I preferred the crazed madman story."

Jim muted the TV.

"Crazed madman? Madwoman, more like. *Doof!*" He reeled as if from a head blow. "Oh yeah," he slowed his words, "that's right; the wall's made of concrete. That'll be why my head hurts." He crossed his eyes, then uncrossed them and cackled.

She rounded on him. "What, and that's funny? Look at her! My sister could've died, and you think it's *funny?*"

He frowned. "Well, it is kind-of funny, don't you think? Hold on—I can feel a joke coming on." His eyes lit up, alien-like. "What did Becky say when she hit the end of the swimming pool? You're a hard act to follow!" He hooted at his own humour. "Or . . . what's Becky's favourite song? *All in all you're just a-nother head in the wall!*" He slapped his thigh, laughing manically.

She eyeballed him. "There's nothing funny about a head injury."

His laughter withered and died.

She lanced him with her glare. "And what about me?"

Her? Funny, there I'd been, thinking it was all about me for once.

"Why didn't you ring me as soon as it happened?" she demanded. "I am her sister, after all."

He looked stricken.

Poor Jim. It wasn't his fault she'd had a bad day.

"Give him a break, Dan," I said. "He's not used to playing Florence."

"He's not used to playing human."

Jim dragged himself upright, flicked off the TV, and left the room. His silence bothered me more than his jokes.

"Typical." Dani rolled her eyes.

Yeah. Typical Dani, turning my accident into something about her.

I felt torn. Thanks to Dani, Jim was upstairs feeling misunderstood, while she sat down here doing her usual melodramatics.

Still, she was my sister.

On cue, her baby blues welled again. She reached for a fresh tissue. "I should be working," she said, voice wavering. "I'm on deadline this week."

"Dan, it's night-time. Work can wait. Tell me about your break-up."

She hugged her glass, opened her mouth to speak, then exhaled and closed it again. Which was very unlike her. Her blow by blows of he-said-she-said usually lasted hours.

"Hey," I said, "if you don't want to talk, that's okay. We can just sit."

She nodded and whispered, "Thanks."

For a while she swirled the amber liquid in her glass, watching it with a glazed un-Dani-like expression.

I gave her arm a gentle squeeze. She looked up at me with a watery smile, then drained her drink. I refilled it yet again, wondering if I had enough brandy to see Dani through her crisis.

"Any chance you guys can work it out?" I asked.

She shook her head.

"Oh."

More brandy-gazing.

"Well, if there's no going back, you need to move forward. Forget him, Dan. He's history."

Her face crumpled. Clearly she hadn't relegated him there just yet. Interesting. As far as I could remember, it had always been Dani doing the chasing, Dani deciding when it was over, Dani delivering the Dear John speech. This time, somehow, she'd lost the power.

Hell, maybe she'd fallen in love.

I grabbed her hand in mine. "Hon, I know it hurts. But you'll get through this."

We all do, I wanted to add.

She shook her head, disagreeing, then started wailing and wringing her hands. Shakespeare would've applauded.

"You will," I insisted. "And I'm here for you, all the way."

I gave her a minute or two for her dramatics, then tried again. "Will revenge make you feel better? We could . . ." I thought quickly. "Throw rocks at his windows? Take out a full-page ad? Ooh! Basic Instinct! Let's boil his bunnies."

She gave a hiccup-y giggle. I handed her a tissue.

"Thanks." She blew her nose.

"Want to go for a walk?"

She sighed.

"Down to the pub, maybe?"

She shook her head, looking morose.

"Okay, let's catch a movie."

She slumped even further in her chair.

"Right. Shall we just stay here, then?"

"Becs, I can't face the world just now. I'm all messed up."

Did she mean on the inside or the outside? I wasn't sure.

"Look at me! I can't go out looking like this." She indicated her face, practically flawless in spite of her tears. "Can't I hang out here a while?"

"Sure. Whatever you want." What else could I suggest? "Want to watch some TV, then?"

She shook her head again, and I gave up.

"Right. Well, I'll get you another drink, and how about you curl up in my bed for a bit while I do some work? I need to write up next week's lectures."

She shrugged. "Whatever."

Then she straightened in her chair. "I could proof-read them for you."

I stared at Dani, aghast. Her spelling and grammar only barely verge on adequate. Really, she should never leave home without a spell-check facility.

Her shoulders sagged. "Or not."

I bit my lip. It would at least give her something else to think about.

"Great idea," I said, with far more enthusiasm than I felt.

CHAPTER SIX

"Coming for a drink, Jebecca?" Sal stood in my office doorway.

I groaned. "I'm never going to live that down, am I?"

"No." She grinned.

"Didn't think so. I'll settle for a drink, then."

As I locked my door the phone rang. I hesitated.

"Let it ring." Sal checked her watch. "Come on, it's 5.30. They'll leave a message if it's important."

We headed down to Little Tuscany, a nearby wine bar and T&T's local watering hole. Over in the corner our noisy group had already switched to weekend mode.

A wine, maybe two; that's what I needed. I bought a self-congratulatory glass of bubbly, and Sal sat down next to me with a Chianti.

She clinked her glass against mine. "Well, Luv, the first week's always the worst. How'd it go?"

"Great. Even better now it's over. I'm exhausted."

"I hear your first lecture was . . ."—she searched for the right word—" . . . memorable." She smirked.

"Oh." I felt my cheeks colour. Did she mean memorable-good or memorable-bad? I didn't like to ask. "Who'd you hear that from?"

She tapped her nose. "Can't reveal my sources."

I'd heard Sal knew everything about everyone at T&T. She must be a gossip extraordinaire if she'd already had the low-down on me. Maybe she'd been speaking to one of the students. Or—I glanced down the table—Matt, maybe? What had he thought of my lecture? Would he admit to spying on me? My heart fluttered up around my throat.

I leaned closer to Sal and murmured, "Who's Matt speaking to?"

She turned and looked at the quiet young twinset-and-pearls woman at his side. "Oh, haven't you met Amanda yet?"

Sal's voice carried down the table, drawing looks from both Matt and Amanda. I cringed.

Sal smiled at them, unfazed, and raised her glass to her lips. "Amanda keeps herself to herself. Not much of a socialite." She paused. "Actually, she can barely string a sentence together."

"Looks like she's managing nicely with Matt."

"Yeah. He's a sweetie. I doubt Amanda would come to drinks if he wasn't there. I'll introduce you later," she added. "She lectures Year 1 Tourism, like you."

"Really? Oh!" With her tidy, no-fuss ponytail and serious, be-spectacled face, she just oozed librarian—but lecturer? No.

"Her specialty's IT."

Which explained her almost-translucent English Rose skin, a stark contrast to Matt's sun-bronzed tones. They probably didn't have much in common. The thought filled me with pleasure which, a micro-second later, translated into annoyance. Why should I care?

My gaze rested on Matt for a double pulse-beat. He looked like he'd just come from a sunbed. Maybe he had some Greek or Italian or something in him. Though that didn't explain the blond hair. Scandinavian, perhaps.

He looked up and smiled. Heat rushed to my face. Damn. He'd caught me staring. He raised a quirky eyebrow and I smiled back but let my glance slide past him, as if I'd been scanning the whole room, not just him.

I felt his eyes still on me, though, stringing an invisible thread of tension between us. The tension tautened, tighter, tighter, until I couldn't stand it anymore.

I leapt to my feet. "My round. What's everyone having?"

They started calling their orders.

"Want a hand?" Matt stood.

No! Anyone but him.

I shook my head, softening it with a smile. "You're hemmed in. Sal can help instead." I grabbed her by the elbow and hauled her upright. "Right, Sal?"

She looked surprised. "Oh, okay."

"I've got this, Sal," said a male voice at my side.

I turned and came face to toupee with a younger, darker version of Benny Hill. Took a hasty step back.

"I bet you do," said Sal. "Becky, Hank. Hank, Becky."

Hank held my hand in both of his. "Ah. The beautiful Becky."

I gave him a small, don't-want-to-encourage-you smile.

He leaned closer, so close I wanted to take another step back, and engulfed me in a hideous huff of beer breath. "I've heard so much about you."

Oh dear. Shame I couldn't say the same about him. I'd have found a way to avoid him.

We made our way through the now-full room and queued at the bar, trying to dodge people's drink spills and (for my part) Hank's hands. He made small-talk about his incredibly important second-year book-keeping course, and I whiled the time away studying his toupee. Was it even made of hair? It looked very . . . nylon. And every time he turned his head, the toupee looked ready to bark and launch itself through the air at me.

I bit my lip, stifling a giggle. His hair was as disastrous as mine—but at least I'd hidden mine under a scarf. Honestly, why did he bother? He should just ditch the toupee and be done with it. So what if people could see his receding hairline?

We returned with our table's orders, and Hank used the opportunity to plant himself beside me and murmur beer-y nothings in my ear. Fortunately Liz's text came through—*I'm here!*—giving me the perfect excuse to abandon Hank.

"Back in a sec," I said, and headed back through the crowd to meet Liz.

"Hi," I said. "You made it."

"Hi yourself. I figured I could work tomorrow instead."

"But tomorrow's Saturday."

She shrugged.

"You'll work through your weekend, and you were going to work Friday night?" I shook my head despairingly. "No wonder you're single."

"I'm happy with single. Aren't you?"

I didn't answer. We both knew my leap into career-mindedness was a consolation prize. As opposed to hers, which was totally by choice and just the way she wanted it.

Liz reached out and gave my headscarf a tug. "Nice. It suits you."

"Just as well, 'cause the bald patch doesn't."

We reached the table and I did the introductions. "Everyone, this is my pal, Liz. Liz, this is—" I decided she'd never remember so many names "—everyone."

'Everyone' laughed. Liz smiled, but it was her Ice Queen smile, the one she probably used to keep pesky employees at arm's length. For me, it simply confirmed what I already knew. She had no interest in socialising; she was here purely for me, bless her.

Sal offered Liz a quarter of her chair. "Here, Luv, take a seat. I'm Sal."

After the briefest of hesitations Liz pumped a few more watts into her smile. "Hi, Sal."

She attempted to sit but Sal's ample behind didn't make seat-sharing easy, so I shuffled my chair closer and gave Liz some of mine, too.

"Sal's our receptionist," I explained, "and font of all knowledge."

Sal chuckled. "I'm not so sure about that. But I make sure everyone gets to Friday drinks."

Liz, without even bothering to answer, swivelled abruptly to me.

I cringed. Liz was no socialite but that had been cutting, even for her. She should save it for the boardroom. I frowned my disapproval at her.

She chose not to notice. "Well? Where's your ugly boss?"

My frown became a glare. Man, she didn't waste time. "Sssh!"

"Is he here?" She looked up and down the table.

I sighed and made a face at her. "Yes. Five down, opposite side." I indicated with my head.

"Are you going to introduce us?"

"No."

She shrugged. "I'll ask Sal, then."

"*No.*" I gulped some wine. "Maybe later. Great show of moral support, by the way."

She gave me a wink, then turned as Hank imposed himself. She handled him far more expertly than I had, freezing him out and sending him on his way before he'd even extracted her name. With an eloquent glance my way—keep the hell away from him—she turned to Sal again and this time, mercifully, made a real effort.

I felt a rush of gratitude. Idle chit-chat with total strangers had never

39

been Liz's thing, yet here she was, supporting me in my big, scary career move.

And checking out Matt, of course.

"Thanks for being here," I murmured in her ear.

She shot me a smile, and this one was the genuine article, not the least bit Ice Queen, and a reminder of the bond we shared.

I sipped at my wine. The background jazz gave way to something more upbeat and I relaxed, moving with the music. What a week! New job, new workmates, new scarf . . .

New boss.

How old was he, anyway? Mid-thirties, perhaps? What a body! How many of his Recreational Tourism students propositioned him each week? Loads, I bet.

"Go on," Liz teased. "You know you want to."

I dragged my eyes away from Matt and leaned my forehead on her shoulder. Groaned. "Don't. This is hard enough already."

She surreptitiously sized him up. "He's not bad, is he?" Then, with a nod of approval, "Yes. Definitely worth breaking your workmate rule for."

"Sorry, girls," said Sal, following our gaze. "He's off-limits."

"Is he married?" I felt a surge of hope. Of *course* he was married! Good. That was that, then.

"No ring," Liz observed.

"Not married," Sal confirmed.

Bummer.

"But there's a rumour—"

"He's gay." Liz laughed. "Of course he is."

Gay? After the way he'd looked at me this week? No way.

"What's the rumour?" I asked.

Sal leaned closer. "Apparently he's a die-hard commitment-phobe. Long-term for him is a couple of weeks." She glanced his way, then back to us. "Mind you, I know plenty of women who'd take the fortnight."

Commitment-phobe, eh? So that electric looked we'd shared was nothing more than flirtation? A sudden thrill hit my groin. Bring on the flirtation!

Whoa. Hold it right there.

It had been a look, that's all. A look. I needed to rein myself in. *Now.*

No fantasies. No lust. He was my boss, remember? My *boss.*

* * *

Ten-thirty, and only five of us remained. I glanced over at the next table where Matt and some young, nubile thing looked like they were solving world poverty.

She glanced at her watch and sighed. "I really need to go." She stood. "'Night, folks." Then, to Matt, "Thanks for listening."

Was there anyone who didn't love this guy?

"Come and join us, Matt," said Sal, indicating an empty chair at our table.

He smiled and came over.

Liz *tap-tap-tapped* on my foot before giving him the benefit of her warmest, iceberg-melting smile. Her eyes as she glanced my way were full of mischief. My stomach lurched. I bit my lip. Friendly Liz was way more dangerous than Ice Queen Liz.

"Hi. I'm Liz. Becky's pal. And you must be . . . ?"

"Matt," he said. "Matt Frobisher."

"Ah." She grinned. "Scary boss."

He raised an amused eyebrow and drank some ale. "Me? Scary?"

"Hardly," I said, with a scowl for Liz.

She leaned close. "Then how come you've been avoiding him all night?" she murmured.

"I'll tell you what's scary," said Sal, "is how fast my wine keeps disappearing."

I looked at her empty wine-glass, then my own half-full one. Which had I been drinking from? Oops.

"Matt," said Liz, her head to one side, "you look very familiar."

My heart leapt into my throat and tried to hammer its way out. *No, no, no!* I gave my soon-to-be-ex best friend a sharp kick under the table.

"Ow!"

"Do I?" He turned to me, his eyes twinkling with knowledge.

Damn him! I tried to avoid his gaze but my eyes betrayed me and magneted back to his.

"Yes," said Liz, rubbing her bruised leg.

Matt raised an amused eyebrow at me. I grabbed my glass and gulped down the rest of my wine.

"Where from, though?" Liz mused with a cultivated frown.

She swung back to me. I gave a nervous start.

"Don't you think he looks familiar, Becky?"

Damn her, too! I shot her a desperate look.

She gave me a smooth, get-yourself-out-of-this-one smile.

"Um . . ." I didn't know what to say.

His eyes creased at the corners. "We had this conversation the other day, didn't we?"

He leaned back in his chair and grinned at me. Waiting. I felt like a butterfly impaled on a specimen board.

Typical. Every time I lied, it always came back to bite me.

"Well," I stumbled, "I don't *think* I recognise you . . . but maybe I'm wrong." I had to raise my voice to be heard over the people at the next table, who were now belting out the chorus of the DJ's song. I glanced their way, relieved. Freddie Mercury would be turning in his grave, for sure, but any distraction had to be a good one.

Matt leaned close. "They're playing your song."

I blushed. *The Great Pretender.* He grinned and raised his glass to me.

Bastard.

"Have you seen *We Will Rock You*?" Sal asked. "It's unbelievable."

"I loved it," said Liz.

"I haven't been yet," I said.

"Me neither." Matt's gaze remained on me.

"You have to see it," said Sal.

Liz nodded her agreement. Sal launched into 'remember that scene when . . .' mode. Matt and I looked at each other and shrugged.

I cast about for something to say. "I—I guess we should see it. It's had rave reviews."

He looked amused. "Is that your way of inviting me?"

"No! I mean . . . well, I guess we could . . . I hadn't really thought . . ."

Crap.

"Sure," I amended, being very adult. "If you want to. Why not?"

His eyes crinkled at the corners. "Why not, indeed."

"Do you go to the theatre much?"

"Not often. I've usually got enough drama going on in my own life."

O-kaaay. Next topic.

Um . . .

We must be able to talk about *something*. But—what?

He relented. "*Cats* is my all-time favourite. What about you?"

"*Les Mis.*" I gratefully took his lead. "It's amazing. I couldn't get into *Cats.*"

"No? *Cats* is far more original, though, don't you think?"

As we chatted I began to relax. Sal was right: he was easy to talk to, and disagreeing with him became a bit of a game.

He was a die-hard Manchester United fan; I told him football was over-rated. He loved Spain; I preferred Italy. He despised politics; I said it was a necessary evil.

"You're determined to disagree with me, aren't you?" said Matt.

"Of course not."

He raised an eyebrow.

My lips twitched. "Oops."

And so it continued. He thought Ozzy Osbourne was certifiable; I argued he was brilliant. We laughingly agreed, either way, Sharon Osbourne was a financial wizard. Matt couldn't wait to head off to Europe for a ski holiday; I offered to carry his bags.

Oh shit. Why had I said *that?*

"I might just take you up on that." He grinned, and I felt a nervous flutter in my belly. "Speak any French?"

"Um . . . does 'Bordeaux' count?"

He laughed. "It's a good start."

Actually, Bordeaux wasn't a good start. There was nothing good about Bordeaux. Bordeaux was what Mickey and I had been drinking 'that' night. Bordeaux all over my shirt. Mickey all over me. Me all over the boardroom table. My love-life all over the office noticeboard.

Anything French with the boss—any boss—was a bad, bad idea.

Matt picked up a beer-mat, inspected it and put it back down. "So, Becky-with-the-scarlet-scarf," he drawled. "Why do you think Liz recognises me?"

Just like that. I felt winded.

His mobile phone beeped, diverting his attention, thank God. Too stunned to frame a response, I watched his fingers flick over the keypad.

He snapped his phone shut and looked up, then reached over and fingered my headscarf.

"I like your hair," he murmured. "Don't hide it too long."

My face flamed. I opened my mouth but the words jammed in my throat. I closed it again, a goldfish in need of a bowl.

He leaned back in his chair, propping one foot on a nearby chair.

This wasn't good. In fact, it was really really bad. I should go.

But my body refused to move. My breath hitched. I was an elastic band, stretched to snapping-point.

"Well?" he prompted.

How could he sit there so darn relaxed? I hated him.

"W-well what?"

"Are you going to admit you recognised me or—" his eyebrow twitched up "—do I have to drag it out of you?"

I gulped. "I don't see how y—"

"How many laps do you swim?"

"Forty."

He grinned, and I realised how easily he'd trapped me. Damn him! Again.

"Uh-oh," I said, "gotta go to the ladies'."

That's right, Becs. Run. Excellent.

I stood and felt a sudden *whoosh* of light-headedness.

Matt straightened in his chair, reached out a helpful hand. "Are you okay?"

I nodded, steadying myself against the table. "Back in a minute."

I smiled, then turned and made my way towards the toilets. Uh-oh. Shifting floor. How many drinks had I had?

No idea. Bad sign.

I wove and bumped my way to the ladies', lurched into the nearest cubicle, and collapsed gratefully onto the toilet seat.

In the background the relentless *doof-doof-doof* of the music competed with the Friday night crowd. Each *doof* was a nail driving into my skull. I slumped back against the cold stability of the toilet cistern and closed my eyes. How had I become so drunk so fast? I hadn't even been feeling tipsy.

Well. Maybe a little.

I took a deep breath, and another. Maybe I should go home. Yes. Good idea. Shouldn't let Matt see me like this . . .

* * *

Laughter at close quarters.

I groggily opened my eyes, gazed around in confusion, registered where I was. The *toilet?* Nightmare.

Was that a face beneath the cubicle door? How strange. I tilted my head to one side and frowned. It *was* a face. A one-eyed face, squashed like a soft-toy between floor and door. The face grinned and disappeared.

"That's her." A giggle. "She's plastered."

Scrabbling in the next cubicle. Then, above me, a voice. "Becky Jordan, what are you doing?"

I looked up. "Liz?"

"You can't sleep in there. Stand up."

"I din' feel sho good." I did my best to push myself upright, and the cubicle wall did its best to help.

"Hey," said Sal, "unlock the door."

I slid the bolt across. The floor tilted dangerously. She pushed the door open. Liz disappeared from above and materialised behind Sal.

Wow. Three people could fit in a toilet cubicle? Oops—four, if you counted both Lizes. We all spilled out.

"Freedom!" I cried. Right before my legs buckled under me.

"We'll have to carry her," said Sal.

"No," I protested. "I'll walk."

"Really? Funny." Liz didn't laugh.

Sal hauled me up by an elbow. "Grab an arm, Liz. I've got this one. She'll manage if we hold her upright," Sal added, as if I weren't even there.

We lurched out of the restroom and through the throng.

Matt.

Oh *shit*. I'd *die* if he saw me like this.

I looked furtively towards our tables, ready to Stop, Drop and Roll if I spotted him.

So far so good.

"Quick," I muttered. "Get me outta here." And hurriedly made my escape.

CHAPTER SEVEN

I woke up slowly. No change there.

What *had* changed was that someone was using a pickaxe to beat a hole in my head. From the inside out.

I groaned, rolled onto my back and assessed the damage. Lower limbs in working order. Toes accounted for. Left arm—oops, trouble there—a dead weight. Right arm fine, fortunately. Stomach very much the worse for wear. Oh God, dry horrors beyond belief, tongue stuck to the roof of my mouth and twice its normal size. Vile taste in mouth— yuk. Nasty brewery smell clinging to me, and if even I could smell it I must be *reeking*. Memory—not sure. Head—not good. Refer to pickaxe comment above. Today would be tough.

I opened my eyes. Rats. Contacts still in. Gritty to the point of pain. On the upside, by some miracle I'd made it back to my own bed. I lurched into a sitting position, swung my legs over the side of the bed, and registered my lack of clothes.

Shite. I glanced frantically around, and spotted the small pile of clothes neatly arranged over the back of my chair. Crap. No *way* could I have folded those clothes; not in the state I'd been in. I probably couldn't fold them like that *sober*.

Who had undressed me? I held my head in my hands, wishing the throb would ease. Jo, maybe? *Eeeuww*—Jim? Oh no—Matt?

My palms grew sweaty. I felt sick. Not Matt. Please don't let it be Matt.

I forced myself to focus, to think, to find even a sliver of memory. But—nothing. I couldn't even remember climbing the stairs, let alone undressing and crawling into bed.

My heart lurched. Bed. I *had* slept alone . . . hadn't I?

I turned, like a prisoner facing the firing squad, and checked the pillows. Only one side had that slept-in look. I sagged with relief.

Okay, forget it. Somehow I'd made it home, and somehow I'd made it to bed.

I cautiously stood and waited for a stomach rebellion. Nothing happened so I reached for my dressing gown and slippers and crept—for the sake of my head rather than Jim—to the toilet and then downstairs. No sign of Jim in all his morning acerbic glory, thank goodness.

Strong black coffee, that's what I needed. Instant; I couldn't wait for the plunger. As for Jules, the cat-food would have to wait. I ignored his accusing glare and walked through to the living room. Then we slumped at the table, my coffee and me, and tried to remember.

Clearly I'd had far too many champagnes. I remembered talking—flirting?—with Matt, and being bundled into a taxi. I had a vague recollection of struggling to find my keys. No matter; I was inside now.

But I wasn't kidding myself. It mattered. Please, please, *please* don't let it be Matt who put me to bed.

Who else had I made an exhibition of myself with? I sipped my coffee, feeling exceptionally seedy and more than a little sorry for myself. Hell, I'd only been at T&T a week! Any good impressions I'd made would've been well and truly un-made by last night's exploits. What had I been thinking? That I was fifteen or something? I was a stupid, overindulging, pissy old tart who deserved everything that was coming to her.

By the time Jim appeared I'd managed a slow cup of coffee and a fast trip to the toilet. I'd also aborted a shower halfway through after the steamy heat brought on another bout of nausea and dotty pre-fainting vision. I felt like something Jules had dragged in. Half-dead and severely pawed over.

Jim took in the extent of my hangover and literally rubbed his hands with glee. I braced myself.

"Well," he chirruped. "We're up bright and breezy this morning."

I gave him a hollow look.

"Good night, then?"

"I guess so." *Guess* being the operative word.

"What was the big idea, trying to break into the flat? You guys just about put me into an early grave."

"Um—sorry?"

"You don't remember?"

I paused, waiting for the memory to return. It didn't.

"I guess not," I sighed.

"Repeat after me: my name is Becky Jordan and I am an al—"

"Ha ha, very funny."

"Seriously, maybe you should come to a meeting sometime."

I shot him an exasperated look. "Jeez, Jim. It was one night."

"Whatever."

Great. I already had memory loss and a mammoth hangover to contend with, and Jim wanted to do a one-man intervention on me?

Forget it. This was just him getting payback.

I gritted my teeth, closed my eyes, and counted to ten. Twice. Opened them again and sighed.

"Go on, then. Tell me what happened." As if he wasn't about to.

"I hear a racket at the front of the house," he said, with relish and plenty of headspin-inducing arm waves, "come out to sort out the burglars, and you and Liz are watching some big fat mama pole-dance her way up the drainpipe."

Oh. Yeah, I did remember something like that, now he mentioned it.

"What was all that about?"

"Um, I think Sal was trying to open my bedroom window."

"What, a storey up?" He shook his head. "Ever heard of using a key?"

I looked at him blankly. Good point.

He picked a days-old maltezer off the floor and casually lobbed it into his mouth. A standing catch? How did he *do* that?

"Or, hey," he said, "knocking on the door, even?"

"We did." I hesitated. "Didn't we?"

He shrugged. "I never heard you."

I tried to think. My head pounded.

"I don't remember. Does it matter? You probably didn't hear 'cause you were zoned-out on porn sites."

He smirked. "Deflection. Easier than self-reflection."

"Fuck off."

"So what did you get up to last night?" he asked. "Impressing the boss, were we?"

I cringed. Probably the opposite. Which was all good, since I needed to keep my distance from Matt.

But all bad, if I wanted to keep my job. My headache escalated.

"Hardly. Went out for a few drinks with the staff, got waylaid by a glass or two of bubbles, you can imagine the rest." Which was what I was having to do.

Jim cackled. "Good stuff. Shagging your boss on the first date. 'Atta girl, Becs!"

I huffed up onto my high horse. "I did not. And it wasn't a date."

"Well," he countered, with his trademark eyebrow waggle, "you told me to imagine the rest."

"You're sick. Sordid." I sighed, feeling sorry for myself. "Depraved."

"You love it."

"Hardly. I only live with you as a favour to mankind."

"Hey, I'm the one doing the favour. There's only one drunk slapper around here."

"I am not," I said haughtily, "a slapper. I did not sleep with my boss—or anyone else for that matter."

"Not that you remember."

It was taking too much effort to stay on my high horse today. I gave up. "I admit to being a champagne addict, and I admit to getting a bit tiddly. Anything else will have to come through my lawyer."

And I took my hangover back to bed.

* * *

I re-emerged mid-afternoon when Dani rang.

"What are you up to tonight?" she asked.

"Nothing. I'm dying."

"Oh?"

"Hungover," I muttered.

"Oh. I'm sad. Can we be miserable together?"

"Sure. Come round. Just don't expect conversation."

"How about a DVD, then? I've got *The Notebook* and *Ghost*."

"Yeah, whatever," I said, unable to muster any enthusiasm.

"Or we can hire one."

"Yours will do. I'll make Jim go for curries."

"Yay!" she said. "Saturday night in with my sister."

So much for being single and living it up.

Needless to say, Jim disappeared into his room when he saw the DVD titles, but not before he'd suggested a threesome instead.

Dani looked like she'd swallowed a fly. "You'll have to kill me first."

"Okay," he conceded, "I get it. You don't like to share. Me neither. Come on then, get your toosh upstairs and I'll give you a quickie before the DVD starts."

He strutted out the door. "I'm horny, you're horny, wanna toot my horn for me?"

We hurled abuse up the stairs at him then settled on the couch with our curries.

"Your house-mate's a creep," said Dani.

I laughed. "He's all talk."

What I'd give to see her call his bluff. She'd chew him up and spit him out.

Dani produced a bottle of wine and popped the cork. I eyed the shiraz with trepidation.

"Hair of the dog," she said. "It'll be good for you."

"You think?" I took a tentative sip. It tasted like medicine; maybe it really would have health benefits.

"How's your new job?" she asked.

"Mmm."

Her eyebrow shot up. "*Mmm* good or *Mmm* bad?"

"A bit of both."

I told her about Sharon's scary colour-coded files. "Everyone says she's a brilliant lecturer." I chewed my food, tasted nothing. "All I've heard is how much everyone loves her, what a natural she is, how much she'll be missed. I hate her."

"I bet you love her files, though."

"Every time I look at them I just hate her more. How will I ever fill her shoes?" I forced down some more curry. "Does this taste like cardboard or is it just me?"

"It's just you."

"Hey, you'll never guess who else I met."

"Who?"

My hangover receded while I delivered the big news. "The guy who

50

saved me at the pool."

She frowned, fork halfway to her mouth. "What? You had to be saved? You didn't say it was that bad."

Not that she'd given me the chance.

Her eyes glowed. "That's just so romantic." She put down her still-laden fork. "Is he hot?"

I grinned. "As sin."

"What's his name?"

"Matt Frobisher."

"He even sounds hot. So have you . . . ?" She leaned forward, like a reporter sniffing out a front-page story.

My grin dissolved. "No."

I reached for my glass and took a sip. Shuddered. Sipped again. "He's my boss."

The reporter slumped back, disappointed. "And?"

"I made that mistake once. I won't be the fool twice."

She raised an eyebrow. "I get it." She picked up her fork again. "He looks good but he's a social disaster?"

"No!"

"Arrogant? Dull? Cross-dresser?"

If only.

"No, he's fantastic." I sighed. "But he can be someone else's fantastic. I'm not interested. Not while he's my boss."

"But why would you hand him over to anyone else? That's nuts. No, masochism!"

I folded my arms. "I'm not going there. It'd just end in tears. He's not worth my job."

"Hey, Becs, if I were you—"

"Well, you're not," I snapped, my headache returning with a vengeance.

I repositioned myself somewhere closer to horizontal, a cushion behind my head. Looked across at Dan, who had a constipated look on her face, and felt guilty.

"Aw, sorry, Dan. I just need paracetamol." I made do with a mouthful of curry. "Let's talk about something else. How's work?"

Her fork made patterns in the food. "Okay."

I watched her re-load her fork and wondered if she'd ever get around to actually taking a mouthful. No wonder she's so skinny. I knew better than to comment.

"You're coping okay with the whole work-Ex thing?"

Dani gave a tight smile. "I guess. I have to, really. He's a major client so I either suck it up or hit the dole queue."

Which just proved I was *so* doing the right thing by not getting involved with Matt.

Her eyes welled up. "I need this job. I'm skint as it is."

Actually, her bonus alone would probably keep a small African nation in food for a year, but now wasn't the time to argue the point. Even I could see her work-hard play-harder lifestyle demanded large and frequent cash injections.

I set aside my plate, sat up and reached over to clasp her hand. "Dan, it's okay to feel sad or stupid or angry or reckless or anything you damn-well like. You're grieving. It'll take time."

"I refuse to grieve over that jerk," she said with venom.

"But you're human, and you're hurting. Don't expect to get over him instantly. It doesn't work like that."

She looked at me with her sad, sad eyes and I wished I could take on her pain so she didn't have to feel it. Which was silly, of course, because she was a grown woman making her own decisions and living her life exactly the way she wanted.

"How about a holiday, hon? There are some great last-minute deals to the Mediterranean just now."

She shook her head. "Work's too busy. And what would I do, apart from lie on a beach all day?"

Lying on a beach all day sounded just fine to me. "Okay, well, maybe you should get some counselling. Have you had any before? No? No harm in trying."

"So you think I'm losing my mind?"

"No! Not at all. I just—"

"Forget it. I'm not doing counselling. Why would I tell a complete stranger all my problems?"

I could have explained precisely why, but she wouldn't have listened. "Or . . . I know! Let's take a kickboxing class. We get to spend time together, we get fit, *and* we get dangerous. Any more jerks and we'll kick them into submission!"

She fell about laughing. "Kickboxing? For God's sake, Becs, I'm fine." Her laughter faded to nothing. "Truly. I'll just keep away from his side of town for a week or two . . ."

She gulped at her wine, avoiding my eyes, then leapt up and busied herself with putting in a DVD. "Come on, then, let's see some Patrick Swayze love." She grabbed the remote and pushed 'play'. "I wouldn't mind someone like him in my life."

"He's dead," I said flatly.

"He was dead in *Ghost*, too. But if that's not love I don't know what is."

I allowed myself a moment's fantasy. Matt, hanging around T&T, singing at the top of his voice until someone—Sal, probably—tuned in and let him use their body so he could have at least one snog with me.

Problem One: Matt would be dead. I didn't fancy that.

Problem Two: I didn't fancy a snog with Sal, either.

Problem Three: I didn't do personal relationships with SSW's. Dead *or* alive.

So there it was. We could watch soppy movies all weekend but it wouldn't change a thing. No Patrick Swayze for her, and no Matt Frobisher for me.

CHAPTER EIGHT

"It's a beautiful Monday out there, folks. London's turned into a tropical paradise . . ."

I lay half-awake, listening to the radio, thinking about the day ahead. A tendril of memory whispered across my mind. A remembered dream? Something from my past? I struggled to hold onto it.

The memory solidified and my stomach did a nasty flip. Flashback.

Little Tuscany. *Hell.* Friday night. Wide awake now, my heart clunking against my ribs, the scene replayed. Me, drunk as a skunk, everybody's best friend. Deep in discussion with Sal, spilling my soul, 'fessing up about Matt. Sal listening avidly, excitement in her eyes.

I hauled myself into a sitting position and rubbed a hand over my face. Gazed into the middle distance, trying to get it all clear in my head. What had I told her, exactly? The swimming accident? Trying to track down his name and number? Oh *no.* Had I told her about all my x-rated fantasies? Would I? No, no, no! I couldn't possibly have been that stupid.

The images kept coming. Sal, a consoling arm around me, engrossed in the drama of it all. Me, maudlin with the drink, latching onto her reassuring words as if they were gold. Sal buying more champagne. *"This'll help you forget, Luv."*

Blast. It all felt too real.

I dragged myself in to work and scuttled out of the lift, past Sal's desk. She wasn't there, thank goodness.

What would she do? Keep it to herself? Or—more likely—have a field day, gossiping to all and sundry about Matt's latest stalker?

I ducked my head and hurried down the corridor. Sure, she was nice, but I didn't know her well enough to be telling her all my secrets. Cripes. What if she told *Matt?*

I increased my pace. Well. Clearly I would have to kill her.

But what would that solve? He'd still know, and he'd still be my boss. Fine. I could kill him, too.

Assuming Sal had blabbed to him. Which she might not have.

I reached my office, threw the key in the lock and leapt inside, whipping the door shut behind me. I leaned against the door, feeling very *Get Smart*-ish. Matt. Must not see Matt. I turned and snuck a quick peek through the glass—nothing, nobody—then quickly snaked an arm out to slap up my 'back in an hour' sign. Snipped the lock for good measure. There. Now, if I hid in here all day, I might just manage to avoid him.

Which left just one problem: I was trapped.

I dropped my bag on the floor and sat at the desk, berating myself. Stupid lush. What had I been thinking? Drinking to put myself at ease was one thing, but drinking without food for hours on end until I fell in a sodden heap on the floor—that was quite another.

And Matt. How could I explain myself to him? What must he think of me? How could I even look him in the eye?

Was Jim right? Did I have a drinking problem?

For goodness sake! Of course not. I had an off-switch. I'd just chosen not to flick it, that's all. But I could if I wanted. Any time. No problem.

Besides, Jim had been kidding. He didn't really think I needed AA.

I logged on to my computer and watched it grind to life. Saw Jim's face when I'd faced him Saturday morning, the expression in his eyes belying the lightness of his words. Maybe he did think I needed AA.

Fine. If my idiot house-mate was going to go all hyper-sensitive on me, I'd just have to show him he was wrong. Moderation it was. Whatever. I'd be so utterly moderated he'd wish he'd never mentioned it.

The phone blinked red at me. My first ever voicemail at T&T, which should've been exciting, but Ms Moderation didn't do excited; not when she was miffed with her house-mate.

I reached for the handset then hesitated, suddenly dry-mouthed. What if it was Gary, delivering a verbal warning?

"Hi there, Rebecca Jordan," said a smooth male voice. "Charlie Hollingworth here. Remember me?"

I gripped the receiver tight, my blood pumping loud in my ears. Not Gary. Worse. I'd buried that name fathoms deep in my past.

"I was thinking we should catch up, talk about old times," Charlie continued.

Catch up? Old times? He must be kidding. I was about as likely to enjoy his company as I would Hannibal Lecter's.

He rattled off his number, but I was fourteen again, and hurting. The day after my first date—my first date *ever*—and Charlie does far worse than kiss and tell. He puts it about that I'm a terrible kisser. A terrible kisser with dog breath. How will I ever live it down? Despair. Disillusionment. Soul-deep shame.

"Call me."

Well, I wasn't fourteen anymore and I'd long gotten over my shame. Had he gotten over being an arrogant, chauvinistic ass? Not likely.

I erased the message, but that didn't stop it replaying over and over in my head. Why, after all these years, would Charlie Hollingworth suddenly be phoning? Surely I'd had enough scuzzballs for one lifetime, without one of them coming back for seconds?

How had he found my work number, anyway? I hadn't been at T&T long enough for them to even update the website.

More disturbed than I wanted to admit, I turned to my computer and scanned my emails, looking for something to cheer me up.

I stared. An email from him, too? Wasn't he being rather . . . persistent?

I shook my head at my own paranoia. He was probably making sure I'd got his message.

I got it, all right. *Delete.*

I scrolled on down, stopping at one from Liz. '*FW: Personality Test— identify your perfect man!*' With the inevitable one-liner, "Worth a look."

Far more worthy of a look than Charlie Hollingworth. Quizzes were fun, and harmless. I pressed print.

Then gasped. No! Not the communal *printer!* Shite! I desperately tried to cancel the print-job but it was too late; the bloody thing had printed. Great. Now I would have to unlock my door and walk all the way down the corridor, past *hundreds* of offices, Matt's included, to pick it up.

What if I just didn't collect it?

Not an option. Someone else would see it, and it had my name on it, and the fallout from that just didn't bear thinking about.

Why, oh why, had I pressed print?

I opened my door, looked left and right, said a quick prayer and started down the corridor. I held my breath and tried to blend into the wall as I passed Matt's office, then picked up the pace a little once I got past the danger zone. It was all I could do not to break into a run as I rounded the corner and saw the printer ahead.

"Morning, Becky."

I reared back in horror. My heart lurched into my throat. I halted mid-stride. Gary. The Big Boss. Stationed right beside the printer, dammit. I smiled a tight hello and forced myself forward.

"How was your weekend?" he asked.

What did he know? What had he seen? His expression told me nothing so I played it safe. "Fair to middling."

He picked up a page as it came off the printer. Horrified, I snatched it out of his hands.

He blinked in surprise. "Er—"

"That's mine," I said. Scanned the text. *'Cost Effectiveness Report . . . Tourism & Travel, Gillingas College . . . Executive Summary'.*

My toes curled with embarrassment.

"Oh." I thrust the paper back at him. "Sorry. My mistake."

He gave me a quizzical look. "That's okay."

He paused, watching the printer do its thing. "I hear you made it to Little Tuscany for Friday drinks."

My heart plummeted the length of my body, coming to rest near my ankles. So. Sal *had* got to him already. This was bad, bad news.

He picked up another half-dozen pages from the printer then turned back to me. "Did you enjoy yourself?"

I searched his face and he gave me an easy smile—or was it more shark? I couldn't tell. I stretched my lips in imitation.

"Yes, thanks." I gulped. "Have you seen Sal this morning?"

"Not yet."

Thank God. Now I just needed to find her and convince her to keep her trap shut. Threats? Not my thing. Bribery? Absolutely. Whatever it took.

Gary glanced over my shoulder.

"Ah, Matt," he said, raising his voice. "Just the person."

My heart surged all the way back up to my throat again, like some half-dead beast frantic for refuge. I heard his footsteps behind me. Desperation curdled in my belly.

"Here's a copy of that report I drafted," Gary continued. "Could you have a look at it and give me your thoughts?"

I stepped to one side.

"Gotta go," I murmured to Matt's feet, and scarpered.

It was only when I was safely back in my office, deep-breathing myself back to normality, that I realised I hadn't collected my printout.

* * *

"Sal? Hi. You're there. Great. Don't move. I'll be down in a second."

I hung up and, before I could change my mind, stepped out of my office. I had to speak to her. Now. Get this whole Friday mess cleaned up and persuade her to keep my secrets secret.

As I headed towards reception her raucous laughter met me halfway up the corridor. In spite of myself I grinned, enjoying the sound. She really was the life-blood of T&T.

Oh joy. Here came Hank.

I stepped to one side, making room so he could pass. "Hi." Be nice, but don't encourage him.

He waggled his eyebrows. "Hi yourself," he said, and winked one of those I'm-too-sexy kind of winks that, on him, was just plain creepy.

I didn't stop to chat.

As I rounded the last corner, there he was. Matt. Right there, at Sal's desk. Leaning against the counter, laughing with her.

"Can you believe it?" she spluttered, dabbing at her eyes. "But what could I say? *I* didn't want to be the one to ruin her week. Figured I'd leave that to you."

I veered sharply away and escaped into the ladies'. Locked myself in a cubicle. Sat down. Stood up. Beat my head against the door a couple of times. Felt the walls closing in. Let myself out and paced back and forth.

Stop being silly; it hadn't been about me.

Ha! It had, and I knew it.

But it had just been one comment. It could've been about anything.

I'd have to resign.

"Oh for Pete's sake!" I said out loud. "Get a grip of yourself."

A toilet flushed and I suddenly realised I wasn't alone. I hastily stepped up to the mirror and patted at my hair. Amanda emerged behind me. She gave me a strange look as she approached the washbasin, but said nothing.

"Amanda! Hi," I said, falsely bright. "I just gave myself such a fright. Almost fell flat on my face. These floor-tiles are really slippery."

She looked at me, then down at the tiles, then back at me.

"Oh," she said, and left without another word.

I watched the door swing to. Had that gone okay?

Sure—except she now thought I was a lunatic.

I waited a few heartbeats and followed. Matt was no longer at Sal's desk so I took a deep breath and approached.

"Hi, Sal."

She looked up from her typing.

"Hi." She leaned forward and stage-whispered, "On a scale of miniscule to colossal, how was your hangover?"

"Enormous."

She laughed. "I'm not surprised. Oh!" She handed me a note. "Phone message for you. He didn't want to be put through to your voicemail. Charlie someone."

My jaw tightened. "Thanks."

Was he stalking me or something? Seventeen years on and suddenly I got three messages in one day? Talk about overkill. Either he was up to something, or dying.

Dog breath.

I crushed the note in my hand. Let him rot in hell.

I shoved Charlie's imminent death out of my mind and focused on the bigger issue: shutting Sal up. "Are you free for lunch?"

"Sure. But not until I've finished this pile." She patted it. "How about a late one? Two o'clock. Can you wait that long?"

I didn't have much choice, so I plastered a smile on my lips. "Sure. See you then."

She nodded, her fingers already back at the keyboard.

Two o'clock! That gave her three-and-a-half *hours*. Plenty of time to destroy my reputation.

And there wasn't a damn thing I could do about it so I might as well put it out of my head. I high-tailed it back to the sanctuary of my office. Stooped to pick up the note somebody had slipped under my door. Wandered in, starting reading.

The missing printout.

My stomach flip-flopped. Who'd picked it up? Heat rushed to my face. Not Gary, I hoped.

I read the scrawled handwriting at the top. *Found this at the back of Gary's report. Figured it was more useful to you than him. PS Have you tried the quiz?*

My whole body crawled with embarrassment as I read the name scrawled at the bottom.

Matt.

* * *

Sal and I met at *Julio's*, a bustling café one street over from T&T. By the time she arrived I was already there, table secured, order placed and conversation planned.

"Hey! She lives!" Sal sat down and placed her order number on the table between us. "How was the rest of your weekend?"

"Quiet. Very quiet."

She laughed. "I bet. Your house-mate was interesting."

"Interesting? Pain in the neck, more like." I stopped as the waitress gave me my muffin and coffee, then turned back to her. "Jim told me he'd met you."

She watched as I sliced my muffin into quarters then eighths. "He seemed rather . . . offbeat."

I smiled. "He's okay. Just individualistic." I picked at my muffin.

"No kidding." Her panini and coffee arrived and she attacked them with gusto. "It was the Bart Simpson boxers that gave it away."

I snorted. *Bart Simpson* boxers? I'd remember that the next time he threw insults at me.

"I mean, hello. My six-year-old nephew wears Bart Simpson boxers." She chewed and gestured and talked at once. "I didn't know whether to whip him onto my knee for a cuddle or call the cops and report him." She chuckled, took another bite of her panini, then washed it down with coffee.

"Bart Simpson boxers?" I echoed. "Are you sure?"

Not that I should be surprised. This was Jim, after all.

"Absolutely. You don't remember?"

I shook my head.

"Guess you had to be there. Oh!" She waved a hand. "That's right. You were."

She laughed then shovelled down the last of her panini.

Out and out fear swirled in my gut. With methodical precision I chopped each eighth of my muffin in half. Sixteen bites. How on earth did I broach this whole Friday night secret-sharing session with her?

I popped bite number one in my mouth. I didn't give a hoot about Jim and his Bart Simpson boxers, but I needed to know *right now* exactly what I'd told Sal and how much of it she'd passed on.

I ate a second piece of muffin. If I couldn't get her to keep her trap shut about Matt, I needed to work out a plan B. Fast.

"He's skinny, isn't he?" she said.

"Who? Matt?" Hell, no. Well-built in all the right places.

She snapped to attention. "No, I meant Jim. But since you've brought Matt up . . ." She pointed her fork at me. "You two looked very cosy on Friday night. Fast work, Girlfriend."

I shifted in my chair, stuffed two pieces of muffin in my mouth.

"No cosier than I got with Hank," I mumbled. Swallowed. The food went down about as well as her words. "Which reminds me, thanks for the warning, *Girlfriend*."

"Touché. You're right. Sorry. I should've said something. Several people have made formal complaints. I think he's on a cautionary. Don't take any crap from him."

Then she narrowed her eyes. "Ha! Nice deflection. You almost had me, there. Tell me about you and Matt."

"What's to tell? We were just talking."

"U-huh. 'Just talking'." She drew quotation marks in the air. "You 'just talked' for so long I reckon you swapped your whole life histories."

She paused. Her face grew sombre. "Just don't get too hung up on him, okay?"

The world tilted.

"Why not? Not that I would," I hastened to add.

She shrugged. "What's to say? Great lecturer. Great sportsman. Great body. Great waste."

I held her gaze. Eventually she looked away.

"Look." She sighed. "He's more interested in his mountaineering than anything you have in mind."

I blushed uncomfortably. They *had* been talking about me. I took refuge in my muffin, dabbing butter on the remaining pieces with obsessive intensity.

Now. I had to do it now, before I lost my nerve.

I carefully placed my knife on the plate. Adjusted it to a jaunty sailor's cap angle. Took a deep breath.

"Sal, about last Friday." I hesitated, then plunged on. "We talked, you and I, and . . . see, there are things I told you that . . . well, I shouldn't have said. Things that needed to stay in my head. Stuff about my past." I paused, and looked directly at her. "And stuff about Matt. Sal, I really need you to forget everything I said."

She leaned forward. "Hey, don't get me wrong, Luv. It's not as if he's told me he's not interested in *you* or anything. It's just . . . look, he may be T&T's most eligible bachelor, but he's also T&T's most determined bachelor. Every woman I know is in love with him—the queue's out the door—but he's just not a relationships kind of guy."

Relief washed through me. I could cope with the heartbreak as long as it wasn't paired with humiliation.

"Sal, promise me you won't breathe a word to anyone. It was the drink talking."

"Yeah, drink has a way of bringing out the naked truth in us all." She gave me an exaggerated wink. "Bet you wouldn't say no to a bit of Matt's naked truth."

I choked down the rest of my coffee. "I'd better go."

"You're running away."

"Yep." I stood. Gave her a closed-lip smile. "But you're wrong. I'd definitely say no. He's my boss, not my lover." I turned to go and stopped short against a wall of six-foot-plus chest. "*Oof!*"

"Who's not your lover?" Matt asked, smiling as his arm shot out to steady me.

Heat flooded my cheeks, spilling down my neck and through my limbs, pooling in my toes. I blushed so hard I may as well have been rotating on a spit. Any second now my skin would do a reptilian peel.

"Oh," I stammered, taking a quick step back. "Nobody. No one. I don't have a lover."

"She's working on it," piped up Sal.

Oh *God.* Shut *up*, Sal. How could I not have sensed him there? How could she not have warned me? I threw her a thinking-of-killing-you glance and, without waiting to hear Matt's reply, dodged around him and shot out of there like I had Jack The Ripper after me.

CHAPTER NINE

I sorted the mess of papers into rough piles on my desk, working my way through a mental To Do list.

Background notes—tick. Course outlines—tick. Avoid Matt—tick. Lectures for weeks one through six—tick. Lectures thereafter—work in progress. Avoiding Matt—another work in progress. Assessments—

Assessments!

I gnawed at a hapless nail, drawing blood. How could I have overlooked the assessments? I had to have them submitted for printing by—when? I checked T&T's schedule. Did a double-take. Checked my desktop calendar. *Tomorrow?* My stomach plummeted. Good grief. I had no chance. I'd been working like a dog as it was, trying to get ahead of all the planning and paperwork. I couldn't possibly have finished the assessments as well.

Or could I?

A little demon in my head mocked me. I'd been time-wasting. I'd been running in circles, achieving nothing. I'd been trying to do a job I had no hope of performing effectively.

Stop it! I stood and paced the small width of my office. This wasn't about me being incompetent, or a failure. I simply had too much to do in too little time.

I stopped pacing and stared out the window. Inhaled deeply and slowly. S-l-o-w-l-y let the breath escape.

There was nothing for it: I'd have to beg.

No point putting it off. The sooner I fronted up to the problem the sooner I'd be able to get back to work. I strode down to Gary's office before I could change my mind, rapped on the door.

Gary looked up from his work and smiled. "Morning, Becky."

"Hi." I managed a nervous lip-twitch.

"You're not wearing a scarf anymore."

I blushed. "My hair's grown back a bit now."

He nodded. "That's good." Another smile, and he continued hammering his keyboard.

I waited in silence, unable to bring myself to interrupt him yet, equally, unable to leave. My hands found each other and wrung together.

Finally he stopped typing long enough to ask, "You're settling in okay?"

"Yes." I sighed. Paused, then, feeling the need to elaborate, added, "I'm really enjoying it."

Even I could hear my lack of enthusiasm.

He chuckled. "I see." He swivelled away from his computer and gave me his full attention. "Are you going to tell me what the 'but' is?"

I blushed.

"Well, yes, there is a 'but'. Nothing major," I assured him. "At least, I hope not. Well, it's not for me, but it might be for you, but I hope not"—the words tripped over themselves—"only I didn't mean for this to happen but it just has and I'm really sorry but you see I'm stuck in a bit of a bind and—"

"Becky." He held up a hand. "How about you just tell me the problem and I'll see what I can do to help."

I exhaled. "Sure. Sorry. It's the first-year Assessments deadline. I don't think I'm going to be able to meet it."

"Is that all? I'm sure we can work a way around that. But it's not really me you should be speaking to. Matt oversees the course so you'll need to talk to him."

I felt the colour drain from my face. I'd managed to avoid Matt quite well these past couple of weeks. It had almost become manageable. But now . . .

"Oh. Of course." I backed towards the door. "Sorry to bother you."

"No bother at all. I'm pleased you're enjoying T&T. And don't worry, Matt knows you've been under pressure. I'm sure he'll come up with a workable solution."

All very well for Gary to say, but he wasn't seeing it through my eyes. For me, Matt represented problems, not solutions. Even being in the same room as him was a challenge.

I trudged down to Matt's office, hoping he wouldn't be there. No such luck. He looked up and saw me as I raised my hand to knock.

"Hey, stranger," he said, then did a double-take. "Wow. You lost the scarf. You look fantastic."

Blushing seemed to be a recurring theme today. "Er, thanks."

My mind went blank. What was I doing here?

Matt sat up straighter in his seat. "I haven't seen you for days. Where have you been hiding?"

It was too close to the truth. My blush deepened, approached beetroot. "Oh, you know, around. Working hard. Trying to get on top of all the planning." I shuffled my feet. "That's why I'm here, actually."

"Oh? You need a hand?" He indicated a chair and I sank into it like a fox hiding from the hounds.

"Not really. Just an extension."

He cocked an eyebrow at me. "An extension, eh? That'll cost you."

"Sure, whatever it takes. The printing deadline for assessments is tomorrow and, well"—my eyes darted around the room before returning to him—"there's no way I'll be able to meet it. I know deadlines are important," I added, "and I promise it won't happen next year, but what with just starting in the job and all—"

"Ah." He grinned. "The new-kid-on-the-block excuse."

He must've heard so many excuses from students over the years, probably far more creative than my own pathetic attempt. I shifted uncomfortably. "I'm really sorry, I know it's not good enough and I feel terrible, but—"

"So what's an extension worth these days?" He leaned back in his chair, rested his feet on the desk.

He winked at me and I did a double-take. Duh. I was such a ditz. He'd been teasing me all along. Come on. He wasn't a monster. What had I been thinking? I'd blown this whole sexy-boss situation way out of proportion. We were friends. Not even that: colleagues.

I rotated my shoulders to release the tension and matched his grin. "Okay, I'm desperate. Name your price."

"Hmm." He clasped his hands behind his head and leaned back even further. "Will a week do it?"

"Hey, three days will do it. A week would be luxury."

"Okay. A week it is. That gives you time to buy me that drink you now owe me."

"Thanks! I'll buy you two."

I trotted back down the corridor with a lightness of step only partly due to my extension.

* * *

The phone rang and I looked up from my work. Really, I had so much to do I should just let it ring. But—I stretched my arms skyward—I needed a break. This was as good an excuse as any. I took the call.

"Is it just me," said Dani, "or are all the good men taken?"

Matt swam across my vision. "It's just you."

She sighed. It seemed to come all the way from her toes.

I deleted the latest Charlie email unread, then pushed myself back from the computer, concentrating fully on Dani. "Want to talk about it?"

"Not really."

"O-kay." I glanced at my work. She'd take it the wrong way if I said I was busy, but it was tempting. "Why are you ringing, then?"

"Fred says I have to keep working with my Ex. The bastard."

"Who? Fred or the Ex?"

"Both."

I gazed out the window at the hazy London skyline. I didn't know about the Ex, but Fred had seemed nice enough on the few occasions I'd met him. Firm but fair.

"Dan, maybe it's just that you're the best person to work with this client. I don't think Fred's the bastard here."

Silence; so heavy I could almost hear her loading the bullets.

"What?" she finally spluttered. "You're saying *I'm* the bastard? Thanks a lot."

"No! Of course not. I'm just saying Fred's got to do his job. If he doesn't keep his clients happy, they won't pay."

"So now I have no rights, is that it?"

I should never have taken this call. "Dani, you know I don't mean that. But how bad can an occasional meeting be? Really?"

"With an ass like him? Bad."

"Last week you loved that ass," I reminded her.

"Yeah, well, this week I hate him. He can't have it both ways, you know."

Both ways? She wasn't making sense. "What do you—"

"Either we're together or we're finished. If we're together, he'd better ditch the wife."

"Wife?" I sat up straighter in my chair. "Are you saying this guy's married?"

"Yes. Married. Which makes *me* single."

Well, hell, I guess it did. "Did you know that when you got involved with him?"

"Oh course I didn't damn-well know that! Jeez, what is it with you?

I blinked. Boy, she was fiery today.

I tried another tack. "What do you mean, he can't have it both ways?"

Another sigh. "He's being a jerk. Tried to kiss me in our meeting today."

"Come on, Dan. You've got a black belt in handling men. Why didn't you just tell him to back off, it's over and he needs to get used to it?"

She was silent a moment. Then, "It's not easy to say that sort of thing, Becs."

"Better to say it than have him bugging you forever."

"Hmm."

"Unless you want him bugging you, that is."

"*Hello.* He's married, so we're finished, okay? He needs to get that into his skull and so do you."

When had this become about me?

"Sis," I said, "are you okay?"

She sniffled in my ear. "I'm fine."

"Aw, hon. First you had to ditch him and now you're having to fend him off. He's being a total jerk, Dan."

"Yeah."

There was a silence. Then she added a soft, "He's still a good kisser, though."

"What? Dani, just make your mind up."

"I have. It's over. He's married, and that's all there is to it."

"Then mean it."

"You have a nice day too," she said, and hung up in my ear.

I dropped the phone back on its cradle and wearily moved to the window. Leaned my forehead against the coolness of the glass and watched all the normal people on the street below. Their lives looked so uncomplicated. I craved uncomplicated.

* * *

Uncomplicated? That was what I wanted? Then why on earth was I back here at the Riviera?

I stared down at the water, panic rampaging through my veins. So what if Liz had been putting the pressure on?

But she was right: it had been weeks now, and the sooner I got back into it the easier it would be.

Only—not yet. This was too soon.

Okay, time for some logic. What did I think might happen? What was I scared of?

Well, death, for starters. Or loose bowels, panic attacks, sudden onset of cramp, general embarrassment . . . So much could go wrong.

O-kaaay. That hadn't worked.

Positive thinking, then. What good could come out of this? Um . . .

. . .

. . .

Well, at least it would shut Liz up. That would be good.

And if it didn't kill me, maybe I'd get over this ridiculous fear of swimming I'd developed.

"Come on, Becky, you can do this." Liz held my hand, tugging me gently towards the pool.

And if it *did* kill me, it would all be academic.

Please let me be somewhere else. Anywhere else.

I took a shaky breath, then another. "I don't know if I can, Liz. I think it's too soon."

I raked the fingers of my Liz-free hand through my hair.

"No," I decided. "I can't. Sorry."

She turned and looked directly into my eyes. "Becs, you had a fright."

I returned her gaze tremulously.

"Yes, okay, a bad one. But you need to get back on that bike and ride it again."

"I'm scared," I said. In case there was any doubt.

"You'll be fine. Truly."

"But look at me." I pointed out my knocking knees. "I'm a wreck."

"I'll be with you the whole way. I promise."

I closed my eyes, praying for divine intervention. A major quake should do it. As usual, nobody upstairs listened. I'd have to get myself out of this mess, dammit.

When I opened my eyes, Liz gave me a reassuring smile. "Just follow me. Everything will be fine."

I shook my head. No. Everything would not be fine. Being here was a mistake. A big mistake.

I extracted my hand from hers and backed away from the water's edge.

"Sorry." Tears blurred my eyes and I angrily dashed them away. "I can't. I just can't."

I turned and ran.

Back in the changing room I slumped on a bench and let my tears fall. My knees continued to quake. What was wrong with me? It was only water, for heaven's sake. It wasn't as if I couldn't swim.

I waited, blinking my tears away and deep-breathing until the shaking subsided. Then I dressed, dragged a comb through my hair, checked my eyes in the mirror. A bit red, but I'd get away with it. Mascara and lipstick, taking care not to let my hand shake, then I checked the result. It'd do.

Six-thirty. It would be a very early start. But that wasn't such a bad thing; I had plenty of work waiting at T&T.

Huge black clouds gathered overhead. I scowled at them. Fantastic. I was going to get wet regardless. Today sucked.

With a quick txt to Liz—*sory xx gon 2 wk, talk l8r*—I high-tailed it for the underground.

Seconds later the phone rang. I sighed. If she made me cry I'd scream.

"Liz, I—"

"Finally," said a very male, un-Liz-like voice. "Becky Jordan, how are you?"

My words jammed in my throat, blocking the air. Charlie.

I slowed.

Hang up. Just hang up.

My ears strained for his voice.

A car horn blared at me as it whizzed past. I gasped. Realised I'd stopped in the middle of the road and scooted back to the safety of the pavement, pulse pounding. He wasn't worth getting killed over.

He wasn't worth anything.

"I'm great, thanks for asking," he said, laughter in his tone.

I thought of all his quasi-stalker calls, and my jaw clenched. All the fear I'd been feeling minutes earlier transmuted into fresh, raw anger. How dare he? And how had he got my mobile number? My grip on the phone tightened. I dragged in some air, and it fuelled the fire in my belly.

"Charlie bloody Hollingworth."

"Hi, Becky. It's been a long time. How's it going?"

Obviously he thought I was up for a friendly chat. I'd give *him* a chat. "It was going just fine until ten seconds ago."

He hesitated. "Have I rung at a bad time?"

"Yes."

"Sorry. I'll call back later."

What, and leave another stalker message? "Don't bother."

"You're right. Easier for you to call me. You've got my number, right?"

Talk about presumptuous. "No, and I—"

"Have you got a pen, then? I'll give it to you again."

He just didn't get it, did he? "Why would I want to ring you? You're a stalker."

"Sorry?"

"You heard me."

"Becky, this is Ch—"

"Jeez, Charlie, what's going on here? You turn up after half a lifetime, bombard me with calls and messages, and you think I'm going to just drop everything for you?" I'd done that once, and look where that had got me. "I'm not, okay?"

"Hey, I just wanted to say hi."

"Well, you have. So thanks for calling, have a nice life, and now you can piss off and leave me alone."

He said nothing, and I was about to end the call when his voice came through again, quiet this time. "Would it help if I said sorry? Because I

71

am."

Man, what did he think I was—some paranoid delusional, still holding on to something from my *childhood?*

"I don't know what you're talking about," I said through stiff lips. *Liar.*

He sighed. "Fine. Have it your way. I thought we were old enough to get past all the bullshit, but maybe not."

"Oh, please. The only bullshit is the stuff coming out your mouth." I gave up trying to be polite. "You know what? You make me sick. You're exactly the way you always were. A worthless piece of shit."

. . . Who tells the whole school I have dog breath and breaks a girl's heart.

I could hear the anger in his voice. "Considering you don't know a thing about me, that's a bit fucking harsh."

"Well, if the shoe fits . . ."

A pause, then a chuckle.

"Oh, you think it's funny, do you?"

He cleared his throat. "Becky, you're acting like I want to kill you, not call you."

"Go to hell." I snapped my mobile closed and marched towards the station.

Jerk.

The naïve teenage Becky had thought him devastatingly attractive seventeen years ago. The older, more experienced Becky knew better.

CHAPTER TEN

I arrived at T&T, thoroughly grumpy and desperate for distraction. E-mails first, and so help me, if there was another freaking message from Charlie I'd take out a front-page ad. about his stalker tendencies.

A punching bag. That might help.

Men.

I strode towards the lift, running the last few metres to catch the doors as they closed.

"Thanks," I said, glancing at the other occupant.

My heart somersaulted.

"Hi, Matt."

He smiled. "Morning. You're here early."

Did he think I was trying to win brownie points? I forced the blush down before it reached my cheeks and returned his smile. "Yeah, it's all those deadlines."

I turned to face the doors which, typically, were now closing so sluggishly the stairs would've been faster. My fingers twitched impatiently. Come *on*. If I had to share the lift with him, at least make it quick. I stabbed at the Close Doors button but Matt did, too, and our hands met in a fleeting touch.

Tingles shot through my fingers.

I jerked back with a muttered, "Sorry." Wished Scottie—anyone—would beam me up.

The doors shuddered shut.

"Don't kill yourself just to meet a deadline," he said. "Do you need more time?"

The lift began rising as if it had to fight for every inch.

"No, no, I'm fine." Why did he think me so incompetent? "I don't usually come in this early," I continued, "but I was awake so figured I may as well be working." Not that I'd make that mistake again. I should've braved the swimming pool, after all.

My nose twitched. Nice after-shave.

Which I shouldn't be noticing. Just like I shouldn't be noticing his proximity. I inched surreptitiously to increase the distance between us, watching the lift's interminable progress on the display. I risked a quick glance . . . *bollocks!* Our eyes met and his eyebrow twitched upwards. I bit my lip.

He looked at the floor, smiling to himself. I followed his gaze down, past his strong square jawline, over his chest (look at those *pecs*) . . . oh boy. My mouth went dry, my face heated. Blood pounding, I looked further south. Forgot to breathe as I took in his chiselled abs—dammit, why did he have to wear such a tight t-shirt?—lower still . . .

I looked abruptly away, furtively fanning my face. What was I doing? Talk about cats on heat. In my peripheral vision I saw Matt glance my way and knew my cheeks were scarlet.

He said, "Are you all ri—", but at that moment the elevator jolted severely, once, twice, then jerked to a halt. His question remained unfinished.

We both looked at the doors, waiting for them to open. Nothing.

"Um . . ." I said.

Matt pushed the Open Doors button. They didn't.

"What the . . . ?" He gave the Level 5 button a prod. Nothing.

"Are we stuck?" I asked, not quite believing it.

"Looks a bit like it." He randomly pushed a whole series of buttons then gave the doors a kick for good measure.

"What, stuck as in *really* stuck?" My heart thudded loudly in my chest.

Hands on hips, he eyeballed the doors. "Yep."

I told myself everything was fine, but my body disagreed. I'd never classed my small-space nervousness as claustrophobia before, but I'd never been trapped in a lift before, either. This felt a whole lot different to jumping in at ground level and leaping out a few seconds later.

Maybe I needed to re-think my claustrophobia status.

"I could really do without this." My voice warbled.

He gave a wry smile. "I know how you feel."

Actually, he didn't have a clue. Dry mouth, clammy hands, and my chest felt like it was shrink-wrapped in plastic. Just keeping each inhalation measured took concentrated effort.

"I've got to get out of here." Then, feeling his sharp glance, I pulled myself together and scrabbled for an excuse. "I need to prepare for my eight-thirty lecture."

He indicated the *Phone—Emergency Use Only* label on the wall.

"No panic. We've got a phone," he said, confident and not at all claustrophobic. "A quick call to the technicians should sort it."

He opened the flap. "Oh." The bare wires stared out at us. "That's a bit inconvenient."

Inconvenient? It was a damn sight more than a bit bloody inconvenient. My chest constricted. I took several deep breaths, trying to stay calm.

"Don't worry, you'll still make your lecture. We'll find a way out."

"Super," I said, but my heart wasn't in it. This lift looked *impossible* to Houdini out of.

"Hey!" I said, suddenly excited. "I've got my mobile."

"Excellent." He patted my back as I ta-dah'd it out of my bag.

Our enthusiasm was short-lived, though: no reception. I dropped my useless scrap of technology onto the floor, slumped against the wall, closed my eyes and tried to magic myself to the Greek islands. Or anywhere. Just get me out of here.

No genies came to the rescue. I opened my eyes and we were still in a metal box, stuck in limbo I-don't-know-how-many feet in the air.

Matt reinspected the buttons. Nothing. I inspected the ceiling. No CCTV.

"This is ridiculous," I said through gritted teeth.

How were we going to escape? Because we would, right? Cold fear trickled down my spine. We *had* to. I couldn't take much more of this.

A quick scan of the elevator's fitness certificate confirmed it was serviced and good for another six months. Funny. I turned my attention to the roof, looking for the trapdoor you see in the movies. Not that I particularly fancied surfing on top as the lift went into free-fall, but if we were about to free-fall I didn't fancy being in here, either. Surfer or cave-girl? I felt dizzy with the enormity of the choice.

But there was no trapdoor, so no choice. Absurdly, I felt disappointed.

I faced the doors again. This was it. Our one and only exit.

Only not today.

"Let's try shouting," I said. "Surely someone will hear us."

Like who? T&T wasn't exactly heaving with people at seven o'clock in the morning.

Matt nodded. "Worth a shot."

He drew a deep breath, then bellowed at the doors. "HELLO! WE'RE STUCK! HELP!"

He kept at it for a couple of minutes, and I did my bit and hammered on the doors whenever he paused for breath. Eventually we stopped, listening for signs of help—or even life—on the outside.

Silence.

I ran my fingers up and down the door seals. "These doors are, like, *vacuum*-sealed. How on earth do we get them apart?"

We had to open them. Or at least break the seal and let in some god-damn air.

"Here, let me have a go." His arm brushed against me, sending a *frritzz* of electricity through my body. My breathing, already laboured, hitched in my throat. Had he felt that, too?

I stepped aside to let him work on the doors, but now, as if the *frritzz* had fried my eyes, I couldn't shift my gaze from him. He strained to prise the doors open and I stood by admiring his biceps. His *biceps*, for crying out loud. What was wrong with me? Did claustrophobia make you horny? If so I was in big trouble.

Why couldn't this job have come with a boss who was paunchy and balding?

"No joy." Matt turned and leaned against the doors, arms folded, looking very relaxed about it all. "Sorry."

"So." I gnawed on a fingernail, unsure whether I was worried more by the stuck doors or my reaction to Matt. "I guess we just sit back and wait."

"Yep."

"And twiddle our thumbs."

"Something like that."

But his tone told me he had plans far bigger than thumb twiddling. My fault: he must've caught me ogling him. But one plus one didn't make a sexcapade. He had a hot body; I'd admired it. That's all.

Anyway, we didn't have time for any of that. This was an emergency, for God's sake! Any minute now we might be dead.

And yet . . . a pulse pitter-pattered in my throat. If we really were about to die, why waste our last moments thumb twiddling? Heat rushed through me as I imagined it. Oh yeah. I wanted to feel his body against mine, his hair tangling in my fingers.

I wanted to *live*. But if we really did have to die today I'd far rather be snogging Matt when it happened.

I felt his eyes on me and had the sudden spooky feeling he'd just heard my thoughts. I licked my suddenly-dry lips. Dodged his gaze and gave myself a good talking-to. Yes, I was panicking. No, that did not give me licence to jump my boss. Yes, he would still be my boss tomorrow. No, we would *not* be dying today.

We would not be dying today.

So I put a lid on my lust, cast about for a G-rated time-waster, and met his gaze.

"Let's play *Two Truths And A Lie*," I said.

CHAPTER ELEVEN

"I have to warn you," said Matt. "I have a great poker face."

That sounded like a challenge if ever I'd heard one. I made a moue. "I hear my face is a dead giveaway."

"I'd noticed that."

My cheeks burned. Had he just seen all my x-rated thoughts in my eyes?

He continued with barely a pause. "By the way, your hair looks great without the scarf."

If I blushed any hotter my toes would snap, crackle and pop. Matt was rubbing salt in my ridiculous little lie and we both knew it.

"You start," he said.

"No, you start. You're the boss." And best I remember that.

"Okay. Let's see . . . fact one: I got engaged once. It lasted eight days."

I blinked in surprise. Really? I studied his face. Truth or lie? He studied me back, poker face *par excellence.*

Hadn't Sal said he was a determined bachelor? Determined bachelors didn't get engaged. It must be a lie.

Then again, maybe the failed engagement created the determined bachelor. Which would make it the truth.

His eyes twinkled. "What do you think? Truth or lie?"

I held his gaze. His expression told me not a damn thing, so I went with my gut. "Truth."

"Well done. Your turn."

Not so fast, Buster. I wanted to know more. "Can I ask what happened?"

"Sure, you can ask. I asked myself the same question."

He shot me a lopsided smile. Looked away. Looked back again.

Exhaled. "Let's just say I don't like sharing."

I grimaced. "Ouch. Did she tell you or—"

"It was more show than tell."

I swallowed. Had he seen her with the other guy? He didn't say, and I didn't ask, because that was getting a bit too personal.

Truthfully, I was surprised he'd even mentioned being engaged. But this game always dredged up unexpected gems.

Unfortunately, it hadn't revealed a way out of this wretched box. I pushed my hand against my chest, hard, as if the external pressure might somehow ease the pressure within.

"Are you okay?"

I blinked, started. "Fine, thanks."

A whopping great lie, of course, but I didn't want him to know how much I wasn't coping. I checked my watch. We'd been trapped in here thirty minutes. As in, half an *hour*. Where was a technician when you needed one? Or an inhaler?

"Fact one: I wish I could swap places with my sister."

"Because she's not stuck in a lift?"

I gave him a rueful grin. "Yeah, that too."

He looked at me for one beat, two. My pulse kicked up. I felt naked, exposed.

Eventually he spoke. "That's the truth. But why?"

"Never mind," I muttered. "Your turn."

"Hang on, back up a bit. What's with your sister?"

I should never have suggested this stupid game. "Nothing. She's just got an awesome job . . ."

"As do you."

". . . And she's absolutely gorgeous . . ."

"As are you." Said with a gentle finger's-touch to the tip of my nose. My body warmed.

. . . And no way would I tell him the other reason. She'd always had a way with men; I'd always been a bumbling idiot. But I'd take that with me to my lift-plunging grave.

"Hey," he said. "Don't change. You're perfect just the way you are."

I couldn't decide if my heart's over-loud *thunk*ing wasn't solely about confinement anymore.

Confinement . . . confinement . . . The thought tripped in my mind

79

like a broken record. "Your turn."

"Fact two: I run a weekend outdoor ed. centre for at-risk teens."

I stared at him. "Wow. Really?"

"Maybe. Maybe not."

That wasn't the sort of thing you made up for kicks. It had to be true. I gave him a slit-eyed look. He grinned back.

Then again, maybe he was just an extremely good liar.

Truth or lie? Instinct told me there was a lot more to this man than hot womanising boss. He was kind and warm-hearted, and he seemed to genuinely care about people, me included. But could I see him devoting his weekends to problem kids?

"It's the truth."

"You're sounding very confident there, Ms Jordan."

I smiled. "Yes. But I'm right, right?"

"Right."

I liked Matt. I liked his looks, I liked his company, I liked the way he made me feel special because I was me. And I *really* liked this other side to him; this giving, nurturing side I kept catching glimpses of.

I wanted more. That wasn't good.

"Tell me about this centre of yours. What sort of stuff do you do?"

"Lots of team building, trust and confidence activities. I'll show you some time if you want."

As in, socially? No way. Bad, bad, *bad* idea.

"Yes," I said. "I'd like that." Which just showed how stupid I really was.

"Excellent," he said, and his smile sent pleasurable little tingles all the way down my spine. "Your turn."

He stretched his arms out sideways, and his hands made contact with both lift walls.

Both walls? The tingles stopped dead. Uneasiness descended. God, this lift was tiny. Really tiny. I swallowed. Was it strong enough to take our weight? For how long? What about oxygen? How long until we'd used it all up?

Fear crept through me, cold, clammy, crushing. I screwed my eyes closed and brought a defensive hand to my throat. I'd better forewarn him.

"Fact two," I said. "I'm not feeling so good. I sometimes get a bit

80

claustrophobic in spaces this small."

"Christ! You should've said." With one stride he closed the gap between us. "Becky . . ."

My eyes flew open.

"It's okay." He clasped my shoulders. "We're going to be fine."

I tasted bile in the back of my throat. *Please* don't let me vomit. If the lift didn't kill me, the shame would.

"Do you think there's enough air in here to last us?" I couldn't keep the alarm out of my voice.

"We've got plenty of air. It's well ventilated in here." He stroked my arms reassuringly.

I rested my forehead against his chest, so strong, so solid. "I hope so." My voice was muffled.

His own voice rang clear and confident. "I know so."

He held me close and I felt safe, secure, protected. The nausea abated. For a while I stayed exactly where I was, against his chest, cocooned in his arms, because here I could cope with anything— claustrophobia, lions on the loose, alien visitations, SSW's . . .

I sighed and lifted my head to thank him, but his lips brushed my forehead and my words dissolved. Our eyes met. My insides turned to jelly, claustrophobia forgotten.

"Becky." My name was a sigh on his breath. He caressed my cheek.

My breath caught. I couldn't drag my eyes from his. Long seconds passed. Blood pumped, hot and loud, in my ears. Every nerve ending stretched to breaking point.

I braced my hands against his chest but, instead of putting distance between us, it somehow drew us closer. Heaven.

No: *danger.*

I arched back against his encircling arm, but the movement dragged my hips against his.

Matt's eyes darkened and dropped to my mouth. Raw heat flooded me.

He lowered his head millimetre by tortuous millimetre. I trembled. At last our lips grazed. My nipples hardened against his chest.

He drew back slightly. His gaze held mine, searing me, branding me. His.

"Becky," he said with a break in his voice, and his mouth came down on mine in a hot, demanding kiss.

Desire stormed through me. Dizziness threatened. My arms snaked around his neck, and our bodies locked even closer. Close enough to feel every lean, hard inch of him. Our kiss deepened and I tasted peppermint and coffee and something uniquely, deliciously him.

When eventually we drew apart, both of us breathing heavily, Matt rested his forehead against mine a few moments.

"Jesus," he said.

We kissed again, but this time it was less urgent and more emotional; slow and soft and intimate.

He cupped my face in his hand, then ran his thumb over my sensitised lips.

"Jesus," he repeated, then took my lips in a soul-deep kiss. His thumb caressed my throat, my neckline, trailing inexorably closer to my breasts.

I forgot to breathe. My nipples ached for release. My fingers dragged through his hair. Through the fabric of my shirt, his thumb sought first one ready breast, then the other. I gasped, shuddered, arching into his touch. What was it about this man? Any closer and we'd be in each other's skin, but it wasn't enough. Not nearly enough.

He slipped his hand up under my shirt and over my ribs, cupping a breast. His groan, raw and sensual, did delicious things to my body. Oh yeah. I'd take a fortnight of this, even knowing he was my boss.

My boss. The thought whipped me back to reality with stopped-by-the-cops speed.

Would I never learn?

"You're trouble," Matt murmured, his lips in the hollow of my neck.

Why, oh *why*, did he have to be my boss? I came to, feeling like the cat that almost got the cream, only to have it whipped out from under its nose.

"Your claustrophobia's got a lot to answer for," he said.

The C-word was a thumping return to reality. Passion? What passion? I was stuck. In mid-air. Suspended in a little box. With no space. No air.

Suddenly the pressure in my chest was overwhelming. How had I managed to breathe all this time? I needed air. *Now.*

I pushed my hands against him, hard, and backed up, desperate for breathing space. Came up short against the wall and stared at him with naked terror, my breathing shallow and far too rapid.

"Oh shit," he said. "Fuck. Stupid comment."

He hesitated. "I don't suppose another kiss would help?"

I strained for air, unable to respond, my palms flat to the wall. How could he even joke about it? I slid down the wall, planting myself on the floor, and my mood came down with me, unleashing the full force of the claustrophobia I'd kept in check until now. Panic rose in my throat. I closed my eyes to block out the reality of my confinement, hands pressed flat against the floor, my back rigid against the wall. This was the longest I'd ever been trapped in a small space. Tears slid down my face as I fought not to be lose myself in a mindless screaming frenzy.

Matt crouched down in front of me.

"No, no, no, no, no," I moaned.

He gathered me into his arms and I fell apart, clawing at him as I sobbed and wailed and screamed into his shirt. I clung to him, one minute pleading with him to get me out of this hell, the next beating my fists against his chest and blaming him.

As I teetered on the edge of complete hysteria, he pulled me away from him and held me firmly at arm's length.

"Becky," he said then, with a gentle shake, *Becs. Stop.*

I couldn't. I'd gone well past the point of self-control. The sting of his hand on my cheek wasn't pleasant, but it was effective. I gasped, my eyes wide in shock and hurt and disbelief.

"Sorry, honey, I had to do that. You were hysterical."

I was no longer hysterical, but I was dizzy and nauseous and there wasn't enough air.

"Becs, slow down, you're hyperventilating."

Great. A medical condition. Just what I needed. I closed my eyes again, one hand to my forehead.

"Come on. Slow. Down."

What was happening to me? Why did I feel so ill? What did he mean, slow down? The tears started again, accompanied by big, blubbery, I-can't-cope-any-more sobs.

"Becs, listen to me," he said, more gently. "You're going to be fine. You just need to breathe. Slowly."

Dizzy blackness threatened to overwhelm me. I slumped back any old how.

"Whoa, careful." He grasped my shoulders and eased me to the floor. "Lie down, it'll stop the dizziness. Knees up. That's it."

He stroked my hair, and it felt stifling and reassuring all at once. "You're okay, Becs. Just take it easy."

Take it *easy*? How could I? I felt sick, I felt faint, and I couldn't breathe. It was like the pool all over again, minus the water.

"Becs, listen to me. Can you open your eyes?"

I shook my head.

"Okay, that's fine. I need you to listen. Can you do that for me?"

A brief nod.

"Great. We need to slow your breathing down, and we're going to do it together. Deep breaths, Becs. You're going to be fine. Breathe in . . . and out. That's it. In, two, three; out, two, three. There's plenty of air, don't worry. Deep breaths. Keep going." A shoulder squeeze. "Good girl. Slow breaths."

We carried on until I was breathing normally again. I tentatively returned to a sitting position.

"Are you okay?"

I opened my eyes and looked into his. "No," I whispered.

The very fact I'd answered, though, told him I was coping again.

"We're getting out of here, don't you worry," he said.

With another quick hug, he stood and faced the doors. He squared his shoulders and began an unrelenting frenzy of shouting and hammering—hell on my tension headache but probably a great release for him.

It was only a matter of time before his efforts paid off. More and more people were arriving in the building and eventually a guy on the fourth floor, waiting for a lift, heard Matt's tirade. Some yelled explanations about no phones and jammed doors, and our link with the outside world dashed off to raise the alarm.

Matt sat down beside me again and gathered me in his arms. The sure, steady beat of his heart and his comforting body heat gave me the strength to hold myself together a little bit longer.

When the technicians finally arrived and released the doors I prostrated myself on the floor, my head at the opening, sucking in greedy lungsful of fresh air, heedless of the flock of interested bystanders watching on.

With the lift jammed halfway between floors, we had to jump down to the fourth floor; a graceless exit by me—and a black mark against wearing high heels—but an exit nonetheless.

Show over, people drifted off to their various offices and lectures. I looked at Matt, shattered. He smiled and draped an arm around my shoulders.

I leaned into him, exhausted. Was it just me or was there something Superman-ish about his presence whenever I needed rescuing?

I stiffened against him. And there I went, doing it again. Fantasizing. Turning him into a superhero in my head, exactly the way Liz said I always did.

A hot, awkward blush swamped my face. This man, a man I'd fantasized about for weeks, an SSW and a damned nice guy—what had I just put him through? Torture, that's what. I'd taken advantage of his good nature. I'd manhandled him, stuck my tongue down his throat, forced him to kiss me, then topped it off by throwing a screaming wobbly and showing him how truly unstable I was.

Uncomfortably aware of his proximity, I whirled out from under his arm. "I'm sorry. God, how embarrassing."

"Why? You couldn't help it."

I shook my head, too mortified to speak.

"Come on," he said, "forget it. How about a coffee. We'll take the stairs, eh?" His eyes twinkled.

I couldn't forget it. I'd never forget it. This was, without doubt, the most mortifying day of my life.

I opened my mouth to speak, but nothing came out. What could I say that wouldn't show me up for the fantasizing idiot I was? I ducked my head and, before he could see my tears of shame, fled.

CHAPTER TWELVE

I wandered into the lounge, stopped, stared, then rounded on Jim.

"What's that you're watching?"

"Nothing." He flicked off the TV, guilt plastered all over his face. "Maltezer?"

"No. Don't change the subject."

It had been a poker game, I was sure. I snatched the remote out of his hands and turned the TV back on, double-checking it hadn't been a DVD. Nope.

He tossed up one, two, three maltezers in quick succession and caught them all in his mouth.

Show-off. I pointedly ignored his exhibition, channel-hopping in search of the evidence. A-ha. No poker. That could only mean one thing.

I stood over him, brandishing the remote in his face. "Have you got something to tell me?"

He reclaimed the remote and hid it under his backside. Farted on it, in case I was tempted. "I made the Olympics. Maltezer Tossing. It's a new field event."

"As in, caber tossing for puny boys?"

"Mock all you like: Maltezer Tossing is huge. People were desperate to get on the squad."

"I'll give you bloody desperate." I snatched his precious sweets off him and held them aloft. "What's with the cable TV? Own up, white guy."

He folded his arms. "Bite me."

I wrinkled my nose, then gagged. "Jeez Jim, that's disgusting."

He smirked. I lunged for the remote. Lunged away again, cursing his backside. He cackled.

"Ha!" I pointed at the decoder box. "What's that?"

"Anti-terrorist device. Compulsory issue. David Cameron's watching our every move."

"Funny." Cameron would be gutted he hadn't thought of it himself.

Jim brought the remote out from under. The card game reappeared.

"I am *not* helping fund *your* entertainment."

"Why not?"

I looked at him in exasperation. "Why should I?"

"Fine. Fuck off, then. I'll get another house-mate." He stole back his maltezers.

"Like anyone else would bother. You stink. Your farts kill small children. You have no social graces. You don't cook. You don't clean. In fact," I expanded, "you wouldn't know a bottle of *Cif* if it leapt up and hit you in the head. You leave your shite all over the flat. You have bad B.O. You eat all my food . . ."

He burped. "You love me."

"And by the way, it was my flat first. So *you* fuck off."

"Man. It's only Sky. What's your problem?"

"You." I slammed the door on him, knowing full well what—who— my problem really was.

Matt.

Since Day One he'd spelled danger for me, and I'd known it. But it was my dream job. I'd thought I could handle it, keep things professional. But keeping things professional wasn't proving as simple as I'd thought.

Turned out I couldn't trust the lift. Or Matt.

Or myself.

Poor Jim. I was a snarly, bad-tempered old cow, and he didn't deserve to be my sacrificial lamb.

I'd better apologise.

* * *

"Here." Dani thrust a glass of wine at me. "You look like you need this."

"Do I ever." I unbuttoned my coat and sank into the lounge chair she'd saved for me. Took a large mouthful of Sauvignon.

"Hey." She looked at me more closely. "Is everything okay?"

I made a moue. "Not enough sleep." Which didn't even begin to cover it, but what was the point? Dani wouldn't understand.

"Poor you," she chirped. "Sounds like you need a couple of early nights."

Early nights wouldn't help one bit unless I found a way to banish Matt from my head.

She skim-read the bar menu and passed it my way. "Want to order some food?"

I shrugged without looking at it. "Whatever."

Matt. He'd taken over my mind like a rash. Scratching just made it worse.

She exhaled. "Put a smile on your face, would you? You look like you've been slapped with a wet fish."

"Sorry." I straightened in my chair and made a determined effort. "What movie do you want to see?"

"A thriller." She held out her flawless fingernails, blood-red tonight, and inspected them. "I've got revenge on my mind."

I jollied her along. "In that case, let's go chick flick instead. I don't want to be an accessory to whatever you're planning for your Ex."

She grinned. "Okay, a tame old chick flick, then. And we'll work out how you can snare Matt."

I grimaced. "Or not. How about . . ." I scanned the feature list. "*Not The Marrying Kind*? I hear it's good."

Her mobile rang. She glanced at the number. "Sorry, it's a work call. I'd better take it."

"Sure."

"Dani Jordan speaking." She covered the mouthpiece with her hand. "Get the tickets," she mouthed. Then, into the phone, "Oh, hello. That's strange. Didn't you get my email?"

I joined the ticket queue. What to do about Matt? This whole situation was getting out of hand. I couldn't hide at home forever: I had lectures to front up for, a job to do. A *great* job. And honestly? Anti-commitment boss versus job-of-a-lifetime? It was a no-brainer.

"Next, please."

Fine. I just needed to decide he was ugly, nasty-minded and a total turn-off. None of which were even close to the truth.

Tickets bought, I returned to my chair. Sipped at my wine.

Hypnosis, maybe?

I shuddered. No. What if the hypnotist slipped up and I ripped off my clothes every time Matt appeared?

With an apologetic smile, Dani stood and walked to a quiet alcove where she continued her conversation in low, urgent tones.

Maybe I should ask Dani for advice. She'd been there done that with men. If anyone would know what to do, she would. And if not . . . well, at least she'd have a box of tissues.

On the other hand, look at her. The tilt of her head, the agitated gestures, the tension in her body. She had enough stress in her life already, without taking on mine as well. Besides, somehow it felt all wrong to be crying on her shoulder when it usually worked the other way.

Phone call over, Dani returned and tasted her wine. "Nice," she decided. "Sorry about that. Another cranky client."

"Speaking of cranky clients," I ventured, "how's it going with your Ex?"

"As in, has he begged forgiveness and promised to be eternally mine?" Dani downed the rest of her wine. "Hardly. Not that I'd believe him, anyway."

She stood and pointed at my glass. "You want another?"

I shook my head. Jim would've been proud of me.

When Dani returned from the bar I told her about my quasi-stalker. "You won't believe who it is."

"Prince William?" She flicked open her mobile.

"Charlie Hollingworth."

Her focus snapped back to me. "*What?*"

"From school. Remember?"

"I remember." She compressed her lips, snapped her mobile shut. "You're right. I don't believe it." Then, after a sizeable swig of wine, "What was he ringing for?"

"Just to catch up, I think."

Her eyes narrowed. "After all these years?"

She shook her head. Her talons *click-click-click*ed against her wineglass. "He's got a freaking nerve."

"That's what I told him."

Abruptly she stopped tapping. She stared down into her sauvignon with the sort of intensity she usually reserved for shoe-buying. "Did he mention me?"

I frowned. "No. Was he meant to?"

"No." Her foot started that annoying bouncy thing she always did when she was agitated.

My frown deepened.

"Forget it." She looked away. *Click-click-click* went her nails again. She scanned the room with jerky movements.

What was going on? Our mums had been friends, so she would've known Charlie, but she'd been several years behind us in school. He'd barely have known she existed. Unless . . .

"Dan, did you have a crush on him or something?"

"Don't be bloody stupid!"

I blinked. Settle, Petal. Sure, she knew about the Dog Breath thing, knew I disliked him . . . but if this was purely sister loyalty, wasn't she taking it a bit far?

The silence grew.

I reached over and gently shook her arm. "Hey. Dan. Don't be like this. He didn't have time to mention you, that's all. I hung up on him."

For a few heartbeats the only sound was the staccato of nails on glass.

"Good," she said. "That's all he deserved."

Her face darkened. "What a bastard. After everything he's done, he turns around and pulls a stunt like this."

"What do you—"

"How dare he!" she exploded, and so did her glass as she slammed it down on the table.

I jumped.

Heads turned. She stared balefully back at the patrons.

What the . . . ? Dani'd always had a temper, but even for her this was over the top. Blushing on her behalf, I scrambled to pick up the shards.

What had just happened? Why had Charlie's name triggered such an extreme reaction? I frowned up at her.

She intercepted my gaze. "What?"

"Would you like to smash mine as well?" I pasted on a grin, trying to diffuse the tension. "Maybe I could line up half a dozen? You want them full or empty?"

After a moment, her shoulders eased. She managed a wry smile. "Good idea."

Another pause, then her lips twitched. "I'll wait 'til you've cleaned up that one first."

Our eyes met, and we both laughed.

"Look at them staring," she said.

We laughed harder. The more people stared the harder we laughed, until our sides ached, tears streamed down our faces, and we were no longer even sure why we were laughing.

I gasped for breath. "Is it PMT or post-man-itis?"

"Probably both." She dabbed at her eyes, then reached over and stole my wine-glass. I decided her need was greater.

"Anyway," she said, all calm-after-the-storm, "forget Charlie. Have you snogged your hot boss yet?"

The inevitable blush rose in my cheeks and I looked away. Too late. She'd seen it.

"You dirty dog! Tell me *everything*. When?"

"Ten days ago."

Another eyebrow twitch. "Not that you're counting. Where?"

I hesitated. "The lift at work. It was crazy but . . . we got stuck."

"You what?"

"Stuck. As in, mechanical breakdown. Stuck between floors. Doors wouldn't open." I shuddered. "It was awful."

"Why? I thought you said he was gorgeous."

I sighed. "He is. Easy to talk to, too."

"Well," she said matter-of-factly, "that's good. At least you've got him out of your system."

"Mmm. I don't think it worked. Getting him out of my system, I mean."

"Why not?"

"It felt too right," I said miserably.

"Go for it. You're both consenting adults."

"Yeah, but he's my boss. And I'm not about to screw up this job on an office fling."

"Who kissed who?"

"What?" Then, catching up with her, "Oh. I kissed him."

This time the blush flooded all the way down to my toes. Why on earth had I thrown myself at him like that? I looked at her, stricken. "Oh God, you're right. He just put up with it because he couldn't escape. What must he think of me?"

"He'll be thinking you made his day."

"Hardly. Not after I got claustrophobic and had the screaming panics on him."

Her amusement turned to horror. "Did you really? You poor thing. Was it bad?"

I nodded. Hid my face in my hands. "I'm so embarrassed. He'll think I'm completely unbalanced."

"I doubt it. Did he kiss you back?"

"Well, yes . . ."

"Did he enjoy it?"

"How should I know?"

She raised an eloquent eyebrow.

I remembered the hard feel of his body against mine, the look in his eyes, the urgency of his lips. I chose a fingernail and bit it. "I guess so."

"Then stop being silly. Have you seen him since then?"

I folded my arms, huddling deep in my chair. "I've been avoiding him."

Agitated, I unfolded my arms, rasping my palms back and forth along the chair arms. "We've talked a couple of times, but only about work. Only when I have to."

She raised an eyebrow. Said nothing.

"What?" I demanded.

"Chicken."

"No, realistic. The less I see of him the better. This job is too good to walk away from, and no way can I let him do a Mickey on me. So I need to get over him. Fast."

I stared glumly at my wine-glass in her hand, then leaned over and swiped it back, emptying it in one greedy mouthful. "Any suggestions?"

Dani looked at her watch and stood. "The movie's about to start."

We linked arms and walked into the theatre.

"For what it's worth, Becs, I think you need a man to get over a man. Get out there and have sex."

She would say that.

"Yeah. Lots of it. Don't be fussy. Get laid," she instructed. "You'll soon forget your horny old boss if you're getting plenty elsewhere."

Casual sex? No. This was me we were talking about. I'd probably choose a complete jerk and have to fend them off with pepper-spray.

CHAPTER THIRTEEN

I graded the essay I'd just read, glanced at my bedside clock, picked up the next. Matt's face swam across the words, and I sighed. Knowing I needed to stop behaving like an obsessive, lust-ridden teen was all very well; it was the actual stopping that counted.

Easier said than done, of course.

I played pen acrobatics as I read. Made it to the end of the paragraph before my eyes glazed over. Was Matt marking, too? Lecturing, maybe. I bet he was a charismatic lecturer. Confident, funny, friendly, attentive, warm eyes, hot body . . .

Enough already! Who cared what Matt was doing? Not me.

Okay—lie. I did care. But I shouldn't. And I wouldn't, once I'd worked out how to wipe him from my mind.

Essays, Becs. They weren't going to mark themselves.

Jim's voice drifted up the stairs. Talking to himself again, eh? I listened for a moment but couldn't quite make out the words. Was he arguing with the TV? Pretending he was Shakespeare? Talking dirty with the dishes?

Whatever. I scribbled a comment in the margin, turned the page. Actually, this essay was good. Maybe I'd be able to award an 'A' today, after all.

Jim rapped on my door.

"What?" I kept reading. "If it's not critical to life as we know it, go away."

"Does coffee count?"

I started. My pulse galloped. That wasn't Jim. That was Matt. What was he doing here?

Crap. I looked down at my sloppy tee and sweats (disastrous), around the room (tornado), down at my hands (shaking). The window wasn't an option; the drop to ground level would be a bone-breaker. Could I hide under the bed?

Sure, but I'd already spoken so it wouldn't look good for my sanity. I was screwed.

The door opened and there stood Matt, bearing two takeaway coffees and the sexiest say-you-love-me smile.

"Cappuccino, no sugar," he said. "Just the way you like it."

I blinked. He knew that?

"Thanks." I tried to keep the suspicion out of my voice but the fact was I *was* suspicious. Matt visiting me at home smacked of ... something. I wasn't sure what.

"You're welcome."

Maybe this was his way of saying let's-be-friends, of acknowledging things had gotten out of hand in the lift?

Then again—his body language wasn't begging for remorse. Far from it. Nervous anticipation tickled my throat.

Nuh-uh. We weren't going there. I deftly magicked my anticipation into annoyance, and directed it straight at the threat. "How did you get my address?"

"You gave it to me, remember?"

Um ...

"After drinks at Little Tuscany? You texted? Invited me over?"

It didn't ring even the teensiest little bell, but I wasn't about to let him know that.

"It wasn't a lifetime invitation," I said, which sounded plain rude, even to my ears.

Amusement tugged at his lips, and my jaw tightened. Didn't he see the whole point of me marking from home had been to avoid him? We needed professional distance, yet here he was, standing in my doorway with that come-to-bed look in his eyes and that coffee fix in his hand, and if he thought his being here was conducive to me getting any work done ...

"Come on, then. A five minute break won't kill you." Matt headed back downstairs, coffees in hand, apparently confident I would follow.

Tempting as it was, staying in my room would have been petty, so I trailed downstairs after him. Purely for the cappuccino, of course.

I found him in the living room, feet up, already reclining in Jim's favourite chair and looking like he owned the place. Why couldn't he do the boss thing properly? Be formal . . . wear a suit . . . stay at work . . .

Hands on hips, I eyeballed him. "What exactly are you doing here, Matt?"

"Checking you're still alive."

I perched on the arm of a chair and folded my arms. "I'm still alive."

"So I see."

"Job done, then."

His eyes creased at the corners.

I toe-tapped. He sipped his coffee, completely unperturbed, watching me watching him.

I broke first.

"I'm not bunking off work, you know. I am marking. Ask Jim. I've been at it all day."

"Hey, no problem. I'm not bothered either way."

"Then why are you here?" Because I doubted house calls were in his job description.

"I just wanted to . . . make sure you're okay."

The sudden solemnity in his voice echoed along my veins. My determination faltered. I met his gaze, wondering where he was going with this. Because if he was about to talk kisses and lust and office flings . . .

"That bout of claustrophobia was bad," he said.

My jaw relaxed. Claustrophobia I could do.

"And since then," he continued, "you've made yourself pretty scarce. I just wondered . . . you're not scared to go in to work, are you?"

Too right I was. But not the way he meant. I reached for my coffee and took a sip. "No, not at all."

"Really? You're sure? I thought maybe you were struggling to be in the building."

I was, but again, not for the reason he thought.

"Thanks, Matt. That's really thoughtful of you. But I'm fine." I dredged up a smile. "Truly. I just need quiet when I'm marking."

Another long glance and he seemed to accept my explanation. "All good, then."

"Right." Suddenly business-like, he finished his coffee, strode out to the kitchen, binned the cup, strode back in, and flexed his shoulders like a boxer ready to fight. "What's the plan?"

"Bum on seat, pen in hand. That should do it."

He shook his head. "We need far more strategy than that. Here's the plan." He ticked it off on his fingers. "We mark for an hour, break for fifteen minutes, mark another hour, break for dinner, mark another hour, then we stop for the evening. Sound good?"

No, it sounded like I was missing something. I narrowed my eyes at him. "What's with the 'we'?"

He shrugged. "You're not the only one with marking to do. And if you think you're getting interrupted here, you should try it at T&T." He reached behind the couch and pulled out a bulging holdall. "So I stole your idea. As of now I'm marking from home, too."

I felt a sudden urge to laugh. "Er . . . I think you're in the wrong house."

"Oops. Oh well, I'll just work here. That okay?" He indicated the dining table.

No, absolutely not. "Sure."

This was nuts. Only I could wind up home alone with my hot, must-be-avoided boss.

"Jim's just headed out," said Matt, "so I won't be in anyone's way."

"You know Jim?" It all got weirder by the second.

"No. I met him when he opened the door." Matt *thunk*ed his holdall on the table, stretched for the ceiling, cracked a few knuckles, sat. "Anyway. Time for work."

He glanced across at me. "Go on. Shoo. See you in an hour."

Was he for real? This time I couldn't hold the laughter in. "Sure. Come on in. Take over my house. Run my life. Want me to peel you a grape while I'm at it?"

"Two. You'll thank me when your marking's done. And by the way, this is a race. First to twenty essays chooses takeaways."

He sat down, picked one up, threw me a shark's grin. "I'm gonna whip your arse."

* * *

"Read, dammit," I muttered, but the words blurred.

I slapped my pen down, rubbed my eyes, grabbed at my hair.

Seriously, *handwriting*? In this day and age? All I could hope was that Matt had a few handwritten essays, too. Word by word, I flogged my way through the first paragraph's appalling scrawl, then paused to check the time yet again. Had I really only been marking forty-five minutes?

Still, that wasn't bad. Another fifteen and I could go downstairs for a chat. Or not. Up to Matt. I wasn't bothered either way.

. . . Who had he been engaged to, anyway? Had he broken it off, or she? Him, probably. Stupid woman, sleeping with someone else. She had Matt. What more could she want? If I was engaged to a guy like Matt I wouldn't be looking at anyone else. Or letting anyone else look at him.

Huh? I re-read the paragraph, wrote a comment.

. . . The lift. Claustrophobia . . . I shuddered at the memory. Thank goodness Matt had been there with me. He really was an amazingly caring guy. A real modern-day hero . . .

Damn him! Now I'd read the same paragraph four times.

. . . That kiss . . .

I reached the bottom of the page and realised I hadn't absorbed a single word. Ridiculous! I tossed my pen aside and wandered over to the window. Pressed my forehead against the cool pane.

Knowing Matt was downstairs, having him treat my home—and me—with such familiarity . . . It just wasn't working. I needed distance, and sanity. But he was invading my dreams, my thoughts, my work; everything.

Enough already. With gritted teeth I retrieved my pen and started again.

At this rate I'd be marking until Christmas.

* * *

He leaned against my doorjamb, his thumbs hooked in his jeans and a smile playing around his lips. "One hour down, two to go. How'd you go?"

I sighed, put down my pen, and leaned back in my chair, massaging my neck. "Eight. You?"

"Ten."

He walked towards me and my heart lodged in my throat. Matt in my *bed*room. I shoved my hair off my face with hands that weren't quite steady, and smiled up at him. He was right here, so close. Lift-close. Too freaking god-damn close.

"You're winning." I hoped my heart, too fast and too loud, didn't drown out my words.

He stood behind me and, with a hand on each of my shoulders, leaned in, apparently reading my latest essay. My breath hitched.

"We're both winning," he murmured.

And, really, there was only one way I could take that comment.

I had decided our lift kiss was simply Matt trying to distract me, that he'd kissed me out of duty rather than desire. Maybe I'd been wrong. Which meant I now needed to rethink how I felt about Matt, work, life.

I swallowed, tried to breathe, failed.

Backup plan: back off.

I spun around in my chair, forcing him to take a backward step. "Let's go outside. We've only got thirteen minutes left and I don't want to spend it in here."

"Shame. I quite like it in here."

I met his gaze, saw the intent in his eyes, and high-tailed it to the door.

"Fresh air," I said. "That's what we need."

Or cold showers.

* * *

I didn't need to turn; my pulse told me who was there, yet again.

"Coffee? Juice? Cider?" Matt asked.

I glanced across at him. "No, thanks."

"Cream donut? Chocolate? Apple?"

I smiled, shook my head. "No. Go away. The hour's not up for another"—I checked my watch—"thirty-three minutes."

He left with a chuckle and a wave, and I congratulated myself on not giving in to any of his delicious temptations.

* * *

Matt again. "I'm on fifteen. How about you?"

I raised an eyebrow at him. "Not telling. And don't think I don't know your game, Buster. You're trying to psyche me out with all these updates. It won't work, you know."

"Pity." He walked over to me, hovered, picked up an essay. "Hey, you'd better double-check this one. I think the grade's wrong."

I narrowed my eyes at him. "That won't work, either."

Jules, curled up on the desk beside my papers, opened one eye and looked at Matt.

Matt reached out and scratched Jules behind the ears. "So you're the secret weapon, eh? What's your name?"

"Jules," I said.

Jules rose, stretched, and moved closer to Matt, smooching under his hand like the traitorous beast he was.

I shook my head in disgust. "Jules has loose morals and very bad taste in people."

Matt grinned. "Unlike you."

"Exactl—"

He crooked a hand around my neck, bent close, and brought his lips down on mine in a breath-stealing, tongue-probing, fiery French kiss. A kiss that lasted just long enough to render me swollen-lipped and aching with need.

My body might be treacherous and weak, but that didn't mean I was about to let him win his marking contest.

I drew in a shaky breath. "Reckon you must be worried if you're resorting to measures this desperate."

He laughed, chucked my chin, and headed for the door. "You're a hard nut to crack, Becky J."

* * *

"Ha!" I wrote the grade with a flourish, threw down my pen, and flung open my door. "Twenty! I win!"

I danced downstairs and into the lounge. "Ta-dah! Twenty! Thank you, thank you . . . Where are you?"

"I demand a recount," said Matt from behind me.

I turned.

"Me too," said Jim.

My jaw dropped.

There they sat, maltezers in hand, drinks within reach, and guilty grins on their faces.

"I'm still marking in my head," said Matt, looking like he'd been caught stealing sweets at the corner shop.

"He's just being sociable," said Jim between chews.

"And you left me slogging away upstairs." Hands on hips, I glared at them. "Bastards, the pair of you."

"But you won," said Matt, "so you'll forgive us."

"Me, maybe," said Jim. "You? No chance. She'll make you pay. For. Ever."

"Have a cider." Matt passed me a bottle. "You won so it's your choice of takeaways. I'll even pay. Forgive me now?"

I drank some cider, thought about it, and decided, no, I didn't forgive him. I really did feel put out. Which was pathetic, of course, since I had nothing to feel put out about. So what if Matt had taken a break?

"Damn," said Matt, his eyes on me. "You're right. She's got murder on her mind."

"Don't be silly," I said, but it came out sharper than I'd intended.

Jim cackled. "It's the Punch and Judy show."

I gave him the evils. "I'll bloody Punch and Judy you."

"Sorry, Becs." Matt adopted a lost-puppy look. "It was Jim's maltezer trick that did it. Have you seen it? It's great." The puppy's eyes gleamed. "Watch this."

He tossed a maltezer in the air, caught it in his mouth.

Excellent. He could do it, too. I was the only plank on the planet who couldn't catch a maltezer.

"Yes, yes." I sighed. "I've seen it. Many times."

"You have to admit, though, it's brilliant. Hey, Jimbo, next stop YouTube. You'll go viral, for sure."

Jim burped.

"Well said, old man." They clinked bottles.

How was it that a good solid burp seemed to help men bond?

I sniffed. "Whatever."

Matt looked my way and patted the couch beside him. "Come here."

I compressed my lips. "No."

"Fine. I'll come to you."

He hauled himself upright and came to stand in front of me.

I sipped at my cider and sulked.

He touched my nose. "Are you really angry with me?"

His eyes searched mine.

I had been angry only moments earlier but now, for the life of me, I couldn't remember why. Languid heat spread through my body.

"No," I said.

His lips turned up at the corners. He moved in close, so close his body heat invaded mine.

"Damn," he murmured. "I was hoping we'd have to make up."

My heart tried to beat its way out of my throat. I couldn't break away from his gaze.

Jim flicked on the TV. "Get a room."

Which was exactly the reminder I needed. With gargantuan effort, I stepped back and away.

"Dinner," I said. "Takeaways. Now. Some of us need food. And I choose Indian. It's going to be vindaloos all round, thanks. No more Mister Nice Guy."

CHAPTER FOURTEEN

Matt had been cunning. He'd suggested the outing as if it were an afterthought, casually tossed back at me as he left. Tired, my guard down, I'd agreed without stopping to think.

Now, though, I'd had plenty of time to think, plenty of time to come up with a reason for cancelling.

So why hadn't I cancelled?

"I must be mad," I said, with yet another glance at the clock.

"Probably," agreed Liz.

I picked at a fingernail. "I should've said no."

Which would've stung, because I really did want to see Matt's outdoor ed. centre. But, with the whole situation becoming increasingly complex, 'no' was the obvious response. The thinking woman's response.

"But you said yes," said Liz.

Indeed. So, in the absence of any thinking . . .

"You should shove me in a tower and call me Rapunzel." I opened a bag of maltezers, jammed some in my mouth.

"Wouldn't work. Your hair's too frizzy."

"Good. I don't want to be rescued." I proffered the sweeties.

She took a couple and winked. "Sure you do. And he'll be here in ten."

My stomach plummeted. I swallowed. "Oh God. Don't remind me. This is worse than my first date. Quick, distract me or I'll throw up."

"Stay single. It's cleaner. Less vomit." She leaned against my window, looking out over Brodrick Road.

I arched a sceptical brow. "You being a shining example of vomit-free singledom?"

"Yes." Haughtily. Then, "How's your sister coping with singledom?"

I thought of Dani's pre-movie meltdown. "Not so well. She went a bit nuts two nights ago."

"Your sister's always been nuts."

"True. But this was serious peanut slab material." I described our chat, my mention of Charlie, her reaction. "One minute she was fine. The next, psychotic."

Liz grinned. "Why so surprised?"

"Well." I sat on my bed, leaned back, lollipopped a maltezer towards my mouth. Missed by a country mile. "There was nothing to be psychotic about. She barely knows Charlie."

"Maybe she missed this month's bonus."

"Doubt it." I passed Liz the maltezers.

She took a couple, handed the bag back, shrugged. "Dani's OTT about everything."

But not usually over nothing.

"Maybe they had a fling," I said.

Liz broke her sentry duty long enough to shoot me a raised brow. "Works for me."

"But they didn't even know each other in school."

She shrugged. "They could've hooked up later."

I thought about it. "No," I decided. "She would've told me."

"PMT?"

"If that was only PMT, she'll need locking up come menopause."

Liz laughed. "Or sooner."

Indeed. I flicked up another maltezer. Failed. Fished it out of my bra.

"What *are* you trying to do, Becs?"

I exhaled, frustrated. "Jim can catch maltezers in his mouth. So can Matt. I'm going to learn how if it kills me."

"At this rate it might. Here. Give me one."

She shook a few into her hand. Lobbed one up. Caught it in her mouth, oh my God, just like that. Lobbed another. Chewed on that, too.

I stared.

"It's not that hard."

I glared.

"See?" Up went another one, and cleanly down into her mouth.

She grinned.

I snatched the maltezer packet back. "I hate you all."

The Saturday morning stillness was shattered by a deep-throttled roar.

Liz looked out the window and turned back to me, eyes gleaming. "Time to play."

My heart hammered.

She swiped the maltezers. "Guess you won't be needing these."

I swallowed. Felt as if my throat were jam-packed with the sickening little balls. Moved to the window and, half-hidden by the curtain, checked for myself.

A motorbike pulled up outside. The engine cut. Matt dismounted and removed his helmet in one fluid movement. Jules materialised beside him and Matt spent a few moments stroking him. Then, as if feeling my gaze, he looked up at me and smiled. My pulse leapt. I fought the urge to leap out of sight and smiled back.

Then turned to Liz and groaned. "This is *so* not a good idea."

"Go on." Liz dismissed me with a flap of the hand. "It's too late to back out now. I'll hide up here until you've left."

Matt approached the front door. Dry-mouthed, I took one last look in the mirror, decided it was too late for plastic surgery, and headed downstairs.

The doorbell rang, and Jim's voice carried from the living room. "Check him *out*. Oo-ooh-*wee!*"

I cringed. "Jim . . ."

Ignoring the urge to run, I pasted a smile on my face and opened the door. My already-short breath disappeared altogether. Hot *damn*. Leather-clad biker Matt was way, way better than jean-clad boss Matt. This version was even better than bare-skinned swimmer Matt.

"Hey you," he said.

"Hey you," I repeated, with amoeba-like repartee.

He leaned against the doorjamb, all black-panthered power. "Ready?"

I nodded.

"You have a scarf?"

I hooked a thumb through the woollen folds. "Yes."

"Good. You'll need it."

Through the wall, Jim's falsetto rang out. "Is that a box of condoms in your pocket or are you jus—"

I shoved Matt down the steps ahead of me, and slammed the door behind us.

He looked at me, chuckled. "Steady on, Tiger. There's no rush."

"Sorry."

I wasn't, not one bit. If he'd heard Jim's condom comment I'd just die.

"Let's go," I said, and fast-walked to his motorbike. If Jim came out to chat, so help me, I'd stab him with my house-key.

Matt handed me a helmet. My fingers fumbled. The helmet slipped. I lurched, juggled, regained control. Slow down, Becs.

"Have you ridden before?" he asked.

Was it that obvious? I shook my head, suddenly nervous. Heaven only knew what I'd been thinking, agreeing to this.

"Here. I'll help you." He showed me how to secure the helmet, positioning my scarf for best protection against the wind, then put on his own helmet.

His eyes creased at me through his visor. "Don't worry, Becky, you'll love it. Just hang on tight and lean into the corners with me."

He started the engine, then patted the seat behind him. "Jump on."

With a quick glance up at my window—and an even quicker glance away when I saw Liz's smirk—I sat behind him, careful not to touch him and feeling like I had too many hands.

"Shuffle in," he said.

Shit. I edged closer. Our thighs touched. I tried not to think about it.

"No, closer."

Closer? Any closer and we'd be in each other's clothes.

I tried not to think about that, either. But with my girlie bits now wedged against his arse, it was hard to think about anything else.

"That's it. Now, put your arms around me."

My last defence crumbled. I gave in and hugged him close, suffused with heat and desire and bad-girl-itis.

He gave me a thumbs-up and we were off.

I moulded my body to his, trying to move in synch with him, and by the time we were out of London I felt like a pro. Then we hit the M25, freely flowing without the weekday traffic, and Matt opened throttle. The wind whipped at my hair and clawed at my clothes as we slip-streamed between cars, and I laughed out loud, intoxicated by the heady combo of speed, danger and lust.

Through Leatherhead, we wove our way down ever-narrowing B-, C- and probably D-roads, finally swinging into what looked to be a wooded farmer's track. Half a mile further and we emerged into an oasis of activity in the peaceful countryside.

For a moment I said nothing, taking it all in.

To our right lay a cluster of old farm buildings, converted and renovated for the Centre's purposes. Directly ahead, facing the carpark, was reception. But it was the grassed area to our left that really grabbed my attention. Several activities were visible, all of them hosting groups of eager kids—a climbing wall, a tyre obstacle course, some blind-man's buff rope activity, and a scary-looking high-wire thing up in the trees.

I took off my helmet and stared. "Do people really attempt that?"

"You can have a go yourself if you like."

I gulped. At that height? Without a safety net?

He saw my expression and grinned. "Don't worry, nobody's going to force you."

"Is it safe?"

"We haven't had any deaths yet. A couple of broken legs . . ."

My eyes widened.

"Just kidding." He winked. "Clients are more likely to return if they leave in one piece the first time."

Another appalled glance at the high-wires, and I let Matt lead me up the steps of a modest brick building into reception.

The woman behind the counter beamed at him. "Morning, Sunshine. You're popular today. Two messages and an invitation." She handed them to him, then smiled at me. "And you've got company."

"Yes," he said, giving her not even a hint of who I might be. "I'm showing Becky around."

She eyed me surreptitiously, clearly trying to categorise me. Business associate or personal friend? She opted for respectful professionalism and turned back to Matt. "They need an RSVP to the invitation today if possible."

Matt nodded, glancing over the messages. "Okay, tell them yes. I'll get back to you later about the other messages." Then, to me, "Come on, let's check out what the kids are up to."

Back outside, we wandered from activity to activity, listening in as the tutors instructed their groups, watching as the teens tackled the challenges.

We stopped at an obstacle course where everyone was working in pairs.

"This is a trust exercise," said Matt.

The pair nearest us inched their way up a wooden slope and down the steps on the other side. It looked fairly straightforward—until I noticed one person was blindfolded.

"The blindfolded person has to trust their partner," said Matt, "or they won't be able to finish the challenge."

"And if they don't?"

He shrugged. "Their loss. They feel left out when everyone else is buzzing about it afterwards. That's incentive enough at this age."

The tutor walked over.

"These guys are doing well," said Matt.

He nodded. "They attempted it yesterday as well, but they're all far better at the trust thing today." He turned to me. "Want to have a go? I've got a spare blindfold."

Matt raised an eyebrow at me.

Why not? Today seemed to be all about new experiences. So I let Matt blindfold me.

I yelped. "I can't see a thing."

He chuckled, checked the knot was secure. "That's the whole point."

His hands left my head, and I felt very alone in my dark little world. Alone, but not truly alone. I sensed him near. Where, exactly? An ever-so-faint breeze drifted past. My pulse raced. My stomach tightened. He was close, very close. I reached out a tentative hand, and found him. Or, at least, his jeans. His nicely filled . . .

Shite.

Matt drew in a sharp breath.

I whipped my hand back, but it was too late. The damage was done. I'd just groped Matt. Big time. In broad daylight. And we both knew it.

Matt cleared his throat. Another guy—please, not the tutor— chuckled. My face burned so hot that, any second, the blindfold would surely burn.

"Oops," I said. Which didn't even begin to cover it.

Matt's voice was full of humour. "It'll keep."

"I'll leave you guys to it," said the tutor, and we all knew he meant three was a crowd. Which it absolutely wasn't. Hell, no. Three was good. Three was a safety net.

"Please stay," I wanted to beg, because God only knew how I was going to play it cool with this charismatic wild card who'd just blindfolded me and seemed about to lead me badly astray if I didn't watch myself.

But the tutor left and I said nothing to stop him. Then cursed myself for being the weakest-willed woman in the world.

Matt took my hand, his thumb drawing circles on my fingers. I couldn't think past his touch.

"Let's go," he said. "How are you doing so far?"

Aside from drowning in lust? Just dandy.

"Take three steps forward."

I wiggled my fingers to stop his thumb's caress. It was too distracting. "Like this?"

"Yep, good. Now, in front of you are three tyres, one after the other. We need to walk through those." He talked me through the mechanics and I followed his instructions to the letter.

"I feel like I'm about to fall flat on my face."

"You're doing brilliantly."

"I can't imagine what it must be like for anyone who's blind."

"Yeah. But people are amazingly good at adapting."

Just as I sensed a slight chill, Matt said, "We're walking through some trees now. You might brush against some—"

I shrieked and threw up a hand, warding off—oh. A leaf. I giggled at my idiocy.

"Sorry." I shuddered. "It felt like a creepy crawlie."

"I should've told you where we were sooner. Tree root," he warned.

I stumbled on it anyway. "Blindness sucks. I couldn't do it. Not for real."

Matt gave my hand a gentle squeeze. "You could if you had to."

He paused. "But I know what you mean. Take away my legs . . ." He exhaled. "That would kill me."

I tried not to think about his legs. "People adapt, remember?"

His voice grew harsh. "Yeah, but not always in a good way." It didn't feel like casual conversation anymore.

We emerged into sunlight and warmth, but Matt remained silent and the air between us felt heavy. What—or who—was he thinking about? Life in a wheelchair? Somebody he knew? A kid he'd worked with?

"Want to talk about it?" I asked.

"No."

Okay . . .

"Sorry," he said, his voice gruff. "Another time, maybe."

Which implied he wanted us to spend more time together. A little zing of pleasure vibrated through me. Then, close on its heels, guilt that I felt pleased. I shouldn't want to spend more time with him. I couldn't *afford* to want that. Matt put too much of me in jeopardy. My career. My heart. My self-worth.

"Right, Ms People Adapt," he said, back to his normal bantering tone, "enough of that. We now have a tiny little gap to squeeze through so you'd better come close." He tugged my hand.

I approached cautiously, my free hand feeling in front of me at a very careful chest height to prevent another mortifying moment. I stopped when I touched him.

"Sorry," he said. "The gap's really, *really* small." He pulled me tight against him.

We edged sideways towards the gap.

"That should do it," he said.

This gap had better be worth it. With my cheek against his chest and my boobs squashed against his midriff, this was yet another brilliant example of how *not* to avoid Matt.

My palms felt clammy. My breath came in ragged bursts. My body was on fire.

"How are we doing?" I asked.

"Almost there. Breathe in." He held me so close I couldn't tell where I ended and he began.

What I could tell was that he was as turned on as me.

Our hips ground together. I didn't dare breathe. Any more of this and I'd be a whimpering orgasmic mess.

We crab-walked a little longer, every step taking me closer to the edge of sanity. His strength, his body, his smell, his touch . . . It was all too much. I bit down on my lip, hard.

Finally we stopped.

"Gotta love those gaps," he said, sliding his hands up my quivering body, over my shoulders, on to my face. He slipped the blindfold off, and even that felt like a caress.

I opened my eyes and stepped out of his embrace. Missed his body heat, told myself I didn't. Looked around and saw we'd in fact covered far less ground than it had seemed. There were the trees, but . . .

I frowned. "Where's that gap we had to squeeze through?"

Matt grinned.

"What?" I rounded on him. "You're telling me there was no gap?"

He shrugged.

I glared at him. Gave his arm a slap, then laughed in spite of myself. "You conniving—"

"Hey, you copped a feel. I owed you."

* * *

"Well?" said Matt. "Are you going to try the high-wires?"

I looked up at them and shuddered. "Am I hell."

"I'm scared of heights and I've done it. What's your excuse?"

"A freakish desire to live?"

"Tell you what, I'll personally guarantee your safety. I'll escort you up there myself."

I eyed him sceptically. "What, and look after me like you did at the non-existent gap?"

He chuckled. "I kept you safe."

Actually, he'd led me onto hazardous ground—not that I was about to tell him that.

"I think I'll pass this time. Thanks all the same."

"Chicken."

"Yep."

"See," he said, linking arms with me as we headed back to reception, "it's all about self-belief and trust around here. Stick with me and you'll be scaling those high-wires before you know it."

I laughed, mostly because I couldn't think of a suitable response. He so knew how to sweet-talk a girl.

Why was it again I'd decided not to get involved with this man?

"I'll just check in here," he said, "and then we'll head back. Want to stop off for a pub lunch on the way back?"

"Sure." May as well bask in his attention a little longer.

We re-entered reception, but this time the receptionist didn't greet us with smiles. With not so much as a glance my way, she said, "Steph," and handed Matt another message.

His lips compressed in a thin line. His jaw tightened. His arm abandoned mine. In less than a second he'd shed his relaxed-charming-guy skin altogether and became a whole different, cold, business-like beast. I shivered.

He shared a look with her—what were they not saying?—then turned abruptly to me. "Change of plans. I'll drop you home. Something's come up."

I blinked. Took the bucket-of-cold-water effect of his words on the chin.

Well. That would teach me for having such a good time that I expected it to continue.

"Sorry," he added, and it was such a blatant afterthought that my own jaw clenched as tight as his.

"Don't be." Even as I said it, he was dialling on his mobile phone.

I zipped up my jacket, about-turned and marched outside. Who was Steph? And what could be so important about her that it turned Matt into a stranger?

I stood by his bike and resisted tapping my foot while I waited. See? This was what happened when you went against your every instinct and followed your bloody heart. This was insulting, should never have happened, and was entirely my own fault.

I shoved on my helmet and yanked at the straps. When Matt joined me I couldn't look at him. I was furious, and couldn't decide whether to direct it at him, this Steph woman, or myself. So I sat wordlessly at his back, resenting having to hold him but doing it because I'd resent falling off more.

I tried to ignore the warmth where our bodies touched, tried not to feel turned on by his proximity. Failed on both counts.

By the time we reached Leatherhead I was desperate to escape the torture. I tapped his shoulder and waited for him to look back at me.

"Drop me here. I'll take the train."

He shook his head.

"I mean it," I yelled. Yelling felt good, even if the wind carried most of it away.

"Forget it. I'm taking you home, okay?"

He picked up speed.

Fine. Whatever. It wasn't like I had any bloody choice. So I let him drop me home, thanked him because my upbringing demanded it, and walked away before he could speak because suddenly my anger had dissipated and I was left with the nagging worry this was somehow my fault and I needed to apologise or be a better person or lose some weight or look more cool or . . .

And I mustn't go down that oh-too-familiar road yet again. Because I was better than that, right?

Screw Matt for making me doubt myself.

But screw me more, because really, the only person who could make me doubt myself was me.

What had happened? Our day out, our friendship, our maybe-something-more . . . It had all been going so swimmingly well. What had that message said? Why had Matt looked so grim? And who was Steph? A work contact or a personal friend? A stalker? Some date he'd left in the lurch?

One thing was sure: if Matt could disconnect from me so easily, I needed to get over him. Fast.

CHAPTER FIFTEEN

I emerged from the underground into the early-morning chill and fast-walked toward T&T. With all the essays marked, today was my first day back in at work, and my nerves were as jittery as they'd been on my very first day. Probably because I'd now be seeing Matt around every corner.

The more I thought about him the faster I walked. He was my boss so I couldn't avoid working with him. He'd be constantly there, liaising with me, looking over my shoulder, coordinating my every move. Would I cope?

Of course I would. I was a big girl now and I'd work with Matt the same I would anyone else. Grief, he wasn't *that* good-looking. He had a crooked nose, for starters. And he might seem caring and fun and a brilliant guy all round, but I'd seen the other side of him. The side that didn't hold with niceties or explanations or emotions. The side that had no problem dispensing with me when other, more pressing Somethings got in touch.

That had hurt, but at least I'd found out now rather than later. Besides, it had been a timely reminder that getting involved with a workmate was a stupid idea. I'd lost sight of what was important: my job.

I crossed the street and marched on. Dani was right—this was hormonal. A Friday night fling should fix it.

And if it didn't, I'd ask the doctor for drugs.

"Morning, Becky."

I turned and drew up short. *Charlie?* My heart *kdomp*ed, then skittered into high gear. Emails, phone messages, and now this?

"Charlie. H—Hello."

He looked a lot older than I remembered—but, then, didn't we all? He wore it well, though. Too well. Bastard.

"Fancy meeting you here," he said, flashing that lopsided, heartbreaker smile I remembered so well.

"Fancy." This wasn't coincidence. It couldn't be coincidence. Even I knew that.

He raked a tanned hand through his dark, Gerard Butler-ish hair. "You work around here, do you?"

Like he didn't know.

I nodded, but my guard stayed firmly up. I knew he'd done his research. I knew he'd hunted me down. I didn't know why, of course, but he'd never been the secretive type. He'd tell me if I asked.

I thought back to our phone conversation; In particular, my out-and-out hostility. It had felt good at the time, but now he was standing in front of me it didn't feel good. It felt childish.

Why hadn't I just asked him what he wanted? It would've been the mature thing to do. A damn sight more civil than accusing him of stalker tendencies and blowing him off.

I'd been so busy obsessing about my schoolgirl humiliation I'd ignored the probability he might've grown up. I'd knee-jerked.

The silence between us grew.

Worse, he'd known I was knee-jerking. My toes curled with fresh embarrassment. He'd known I was knee-jerking and he'd known precisely why. He'd even offered me an apology; not that he should've needed to after seventeen years. Pretty decent of him, actually. And I'd thrown it back in his face.

I owed him an apology.

"Um," I began, just as he said, "How—"

We both stopped, not wanting to interrupt. Our eyes met, his crinkling with what appeared to be amusement and mine, thoroughly embarrassed, darting away. Now would be a good time for an elephant to round the corner and trample me underfoot.

"You first," he offered.

Rats.

"Okay." I hesitated, awkward. "I was going to say sorry."

He raised an eyebrow and waited.

"I was really rude the other week."

"Hmm."

I laboured on. "I was upset, and angry, and I jumped to conclusions.

Sorry."

He gave me a winning smile. "Apology accepted."

I allowed him a tight smile and walked on, not wanting to prolong the agony. But Charlie obviously had other ideas; as I moved, he moved, and my path remained blocked.

My jaw tightened. I frowned up at him.

He raised an eyebrow. "Not so fast, Becky Jordan."

What more did he want from me? I was drowning in my own embarrassment. Wasn't that enough?

"I owe *you* an apology, too. A big one."

He looked me in the eyes, and my belly did a nervy flip. I remembered those eyes, that look. I'd been smitten, absolutely smitten. Suddenly emotional, I didn't trust myself to speak. But I didn't trust him either. So I watched and waited.

"I should've said this years ago, but . . ." He shrugged. "Look, I was young and stupid. Shot my mouth off. Nothing I said was true. You know that, right?"

He reached out and took my hand. "I never meant to hurt you."

Maybe not now, but back then . . . I tried to reclaim my hand, but his grip tightened. He gathered it in to his chest (gosh, quite muscular), and my pulse stuttered like a startled rabbit.

"So . . . is that okay?" he asked.

I hesitated. I'd carried that *Dog Breath* taunt with me a long time.

Then I noticed his expression, all anxious-young-boy. Come on. Was I or was I not wearing big-girl panties?

"Apology accepted."

"Excellent." The anxious young boy disappeared. "Let's go, then." Charlie The Confident linked an arm through mine and started walking.

"Hang on—what?"

"I'm going to buy you coffee."

"I—I don't think that's a good idea."

"Why not? It's just coffee."

"I know, but—"

He gave my arm a squeeze. "But nothing. Let's start over. Be nice to each other. Catch up."

Hell, this hadn't been in my Apology Plan. It wasn't even in my *Life* Plan.

"Charlie, you don't have to do this."

"I know. But I want to. And I think you do, too."

The man was incorrigible. Not unlike a steamroller. I shot him a sidelong glance and he grinned back at me, every bit the dark attractive rogue.

Oh, what harm could it do?

I relented. "Fine. How about *Julio's*?" I indicated the café as we drew level. "Their coffee's pretty good."

"I have a better idea." He turned, guiding me across the street. "Let's go in my car. I'll drop you back afterwards."

I started to argue, then he *bleep-bleep*ed the alarm and I realised which car he was referring to. A powerful-looking sports car—low, sleek and black, with a back seat even a midget would feel cramped in. Then I read 'Carrera' on the rear.

My mind scrambled. Since forever, it had been a dream of mine to ride in a Porsche. This was on my bucket list. I had no lectures or appointments coming up, nothing that couldn't be done later. A shiver of anticipation shimmied up my spine.

"Okay," I said, keeping my voice casual.

Work could wait an hour.

* * *

He revved the engine and shot me a flirtatious grin. "Buckle up."

It was just like old times. Well, not quite. I'd grown boobs and he'd grown facial hair. But there was still a spark, and I was fairly confident he wouldn't call me Dog Breath today.

"Nice car," I said, caressing the leather upholstery.

"She'll do."

Understatement of the century. What I'd have given to have a car like this. I'd never let Jim near it, of course; not without shoving him through a decontamination unit first.

Cool at first, the leather quickly warmed, moulding readily to my shape. I inhaled. Real leather. *Porsche* leather.

"It seems such a waste having a Porsche in the middle of London," I said.

"True, but once I'd seen her there was no going back." He changed gear, whipped into the next lane. "I try and do all my site visits by car."

"Site visits?"

"I'm a landscape architect. Sunny days I watch other people work. Rainy days I stay inside and doodle."

"Sounds more like play than work," I said, looking at him with fresh eyes, because the Charlie I knew wouldn't have downplayed his role in anything, much less his career. But this Porsche hadn't just dropped from the sky, and his family weren't moneyed.

Maybe he really had changed.

The thought was unsettling. Had I been wrong to hate him all these years?

But Dani hated him, too.

Maybe we were both wrong.

What was that all about, anyway? Why did she dislike him so intensely? Was it sister loyalty gone mad, or something about her?

Even as I thought it, I knew the answer. She'd always lived life in the 'something about her' lane. Chances were nothing had changed.

Only one way to find out. "Have you caught up with Dani recently?"

Charlie glanced sharply my way, then concentrated on the road. For a moment he didn't answer. The silence prickled my skin.

"We've bumped into each other a few times."

As in gentle bumper-to-bumper whoopsie? Or something more head-on, fatalities-involved-ish?

"Why do you ask?" He fiddled with the car stereo, not meeting my eye.

Was he hiding something?

Fine. If he was going to give me nothing, I'd give him nothing back. I wouldn't mention shattered wine glasses or hurt expressions or strong reactions to his name.

"No reason. I just wondered."

He threw me a wry smile. "What with London being so small and all."

"Something like that."

We lapsed back into silence. I gave up thinking about Dani—she was entitled to her feelings—and watched the scenery instead. It took me a while to register we were on the M23, heading south.

"Charlie, I thought we were going for coffee."

"We are."

"And how far away, exactly, is this café?"

He winked, smiled. "Oh, a few miles. Don't worry, it won't take long in this baby." He patted the dashboard.

"But I have to be at work in . . ."—I looked at my watch—". . . thirty minutes."

"Really?"

"Are you kidnapping me?" I asked, only half-joking.

"What? No! You wanted coffee. I'm just making sure you get the best."

"Okay, Buster. Give it to me straight. Where exactly are we going? Because if you're taking me further than the local coffeehouse—which," I added, spotting the exit to Crawley, "looks fairly likely—the least you can do is tell me. Some of us have work commitments."

"It'll spoil the surprise if I tell you," he stalled. Then, seeing the look on my face, "All right, all right. It wouldn't be much fun if I had to drag you there kicking and screaming."

"Indeed."

I waited.

"Can you take some time off work?" he asked, eyes on the road. "Say, most of the day?"

I gaped at him. Where on earth was he taking me?

"Most of the day?" I spluttered. "Are you crazy?"

"A little." He shrugged. "Want me to turn back?"

I compressed my lips, said nothing, and watched him.

He glanced at me, his laughter lines deepening, and kept driving. "Come on, Becky. It's a lovely day out there. You know you want to."

I hesitated. Friday. I didn't have any lectures today. And he was right: it was a stunning morning. What if I called in sick, just this once? I probably could take today off without the world coming to a halt. I'd be able to catch up over the weekend.

Maybe this was exactly the distraction I needed to get over Matt. Time spent with another guy. Nothing romantic, obviously—we'd been there done that years ago, with disastrous results—but I quite liked the idea of a few hours with Charlie. No strings. No expectations. Just time out with a friend. And his Porsche, of course.

On the other hand, did I want to waste any time at all on a man who apparently thought I could, and would, drop everything for him at a moment's notice? What arrogance!

He gave me a winning smile. "I really can't think of anyone I'd rather take the day off with."

Arrogance—or charm?

"Live a little, Becky. You'll enjoy it."

And butter probably didn't melt, either . . .

"Fine. Okay. Yes, I could take a few hours off." I paused, and narrowed my eyes at him. "Thanks for asking."

He acknowledged the jibe with a wry twist of mouth.

"But I need to make a phone call first."

He pulled into a lay-by and I rang Sal. "Hi. Listen, I . . . I've got a migraine. Spotty vision, screaming head, the works. Could you reschedule my meetings for me?"

I organised it all with Sal, but when she asked about the traffic noise I pleaded bad reception and hastily hung up. I grimaced at Charlie.

He chuckled and headed back onto the motorway. "Good girl. Right. Coffee, here we come."

"If I get a migraine out of this," I said, "I will hold you totally responsible."

CHAPTER SIXTEEN

We entered the village and slowed to a crawl.

I read the sign. "Bosham."

"Pronounced Bozz'm."

Bathed in glorious sunshine, the village was picture-perfect postcard material. Charming cottages, beautiful gardens, the odd thatched roof, and the rusts and yellows of autumn added a golden glow to it all.

"It's lovely!"

He smiled. "It gets better."

We reached the end of the lane and I gasped. Before us lay a large expanse of estuary, swampy and windswept, its saltmarsh-and-pebble bed partially exposed.

"Amazing," I breathed.

Charlie pulled over and parked next to a centuries-old stone wall. "The tide's coming in. Perfect."

We continued on foot, exploring the waterfront, the cobbled high street, the quaint little shops.

"This place is stunning," I said. "I didn't even know it existed."

"Bosham's been around a very long time. You know the legend about King Canute commanding the waves to retreat?"

"Mm-hmm?" Only vaguely—not that I was about to admit it.

"That happened right here, in Bosham."

"Really? Wow! And did they?"

"Did who? What?"

"The waves. Did they retreat?"

He chuckled. "No. The King got his feet wet and discovered Nature didn't take orders, even from a king. Still doesn't. See?"

He pointed out a battered, weather-beaten sign. *This road floods each tide.'*

I stared at the sign, then him. "No way."

"If we stay a few hours you'll see it." He tugged my hand. "Come on. Let's find a coffee." He glanced at his watch. "And brunch?"

On cue, my stomach grumbled. "Good idea."

We headed towards the cluster of waterfront cafés. Ultra-aware of his hand clasping mine, I tried unobtrusively to extract it. But Charlie had other ideas. He squeezed my hand.

"What's the hurry? Slow down." He stopped and turned me bodily to face him. Brushed a strand of hair off my face. "Enjoy the day."

His gaze, intense and frankly appraising, left me in no doubt what he meant.

Butterflies fluttered in my throat. I swallowed. Coffee I could handle, but Charlie with that look in his eyes . . .

He tugged me closer.

"Charlie, I—" I pulled back. "Okay, what's the deal here? Are you terminally ill or something?"

His grip loosened. He frowned. "Sorry?"

"Are you dying? Just tell me, Charlie. I can take it."

His lips twitched. "Do I look that bad?"

"No! It's just . . ." Crap. Me and my big mouth. I plunged on. "I don't get it. You haven't made contact all these years, so why now? Are you taking some new-age course or something? Purging the past?"

He laughed. "Does there have to be an ulterior motive?"

Wasn't there always with men?

"Maybe I just thought it would be nice to see you again," he said. "Which it is." Somehow the space between us disappeared. "Very."

He did that intense-gaze thing again. I decided I'd better spoil the moment before things got out of hand.

"I don't know about you, but I'm starving." I twisted out of his arms and bolted for the cafés. "Come on."

I glanced back to make sure he was following and caught myself ogling. God. After all these years he still looked good enough to eat.

But looks weren't everything. I turned away, sucked in some air, and kept walking. Fantasy Becky could stop right there. No day-dreaming allowed. I wouldn't think so much as one little thought about those eyes, that hair, the whole package. I'd cast him as the villain for too long to suddenly throw him into any other role.

* * *

The shadows lengthened, and Charlie checked his watch. "Fancy a drink before we head back?"

"Sure. Why not?"

We drove inland a few miles and stopped at the Highwayman's Rest, a thatch-roofed, whitewashed affair with ancient wagon-wheels propped against one wall. Charlie ordered drinks while I chose a booth near the fire.

He handed me my drink and sat opposite, kissed his beer against my cider. "Cheers."

"Cheers. Today's been fantastic, Charlie. Thanks so much."

"The pleasure's all mine. And thanks to you, too."

"For . . . ?"

"For letting yourself be led astray."

I arched a brow at him. "I've never bunked off work before."

I thought about it, grinned. "Then again, I've never been offered a trip in a Porsche before, either."

Charlie gave an exaggerated sigh. "That Porsche. It's nothing but trouble. Ladies will do anything for a ride with me."

"Is that right?"

His eyes creased at the corners. The double *entendre* hung between us. I thought of the Porsche, thought of him, and suddenly had an image of us parked up in it. I blushed, ducked my head. Now he had me spread-eagled on the bonnet, skirt rucked up to my waist . . .

What?!

No he did not. My blush strengthened. He had me sipping cider and making polite conversation in a well-lit, family-friendly pub, and his 'ride' comment certainly hadn't warranted a car bonnet fantasy.

Disturbed and embarrassed, I engrossed myself in the fire, but my skin prickled with the imprint of his gaze. The flames leapt and danced like lovers. The silence lengthened. Schoolgirl awkward, I studied my cider, twirled the glass in my hand, then took a fortifying swig before finally looking up.

He threw me an easy smile.

I smiled back. See? No need for nerves. Charlie knew perfectly well we were just pals. My mind was in the gutter, but that was my issue, not his.

His gaze slipped from my eyes to my mouth.

My blush returned tenfold. Okay, that hadn't been a pal look.

His gaze continued on down and my nipples, traitorous little attention-seekers, hardened in quick response. I folded my arms over the evidence. Too late; he'd noticed. His eyebrow quirked suggestively. Was it just me or was that log fire burning hotter than ever?

He crooked an arm along the back of his bench. His eyes, at once teasing and challenging, roamed back up from my chest until our gazes locked.

I swallowed. This whole distraction thing had worked perfectly until now—but precisely how much distraction did I want?

Come on, less of the Miss Priss! Didn't I want as much distraction as I could get? How else would I ever get over Matt and on with my career?

Charlie bought another round of drinks, refusing to let me pay. We chatted about our careers, hobbies, lives. A waitress threw more logs on the fire. We swapped memories from our teens. No mention of dog breath. Patrons finished their drinks and moved on. Others arrived and ordered meals.

"So, Becky-all-grown-up, is there anyone special in your life?"

I choked on my cider. Cleared my throat. Started to speak, reconsidered, then finally settled for, "No. You?"

"Not now."

I raised my brow at him. Not now as in 'no longer in a relationship'? Or not now as in 'not while I'm talking to you'? Not that it was any of my business. "You're . . . ?"

"Separated." His hand cut through the air. "Well and truly. Soon to be divorced."

"Ah."

"I'm better off without her. The Estepona villa, though?" He grinned. "That's a loss."

"I bet."

He shrugged. "There'll be other villas."

I had to laugh. He played the arrogant ass so well, but if there was one thing today had shown me it was that Charlie had definitely improved with age.

"Hollingworth!" A voice boomed. "I'll be darned. What a

coincidence."

I looked towards the voice and froze. Felt my face blanch. Dani's boss? What was he doing here?

If he saw me here with Charlie and it got back to Dani . . . well, it could go either way. It might be yay me for taking her advice—or boo me for hanging out with the guy who'd provoked her glass-smashing frenzy.

I wasn't a betting woman.

But it was too late to make myself scarce. Here he came, straight for our table. I pasted a smile on my face.

Charlie stood. "Fred. Great to see you, man."

They did that male camaraderie back-clapping thing, then Charlie stepped back. "Fred, I want you to meet Becky. Becky, Fred."

"Becky?" Fred's mouth dropped open. "Hi."

I found my voice. "Hi, Fred. Fancy meeting you here." It could only happen to me.

"Oh. You know each other?" Charlie grinned, gave him another back-clap. "Small world, eh?"

"It sure is." He looked from me to Charlie and back again. Blinked. Scratched his chin.

I felt like I'd taken a head shot with a stun-gun.

"Becky and I went to school together," said Charlie, answering Fred's unspoken question. He gestured for Fred to sit in the bench he'd vacated then squashed himself next to me.

"Really?" Fred's eyes locked on Charlie's arm, hooked over the seat behind me.

Charlie's fingers grazed my shoulder and heat flooded my cheeks. I knew exactly what Fred was thinking, and if *that* got back to Dani I'd never hear the end of it. *'You dirty dog'* would be followed by *'Thought you couldn't stand him'*—or, worse, the loyalty card, *'You know I can't stand him'*.

I took refuge in my cider.

But what if she told Mum? One whiff of this and Mum would be in Mrs Hollingworth's ear and they'd both have us married off before you could say 'that lovely young man'. And all we'd done was coffee!

"Fred's down here on business," said Charlie, playing footsie with me under the table.

"Terrific." I gave Fred a tight smile. "Food, anyone?" I picked up the menu. "Steak and Guinness pie? Scampi?"

"Great idea," said Charlie, leaning close to read over my shoulder.

He beckoned the waitress over and we placed our orders.

"Nothing for me," said Fred.

"You work down here often?" Charlie asked.

They started talking shop and for a while I stayed tuned in, worrying about Fred and what he may or may not say to Dani. Eventually I relaxed—what would be would be; cider had a way of making life seem so much simpler—and my mind drifted. What a lovely day. Bosham had been such an unexpected discovery. Ditto the grown-up Charlie. Imagine if I'd gone through my whole life hating him without even knowing him.

Our meals arrived, we ate, they talked. And now, with a full belly, I felt very mellow. Mellow, and sleepy. I hoped Charlie wouldn't mind me snoozing on the drive home.

Fred stood. "I'd better go. See you back in London."

We watched him leave.

"Fancy meeting him here," said Charlie.

"Yes, fancy." I smothered a yawn.

He turned my wrist over and checked my watch. "Hey, it's getting late. Want to stop over at a B&B for the night?"

I snapped my head around, my pulse lunging into a gallop. He returned my gaze evenly.

Sexy mouth.

What was it Dani had said? Find a man to replace a man?

Heat washed through me. I rested my head against the back of the booth and closed my eyes. Well? Why not? As a Matt-replacement I couldn't do much better than Charlie. And what better way to finally, permanently, put that Dog Breath incident behind me?

I smiled to myself. Had Charlie really just managed to engineer an overnighter out of a coffee outing? Well played. Very well played.

"Feeling sleepy, huh?" I asked.

His lips whispered across my ear and I jumped.

"Only if you are," he murmured.

I turned my head and there were his lips, only a hair's breadth away. His gaze fell to my mouth. My breath hitched. Awareness, a moth's fragile flutter, flickered against my ribs.

126

"Desserts," drawled the waitress, "coffee, or do you want the bill?"

Charlie's eyes didn't leave my lips. "I think we'll go for the bill."

He threw some notes on the table, stood, and took my hand. "Let's go. There's a B&B over the road."

* * *

My mouth went dry as I took in the enormous bed. Did it have to be so damn prominent? "Well. Here we are, then."

"Yep, here we are." He removed his coat, tossed it over a chair.

I looked at the coat, then at him, and felt a wallop of guilt. Crap. I sat down abruptly on the bed. What was I doing? Since when had I turned into a dirty slapper? I couldn't share a room with him.

"Coffee?" He rummaged around in the sideboard and pulled out a kettle.

I cleared my throat. "Sure."

For goodness sake! I had nothing to feel guilty over. This was the only room available. We had to sleep somewhere.

But sharing a bed with him?

Sleeping together didn't have to mean sex, though.

Yeah, and who was I kidding?

Okay, so maybe we would have sex. So what? We'd had a fantastic day. This was a moment in time, nothing more, nothing less.

He took the kettle into the *ensuite* and filled it with water. Re-emerged and plugged it in.

But—casual sex? Me?

Why not? We were consenting adults.

The kettle boiled and he poured two coffees. Gave one to me then sprawled on the oversized three-seater beneath the window. Patted the cushion beside him.

I hesitated, then got over myself and joined him on the couch.

He shifted in his seat, as if to make room for me, but somehow his knee ended up touching mine. "I've enjoyed today."

"Me too." I sipped at my coffee, every hair on my arm alert to his nearness.

He reached out and gave one of my frizzy curls an experimental tug. The curl pinged back. He bounced my curls lightly against his hand. "I

127

remember those curls."

And I remembered his touch. A delicious shiver rippled through me.

"Cold? Here, I'll warm you up."

"I'm fine."

But he took my coffee anyway, placed it on the table, then drew me into the circle of his arm.

I hadn't been cold to start with, but now I felt damn-near feverish. And maybe I was. Why else would I be getting this cosy with a guy I'd hated almost twenty years?

"Better?" he asked.

I exhaled, trying to steady my pulse. Nodded.

He relaxed into the couch.

"Becky, Becky, Becky," he said, as if I were some perplexing problem he couldn't quite get his head around.

"Yes?" In my peripheral vision I could see him looking at me.

His fingers tangled in my curls. "Do you trust me?"

I turned and made eye-contact with his mouth. My heart tripped then raced. "No way."

"Wise girl." He stood and, taking my hands in his, pulled me up with him.

I gave up trying to breathe. "Wise? Or just really stupid."

His arm tightened around my waist. "Let's be stupid together."

And his lips, some seventeen years late, came down on mine.

What started as a kiss quickly became far more physical and I decided that, stupid or not, a horny-as-hell shag was absolutely what I wanted tonight.

CHAPTER SEVENTEEN

The light through my eyelids told me it was morning. I lingered on the edge of consciousness, caught in that warm, fuzzy state where reality and fantasy blend seamlessly. I shifted in the bed and my hand came up against something solid. Something human.

Charlie.

My heart hammered. Fully awake now but desperate not to wake him, I gently removed my hand from his shoulder.

I relaxed into the sheets, trying to keep my breathing regular. What to do? Lie here and play dead until he'd woken and showered, or creep out of bed and hide in the bathroom myself?

I carefully turned my head a couple of degrees, then opened one eye. Charlie smiled back at me. Amused. Benevolent.

Shit. I slammed my eye closed.

What do you say to the guy you've just spent the night with, shamelessly screwing every-which-way into the wee small hours, whom really—when all's said and done—is nothing more than a convenience?

And here I lay, stone cold sober, with not even a smidgeon of hangover. Which ruled out dashing to the loo, vomiting heartily until he left in disgust, then catching a quiet train home. No, I had to face this one head-on.

"Morning," I muttered.

He grinned. "Morning, Beautiful."

I turned my head and opened both eyes at him. There was far too much sunlight, and he was far too focused. Rats. I blinked hard and rubbed my eyes.

"Thanks for coming, Becky," he said.

I rolled my eyes, though not at him. He chuckled. Then stopped as I pulled first one then the other eyelid down over my still-rolling eyes.

"Are you okay?"

I released my eyelids. "I didn't take out my lenses last night. They need to re-lubricate."

Another chuckle. "Sounds like fun. Can I help?"

"Funny." He was enjoying this whole morning-after thing far too much. I closed my eyes again, but my skin goosebumped under his steady gaze. "Um, about last night."

"Mmm?"

I felt like I needed to say something—but what? Acknowledge that coffee had evolved into something considerably more intimate? Reassure him that I, Ms Modern, posed no threat to his bachelorhood?

Shite. Our families went back way too far for him to be good one-night stand material. And he'd proved himself a one-hundred-per-cent Genuinely Nice Guy, yet another indicator he was absolutely the *wrong* choice. You don't do one-nighters with GNG's who know your mum.

I opened my now-fully-functional eyes and the GNG was still there, lying butt-naked beside me, a smile dancing on his lips.

"Well, see, I—" I stopped, rephrased. "I just wanted to—"

Damn. Why did this have to be so awkward?

Without any awkwardness at all, Charlie leaned close and planted a kiss on my nose. "You just wanted to . . . do it all again?"

"No! I—"

"Shame." He gave me a lopsided grin. "Ah well. You make the coffees, then."

I abandoned my morning-after speech and forced myself to relax. "Sorry. I'm shattered. Can't move."

His grin broadened. "Shall we test that?"

"You've got a one-track mind." I wrinkled my nose at him. Stretched, cat-like, and noticed a few aching muscles.

I shot him a sidelong look. "Coffee with you should be against the law."

He traced a finger down my collarbone and over my breast. "You like the idea of being cuffed, huh?"

"No!"

I had a sudden image of Matt, standing before me with a glint in his eye and cuffs in his hand. Delicious heat uncoiled within me. My pulse kicked up.

"Methinks she protests too much." Charlie's hand travelled down towards my waist, taking the sheet as it went.

I tugged the sheet back up. He probably had a point, but unless Matt was the one doing the arresting . . .

Charlie flipped me onto my back, whipped the sheet away, and moved on top of me. His lips hovered over mine. "Want to play cops and robbers?"

Matt reappeared, and this time he was wearing nothing but a policeman's hat. He cuffed me and kissed me and . . .

Oh God. This was wrong. Why was I in bed with Charlie, when all I really wanted was Matt?

Charlie locked my arms above my head, his free hand moulding my left breast, his tongue probing my mouth.

I'd never felt more turned off. I turned my head away. "Stop. Charlie, I can't."

He paused. "What's wrong?"

"Nothing. Everything. Shit." I tried to move out from under him but was trapped by his weight. "Can you get off me? Sorry."

He rolled aside and I pulled the covers high, feeling like a born-again virgin.

"Sorry," I repeated. "It's . . . I'm not in the mood. Sorry."

Which didn't even begin to cover it, but I could hardly tell the man with whom I'd just spent the night that I was fantasizing about someone else.

For a moment Charlie lay rigid beside me, hands behind his head, lips clamped and jaw locked as he stared at the ceiling. Then his mouth relaxed and he chuckled.

I released the breath I hadn't realised I was holding. Phew. The last thing I'd wanted was to upset him.

"Then what," he said, grabbing my hand and hauling it down over his rock-hard erection, "am I going to do with this?"

"I'm sure you'll think of something." I whipped my hand back and scooted out of bed, self-conscious about my nudity. "I'm off for a shower."

I dived for the sanctuary of the *ensuite* and showered quickly, with frequent furtive glances at the door. When I emerged in yesterday's work-clothes Charlie handed me a cup of coffee.

"Thanks," I said, trying not to look at his body and wishing he was wearing more than a towel. "Sorry about before."

He shrugged. "Yeah, me too. I'm off for a cold shower. Unless . . ."

He reached for me, but I fended him off with a light, "Never come between a woman and her coffee, Hollingworth."

"Cold shower it is," he concluded, his smile not quite reaching his eyes.

I felt ashamed. What was wrong? What had changed?

Nothing—except Matt had re-invaded my mind. Everywhere I looked, I saw him. Every thought I had went back to him. My— Dani's—distraction plan had been a total failure. So . . . time to pull out.

I rummaged around for my mobile and sent Liz a text message— *Never take Dan's advice. 1 night stand = bad bad idea.* I re-read the message and pinched my eyes shut, repressing a shudder of shame. How could I ever have thought anything good might've come of it? Stupid, *stupid* woman.

Within seconds Liz replied—*What? You didn't! Who? Details!*

I was still trying to work out what to tell her when Charlie emerged from the *ensuite*, lover-turned-executive. *Ve-ry* smart. It must have shown in my face because he spread his arms, inviting inspection. "Well? Do I pass?"

I couldn't play his game anymore. With a brisk nod I pocketed my mobile, collected my things, and walked out ahead of him.

"What—just a nod?" he said, close behind me. "I hear I look best in a suit."

Oh *please*. Enough already. Remorse mutated into bad temper.

"Don't flatter yourself." I stomped my way down the stairs. "You're ugly, you're crap in bed, and your suit's naff. Let's go."

"Ouch," he said, laughter in his voice. "Careful on the corners. Your nose is growing."

I glared over my shoulder at him. He grinned back, unperturbed, then *bleep*ed the Carrera and strode ahead to hold my door open for me, every inch the gentleman.

"Thanks," I muttered. Now I felt like an ungracious fool *and* a cheap slut.

We pulled out into the traffic and I took one last look at the B&B, scene of our dirty overnighter. Back to London, back to reality, back to

Matt.

No! Not back to him. Work—yes. Him—no. Remember?

I'd chosen my career. Therefore I had to sacrifice him.

"Any plans for the weekend?" Charlie asked.

I started. "Oh. Er . . . no, not really."

Get out of my head, Matt Frobisher.

"Want to do coffee?" Charlie threw me a mischievous grin.

I stared at him. Jeez. How did I end up feeling like an immoral piece of filth, while he came out of it feeling like the man about town?

"No. I've got to go into work."

Work, Matt. Matt, work. Would I never be able to think of one without the other?

"Ah, well, another time, then."

I turned and gazed sightlessly out the window. What was he doing right now? Sleeping? Working? Standing in a shower making love to some other lucky woman? Thinking about me?

Dammit, why did I want that, anyway?

CHAPTER EIGHTEEN

"Hey, Becs."

My heart skipped a beat. Why was Matt at work so early? I didn't want to see him. Not yet. Not until I'd worked out how to deal with him. *He* might be able to switch his feelings on and off at will, but I wasn't so lucky.

The cosmos, however, didn't care if I was ready for Matt or not; here he was. And with the coffee machine still chugging out my coffee, I couldn't even run.

"Hi." I kept my gaze firmly on my mug.

"How was your weekend?"

My cheeks flamed. He'd seen through my migraine excuse last Friday. Or . . . feck. Maybe he knew Charlie. My palms grew clammy.

"Average," I said, wishing I'd pressed *Disappearo* instead of *Cappuccino*. I didn't want to feel ashamed of my night with Charlie, but I did.

"As long as you got rid of your headache?"

"Eventually." I turned sugar-stirring into an art form.

"I'm glad."

He lingered, and my jaw clenched tight. What more did he want? A time series analysis of my pain levels? Or was he trying to psych me into a Charlie confession?

I gave myself a mental shake. Less of the paranoia, Becs. Maybe he'd finally had the decency to feel bad about giving me the flick mid-date, or whatever our trip had been.

Ha! As if. More likely he'd split with Steph and needed someone to take up the slack in his diary. Becky would do.

Second-best Becky. Becky the gap-filler. Just-for-fun Becky.

I glared at my coffee.

Did he really think I'd let him blow me off one week and love me tender the next? Like hell. And now, damn it all, I'd stirred my cappuccino so hard it had become a bloody latté.

I straightened and turned my glare on Matt.

He blinked, frowned, cleared his throat. "You're angry. Was it something I said?"

"No."

"Want to talk about it?"

"No."

He regarded me as if I were a troublesome teen. "Well, if you're going to look daggers at me like that, the least you can do is tell me why."

What—so he could have a good laugh at me? I pursed my lips.

"Come on, get it off your chest. It'll make you feel better. Besides, we have to work together."

Ah, yes, work. Couldn't have *work* being affected, could we?

I ground my teeth. "Is there a problem with my work?"

"No, not at all. I—"

"Then why mention it?"

He exhaled. "My mistake. Forget work."

He raked his fringe up off his face. "Look, I get it. You're upset." He paused. "It's about our trip to the Kinetix Centre, isn't it?"

I hugged my coffee close, said nothing.

"That sudden change of plans really screwed things up, didn't it?"

Suddenly I didn't feel angry. I just felt sad; tearful, even. Didn't he see? Plans changed; that wasn't the issue. The issue was *his* change towards *me*. I bit my cheek.

Matt's eyes, concerned and caring, searched mine. I didn't trust his eyes, though. Not anymore. I didn't trust him.

He nodded, gently took my coffee from me and placed it on the bench.

"Becs, I am so, so sorry." He tucked a wayward curl behind my ear, and a pulse fluttered in my throat. "My life is . . . things are . . . complicated."

I bet. But that's what happened when you were making like Casanova and juggling women.

He rubbed at his neck. "Would you have dinner with me?"

I stared at him. What kind of an arrogant . . . ? "No, Matt, I would

135

not."

"Please. This is important to me." He looked me in the eye. "I upset you that weekend, and I want to put things right."

"Then say sorry and we'll leave it at that."

He rested his hands on my shoulders. "Dinner. Please. Just this once. Don't worry," he added, his eyes creasing at the corners, "I promise I'm not a stalker."

I quirked an eyebrow. He may not be a stalker, but he was my boss. And I doubted very much he was issuing this invitation to the whole of T&T.

"Matt, I don't think dinner's a good idea."

"You didn't think marking together was a good idea, either." Then, seeing my slit-eyed look, "What? You didn't. But you got plenty of work done, and you had a good time doing it." He grinned. "Go on. Admit it."

I allowed him the beginnings of a smile. "Okay, I admit it. It was fun." And it had just made his big freeze so much more painful.

"This will be fun, too," said Matt. "I promise."

I leaned past him and stole back my coffee. Drank a mouthful. Regarded him in silence.

"Say yes," he said. "Quick. Before you change your mind."

"I'm not changing my mind."

He winked. "You just did. I saw it in your eyes. I'll pick you up at seven."

And before I could call him a smug little know-it-all and several other less ladylike names, he was gone.

* * *

The cab pulled into the modest driveway and Matt paid our driver, ignoring the notes I offered. He held the door open for me as if I were some kind of celebrity, then took my elbow, escorting me with easy intimacy along the dimly-lit path. His fingers burned my skin but I didn't flinch from his touch: no way was I going to let him know how much he affected me.

I glanced around. No signage that I could see. It all felt very . . . suburban.

"What restaurant is this?" I asked. "I don't know it."

"Frobisher's." A smile tugged at the corner of his mouth. "Leatherhead's finest."

Frobisher's? As in, his surname? Good grief, his family were restauranteurs? How exciting!

. . . And embarrassing. He'd brought me to an exclusive restaurant, and I'd shown up in this old outfit. I nervously adjusted my clothes. Yes, the sheer green top and black satin pants looked smart, but I was seriously underdressed. I should've gone glitzy.

"You look gorgeous," he said, as if he'd just read my mind.

"Thanks." I gave him a not-believing-you smile. Then slammed my mind closed just in case he really was a mindreader.

He held the door open for me and ushered me in. It didn't look very restaurant-y. No front desk. No maître-d'. And—I shot Matt a quizzical look—was that a TV I could hear through the wall?

He dropped his keys on the console table and shrugged out of his jacket, tossing it over a nearby chair. "Can I take your coat?"

It landed on top of his jacket.

The penny finally dropped. "Oh my God. I'm such an idiot. This isn't a restaurant, is it?"

"No, just my place. Sorry. We can pretend if you like. I'll wait on you hand and foot, and call you Ma'am." His lips twitched. "You can even pay me for it. I promise my rates are reasonable."

I did my best not to blush. Failed. Then felt a fool for reading too much into a perfectly innocent joke.

Matt's eyebrow rose. He chuckled.

Okay, maybe not so innocent.

He showed me into a large, open plan living room. To our left, a large, rustic dining table had been set for two. Flowers. Candles. Wine glasses, three per setting. Impressive. And as for the kitchen . . . I almost drooled as I took in the gleaming surfaces and ultra-modern equipment.

Ooh! Espresso machine alert.

"Mmm, coffee," I said.

"Oh yeah. The best. You'll never want to leave."

Which was fairly cocky of him. But before I had time to frame a suitably cutting response, a wordless shout came from our right. I looked across and saw a basketball game on the massive TV monopolising the far wall. As I watched, the three-pointer that had drawn the shout replayed, the shout replaying with it. In the dim lighting I couldn't make out the shouter.

"Evening," called Matt. Then, to me, "Come and meet my brother."

His brother glanced our way, then paused the basketball before turning to greet us. A small jolt went through me as I registered he was in a wheelchair.

"Becky," said Matt, "I'd like you to meet my brother, Stefan."

Stefan cleared his throat. His mouth twisted and worked. "Hi," he finally said. His left arm jerked awkwardly.

My heart splintered. I recognised Stefan's condition: cerebral palsy. I also recognised the reptilian intensity with which he now regarded me. He was waiting for my reaction. Waiting to see my repugnance.

A childhood friend had suffered the same disorder. To me she was just Kimmy, a loyal mate with loads of spunk and a wicked sense of humour, but most people struggled to see past the physical to the beautiful girl trapped inside. In Kimmy's words, she was the monster everyone avoided.

I gave Stefan an open, friendly smile, one that reassured him I didn't see a monster.

"Hi, Stefan. Nice to meet you."

Unsure if he was up to shaking hands, I didn't proffer my own.

He swallowed convulsively. Tried to get the words out. I waited for him.

"Stef," he said. "Call me Stef."

"Okay. Thanks, Stef."

I stilled. Backtracked. Replayed. Matt's brother. Stefan. Stef.

Stef, not Steph?

I almost laughed with relief. That day at the Kinetix Centre, when Stef had left a message and Matt had been so quick to drop everything, me included, it had been for his brother. His wheelchair-bound brother. Nothing to do with another woman at all.

And me? I'd decided it had been Matt revealing the beast he truly was.

Well, I'd got that right—but I'd interpreted it all wrong.

Oh God, so horribly wrong. How could I have been so stupid? Shame, a burning ball of bile, welled in my belly, smothering my relief, leaving me pink-cheeked and discomfited.

Matt met my eyes with an enquiring look. I shook my head: not now.

Stef said nothing but he also missed nothing. With surprising speed he swivelled his wheelchair, flicking his gaze between Matt and me. His expression sharpened. He focused on me and stared me down, bitterness in his eyes.

I wanted to reassure Stef. My embarrassment had nothing to do with him and everything to do with me. I was the monster. But how could I even begin to explain? Matt was standing right there, and our whole Kinetix misunderstanding still lay like an open chasm between us.

I drew in breath to speak, trusting I'd find the right words. I didn't. In the end I released my breath without saying a thing. Felt like a clown who'd lost his wig.

Thankfully, Matt came to the rescue and filled the silence.

"Stef's my house-mate," he said, resting a hand on Stef's shoulder. "He's the brains in the family and I'm the brawn."

I laughed; all tension release, no humour. "You're the brains, eh, Stef?"

As soon as it was out I wished it unsaid. It sounded brittle.

Stef slid me a look of loathing. I shrivelled inside.

Matt intercepted Stef's look and visibly bridled. He stepped back and glared at Stef with such tight-jawed, potent fury it was a wonder Stef didn't turn to ash on the spot.

Their eyes locked and sparred.

Stef yielded first.

When he finally looked at me once more, it was carefully minus the animosity. He shook his head. "Matt's the brains as well as brawn."

He pulled out a handkerchief with his right hand and wiped the saliva from his lips. "Good at cleaning, too," he added.

This time my laughter was genuine. "Excellent. So he's your slave? I could do with one of them myself."

Stef shrugged. "Have him. I'll find a better slave. He's too bossy."

"It's hard to find a good slave," I said.

"He's lippy, too." Stef's lips twitched up in a smile, his earlier resentment dissipating.

I arched an eyebrow. "I bet he is."

"Different kind of lippy," Matt murmured in my ear, passing behind me on his way to the kitchen.

Before the blush had even found its way to my face, he was speaking again. "Don't mind me. I'll just be out here pouring drinks and *slaving* over a hot stove for both of you."

"Three courses, I hope." I fought cheeky with cheeky.

"Four, if Stef hasn't eaten the after-dinner mints."

I raised an eyebrow at Stef. He snuck his right hand down the side of his wheelchair and brought out a box of mints. My eyes widened. He quietly snuck it back again and covered it with his handkerchief, all the while maintaining a poker face as skilled as his brother's.

I snorted with laughter. "You must give Matt a run for his money."

"Hey, Stef," Matt called. "If you've finished watching the basketball I'll turn on the music."

Stef muttered to himself, but grudgingly flicked off the TV.

"Don't turn it off on my account," I said, but Matt hadn't wasted any time: mellow music already permeated the room.

Stef moved his head a little, in the manner of a shrug. "I'll watch it later."

He checked his watch then excused himself and went over to Matt. Matt hunkered down to Stef's level and they began talking in low voices.

I was suddenly struck by their resemblance. I hadn't noticed it earlier but now, watching them in profile, I could see it in their eyes, their jaws, the tilt of their heads. Even given the huge disparity in their physical conditions, there was no mistaking they were brothers.

Matt came around the breakfast bar, stowed a water bottle under Stef's left arm, made a comment that had them both looking my way. Stef nodded and gave Matt a friendly punch on the arm. I smiled. Brothers first, but friends as well.

Stef returned to my side. "I've got to go. My helper will be here soon."

"Oh. Right." I had no idea what kind of help he meant but I didn't want to offend him by asking. We'd already had a rocky start.

"I thought Matt was cooking for all three of us," I said.

"He is." Stef paused, coloured a little. "Eating isn't easy for me. Matt usually helps." His jaw sawed as he grappled with the words. "My helper's coming over so Matt can have time with you."

The enormity of Stef's reality—Matt's, too—hit me with freight-train force.

"Stef, I—God, I'm . . . sorry."

"For what?" His mouth tightened. His eyes narrowed.

Unexpected emotion thrummed in my throat. "You didn't have to banish yourself like that. I don't want to upset your routine."

He grabbed his handkerchief and swiped at his mouth.

"My routine is a life sentence." His voice was harsh. "It shouldn't be a life sentence for Matt as well."

"I'm sure he doesn't feel—"

Stef about-turned and abruptly left the room.

I watched the door swing to.

". . . like it's a life sentence," I finished.

Unshed tears burned my eyes. I swallowed painfully. What had I been thinking? I shouldn't have made a big deal about it. It was what it was.

Matt reached my side and put a hand on my shoulder. "Are you okay?"

I nodded, but didn't dare look at him.

"He's having a bad day," Matt said.

I nodded again. Clamped a hand over my mouth, hard, trying to keep myself in check. I couldn't have spoken, even if I'd wanted to.

"You're not okay." His fingers came around my nape, tangled in my hair.

I turned into his chest and Matt held me close, his chin resting on my head, one hand gently stroking my hair. For a few moments I stayed there, motionless, taking refuge while I pulled myself together. Then I stayed there a few moments more, savouring his nearness.

What was it about these Frobisher boys? One way or another, they were drilling right through to my emotional core.

When I finally straightened and moved back a little, he said, "I'm sorry. I should have warned you."

"No. *I'm* sorry. I didn't mean to upset Stef. I should've thought before I spoke."

Matt gave me a brief squeeze then held me at arm's length so he could look me in the eye. "Stef over-reacted. He's lived with this a long time, Becs. He knows you were being supportive. He's just grumpy today."

"He's got every right to be grumpy. Honestly, I don't know how he does it."

He smiled, took my hand and led me to the table. "Come on, let's eat. I've prepared a top notch meal for you and I want you to enjoy it. Besides, I'm not sure my date should be spending the evening crying over my brother."

CHAPTER NINETEEN

The entrée, an exquisite scallop concoction, sent my taste buds into raptures. Those scallops . . . that citrus chilli sauce . . . surely Matt could not have prepared that himself? Yet there he was, back in the kitchen and cooking the main, not a catering box in sight.

Fascinated, I sat and watched from the safety of the breakfast bar. He worked the space with a dancer's skill, never missing a culinary beat as he reached for a pan, filled it with water, fired up the gas hob, tossed the salt grinder from hand to hand with barman bravado, winked at me, flourished the salt over the water, then turned his attention to the oven.

I tried to imagine Matt doing the same in my kitchen and choked back a laugh. No room for artistry in there. He'd have to wedge himself in. Compared to this designer model, the pokey little cupboard Jim and I called a kitchen was truly pitiful.

Matt took a tray of freshly-baked ciabatta rolls from the oven. My mouth watered. They smelled divine. Could my own oven bake something like that?

Did my own oven even work?

He picked up the wine bottle. "Refill?"

"Please." I pushed my empty glass across the island bench towards him.

He topped up both our wines then came around the bench, returning mine with a smile. I accepted the drink, along with the inevitable *frritzz* as our fingers touched, and took a sip.

Now I knew Matt's reason for cutting short our Kinetix Centre trip, I was finding it very easy to relax and enjoy his company. Too easy.

I smiled at him over the top of my glass. "What other hidden talents do you have?"

He leaned against the wall, all casual cowboy in jeans and tee. Black jeans today; an indecently good fit. And best I didn't think about that particular talent. I forced my eyes north.

Matt's mouth curved. "Guess you'll just have to wait and see. Can't give too much away in one date."

That D-word again. My stomach flip-flopped. This was a *date*. With my *boss*. The thought jammed in my mind like a scratched CD.

He thrust his free hand in his jeans pocket and the fabric tightened. My breath caught. My blood warmed.

I was such a goner.

Matt contemplated his wine, and I contemplated him. I contemplated him so hard that when he looked up I started.

"Have you signed up for Conference Week?" he asked.

"Nuh-uh."

"You know registrations close on Friday, right?"

"Yes, but . . ."

I blew out my cheeks, forced myself to focus on his words instead of his body. "I'm not really bothered, Matt. I've never gone before. Sales targets always came first."

"You don't have sales targets now."

"True. Are all our lecturers going?"

"You bet," he said. Conference Week coincided with a lecture-free week—a deliberate ploy so T&T's lecturers could attend. "You shouldn't miss it, Becs. As far as conferences go, it's a must. Fantastic professional development."

My lips twitched. "Professional debauchery's what I heard."

"Guess you shouldn't miss that, then."

"I'd better not commit until I've checked all my looming deadlines," I said, straight-faced.

He laughed. "Touché. I mean it, Becs. Forget the deadlines. Just come."

Matt swirled the wine in his glass, studied it, sampled it, then looked at me. "It wouldn't be the same without you."

Our eyes locked. The air crackled with tension.

He opened his mouth to say more but I had a sudden attack of teenage nerves and leapt in ahead of him.

"Your water's boiling." I indicated the pan.

He gave a grunt of acknowledgement and hauled himself off the wall.

144

Then stepped close, very close. So close I could see the fabric of his tee vibrating in time to his heart.

With a gentle hand he tilted my face and looked into my eyes. My mouth dried. His thumb caressed my cheek, leaving a trail of heat in its wake.

"I'm not going to beg, but . . . come to conference."

He held my gaze a moment longer, then went out to the kitchen and busied himself at the stove.

Full of nervous tension, now, I stood and wandered the room. I paused here and there to touch a plant, straighten a cushion, run a finger along the back of a couch. I stopped to admire an oil painting. Its vivid colours dominated the living room wall. I cocked my head this way and that, trying to make sense of it. "Okay, I give up. What is it?"

He glanced up. "No idea. A squashed head? Split watermelon?" He shrugged. "Maybe it's just a paint splodge."

I laughed. "Nice analysis, Mister Frobisher."

"Stef bought it. Art's not really my thing."

Which, actually, was reassuring. I'd finally found something he wasn't an expert in. It made him seem more real.

I returned to the breakfast bar and hovered. Art may not be his thing, but cooking definitely was. I inhaled, savouring the aromas. "Need a hand?"

"No, this is almost done. You could take these to the table for me, though." He put a green salad and a basket of rolls on the breakfast bar.

"Thanks," he added, with a just-for-me smile.

It was as I took the salad through that I noticed the photo frames. Clustered on the sideboard, they fired my curiosity. The rest—artwork, cushions, furniture—could have graced any modern man's home. But these photos, all higgledy piggledy with their non-matching frames? They were personal.

Photos offered insights into the people they belonged to. What would these tell me about Matt? Nosiness got the better of me.

My eyes immediately latched onto the largest photo. Matt in a triumphant man-conquers-mountain pose, backpack at his feet, grin on his face, snowy peaks at his back. Determination, success, and love of the outdoors. Nothing new there. I moved on.

To the right stood a shot of the two brothers, taken years earlier.

Matt, smiling and broad, next to Stef, then a teenager, solemn and slender. The contrast between the boys couldn't have been greater, yet once more I was struck by their uncanny resemblance.

A much older image caught my eye, the colours yellowed, the focus less sharp. I picked it up and held it to the light. The boys were young this time, but their eyes were still unquestionably Matt and Stef. They sat, one on each knee of a giant of a man, his sheer size accentuating Stef's tiny frailty. The man could've been Matt; Matt with a number one buzz cut.

This was their dad, then. I smiled at him as he smiled at me, hugging the boys close, his love plain to see.

I scanned the other photos, but nowhere could I see someone who might be Matt's mum. Where was she? What had happened that these photos weren't telling me?

Matt placed our meals on the table with a flourish. "*Voilà*. Dinner is served."

"And wine to match." He set aside the first bottle of wine, opened a fresh one, and half-filled the second of our three glasses.

I held up the older photo for Matt to see. "Your dad?"

He smiled, nodded, and held out my chair for me.

I joined him, self-conscious as he helped me with my seat. "You don't have to play waiter all night, you know."

"No? I was hoping for a good tip later on."

I bet he was. And I wouldn't mind giving him one, either—which meant I was right back at square one on the whole Affair *versus* Career debate, dammit.

"Where did you learn to cook?" I asked, with the most unsubtle subject change ever.

"I've been playing in the kitchen as long as I can remember. Dad cooked all the family meals, and I used to help out." He gave a wry smile. "Actually, I probably wasn't much help at all, but Dad made me feel like I was helping."

"Well, this salmon is divine. Here's to Dad." I raised my glass. "He taught you well."

Matt's glass met mine. "He taught me all sorts of things."

"Like what?"

"Stuff."

Matt fell silent, and I wondered what was going on in that head of his.

Time for another subject change. "Stef looks pretty frail in those early photos," I said.

"He was."

"Is he able to walk?"

Matt reached for a ciabatta roll. "When he gets over himself and makes an effort."

I started to speak, then thought better of it. Then thought again and said it anyway. "I'm sure he's doing his best, Matt. I mean, it must be really hard for him. Every day's a challenge."

"Of course it's bloody hard for him." He stabbed his knife into the roll. "But life is hard. You either lay down and die, or you tough it out."

He was right, of course. Still, I could see how, faced with Stef's daily struggles, the lay-down-and-die option might have some appeal.

Matt sighed, put down his knife. "Look, Stef can walk. It's not easy for him, but if he practised he'd get better. He needs to build up his strength and stamina. His life depends on it. But I can't tell him that. Me, of all people. Imagine how he'd feel."

I said nothing because what could I say? Matt was good-looking, strong and capable; a powerhouse of a man. Stef came from exactly the same genes, yet his body was a frail, twisted, defective, altogether lesser version. It was as if Stef had ended up with all the physical leftovers, and had to watch Matt enjoy the banquet.

It couldn't be easy for either of them.

We chewed in silence.

"You two seem to get on well, at least," I eventually offered.

"We have to."

This time the silence was shorter.

"But yes," he conceded. "I suppose we do get on pretty well."

"Are you alike?"

Matt's face contorted. He looked away.

"No," he said, his tone harsh. "He has a body that doesn't work."

"Hey." I reached across the table and gripped his hand. "Are you alike?"

For a moment he didn't respond. Then, with a deep breath, he met my eyes. "We're so alike it's scary."

I smiled. Interlaced my fingers with his. "Guess he must be a great guy, then."

* * *

I lingered in the kitchen, chatting as Matt stacked the dishwasher.

"Right," he said. "Are you ready for dessert?" He reached around me for a fresh pan.

I wasn't convinced I'd ever need to eat again. Still, dessert was dessert. I sucked in my belly. "Sure. What are you going to wow me with this time?"

He threw me a grin. "The Frobisher Special."

Brown sugar followed cream into the pan. He added a dollop of butter, then fired up the gas.

I watched as he stirred. "Can I help?"

"Sure. If you stir this for me, I'll make the coffees."

He stepped back from the stove, still stirring, and beckoned me over. I moved into the space he'd made and took the spoon from him, trying not to notice the heat of his body at my back.

I stirred but forgot to breathe.

"Like this?" I asked, just for something to say.

"Exactly like this." His breath fell hot on my neck.

I shuddered. Blew out my breath silent and slow, then worked that pan with the sort of focus usually reserved for driving exams or lion taming. The slight drag of my body against his as I stirred was a lesson in hyper-awareness.

He squeezed my shoulders and finally turned away. "I'll make the coffees. Once you've got that melted, turn the heat down low, okay?"

What was a girl to do? All sexual tension and nowhere to go, I kept stirring, casting occasional glances at Matt. He was playing this—me—well. Too well. If I didn't watch myself I'd be jumping his bones by the end of dessert. Which might be exactly what I needed . . .

. . . Or exactly what I didn't need. Let's face it, his reputation as T&T's most determined bachelor had been well earned. I was just his latest challenge. Once that challenge was over he would still be my boss.

But he didn't feel like my boss tonight. And I didn't feel like I was merely a challenge.

"How's the sauce going?" Matt asked.

Cripes. The sauce. I looked down, discovered it was bubbling, and quickly reduced the heat.

"I think it's almost done," I said. Not that I could tell.

Maybe I should taste it, just to be sure. It smelled delicious. And it was loaded to the gunnels with calories, so odds were on it would be sinfully good.

The sauce, thickening now into golden brown nectar, enticed me. *Taste me, taste me.* My finger hovered over the pan. My mouth watered. Another glance Matt's way—not looking, all good—then I quickly touched forefinger to spoon and closed my mouth around the stolen sauce. My taste buds whooped with excitement. This sauce was *miraculous.*

I dipped the spoon back in the pan, blew to cool it, then swiped a healthy finger-load. It was a food quality check, that's all. Nothing to do with my sweet tooth. I withdrew my finger, opened my mouth—

Matt's hand closed around my wrist.

I started, looked up, blushed.

His eyes danced. "Couldn't wait, huh?"

"Quality control." I composed my expression into one of serious scientist.

"Ah. And the quality is adequate?"

"I'm not sure. I'll tell you in a minute."

I tried to raise my finger to my mouth but, instead, it headed away from me and straight towards Matt's mouth. I slitted my eyes at him and pulled harder. He smiled, but still my finger continued inexorably in the wrong direction.

"That's my finger," I said.

"That's my sauce," he countered.

My finger approached his lips. A pulse leapt in my throat.

"I stirred it," I said.

"You certainly did."

Since I couldn't get my finger to my mouth, I'd have to bring my mouth to my finger. I moved my head closer. His eyes met mine over the top of my finger. Sauce trickled down towards my palm. He smiled, then closed his lips around my finger and sucked.

I gasped. Was instantly wet, hot, and ready. The spoon clattered into the pan.

His tongue trailed up and down my finger with seductive intent. He released my moist, sexed-up finger and moved on down to my palm, his tongue claiming every last sweet calorie.

I dragged in a raggedy breath. "Well? Is the quality adequate?"

He looked up. Held my gaze with his dark, dark eyes.

"Oh yeah." My finger stood to attention between us. "The quality is more than adequate."

Stef appeared in the doorway and cleared his throat.

I leapt back from Matt, reclaiming my finger and hiding it from view.

"Hi," I said. "Want some dessert?"

Stef hesitated, flicking a look of enquiry Matt's way. He was asking his brother permission to gatecrash, I realised. Decent of him.

Matt waved him over. "Why not? There's plenty."

Stef ventured closer. "Thanks. What's on offer? It's not . . . ?" His eyes lit up. He wiped his mouth. "Awesome. Granny's date and butterscotch pudding."

"Matt just taught me how to make the sauce," I said.

Stef's eyebrows rose. "He did?"

I nodded. "My hips will never be the same." I wiggled them for emphasis.

Matt cleared his throat, averted his gaze. "Neither will I if you keep that up," he muttered.

Stef glanced at his brother, and his mouth quirked up at one corner. Then, directing his words to me, "He gave you Granny's world-famous butterscotch sauce recipe?"

"Is it really world-famous? Wouldn't surprise me. I can't believe it only has three ingredients." I dipped my pinkie in the saucepan and licked it with deliberation, in case Matt happened to be watching.

Stef sighed. Turned back to Matt. "Bruv. You know this means you'll have to marry her, right?"

Matt grinned. Stef grinned, too.

I couldn't decide whether they were sniggering because the odds of Matt ever marrying were non-existent or because Stef had caught Matt out. Concluded it was probably the former and I'd look stupid if I didn't fight back.

"That's a damn high price for a recipe," I said.

Stef sniggered.

Matt quirked an eyebrow, then proffered a warmed square of date cake. "No price is too high for this pudding, honey. Make sure you pile on the sauce. May as well get value for money."

CHAPTER TWENTY

I sat on my bed, knees hugged to my chest, chatting to Dani's reflection as she adjusted her hair.

"You should've seen him, Dan. He's amazing in the kitchen. Actually"—I smiled to myself—"he was amazing full-stop."

She pulled her hair into an elaborate French-looking style. "Well, at least he fed you up before he tossed in the M-word."

Even as she said it, fresh panic lodged in my throat. I'd thought I could keep things professional with Matt. I'd been wrong.

"It was his brother's M-word, not Matt's. What Matt wants is a quick fling with no strings." I sighed. "And that's so not me, Dan."

She tilted her head to one side, studying her reflection. Murmured, "It's not working." Then, to me, "Are you sure about that?"

"What? Him, or me?"

"Both. Either." Her fingers did some magic and suddenly her hair had body as well as elegance.

"How do you do that stuff with your hair?" I yanked at a couple of my own frizzy curls and sighed. "I can't do anything with mine."

"Product, darling, product." She smiled at her reflection then turned to face me. "Ever heard of taking a risk, Becs?"

"My hair's—"

"Not your hair, silly. Matt."

I huffed. What did she think I was doing? I was working with the man, wasn't I? If that wasn't risk-taking, what was?

Dani sat on the bed beside me and ran her finger down the conference programme. "Hey, a cocktail evening! What will you wear?"

"No idea."

Maybe I should wear a sack. Something really ugly, something that would drive Matt away. Nothing else seemed to be working. I'd done everything I could think of to avoid getting involved with Matt. I'd even executed Dani's distraction plan. But we'd gotten personal. Way too personal.

Dammit, what was wrong with me? Why couldn't I just be happily single, like Liz?

Dani opened my wardrobe. "Come on, show me your glad-rags. Cocktail evenings are fab. Think networking. You've got to knock 'em dead."

"I don't want to knock him dead."

"I said *them*, not *him*. Knock *them* dead." She gave me a sly look. "I'd quite like to meet this boss of yours."

God, no! It was bad enough that I was in lust with him, without my gorgeous sister wedging her stiletto into the mix. She'd end up with the man I wanted, and I'd be the shrivelled, dried-up old spinster who spent Christmases with them and wished her life was mine.

Thankfully, before I could answer she started hauling out clothes for inspection.

"That, maybe? No." She flung it on the bed. "Hmm, this one, then? Oh, God, yuk!" It flew in the same direction. "Good grief, *yellow*?" She shuddered and threw it on the pile.

And so it went on, until she turned to me and demanded, "Where are your clothes, Becs? These are antiques. Cast-offs. It's all so freaking *nineties*."

"Style never dates."

Her derision lanced me. "Then start buying clothes with style instead of cheap price-tags."

What could I say? I hate shopping for clothes. I've always hated it. She'd just summarised my whole approach.

"Nothing ever fits," I sulked. "Not that you'd understand. Your body's so perfect you'd get away with any old scrap of fabric."

"Oh, get over it. Your body's your body and you can look like a frumpy old has-been, or you can"—she struck a pose—"work it."

I slumped next to my rejected clothes. "Whatever."

She grabbed her bag and slung it over her shoulder. "Stop sulking. We're going shopping." She shook her hair loose, made for the door. "Better bring your credit card."

With military precision we descended on Covent Garden.

Dani didn't so much as glance at *Fix*, she even gave *Raquelite* the cold shoulder, and when I suggested *Moreton Spry*—my personal favourite; Mum's, too—she just snorted. "Trinny and Susannah would have a field day."

"Hey, that's a bit rough. It's not like I'm refusing to spend money. I'm happy to buy something." I stopped at a likely-looking window. "What about here? They've got nice evening wear."

"Becky. You need sophisticated. You need stunning. You need more than a high street chain-store look." She strode purposefully on.

I clutched my wallet a little tighter and trotted after her. Maybe this whole shopping-with-Dani thing wasn't such a good idea.

She turned into a close, cobbled street away from the crowds and at last slowed to a measured pace.

"Wow," I said, drawn to the eye-catching window displays. "I didn't even know this street existed."

"At your age that's ridiculous."

"I'm only thirty-one! I'm poor!"

Dani stopped and rounded on me. *Uh-oh.*

"Look."

Yep, she meant business.

"It's all a matter of priorities. Crikey, Becs, it's not about doing the quickest shopping trip ever . . ."

Actually, it was. Get in, spend the money, get out.

". . . It's about finding the right look." Hands on hips, she cast a scathing eye over my comfortable but not-very-pretty garments.

"Hey, less of the evils. These aren't my party clothes."

"Do you want to blow Matt away," she demanded, "or not?"

"Yes. Definitely."

I reconsidered. "Actually—no."

I shuffled my feet. "Oh, I don't know."

She looked at me quizzically.

I grimaced. "It's complicated. But when all's said and done he's my boss so, really, I shouldn't go there. Right," I decided. "I'm not going there. That's it."

She snorted. "Sure it is. So let me get this straight. You're happily single . . ."

A determined nod of my head. "Yes."

". . . And totally not interested in your boss . . ."

A determined shake of my head. "Not anymore."

". . . But you'll show him what he's missing just because . . . ?"

Another nod, this time rather less determined. "Just . . . because."

We didn't have a future—not in the longer-than-a-fortnight sense—but I still wanted him to see me at my very best. Was that so wrong? "Does there have to be a reason?"

Dani flapped a dismissive hand. "Whatever. This is where you buy your dress."

"Fine." I gathered my pride around me. "Let's get it over with."

She ushered me into *Mischief*, an intimate little boutique where all the price-tags were hidden. I felt afraid. Very afraid.

An aging woman with serious mutton-versus-lamb issues approached us. She smoothed her elegant clothes with a heavily-bejewelled hand and offered us a plastic smile.

"Good afternoon, ladies," she said, adding icy emphasis to the last word as she looked me up and down.

Then, far more warmly as her eyes swept over Dani, "I'm Sue-Ann. How can I be of assistance?"

Mission explained, Sue-Ann trotted around the shop gathering armload after armload of garments for me to try on, then hovered like a nosy butler, killing me by degrees with her 'that is so You' comments.

Ever-conscious of my pear shape, I honed in on looser options and figure-hiding dresses. Dani pronounced them 'matronly' and 'boring' and even, with increasing agitation, downright 'ugly'.

"Becs, no! It just doesn't *look* good." She threw up her hands in despair, then rounded on Sue-Ann. "That's it! Stop! No more dowdy stuff. Don't listen to a word she says. She needs sleek, sexy, stunning, *young*. You don't want to look like his *mother*, Becs."

I started to protest, but Dani silenced me with her hand. "I love you to bits, Sis, but you *so* need to get over your hips. Just this once. Trust me. Please?"

I panini-pressed my lips together. It was easy for her to talk about hips as if they were optional extras; she had a model's body and the confidence to match. Some of us had been disguising our 'womanly figure' since before our first kiss. Some of us had gone through our entire teens boyfriend-less because of said 'womanly figure'. Some of us had issues, okay?

"Look," said Dani, "the best way to look slim is to go for clothes with a closer fit. Not slutty, not too tight, just . . . Well, let's try some other options and I'll show you."

"I don't know what his mother looks like," I muttered. "She's not in the family photos."

"Maybe she died."

"So you're saying these clothes make me look dead. Nice."

Fortunately, at that moment Sue-Ann produced another shedload of garments for me to try on, and our petty argument stopped before it gathered momentum.

I tried on another hundred or so outfits, and under Dani's eagle eye a short-list of possibilities emerged. I stopped offering opinions—clearly what I thought was irrelevant—and an eternity later Dani stopped me mid-pirouette and smiled.

"That's it. That's the one." She turned me this way and that, making me look at myself from every angle. "Now *that* is classy."

It was. It was absolutely perfect.

The black silk halter-neck dress with its plunging neckline was subdued—but wow! What a statement. It transformed me into a Fifties screen siren.

"I can't believe it's me." Awed, I stroked my hands over the figure-hugging fabric.

"You have a lovely neckline, and beautiful breasts," Sue-Ann purred. "This dress accentuates everything to perfection."

I stared at my waist. It seemed so tiny. How had that happened? I fingered the black-satin waist band that drew up towards a diamante cluster, accentuating my cleavage.

"These are hand-sewn." Sue-Ann lovingly touched the beads. "Such beautiful detailing. Here." She handed me an amber- and diamante-encrusted clutch-purse. "What do you think?"

I thought it all looked way too expensive but, just for now, I pretended it didn't matter.

"It's lovely." I moved this way and that, watching the A-line hem caress my knees, loving the brush of silk against skin.

"We'll take the purse as well," said Dani.

I hurriedly searched for the price-tag. Found it in an inner pocket. Gasped. Stared at Dani in horror. *No!* Absolutely not. How would I ever pay off my credit card?

Dani's glare dared me to speak. I lapsed into silent panic.

A few nips and tucks were needed—on my body, but we settled for the dress—and Sue-Ann tutted and clucked as she assessed the alterations. Then she said, "Go and have a coffee, ladies. It will be ready in an hour."

Coffee! Great idea.

Dani disagreed. "Shoes," she reminded me. "You need shoes."

My throat closed over. The dreaded 'S' word. Why was she doing this to me? She knew how I felt about it. Trying to find shoes for my size eight clompers was torture *a la* needle-in-haystack. Generally, if they fit I bought them. Fashion and personal taste were optional extras.

I glowered at her.

Dani glowered right back. "Shoes."

She was right. I didn't have pretty evening shoes. Reluctant but resigned, I followed her down yet another pokey back street.

When I re-emerged into daylight, clasping my first ever pair of *Miu Mius*, I didn't know whether to feel ecstatic or depressed. Ecstatic because my sexy black, diamante-detailed, peep-toe stilettos looked gorgeous—and, astonishingly, were a perfect fit. Depressed because I'd now have to beg my po-faced bank manager for mercy, and I wasn't sure he did Mercy.

Dani finally relented and allowed me a quick caffeine fix, but I barely had time to taste it before she hauled me to my feet again. "Time to pick up your dress."

Of course, it wasn't enough just to collect it and go. Both women insisted I *must* try on the dress again, 'with your new shoes as well', to check the alterations.

I paraded in front of them, to cheers (Dani) and clapping (Sue-Ann), then posed in front of the mirror. I giggled with amazement. "Is that me?"

Dani's eyes shone. "You look totally hot."

She'd never said that about me before. Next to her I'd always felt like the frumpy aging sister, but now . . . now I liked my curves. Now I liked standing beside my sister.

Sue-Ann rang up the bill. I handed over my credit card, nauseous. My bank manager would have a purple fit.

I waited until we'd left before I sagged on Dani's shoulder.

"I'm broke!" I wailed. "Flat broke. I'm never go shopping with you again."

CHAPTER TWENTY-ONE

The flight to Dublin took little more than an hour. We'd barely left the ground when Amanda, sitting to my right, cleared her throat. "Do you like flying, Becky?"

I started. She'd spoken? To me? I must've been gripping the armrests too hard.

"It gets me where I'm going," I said.

At least, I hoped so. And best I didn't think about that, since we were in the air.

Then it struck me that maybe this wasn't about me. Maybe this was her way of saying she was scared. Maybe we had something in common, after all. "What about you?"

"Oh, I *love* planes."

Then again, maybe not.

She beamed. "They're incredible. Don't you think it's remarkable that such a huge, heavy lump of metal can stay in the air?"

I glanced out the window. Swallowed. "I guess."

She leaned closer. "See those little flaps on the wings? Have you ever wondered what would happen if they stopped working?"

Shit, lady. Enough already.

"So many plane crashes happen because of the tiniest little malfunction." She held her finger and thumb a millimetre apart, then sighed happily. "Isn't technology amazing?"

I sure hoped so, because our lives were depending on it *right now*. How could I say 'shut it' without being rude?

She warmed to her theme, quoting me statistics I didn't want to know. The guy next to the window eyed her as if he wanted to drive a pickaxe into her skull.

It worked for me.

He inhaled deeply, exhaled and said, "Oh, what glorious fun."

He rummaged around for some headphones and turned his body towards the window, staring down at the London murk.

Lucky him.

I tried once, twice, to politely change the topic, but Amanda just couldn't take a hint. She enthusiastically regaled me with all the gory Lockerbie details. Staines got a brief mention but wasn't really big enough to rock her radar. Spookily, her birthday coincided with 9-11. She knew an unhealthy amount about the Tenerife disaster, considering it had happened before she was born. On and on she prattled. Dates, aircraft, causes—she really was quite the plane crash encyclopaedia.

Flying's not my idea of fun. Planes are flimsy. They rattle, they shake, they make a horrific racket at take-off and even more of a racket at landing, they get buffeted around in the wind and, as far as travel goes, they're not even very comfortable. Add Amanda to it all, complete with air disaster commentary . . . Well, she was tempting fate and I didn't like it. Not one bit.

I prayed for some kind of divine intervention. Make her fall asleep, lose her voice, have a seizure . . . Whatever. Just shut. Her. Up.

The pressure in my chest grew, an enormous doomsday bell reverberating against my ribcage. I could tell I was building up to a good old-fashioned, screaming-heebie-jeebies, we're-all-going-to-*die* moment.

I cast around for Matt. He'd seen me like that; he'd be able to help.

Except his seat was empty. Where had he gone?

Hank caught my eye and sent me a lascivious wink. Slimeball. I pointedly ignored him and settled back in my seat. No way did I want his help.

I took a couple of deep breaths and tried to think happy thoughts.

Okay, the happy thoughts weren't working.

I tried a different approach.

"How do you know so much about air disasters?" Get her talking about herself.

"Reading. Lots of reading. Some people are into horror movies; I'm into plane crashes. I mean, think about it. Isn't it just fascinating that these huge machines can fall out of the sky and get smashed beyond recognition and experts can still work out what happened?"

Fascinating? No. Gruesome.

"Daddy and I used to talk about planes all the time. He was an aircraft engineer."

She fell silent. I sent up a prayer of thanks.

"Until he got blamed for that crash back in ninety-seven," she said.

I jerked my head up, shocked. "Oh no. What happened?"

"A plane crashed, Daddy got blamed, so he hung himself in the bathroom."

I opened my mouth to speak. Closed it again. Freaking hell. Poor Amanda.

I looked across at headphone guy. He met my eyes with an expression somewhere between deer-in-the-headlamps and pass-me-a-sickbag. His music obviously hadn't saved him.

"Anyway," she said, businesslike, "that was years ago. Things have changed since then. But even though technology's so much better, loads of things can still go wrong."

She gave us a run-down on all the 'technical hitches' that could send our plane plummeting down from the sky.

I broke out in a cold sweat. I hadn't realised air travel was still so *risky*.

Headphone guy clapped a hand to his forehead then closed his eyes.

I grabbed the emergency evacuation manual and committed it to memory. Hopefully we'd crash into a nice flat field where we might have half a chance of surviving.

* * *

Miraculously, we landed in Dublin without a hitch. I couldn't keep the smile off my face. All those lilting Irish accents—and I was alive to hear them.

"We're here!" I said. "Who's for a Guinness?" Because dammit, after that flight, I could do with one.

"If the lady wants Guinness," declared Hank, "the lady shall have Guinness."

His arm came around my shoulders. "And so shall I. To be sure, to be sure."

The hug became a shoulder massage. I suppressed a shudder. On the erotic scale it rated right up there with smear tests.

161

I gave him my best fuck-off smile and moved out of reach. Indicated our bags, strewn around us. "Shouldn't we at least check in to the hotel first?"

"And sign up for dinner," said Amanda.

"Dinner? Guinness? Same thing. Me poor Da' was Irish, *begorra*! I'll no' be passing by a Guinness." Hank hee-hawed with laughter, and his toupee moved slightly askew.

I cringed. The toupee was a disaster. And as for that appalling accent, his poor Da' would be turning in his grave.

"Are you going to keep that up all week?" I asked.

"I'd keep it up all year for you," he said, with a lewd grin.

Hank on heat. Just what we needed.

Amanda blushed beet-red and dashed off to get a baggage trolley.

Matt coughed into the silence. "Give us a hand with these bags, Hank."

Then, in an undertone to me, "Don't say a word. You'll just encourage the prick."

Great. With a rutting pig in our midst (thanks, Hank) and minimal odds of surviving the return flight (thanks, Amanda), drinking myself into an AA meeting (sorry, Jim) suddenly looked like an excellent option.

* * *

Being the only other woman in our group, Amanda was my room-mate. Joy. I tossed my bag on the nearest bed and shrugged out of my coat, then watched as she painstakingly shook out and folded her clothes before stowing them all neatly in two of the drawers provided.

"You can have the other two," she offered.

"Thanks," I said with zero enthusiasm. "Maybe later."

She probably had hangers for her clothes and all.

I unearthed the tea and coffee facilities and plugged in the tiny kettle. "Cup of tea?"

Amanda nodded and, smiling, produced a packet of *Blue Ribands* from her hand luggage. "With chocolate wafers."

Yum! Maybe she wasn't so bad, after all. We just needed to avoid any mention of planes.

I went across the hall and knocked on Matt's open door, then

162

ventured in. "Cup of tea? Or would you be looking for something a little stronger?" This in my best Irish accent.

Matt and Roland, the Year Three specialist, were both hunkered down in front of the tiny fridge bar and clearly looking for something a little stronger.

"Has it got legs?" I asked.

They turned and stood as one.

Matt nudged the fridge door shut with his foot, giving me an appraising glance. "Abso-lutely."

Languid heat trickled through my veins. Why couldn't he just creep me out, like Hank? It would make everything so much simpler.

"Sorry?" Roland frowned. He never understood innuendo. Mister Literal all the way, was our Roland.

"Nothing." Matt gave me a disarming smile and I smiled back, my pulse kicking up in spite of all the promises I'd made myself.

He stretched, reaching for the ceiling. Abdominals, rippling lightly, revealed themselves above his belt. Really, a girl could be forgiven for wanting to leap on him right there and then.

"I like the sound of something stronger," interrupted Roland. Which was fortunate, because these were both workmates, and this was still work, and it could just stop right there.

"Stronger than what?" I asked, nonplussed.

He looked at me as if I'd forgotten how to walk.

"Tea, like you said." He indicated the rows of miniature bottles in front of him. "But we'll drink this dry in five minutes."

"Come on," said Matt, "let's find a real bar."

I went back to tell Amanda, and found her hanging the last of her clothes in the tiny wardrobe. And yes, she had brought her own dinky hangers—folding travel ones, no less.

I reneged on my cup-of-tea suggestion. "We've had a better offer. There's a bar downstairs. We're all heading down now. Let's go."

I didn't wait for her.

Downstairs, Hank was already propped up at the bar, looking like he'd been there all year. He downed his whiskey and joined us at the table, but not before he'd ordered, at top volume, "Compulsory Guinnesses all round. When in Ireland, do as the Irish do."

After that it was compulsory Murphys all round. Amanda and I sat out while the boys had compulsory Kilkennys all round. By the time it got to compulsory Let's Start Agains all round I felt rather light-headed.

"I could do with some food," I said.

"That'll just dilute it," said Hank.

Matt shot Hank a derisive glance, so quickly disguised I wasn't sure I'd even seen it. "Dinner's in half an hour. Maybe we should make a move."

"We shouldn't miss dinner," said Amanda. "Just last week there was a news item about this. A really experienced international pilot . . ."

I groaned but she told us his story anyway, which ended rather abruptly after he missed lunch, had a few pre-flight beers, and flew himself and two hundred-odd passengers into the side of a cliff. Lovely. I was just about to ask her how a pissed pilot managed to get through security when Roland cut in.

"Amanda's right," he said. "We should go to dinner. They always have a good keynote speaker on the first night. Kick-starts the week."

Which gave us only half an hour to freshen up for the official opening of Conference Week. I made do with a power nap while Amanda dealt to her hair, pulling it into a bun so tight I expected grey matter to ooze from her ears if she smiled.

In the event, dinner was worth the effort. Excellent food, prompt service, and an unmissable keynote speaker. It whetted my appetite for whatever the next four days might hold.

As for the company, I was having the time of my life. Even Hank was bearable. He and his toupee weren't quite the lady-catcher he imagined himself, but at least he was keeping his hands to himself so I wasn't bothered by his smarmy one-liners.

Meal over, a band set up in one corner. Waiters shifted the tables back, making room for an impromptu dance floor, and a bar of indecent proportions *whoosh*ed its shutters open for business. Good grief, this week would pickle my liver.

"Becky. You're here."

My heart sank. I knew that voice. I turned and forced a smile. "Alyssa." The piranha from my last job.

She looked stunning as ever.

"*Mwah! Mwah!*" She air-kissed my cheeks then held me at arm's length. "Darling, you look fantastic."

Whatever.

"So do you," I said.

"Thank you, darling. We do our best." Her hand strayed up to her already-perfect Cleopatra-black hair.

I self-consciously tucked a wayward strand of frizz behind my ear. "You're still in travel, then?"

"Yes." She sighed dramatically. "Branch manager, now. Can you believe it?"

Actually, no. What—whose—strings had she yanked to pull that off?

"It's phenomenally busy," she continued. "But I like it that way. I feel . . ." She pirouetted her hand as she searched for the word. "*fulfilled.*"

"That's great, Alyssa." I tried to mean it. "Well done."

"Thank you, darling. Anyway, Conference Week is such a good opportunity to think outside the square. You know"—she smoothed her hands down over her hips—"seek out new opportunities."

I wasn't sure quite what opportunities, or even what square, she had in mind but, judging by the dress she wore, they weren't work-related. That neckline alone was a health and safety hazard, plunging so deep it almost reached her navel. What was she thinking, wearing that to a work dinner? And in *Pretty Woman* red? Didn't she realise she stood out like blood in a shark enclosure?

I sighed. Shoved the petty bitch inside me back in her cage. So what if Alyssa wanted to make a statement? So what if she obsessed about her image and took the airs and graces too far? Give the woman a break! She wasn't a nasty person. And sure, that colour would be a big mistake on me, but on her it was a crowd-stopper. Admit it, Becs. She looked stunning.

She put a hand on my arm. "Now. Before you tell me what you've been up to since you left Beacon Travel, do you know that *gor*-geous man over there?"

I didn't need to look. "With the blond hair?"

"Yes."

"That's Matt. I work with him."

"Lucky you." She flashed him a pouty smile. "What does he do?"

"He's a lecturer. Recreational Tourism."

Her eyes gleamed as she inspected him over her wine-glass. "Really? I wonder if he needs a guest speaker. I must ask him."

I did a double-take. Guest speaker? Her? In Rec. Tourism? "I—"

"Recreational Tourism, you say? Let's see. The great outdoors . . . leisure pursuits . . . small business opportunities . . ." She waved a hand. "I'm sure I'll come up with something."

I found my voice. "You might need to ditch the stilettos for a while."

She smiled. "I do have a life outside of work, Rebecca," she purred.

"Now." Her finger tapped her lip. "What could I offer that he won't be able to refuse?"

Plenty, no doubt, given she was such a god-damn Man Magnet.

Without further ado she made me introduce her to my colleagues, and before you could say 'look at her tits' all the men were falling over themselves to get a prime spot next to Alyssa and her cleavage. Within the minute she was at Matt's side, giving him her undivided attention and a D-cup close-up that was every guy's wet dream.

I should have felt pleased. Alyssa was the perfect decoy. With her around he'd soon forget about me. Problem solved. Career saved. Excellent. I should have felt pleased, but all I felt was hurt.

Amanda came alongside me. "You know that plane crash I told you about earlier?"

Which one? I didn't ask.

"Well," she said, looking around, "I'm guessing the number of people here is about the same as the fatalities in that crash."

"I need to go to the ladies' room," I said and bolted.

CHAPTER TWENTY-TWO

I bought another drink and wandered off into the throng, keeping an eye out for Amanda. No way could I spend another second with her.

Every so often I doubled back for a glimpse of Matt—not because I was interested in him, of course, because I wasn't. So what if he was a brilliant lecturer who spent weekends working with needy kids? So what if he leapt tall buildings and took claustrophobic women in his stride? So what if he made me feel alive every time he was near? None of that meant I was into him. I wasn't. Not one bit.

Still. Looking couldn't hurt, right?

I began to feel strangely removed. Although I smiled hellos to people I recognised, stopped to chat with a few, I didn't connect with anyone. It was all a pretence. I was part of this gathering, but not part of it at all.

Was that my mobile? I ducked into an alcove, set down my glass, and took the call.

"Hello," said Charlie. "Fancy a coffee?"

"Charlie. Hi. I . . ."

I should tell him. Thanks but no thanks. Once was enough. It's me, not you. Whatever. Let him down nicely, hang up, and get on with my life.

"Sorry," I said. "I can't. I'm out of London at the moment."

Oh, for crying out loud. I *so* needed to put on my big-girl panties.

"Pity," he said. "Where are you? Somewhere exotic?"

"Not particularly. Just a work conference in Dublin."

"Dublin, eh? I've got a wee place in Killiney. Want me to pop over and kidnap you for a while?"

What—he'd just 'pop over'? Like he had a chopper on standby or something?

Mind you, if he had a house in Killiney he must be loaded. Maybe he really did have a helicopter.

"No," I said. "Kidnapping's out. This conference programme's too good to miss. Let's catch up when I'm back."

I didn't mean it, of course, but he knew that. This was just a game to him.

He chuckled. "Chicken."

"Absolutely. You kidnapped me once before, and look where that got me."

"You loved it."

"I've got to go, Charlie."

He exhaled. "It's hard to find a good kidnappee these days."

I loved his humour. Why couldn't I fall in love with Charlie? Imagine! We'd move in together and, just like that, all my problems would be solved. No more pokey rented flat with second-hand furniture. No more dodging around Jim's dirty dishes and smelly thrice-worn socks. No more desperate matchmaking by my grandchildren-hungry parents. And—the Grand Prize—no more fantasising about Matt; I'd be too busy fantasising about my gorgeous, rich Charlie.

Shame my heart couldn't do the decent thing and love him.

Where was Matt, anyway?

Not that I cared, because I didn't. I couldn't afford to care. Not if I wanted to keep my dream job, and self-respect.

I looked down at my wine glass. Saw Jim's face. *Maybe you should come to a meeting.*

Did he really think I had a problem?

Well, I didn't. I'd show him. Right now, even.

I re-joined the party without my glass. Best I didn't drink any more tonight, anyway. I was feeling maudlin, and drinking in this mood would just make everything worse.

Matt?

Ah, there, found him again.

. . . And there was Alyssa, glued to his side. Selfishly, I wished she would leave with a nasty gastro virus or something. Even though I couldn't have Matt, I didn't want her to have him, either.

But she stayed right where she was. Flaunting her body with calculated sensuality. Standing so close she could probably feel his every breath. I wanted to run away, hide in my room, sulk for a week. But I couldn't drag myself away. Unbearable as it was to watch her reel Matt in, I couldn't stand the thought of leaving and missing it, either.

I grabbed a glass of soda water, just so I had something to hold, something to sip while I tortured myself.

Everyone else made the most of the subsidised booze, and the party gathered momentum. The noise level increased. Not to be outdone, the DJ pumped up the music. Everyone seemed to be losing their inhibitions and finding boogie shoes straight out of *Saturday Night Fever*.

Not me, though. I drank soda water and spied on Matt. Alyssa must've said something witty. He laughed and she joined in, one delicate talon stroking his arm.

Jealousy coiled inside me. I switched my focus abruptly away, then noticed Hank watching me. I blushed furiously, feeling as if I'd been caught in my underwear. He shot me a smug smile.

Crap. He knew.

Of *course* he knew. How could I have let myself be so transparent? I bit my lip, looked away. Then, stupidly, back again. Blast. There he was, still watching me.

Desperate to escape Hank's knowing eyes, I melted back into the crowd, only to trip over a badly-placed chair. I pitched forward and my glass flew out of my hand. Fortunately a waiter with superhero reflexes was passing at that moment. He whipped out an arm to save me, all the while balancing a tray of breakables, then rescued my glass and refilled it for me, bless him. Gosh. Maybe I should marry him. He was helpful, resourceful, light-footed . . . I could do a lot worse.

I groaned. Had it really come to this? Assessing random waiters for marriage? I cringed. Cringed harder at the thought of my klutz-of-the-year stumble.

I glanced left and right. Was anyone staring? Pointing? Laughing?

No, thank goodness. I surreptitiously rubbed my ankle. Ouch. Must've rolled it.

I adjusted my top and sipped from my glass. Oops. The waiter had given me champagne. Hmm. Did I want it? I rotated my ankle and decided yes, in the absence of paracetamol, I did.

I headed towards some vacant seats and rearranged them so I could rest my ankle. Bliss.

Except—what was that creepy feeling in the back of my neck? I glanced around. Nothing. Looked again, and froze. Bloody Hank. *Again.* Goddammit, that man and his toupee were everywhere.

He stared at me with lizard-like intensity. I ignored him but it didn't work; I could feel his eyes boring into my back. I shifted uncomfortably in my seat, looked at him again. He responded with a wink. A full-on, lecherous wink.

Eeeuw. Did he think that was a turn-on or something?

He started towards me and I stood, my now-racing heart telling me what my brain hadn't worked out. This felt wrong. Creepy-wrong.

What did he want? Had he been following me all evening? Did he know my room number? Was he some kind of predator? A rapist? Knife-wielding madman?

Oh, come on, Becs. Less of the dramatics.

I took a deep, calming breath and a deep, calming slug of champers. This was *Hank.* Gauche, ugly, harmless Hank. He wasn't stalking me. He wouldn't know how.

Still, I didn't fancy hanging around, so I hobbled in the opposite direction. Ouch. Blasted ankle.

A hand grazed my side, just above my waist, and I jumped. Calm *down*, Becs.

I glanced back. Shite. How had he reached me so quickly? Panic flared. I jerked away. He grabbed my wrist. Breathless, I tried to break free. For a little guy he was surprisingly strong. I used the only weapon I had, and tossed my champagne in his face. He swore. His grip tightened.

"Prick-teaser," he said, his breath warm in my ear, his potent aftershave smothering me.

"Let go." I yanked my hand back with all my strength, letting the momentum wheel me round, and fled, only to come up short as he seized my upper arm. The wine-glass slipped from my fingers and splintered at my feet.

"Get off me!" Panic transmuted into rage and I spun towards him, lashing out with my free arm.

"Whoa."

Something about his voice gave me a milli-second's hesitation, and he used it to grab my other arm.

"Becky. Slow down."

The voice finally registered. Wrong guy. I stopped struggling. "It's you."

Matt smiled down at me. "As opposed to . . . ?"

He glanced over my shoulder and his smile dissolved. "Ah."

"Hank," he said, with an abrupt head-nod. Then returned his attention to me. "Where were you heading in such a hurry?"

I threw Hank my best fuck-off look. "Anywhere he's not. Let's go."

Hank closed in. "I only wanted to buy you a drink."

I tensed.

Matt turned me bodily away, his arm draped over my shoulder. "I've got this one. Off you go," he added with the dismissive hand-wave a parent gives an irksome child.

Hank started to argue then shrugged. "Whatever. Catch you later, Becky."

"Not if I can help it," I muttered. Glared at his departing back. "Pig."

Matt laughed.

I clapped a hand to my mouth. "Sorry. Not you. Him."

"I gathered that." He guided me with his arm. "What happened?"

"Nothing I couldn't handle."

He threw me a sceptical look. "M-hmm. Then why are you limping?"

I looked down at my ankle, then up at him. Gosh, had he always been that tall?

"I rolled my ankle. Nothing to do with Hank," I added hastily.

"If it was I'd have his balls," he growled, then moved his arm down to my waist, holding me close. It felt nice. Too nice. "You'd better get some ice on that."

Good point. My ankle pounded its agreement. I bit my lip, nodded.

"Here, I'll help you to your room. Pumpkin time for you, I think."

He led me to the lifts and his arm stayed right where it was as we glided up towards our floor.

"A good night's sleep and I'll be right as rain," I said.

"Tomorrow's a busy day, so if you can't walk I'll have no option but to piggy-back you."

I giggled. Maybe I should call his bluff.

The lift came to an abrupt stop and I staggered against him.

His arm tightened around me. "All right?"

I nodded. We made our way up the corridor. Luckily this was the last stretch; my ankle was really hurting now.

"Where did you get to, anyway?" Matt asked. "You disappeared."

He'd noticed! I resisted the urge to do a happy-dance. "Just wandering."

"Having fun?"

"Until Hank showed up." I shuddered. "What a creep."

We stopped outside my door and I swiped my room-card. Nothing. I tried again. Still nothing. I balanced on my good foot, bit my lip. Come *on*.

Matt leaned against the wall, arms folded, and waited.

I turned the card over and had another go.

Oh, for goodness sake. I inspected it as if it had fallen from the sky. "Why aren't you working?" Then, to Matt, "It's not working."

"Here." He took the card and opened the door with ease.

"How'd you do that?"

He shrugged and smiled. "With a gentle touch."

I looked at his hands. Remembered them on my body after my accident in the pool. Oh yeah. Those hands had a lot to answer for.

But they'd also got us into my room. The door closed behind us and I sank to my bed with relief.

Matt rang for an icepack then crouched in front of me and, with great care, removed my left shoe. "Let's have a look at this ankle, then."

"Um, it's the other one."

He removed my right shoe with equal care, cupping my foot in his hands as if I were Cinderella. I looked down at my delicate size eight and snorted. Ugly step-sister, more like.

He shot me a questioning look.

"Ticklish," I improvised.

"Ah."

With gentle hands he turned my ankle this way and that. "Does this hurt? No? How about this? No? Excellent. Nothing too critical, then. I think some ice, then a good night's sleep, and things will look a whole lot better in the morning."

I looked down at Hot Doc and wondered how things could possibly look any better, ever.

The ice was terrific. It calmed and soothed almost as well as his hands.

"Thanks, Doc." I handed him the icepack.

"Any time, Ms Jordan." He tossed the icepack aside and knelt in front of me, checking my ankle again. Gave the well-chilled toes a warming squeeze, then switched to the other foot and gently massaged.

His thumbs expertly worked their way up towards my heel and I sighed with pleasure, a total sucker for a foot massage. His hands continued on up, starting on my leg. What—? Ooh, *nice*. Lucky I'd had that leg-wax last Saturday.

"I could get used to this," I murmured.

"It's better with massage oil."

I bet.

Matt playing masseur? It reeked of my usual fantasies. I reached out an experimental finger, touched him. No, not a dream. Real. He was real. This was real. Hell-sexy real. I should jump him and be done with it.

He looked up and read me like a front-page headline. His hands stilled. His eyes darkened.

A pulse caught in my throat. I braced my hands against the bed, breathless.

And then his hands were on mine, his thighs brushing my knees, his eyes seeing through to my soul.

Slowly, slowly, our fingers laced themselves together in a perfect fit. My body flooded with heat.

I leaned forward and his lips were a hair's breadth from mine. My lips partly slightly in anticipation. For long, tormenting, exquisite seconds he held back, and then at last he kissed me; the merest of sensuous grazes. My lips felt swollen, needy. My heart pounded. My breath came ragged. Our lips met again, with urgency, and I opened my mouth to him, drinking him in, urging him on. He dragged me against him. Our tongues tangled. My head reeled with his heat, his taste, his smell . . .

In one expert movement he lifted me bodily up the modest single bed and laid me back against the covers.

I looked into the depths of his gorgeous brown eyes. Lost myself there.

"Becky," he murmured, and the spell broke.

Screw the job. I wanted him. I wanted him *now*. We kissed fiercely, hungrily, clawing at clothes, frantic with lust, only to be brought abruptly to by a sharp intake of breath. "Oh. Er . . ."

Our heads did a perfectly synchronised snap-around to see Amanda backing swiftly out of the room, eyes and mouth all capital o's. The door clicked shut.

Matt's eyes found mine. I grimaced.

He cleared his throat. "Maybe we should take a rain check." He disentangled his hand from my hair, and somehow even that action was a caress.

I moved my hips against his. "Do we have to?"

He smiled and brought his lips back down on mine. His hand roamed down my back and over my hip, tracing an exploratory finger beneath my panties. I moaned against his lips as his finger trailed lower, and lower, almost there, oh yes . . .

And then, Goddammit, he stopped.

He carefully extracted his hand. "We have to," he murmured.

One last nibble at the hollow of my neck, one last pleasured sigh from me, and he sat up.

I shivered at the loss of contact.

He looked down at me, stroked my cheek. "Let's go to my room."

I brought my hand up to his much larger one, entwining my fingers with his.

"I'd love to say yes, but you're rooming with Roland and if he walked in . . ." I paused, tried to find the words, failed. "Sorry. Guess I'm a prude."

He laughed. "Who would've thought, eh?"

I wrinkled my nose at him. "Anyway, Doc says my ankle needs a good night's sleep."

"He does indeed." Matt pulled a blanket over me and I snuggled into it.

He kissed my nose. "Sleep well, babe."

"Mmm. You too."

His lips grazed mine. "I doubt it."

CHAPTER TWENTY-THREE

Apparently the theme for Day Two was Embarrassment.

Embarrassment when I woke and had to face Amanda and her pearls before the day even began.

Embarrassment when I went downstairs to breakfast and had to sit next to Matt, the air between us thick with undercurrents and Amanda watching my every move.

More embarrassment when Hank, sitting directly opposite, caught my eye and threw me a slimy smile.

Then Roland asked, innocently enough, where Matt and I had disappeared to during the party. I was so engulfed by embarrassment that words failed me and, for a moment, I thought I'd faint. No such luck. Matt, with a brief glance my way, said we'd both needed an early night. I almost fled the table in the loaded silence that followed.

Matt caught up with me as I left the dining room. "What's your first workshop?"

I kept walking. "Can't remember."

"I'm going to Tourism's Impact on Tribal Culture in Asia. You should come with me."

"No."

It felt rude even as I said it. I walked a little faster.

He kept pace with ease. "Becs, what's wrong?"

"Nothing."

"Really?" He stopped, placed a restraining hand on my arm. "Are you avoiding me?"

I stopped, lips compressed, arms folded. "Of course not."

His eyebrow didn't believe me.

I sighed. "Look, I'm feeling a bit . . . awkward." I couldn't meet his gaze. "It's just me. I'm not sure how I should act around you after . . ." I hid my face in my hand. "And Amanda walking in on us like that . . ."

He grinned. "She'll get over it."

"Then having to sit and eat breakfast with her like nothing's happened . . ." I looked him in the eye at last. "That's more than awkward. That's *mortifying*."

His grin widened—clearly mortification wasn't contagious.

"So, right now, yes, I'm avoiding you—*and* everyone else. 'Cause it's the only way I'll get through today."

And, leaving him with his amusement, I took myself off to some mindless workshop on Conservation. Better that than Conversation.

I slunk my way through morning tea, lunch and two workshops. Then, rather than face Amanda up in our room, I left the hotel and hid out in a café for an hour. When I thought the coast was clear I returned and whipped upstairs to change for pre-dinner drinks. No Amanda, thankfully.

I went downstairs and, sure enough, the others were gathered in the bar and on their second round. Boring old soda water in hand, I waved at them all across the bar then made a show of talking into my mobile phone rather than joining them. I needed to find a bit of brazen in me first.

I found an empty booth and this time really did use my phone. "Hi, Liz. How are you?"

"Busy. Stressed." She sighed. "Busy."

Liz was always busy and always stressed. That's what being HR Manager for a major accountancy firm meant. But something in her voice had me worried.

"Are you okay? What's going on?"

"I'd give my back teeth for a week in Ibiza."

I waited.

Another sigh. "I'm fine, Becs, don't worry. It's just . . . we've just been told we're restructuring, and everyone's feeling nervous, and it's on a tight timeline, and there'll be redundancies, and Christmas is approaching, and . . . you know."

Yeah, I knew. Liz was no soft-sap—she wasn't dubbed The Razor at work for nothing—but her heart wasn't made of stone. *That's* what I knew.

"Are you the one issuing the redundancy notices?"

"Yep." She sounded grim. Clenched-teeth grim. Poor Liz. She would feel each and every one of those redundancies.

"Book a holiday, Liz. Soon."

"Yeah. But not until it's finished."

Much as I admired her for being so outrageously conscientious, I wanted to shake her for it, too. Sometimes your strength could be your weakness.

"Liz, just promise me you'll step back if the stress gets too much."

"You know me."

"Yes, I do. That's why I'm saying it. Promise me, Liz."

She promised, but her heart wasn't in it. Her heart was already back at work and there was no point talking further, so I finished the call and joined the others.

As we moved through to dinner Alyssa materialised, greeting my workmates as if she'd known them forever and accepting Roland's invitation to join us. She manoeuvred herself next to Matt, and before I knew what was happening she'd secured a table and organised everyone into seats, with Matt firmly by her side.

What about me? I wanted to ask, but with Amanda's radar already working overtime I couldn't risk a scene. So I found myself at the other end of the table, sandwiched between Hank and the wall. Happy days.

Across from me, Roland and Amanda were in deep discussion.

"Did you know that, Becky?" Amanda asked.

"What?"

"It's six years today since that awful Nigerian plane crash. Sosoliso Airlines. Flight 1145. Seems like yesterday," she added dreamily.

More freaking plane stats. Just kill me now.

"Struck by lightning," she expanded.

"Lightning?" Roland repeated. "Aren't planes meant to be safe from lightning? Like a—what's it called?"

"Faraday cage."

"Yeah, that's it. The lightning hits the outside of the plane and everything on the inside is safe."

"Not this time," she gloated.

And if I had to listen to any more of this I'd be swimming home from Ireland.

Which left Hank.

"What workshops did you go to today?" I asked. Which got us through the entrée.

Over the main he asked how I was finding T&T.

"Busy," I said. "But I'm really enjoying it. Everyone's been so supportive."

"Well, just you let me know if there's anything I can do to help." He winked, and it gave me the creeps the way it always did. "I'm glad you came to Conference. We can get to know each other better."

I opted for a small smile, repressing my shudder. Which soon proved to be a mistake. By dessert his thigh was firmly wedged against mine and, short of burrowing a tunnel through the wall and escaping into the chilly Dublin night, there wasn't much I could do to un-wedge it.

Over coffee he rested a proprietary hand on my thigh and squeezed. I decided enough was enough.

"Take a hint," I suggested pleasantly, removing his sweaty mitt.

He didn't. He grabbed my hand and leaned in close. "Bad girl." He licked his lips. "I bet you'd like a spanking, wouldn't you?"

What? I must've heard wrong.

He gave my hand a playful smack.

O-kay. I hadn't heard wrong. I whipped my hand away, looking to Amanda and Roland for support. But they were so engrossed in their plane crash body-counts they didn't notice my bondage-and-discipline predicament.

With a forced smile and a murmured, "Punish yourself, asshole", I pushed my chair back from the table and bolted.

I skirted the tables and made my way to the opposite side of the dining hall, feeling dirtied and, somehow, invaded. My hands shook uncontrollably. I squashed them under my arms and turned towards the French doors. Yes. Fresh air, that's what I needed. I headed outside.

Potted plants transformed the balcony into a leafy sanctuary. If only this were the Mediterranean. I could do with balmy. Instead I had bracing—sub-Arctic, even—and out here on the balcony my top, sleeveless with a plunging cowl neckline, was nothing short of ridiculous. Five minutes and I'd be a prime candidate for hypothermia. Still, that was preferable to another five minutes with Hank.

I shivered, hugging myself warm as I looked down on the hotel grounds. Uplights strategically highlighted a pond here, a gnarled old tree there. A *petanque* pitch! I must have a game before the week was out.

And then he was there, standing close behind me. His arms snaked around my waist and he nuzzled my ear. I recognised the aftershave instantly. Stiffened, recoiled.

"Mmm," he said in a throaty undertone. "Finally."

"No!" I tried to prise his arms away. "Hank, let go."

His body pressed in on me from every direction. I felt nauseous.

"*Grrrrr.*" He purred in my ear, thrusting his erection against me as he slid his hands up my ribcage. "You know you want it." And he pinched my nipples smartly.

I yelped. Startled, he relaxed his hold sufficiently for me to turn. I shoved him off me. "Stop that."

His eyebrows spiked in surprise, and then he grinned.

"Feisty." He closed in again. "Playing hard to get, eh?"

I watched the individual droplets of sweat gather on his upper lip. Maybe I should just vomit my meal all over him.

"Fuck off, Hank."

He yanked me into his arms and kissed me, smearing those hideous beads of sweat all over my lips. I gagged. How dare he? I brought my knee into his groin. Hard.

Hank stilled, mid-kiss, then doubled over, clutching at his groin. "You stupid bitch."

My rage receded and I stepped aside, wiping my mouth. "Keep your filthy mitts off me. Creep."

I wheeled away—and there was Matt, at the balcony entrance. He looked thunderous.

"What the *fuck* is going on?" he ground out.

I shrank from his gaze, groped behind me for the solid security of the balustrade. "I—"

But Matt wasn't talking to me. Hank eased himself upright, pain etched on his face, as Matt closed the distance between them.

Matt drew himself up to his full height and towered over Hank. "You slimy piece of shit."

He grabbed Hank by the scruff of his neck, almost hauling him off his feet, and thrust his face close. "Touch her again and I'll fucking kill you."

He released Hank abruptly. "If she doesn't kill you first."

A giggle bubbled up in my throat.

Hank shrugged his shirt back into place. "What's it to you?"

"Plenty." Matt stabbed a finger at Hank's chest, staring the shorter man down.

"Becs," he said, his eyes still trained on Hank, "come here."

His voice brooked no argument. I went.

Hank straightened his toupee. "She's a prick-tease. She wanted it."

Behind Matt, I drew an unsteady breath, shaking as my adrenalin rush subsided. "Like hell I did."

"Go on." Matt gave Hank a shove. "Get the fuck inside or I'll finish the job she started."

"Oh yeah?"

"Yeah."

They squared off against each other, eyeball to eyeball, fists clenched, anger rolling off them in clouds.

Finally, Hank glanced at me. "She's not worth it," he muttered, then sloped off inside as instructed.

I sagged against Matt's back.

"I'll have his balls for this," Matt muttered.

Then he turned around, grabbed my shoulders, looked in my eyes, and gave me a little shake. "Christ, Becs."

Judging by his expression, I was lucky not to hear my bones rattle.

"What? It's not like I encouraged him."

"I know."

He exhaled, rubbed at his neck, then gave me a rueful grin. "Remind me not to get on the wrong side of you."

"Only special people get that treatment." I held out a trembling hand for inspection. "There's only so much excitement a girl can take in one day."

He looked me over with concern. "Are you okay?"

I nodded, but my chin trembled.

He drew me close, his body searingly hot against my chilled one. I felt safe.

We stayed like that until my shakes had subsided. Then he ruffled my hair and released me. "You do get yourself into some scrapes, don't you?"

"Hey, I was just minding my own business. What's your excuse?"

"I saw you come outside. Thought I should join you." He grinned. "I figured you'd avoided me for long enough."

I grimaced. "Sorry."

"When Hank followed you, I decided I'd better make it a threesome."

"Some threesome."

"Yeah." He relaxed against the balustrade. "I'm not into threesomes."

We smiled at each other.

"Me neither."

"Here." He shrugged out of his jacket. "Put this on. You're shivering." He wrapped it over my shoulders, stroked a finger down my cheek.

Instant heat seeped through my body. "Thanks." I huddled deeper into his jacket.

"You're welcome," he said, and the wind whipped at his shirt and tousled his hair and it all felt very movie-ish.

Then, as if he'd just remembered the temperature, he said, "Come on, let's go."

But when we stepped back through the French doors he steered me away from the tables.

I frowned. "Where are we—"

"Sssh." He touched a finger to my lips. "No arguments, please. I've got a plan."

"You have?" My pulse picked up as I imagined what his plan might be.

He stopped at the lifts, ushered me in and pushed the seventh-floor button. Then surprised me with, "It's cold out. We'll need coats."

When we reached our rooms he stepped close and removed his jacket from my shoulders. I looked up at him, waiting, anticipating.

He gently turned me away from him. "Coats," he repeated.

Disappointment wrestled with excitement. I unlocked my door, donned coat and scarf, then re-joined him in the hallway.

"Let's go." He slung his black overcoat over one shoulder.

"Where?"

"The real world. You need time out to forget what happened back there."

"Sounds perfect."

The lift took us back down to the lobby.

"And get away from your workmates for a bit, too."

"You excluded, of course."

"Of course." He grinned.

I laughed, heady with expectation—and probably a good dose of delayed shock, too.

CHAPTER TWENTY-FOUR

Dublin by night looked and felt exotic—or maybe it was just my mood.

Matt and I followed our noses through the narrow cobbled streets, jostling against each other as the crowd ebbed and flowed around us.

"I didn't expect it to be this busy," I said.

Matt nodded. "Pre-Christmas mania. Late-night shopping." Then, as we rounded a corner, he added, "Have you met Molly Malone?"

"Sorry?"

He indicated with his head and, following his gaze, I took in the bronze statue ahead. "Oh, she's beautiful."

We stopped for a moment to admire her.

"Prostitute or street hawker?" he asked as we continued on.

I stared at him. "The poor woman has a decent cleavage so she must be a prostitute? Is that it?"

"Hey!" He raised his hands in protest. "Unfair! It's just the local legend. Hawker by day, prostitute by night."

I shot him a disbelieving look.

He chuckled, then draped an arm across my shoulders. "I'm so misunderstood."

Every nerve-ending stood to attention. A fire started in my belly. Was I misunderstanding his arm? I didn't think so. Determined not to frighten it away with any sudden moves, I matched my step to his, leaning into his arm.

Warmth spread through me, and with it, wonder.

How had this happened? Here I was, out for a night stroll with the most delicious man on the planet, and he seemed to want nothing more than to be here with me.

I snuck a glance up at Matt. He looked down at me and smiled, one of those smiles that says far more than words can ever express, and my soul sang. I felt like a princess. A princess who, in spite of all her best efforts, still fancied this knight something rotten. And he fancied me.

Which was either fantastic or a full-blown calamity, I wasn't sure which.

"How about we go somewhere warm and thaw out?" I suggested. Somewhere public. Somewhere I wouldn't be so tempted to rip off his clothes.

We turned back towards Temple Bar, Dublin's bustling party district. Half of Dublin seemed to be here with us, sharing the festive cheer. Christmas screamed at us from every angle. Christmas colours, Christmas lights, Christmas scenes. My heart felt full. Christmas was such a special, special time.

Would I be spending it with Matt?

I hoped so.

"Thanks for this," I said with a smile.

His arm briefly tightened around my shoulders. "I needed to get out, too. Pub or café?"

"Café," I said quickly.

His lips twitched. "You're sure?"

I thought of Jim. "Very. Mrs Boring tonight, that's me."

"You're anything but that, Becs," he said, and something in his tone had me thinking of the ship's-bow scene in *Titanic*.

We picked a café at random and Matt ordered coffees while I found us a window table. For a while we sat in companionable, but oh-so-aware, silence. We drank our coffees, watching the world go by and surreptitiously watching each other.

Across the street, a busker serenaded passers-by with his Nirvana-esque *Silent Night*. I watched the coins drop in his hat. "He's making a good living."

"No thanks to his vocal talents."

"He's not that bad," I protested.

Matt's eyebrow shot up.

"Okay, you're right, he's bad. But it's Christmas. And it's cold. He deserves a break."

"A bleeding heart. I might've known." He shook his head, then leapt to his feet, produced a fiver from his pocket, and strode outside to deposit it in the busker's hat. The busker responded with an earsplitting

Matt returned, grimacing. "Bad idea. What a racket. I blame you."

I grinned, glowing with warmth and Christmas spirit and general happiness. Outside, people strode by, hands in pockets, collars drawn up against the evening chill.

"If you won a million pounds tonight," I said, "what would you do with it?"

"Ah. The humanitarian-materialist test." He paused. Looked down into his coffee, took a contemplative sip. "I'll tell you if you tell me."

"You first."

"Well, I've always thought when I got rich and famous—"

"What?" I feigned surprise. "You mean you're not already?"

"On a lecturing salary?" He grinned. "Hardly. Anyway, when I'm rich and famous I'll set up an organisation—"

"Materialist! I knew it."

"Stop interrupting me, woman! A *non-profit* organisation," he emphasised, "offering—"

He stopped, then pointed his spoon my way. "And you're not allowed to laugh."

What was coming? "Okay."

"Adventure-based courses for physically disabled kids."

My heart melted. "Oh, that's a wonderful idea."

"It's really just an expansion of what the Kinetix Centre already does. But we'd cater for specific needs, and we'd offer live-in options, too."

A lump rose in my throat. I shook my head. "Wow. Humanitarian. Definitely humanitarian."

He shrugged. "Yeah, well, I need the million pounds first, so don't get too excited. The accommodation would be hellish expensive to set up, and as for the health and safety regulations . . ."

His eyes met mine. "Hey, don't get all teary on me. It's just an idea."

I blinked to clear my vision. "An amazing, generous, kind-hearted idea. Is Stef your inspiration?"

Matt stared into the dregs of his coffee.

I waited, but he said nothing. Damn, I'd upset him. Me and my big mouth.

He leaned back in his chair, placed both palms flat on the table. Studied his hands, then finally met my gaze. "Yes. He wouldn't thank me for it, but I'd dedicate it to him."

Relieved I hadn't offended him, and touched at what he'd just shared, I reached out and clasped his hand. "I think it's an amazing tribute to an amazing person."

Matt squeezed my hand, nodded, stared out the window. The streetlamps and Christmas lights cast a golden glow over the cobbled stones, lending a magical air to the street. If I wished really hard, would we be able to stay like this forever?

He turned back to me, his thumb exploring the palm of my hand. My breath shortened. My neckline warmed. Did he have any idea the havoc that thumb was wreaking on my senses?

For a moment neither of us spoke.

"Go on," said Matt, "what would you do with your million?"

"You're so organised that I'm embarrassed to say, now." I laughed, making light of it. "I was just going to put my gear in storage and go to Africa for a year or two. Vaccinate a village or something. I hadn't really thought past the plane flight. You're amazing. You've got it all worked out."

"Tell you what, let's win a million each. You write my health and safety policy and I'll work out your vaccination schedule."

We ordered second cups of coffee. Kept talking.

"So there's you and Stef," I said. "Any other siblings?"

"No. Stef's needs were . . . hard work."

I bit my lip. Hard work didn't even begin to describe what his family—what Matt—had had to deal with. I felt like such a heel. There I'd been, all these years, getting upset and agitated over my sister's dramatics and my parents' blinkeredness. It was just so *trivial*.

"My mother didn't like hard work," Matt added.

"How did she cope?"

"The way she always did."

I waited, but he didn't elaborate and something in his eyes told me not to go there.

"And your dad?" I asked.

His expression softened. "Dad was an amazing man."

"Was?"

"He died when I was twenty-one."

I covered his hand with mine. "I'm so sorry."

186

"It was a long time ago," he said, but his lopsided smile didn't mask the sadness.

"How old was Stef?"

Matt stared out the window. "Only fourteen."

I frowned. That poor wee boy. How had he managed? And how had their mother found the strength to put her grief aside and give Stef the care he needed?

"That must've been so hard for you all. Your mum, especially, with the increased responsibility."

His laugh was harsh. "My mother wouldn't know responsibility if it came fully packaged with instructions."

I took in his words, his tone, his emotion. Wondered just what had happened. "So . . ."

"So life goes on. And when things get tough you remember that someone else always has it tougher."

He said it like a hardened old man, but beneath the words I glimpsed a tearful little boy. My heart ached.

"Dad always said Stef was the bravest person he'd ever met. But I think Stef got that trait from Dad."

Matt lapsed into silence, obviously thinking about his father. I didn't interrupt.

"Dad was a builder, and he loved his work, but he gave it all up to care for Stef."

"He sounds wonderful," I said.

"He was. You'd have liked him."

"I'm sure I would've, if he's anything like his son."

Our eyes locked in an emotional, electric connection that sizzled all the way down to my toes. Surely, steadily, this man was drawing me in, and I was no longer sure I wanted to fight it.

* * *

Matt asked about my family, and I spoke candidly of my childhood, mostly happy yet always tinged with my own senseless feelings of inadequacy. He remembered what I'd said about Dani that day in the lift, and we discussed it more fully.

"You've missed your calling," I teased. "You should've been a therapist."

"And hang out on couches listening to people whine all day? No thanks. Exercise. Breathe. Works every time."

It took me far, far longer than it should have to work out what was going on. Sure, the underlying beat between us was still raw and sexual, but it went deeper than that. We were talking. Really talking. I'd shared things with Matt that I just did not discuss. Ever. And I doubted the things he'd told me this evening were his standard topics of conversation.

This level of connection was not something I'd experienced before, but I liked it. I liked the strange mix of exhilaration and peace that went with it. It felt . . . precious. *Right*.

My breath caught in my throat. My heart thumped hard and fast against my ribs. Shit. I set down my coffee and the china rattled as my hands turned into trembling clumsy paws.

When? Why? How? I'd done everything I could to make sure this *didn't* happen.

Time stood still, waiting for me to catch up. And Matt sat across the table from me, completely oblivious, laughing as he told me about his first snake encounter, backpacking in Australia.

Too stunned to speak, I nodded in all the right places and let him talk. I hadn't felt like this since . . . Well. I hadn't felt like this. Not with Mickey, not with that double-barrelled rich boy I'd wasted six months on, not even with that lecturer back in College.

This was a first. As significant a first as my naïve fumblings with Billie what's-his-name back in the Lower Sixth. No. *More* significant, because this felt like fate. No matter what I'd done to try and prevent it, it would've happened anyway.

"Go on, then." He interrupted my thoughts. "The first time you had sex, where'd you do it?"

I gaped at him. How did he read my mind like that? "I—what?"

"Well, you were off in a dream. I had to get your attention somehow."

I laughed shakily. "Ha! It worked." I struggled to pull myself together. "Um . . . a layby on the M25. Back seat of a VW beetle."

This was a catastrophe. Now I really would have to resign.

He chuckled. "Cramped."

How could I have been so *stupid?* "Hmm? Yes, rather."

I remembered the tangled mess of limbs and underwear, all notions of romance gone as Billie and I tried to work out how to achieve penetration—let alone orgasm—in the close confines of his mother's car. Losing my virginity had been nothing like I'd expected.

Ditto my job-of-a-lifetime.

"I still like beetles." I forced a smile. "You?"

"Oh," he said easily, "I'm not fussed on VWs, myself."

"No deflections allowed. Come on, spill the beans. Where'd you first have sex?"

"Weymouth beach. Summer holiday with the family. Sand in every orifice."

I laughed. "The things we do for sex, eh?" Then blushed, wishing the words unsaid. I quickly manoeuvred the conversation onto safer topics.

Eventually we left the café's cosy warmth and ambled back towards the hotel. I dragged him in to a gaily-decorated women's store to choose a scarf for Dani.

"She helped me choose my Casino Night outfit," I said.

"Mmm. I can't wait to see it." His voice as he said it, all husky male baritone, coupled with the glint in his eye had me instantly weak-kneed.

I paid for the scarf and waited for it to be gift-wrapped, dry-mouthed and *über*-aware of him wherever he moved.

"She'll love it," he said as we left the shop.

"Don't you just adore Christmas?"

His smile was teasing. "Not as much as you."

We stopped in the middle of the Halfpenny Bridge and stood arm-in-arm, looking down on the Liffey river. In the utter stillness of the night air, the streetlamps and car lights reflected perfectly off the water.

"If you could be anywhere in the world right now," I murmured, "where would you be?"

He took his time answering.

"Here."

I tore my gaze away from the water and looked up at him. "Really? Of all the places you've been, this is it?"

"Mm-hmm. Beautiful night, beautiful place, beautiful girl. Dublin's my pick."

He met my eyes, and the heat in his smile lit me from the inside out.

189

"But I'd love to show you an Egyptian sunrise," he added. "That would come a close second."

"Sun*rise*, you say? I don't think so."

"It'll be worth it," he promised.

My heart pitter-pattered. Not *would* be worth it. *Will*. That didn't sound like a Mickey-length fling to me.

Then again, it was only one word. Not much point in over-analysing.

Whatever. I didn't care. This evening would be branded in my memory forever.

Returning to the hotel sometime before midnight, it was the most natural thing in the world for my hand to be in his. And for us to kiss in the lift. And for us to linger over our goodnights in the corridor.

That's when we heard them. Voices, one masculine, one feminine, and both coming from Matt's room.

I put a restraining hand on his arm. "Has Roland got company?"

"I was wondering the same thing."

We waited a minute longer. Whatever they were discussing, it was intense. Then she giggled.

"I think you might be about to interrupt," I said.

Then I had a thought.

"Wait here a second," I said and quietly unlocked my door.

As I'd suspected, the room was unoccupied. And with the dining room closed for the night, it was fairly obvious where my room-mate must be. I beckoned Matt over.

"That's Amanda in there," I said and his eyebrows almost launched themselves off his brow. "Which means a bed is available . . . but"—I shot him a doe-eyed look—"it's in here."

He smiled at me, then, with his come-to-bed eyes. He gathered me close and backed me into the room. "Oh really?"

"I'm afraid so."

The door clicked shut behind us.

"What a disaster." His lips grazed mine.

"I know," I mourned, still backing up.

"How will you cope?" He expertly released my bra strap.

I gasped. "With difficulty."

"But I hope you'll put up with me somehow." His lips were insistent against my neck.

I slid my hands under his shirt and up the hard contours of his back. "I could just close my eyes and go to sleep as usual." Excitement coiled in my belly.

He picked me up and lowered us both onto the bed.

"Well, I'll do my best not to disturb you." His lips explored the neckline of my cowl top, lower . . .

My breath came ragged.

. . . Lower . . .

A pulse kicked in, low and slow.

. . . Mmm . . .

I closed my eyes. My fingers tangled in his hair. His tongue, lapping through the lace of my bra, made hot, wet contact with my nipple. Heat surged through me. I moaned. Guided him across to the other nipple.

"Christ, Becs."

His lips found their way back to mine, but his hand continued where his tongue had left off. He cupped my left breast, caressing the nub into hard arousal. Hot, aching need arrowed down to my core. I gasped. Arched my body up towards him. His erection ground against me, and he groaned against my lips. Lust surged between us. Our kiss grew urgent, our bodies moving as one.

My fingers roamed over his shirt, stroking, searching, dispensing with buttons.

Skin. I ran my flattened palms up and down his exposed chest, in love with his smooth, toned muscles, his sheer masculinity.

He withdrew his lips and looked down at me, his hands in my hair, his eyes on my mouth, his erection against my hip. "Sleepy yet?"

"Very." I pulled him close for another kiss.

He straddled me, lifting me slightly so he could shimmy my top up over my head. The bra followed. I lay beneath him, naked from the waist up.

He traced a finger down my cheek. "You're beautiful."

I felt beautiful, too. Like some divine creature who really was worthy of his adoration. Just as he was worthy of mine.

I reached out and hauled him down on me, needing to feel his skin against mine. Fingers, tongue, penis, lips . . . I felt wonderfully vulnerable. Dangerously vulnerable. Nothing, nobody, had ever made me feel so exposed, so safe.

Nobody came close.

Slick with sweat, desperate for release, my body tensed and pulsed.

"Now, Matt, now."

He smiled. "Not yet."

With deliberate leisure he raised himself on his hands, teasing me with just a flicker of him inside me. "And if you tell me you've got claustrophobia now, honey, there will be big trouble."

A silent scream rose in me. "If you don't hurry up, *honey*, there will be even bigger trouble."

He grinned, unperturbed, then gradually lowered himself down on me, his penis driving slowly—ever so slowly—home until I felt full to bursting, shuddering with exquisite need. He paused to kiss me, so softly, so tenderly, it brought me to the brink of tears. Fear and joy swirled in my mind. Fear that I wouldn't survive this emotional journey, joy that I was taking it with him.

Then his lips left mine and, millimetre by agonising millimetre, he raised himself off me again until he barely penetrated.

I sobbed. Dragged my fingernails down his back, trying to drag him closer.

Again, with sensational control, he slid deeper and deeper within me until we were one. Another pause, another kiss, another quiver as he withdrew.

An orgasm of gigantic proportions swelled within me. I cried out, clawing at his shoulders, holding on for dear life.

"With you, babe." He drove powerfully down, on me, in me, through me, again and again, holding me close, sharing the journey, until we both reached a climax so eclipsing, so monumental it could never, *ever* be passed off as a casual encounter.

Nothing would ever be the same.

CHAPTER TWENTY-FIVE

I woke—and there he was. Right beside me. Sharing my bed.

In our bone-deep, post-coital contentment we'd fallen asleep in each other's arms. Which sounded far more romantic than the reality, because now I needed the toilet and I was trapped under Matt's right leg.

I eased my body out from under him and slid gracelessly to the floor, then tiptoed out to the bathroom. Afterwards, I sat naked on Amanda's bed and contemplated the dark hump across from me. Matt-in-my-bed. This was a dream, right? I leaned forward and prodded the hump. It groaned, moved, and revealed its face.

Matt. Unbelievable.

I glanced at the bedside clock—three-fifteen. If I didn't get a couple of hours' sleep I'd be a mess in the morning. I slipped under Amanda's bedspread and closed my eyes, but sleep evaded me. I kept seeing images of our lovemaking, first in fast-forward, then in slow motion, repeatedly rewinding through those minutes when he'd held me at the brink of ecstasy. Finally, frame-by-frame, I relived the entire evening, starting when he'd helped me get rid of Hank until I fell asleep in his arms.

It felt too good to be true—but there he was, sleeping in my bed, taking delicious to a whole new level. I rolled onto my side and watched him. Minutes ticked by. Peace blanketed me. Sleep didn't matter. I'd get by on love.

Matt rolled over and opened his eyes, glancing sleepily around. His smile as he found me spoke of such intimacy I almost couldn't believe he intended it for me.

He shuffled back a few inches and held the covers open. "Come back. I miss you."

Happiness welled. Suddenly emotional, I blinked back tears.

"Hey." He leaned up on one elbow. "Babe, what's wrong?"

I knelt on the floor in front of him. "Nothing," I whispered. "Absolutely nothing."

He traced my lips with a finger. "Good."

I kissed his finger. "Well . . . maybe one thing."

"Mm-hmm?" The finger trailed down my throat, past the hollow of my neck, and over my left breast. It stopped at my nipple.

I sighed, moving against his hand.

"A single bed," I said, eyes twinkling, "is way too small for us both to sleep in."

He raised one eyebrow. Reached out to lift me bodily on top of him. "Then we'd better not sleep."

* * *

We forced ourselves to turn up for breakfast, mostly to show people we hadn't been kidnapped at gunpoint. We nearly didn't make it, getting seriously waylaid in the shower, but eventually worked out we made faster progress if we kept a wall between us.

Matt went and sat with the others. I stopped at the buffet table to pour myself a juice, hoping it might look as if we'd arrived separately. After dawdling over the food as long as I dared I took my juice back to the table and sat down. Fortunately, Hank wasn't there.

"Morning," I said.

I waited for someone to ask what was wrong—on three hours' sleep I looked and felt ragged—but nobody mentioned it. Eventually I found the courage to glance Matt's way. His clothes looked a bit crumpled, and—oh, cringe! His clothes. He was still wearing yesterday's clothes. Would someone notice? I needed to warn him. Invent a reason for him to go and get changed.

He winked at me.

No, Matt. Concentrate. I widened my eyes in warning, staring pointedly at his shirt. He followed my gaze down then looked back up at me, all raised eyebrow and cheeky grin, clearly misinterpreting.

Typical male: sex on the brain. He didn't get it at all. His mind was still in bed. Didn't he care what anyone else thought?

"I'd better get some food," I said, and escaped over to the buffet cart while I settled my frayed nerves.

Fine. If he didn't care, I didn't care. I returned to my seat and kept my eyes on my plate.

Amanda's voice rang out. "You mean Erebus?"

I glanced down at her, looking so Little House On The Prairie as she chatted about other people's deaths, and it suddenly seemed impossible that she might have been shagging herself silly with Roland—or anyone—only hours earlier. No mussed hair, no heaving cleavage, no shining eyes or sidelong glances or any other tell-tale signs.

She may have been out last night, may even have been the woman we'd heard in Roland's room, but I'd bet Gran's ashes it had nothing to do with sex. At best it would've been a verbal orgy of plane-crash statistics.

Amanda wouldn't get romantically involved. Or indulge in happy-ever-after fantasies. Or sleep with a co-worker.

Amanda wasn't like that. At all.

Why couldn't I keep it simple, like her? Be more doomsday, less . . . Becky?

I needed caffeine. Fast.

As I reached the coffee dispenser Matt materialised behind me, so close I felt every inch of his body against me.

Dammit, how could I think sensibly when he kept touching me? It turned my brain to mush every time.

"I'll have mine with sugar, thanks," he said.

Who cared what anyone thought? I couldn't pretend with him. I giggled. "I bet you say that to all the girls."

"I don't do this to all the girls." He gently blew in my ear.

I moved my head a fraction. "Matt!"

He backed off a couple of millimetres, barely enough for me to turn around. I surreptitiously used my hip to push him back a bit further then turned and glinted at him meaningfully. Handed him his coffee.

"Thanks."

"You are such a chancer!"

He grinned and winked.

"This is *work*, Matt. And we're at *breakfast*. A little restraint, please."

"Sex for breakfast sounds perfect. It'll set me up for the day."

"What will?" Roland asked, pouring himself a coffee.

Matt raised his eyebrow at me and grinned. The question hung.

"He said a good breakfast sets him up for the day." I avoided Matt's gaze. "Me? I prefer a light breakfast and a decent lunch." Then, as if I hadn't said enough already, "I can't take too much at breakfast."

Matt's grin broadened.

"I like as much as I can get at both meals," said Roland.

"Well," said Matt, "if I had the choice . . ."

I rolled my eyes. "You men are all the same. Over-Indulgers Anonymous. See you later." I met Matt's eyes in an electric look. "I need to get organised."

He took the hint and joined me upstairs for a bit more over-indulging, then went back to his room for a change of clothes. I mooched about. What did it mean for the relationship if you slept with someone three times in one day?

Probably nothing more than you both had a high sex drive.

Rats! Look at the time! I pulled myself together, found pen and paper, and headed down to the first workshop. Matt had saved a seat for me.

"This session sounds good," he said as I sat down.

I raised a sceptical eyebrow. "Really? *Travel for the Over 60s*? I wouldn't have thought it would interest a fit, outdoorsy guy like you."

He looked at the facilitator, moved his thigh against mine. "I'm thinking ahead."

The workshop began. I sat there, *über*-aware of Matt's leg against mine. People laughed. What had the speaker said? I made an effort to concentrate. Matt's hand strayed to my thigh. Slowly, seductively, he stroked up, down, up, up. I tried not to notice.

His hand moved across to my inner thigh, hovered. My breath hitched. If he flexed his fingers just a fraction he'd be . . .

I gasped. Licked my lips. Felt liquid heat pooling beneath his touch. I closed my eyes as he continued to stroke, up, down, up, up. My breath came short and shallow. He splayed his fingers, and gently parted my legs. My eyes flew open, and I stared wide-eyed at Matt, the heat in my face nothing compared to the fire he'd lit below.

He steadily returned my gaze, his eyes lust-darkened, his knowing smile daring me to make a sound.

I bit my lip. We really should stop, before—

His fingers slipped inside my panties and my thoughts scrambled.

The room disappeared. It was just me and Matt and his fingers and my . . .

Hell, why was I even here? I wasn't learning a damn thing from this workshop—except that, where Matt was concerned, one touch and I was wrecked.

"What workshop are you going to now?" Matt asked as we finished morning tea.

"I'm not telling. Find your own workshop."

"Grumpy girl." He grinned. "Didn't you get enough sleep last night?"

I threw him a mock-glare. "No more stalking. Go to the workshop you signed up for. I'm here to work."

As the second workshop started, Matt slipped into the seat beside me.

"Sorry I'm late," he whispered.

* * *

We had a couple of free hours before dinner, which was perfect. I desperately needed a nap if I had any hope of lasting the evening.

"I'll just lie there with you," said Matt.

"No way. You won't just lie there and we both know it."

He grinned.

"I'm going for a nap. Alone. Then I'm getting ready. A—"

"Alone. I get it."

I smiled. "I'll see you downstairs at dinner."

"You're blowing me off, aren't you?"

"Yes." I pulled him into an alcove, kissed his nose, and left.

Casino Night. Black-tie event and *the* highlight of Conference Week. I couldn't wait. As we arrived for dinner we would collect our chips, and whoever banked the most at the end of the night would win a holiday package for two. A week in Santorini, no less.

Imagine! If I won I could take Matt for a romantic getaway. I fell asleep, dreaming of sand and sex and glorious sunsets. Two hours later I woke with Matt still on my mind.

I took a long, leisurely shower, letting the water run over my face and down my body. This evening would be amazing, I could feel it in my bones. Slowly, luxuriously, I soaped myself, thinking about Matt. I towelled myself off, thinking about Matt's body on top of mine, then stood naked in front of the mirror, assessing my legs, hips, breasts. I lifted my hair, studying the line of my neck. Traced a hand down my body's curves, feeling sensual and erotic. Marvelled that Matt saw anything desirable in me. Revelled in the knowledge that he did.

With a heightened state of consciousness I opened the wardrobe and pulled my knock-'em-dead cocktail dress off its hanger. I carefully placed it on the bed. Looked at it and felt a bolt of excitement. This evening I wanted to stop Matt in his tracks, bowl him over, make him see me in a whole new light.

I took my time getting ready—so much time, in fact, that Amanda came in, showered, changed and left again before I even finished my make-up. The gods must have been on my side, though, because for once my hair did precisely what I asked of it and stayed up in a loose clasp with only a few tendrils escaping around my face. Bathrobe off, little black dress on. A quick look in the mirror—no, the underwear had to go. There, better.

I took the *Miu Mius* out of their box, lovingly stroked them, then slipped them on my feet. Back to the mirror so I could admire the length they added to my legs. A pair of black drop earrings and Sue-Ann's clutch purse were my only extras.

I went downstairs to dinner, collecting my chips at the entrance. Wow. Our bland conference room had been transformed into a glitzy casino hall. Over in our usual spot I spotted Alyssa, stunning in royal blue as she chatted to Matt.

I refused to feel jealous. I didn't need to feel jealous.

Alyssa smiled as I approached, her fingers tinkling in a hello as her eyes flicked over me in rapid appraisal, like an athlete assessing the competition. I squared my shoulders and gave her a knowing smile—I looked good and she'd noticed—then allowed my gaze to move on to Matt.

My breath caught. A heat wave whipped through me. *Damn*, he looked good in a suit. I'd never seen him in one before but, oh my giddy Aunt Annie, I could get used to it.

For a few seconds he didn't notice my approach, but it was worth it when he did. He did a double-take, stopping mid-sentence to watch me, his gaze intent, his lips pursing in a silent whistle of appreciation. With a murmured something to Alyssa he walked my way, his eyes locked on me. Judging by his expression, my dress had been a great investment. And as for his suit . . .

Within inches of each other we stopped.

Could he hear my heart pounding?

I licked my lips. "Nice suit."

His back shielded us from the T&T group as he pulled me close, a proprietary hand on my waist.

"You. Look. Stunning." His voice, that deep rich baritone I remembered from the pool, seduced me all over again.

"Thanks." I smiled up at him from under my lashes.

"Let's go upstairs."

"Later."

His fingers found mine. "Promise?"

"Absolutely. Trust me, I'm there."

He kissed my fingers, making no attempt at discretion.

"Let's be social for now," I said. Released his hand and walked towards our table, feeling his eyes on me as he followed.

People were taking their seats for the meal, now, and we did likewise, sitting side-by-side so we could touch under the table.

As soon as dessert was over, waiters moved the tables aside in preparation for the games. Casino Night was about to begin. The room buzzed with excitement.

I excused myself and made my way to the Ladies'.

As I reached the restroom Alyssa materialised at my side. "You look fantastic," she said. "You *must* tell me where you bought that dress."

I turned to the mirror. "Oh, some boutique," I said vaguely. "Covent Garden, I think."

"I love Covent Garden." She stood beside me and whipped out her lipstick. "Such reasonable prices, aren't they?"

Hardly.

Two deft strokes over her lips, then she smiled at herself to check the effect. "Matt's such a honey, isn't he?"

Ah. Her real objective. "Yes. He is."

"And *such* good company."

I smiled, fussing with my hair. "Mmm. Especially last night."

Stock still, I stared at myself, horrified. Stupid woman. Shut up!

"Last night?" Her eyebrows shot up. "But he left early. With . . . *you?*" She frowned, pulling her head back, turkey-style, as she studied my face.

My cheeks flamed. "Oh, he, ah . . . took me out for a drink."

"He did?" Her eyes were saucers. "Are you two—"

"He helped me fend off Hank," I interrupted. "Things got a bit out of hand."

"Oh." Alyssa relaxed. "Are you all right?"

"Yes. But I'm glad Matt was there." And in my room . . . And in my bed . . .

"That's so Matt," she said, as if she'd known him forever. "What a *darling*. He's such a gentleman." She headed for the door, interrogation over. "I'll see you at the tables."

I took my time, double-checking my hair and reapplying lipstick before heading back. It was as I walked through the foyer that I noticed him. The casual confidence, the elegant cut of the suit, the shaggy roman crop of hair; all unmistakeably Charlie.

What the hell was he doing here?

"Becky," he called, raising a floppy arm in my direction. The arm floated floorwards, seemingly of its own accord. He lurched towards me.

Cripes. He'd had a skinful.

I stopped, torn. Should I ignore him and speed-walk the hell out of here? Or deal with him now and try to minimise the fall-out?

He let out a low wolf-whistle.

"Buxom Becky!" he roared.

Heads turned, first his way and then mine.

Buxom? Me? My face grew hot. That'd teach me for wearing a push-up bra. And now he'd made me the focus of the whole foyer I no longer had a 'run away' option, dammit.

Suddenly his knees buckled beneath him. By some miracle he managed to stay upright and continue across the foyer towards me. Brilliant. He'd definitely had a skinful. It might've been funny if he'd been someone else's problem.

I took a deep breath and faced the music. "Charlie. What brings you here?"

He stopped in front of me, very rumpled-rich-boy and smelling like he'd bought the whole damn brewery.

"You."

He wrapped his arms around my waist and planted a smacking great kiss on my lips. "Fuck, you're hot."

Not quite up to his usual romantic standards. I stifled a nervous giggle. "Er . . . thanks."

He honed in on my lips again. I quickly pulled my head back, not wanting a second whiskey-laden encounter. He miscalculated and stumbled against me.

My arms automatically came around him. "Oops. All right?"

"Mm-*hmm*." His hands found bare skin and roved over my back.

I braced my own hands against his chest, trying to put an inch or two between us.

"Actually, this is a work function so I should probably head back in." I softened the words with a micro-smile.

"Forget work." One of his hands headed south. "Fancy a shag?"

I ignored his wayward hand, focusing instead on his words. "Um, not just now. Tell you what, I'll give you a call. Leave your number at reception for me." I gently but firmly pushed at his chest.

He leaned into my hands. "Aw, come on, Becky. Leas' gimme a kiss."

Fine. Whatever. Anything if he'd just leave. "One kiss. Then I have to go."

I leaned in and gave him a peck on the lips. His arms came around me in a vice-like grip and he met my peck with a hungry, open-mouthed invasion. *Bleughkk!* I tried to extricate myself but he was like an oversized octopus, all tentacles and suction.

If only I'd had a couple more minutes to haul him off me. If only I'd ignored Charlie from the outset and run the other way. If only, if only, if only . . .

But suddenly it was too late for any of that.

Dark eyes locked on mine. His hands balled into fists at his sides, his body rigid with potent anger. My stomach did a ten-storeys-a-second plunge.

Matt.

CHAPTER TWENTY-SIX

For infinitely long seconds Matt stood stock-still. His eyes bored into mine.

I stiffened in Charlie's arms and quietly peeled him off me. He reached for me again, slurring sweet somethings in my ear, but I paid scant attention. I felt ill. Unable to move, unable to speak, unable to do a single thing to remove the sting of stony stricture from Matt's gaze.

It was as if I'd been struck with paralysis. I felt, heard, saw nothing.

Nothing but Matt. The only man I'd ever truly loved.

And I guess that's the way the gods work. Give a girl a good hair day, take away her man.

Slowly, with great deliberation, he walked towards us, his eyes giving me not even a blink's-worth of freedom. Crap, shit, *fuck*.

The sheer intensity of his gaze overwhelmed me. I began to feel light-headed. Dread, an icy cube of numbness, settled in my chest. The foyer shimmered out of focus. Matt dominated my vision, every angry inch of him highlighted in razor-sharp detail. Razor-sharp detail that shrank into the distance until I was seeing him through a long, glaucomic tunnel. His approach decelerated into slow motion. Roaring static filled my ears.

In the background Charlie launched into song. *"You loss that lovin' feelin', whoa, that lovin' feelin' . . ."*

I pushed Charlie, hard, extracting myself from his embrace. The tunnel disappeared, the static cleared, and suddenly everything was happening way too fast.

Matt hauled Charlie around by his shoulder. "What the fuck do you think you're doing?" The fury in his voice was a caged beast.

"Whoa!" Charlie staggered, righted himself, then looked at Matt, perplexed. "Jus' havin' a bit of—"

"Get your hands off her."

"These?" Charlie inspected his hands closely, palm-up then palm-down. "Woss the plob-rem?"

"Matt." I stepped forward and laid a hand on his arm. "It's okay. He—"

"It's okay?" He rounded on me. "It's *okay*? Since when is it okay for him to maul you? Make a public display of you? Treat you like a cheap whore? He has no right!" He swung back to Charlie, shoved him in the chest. "No fucking right!"

Charlie didn't answer. He had enough to contend with, just staying on his feet.

In my peripheral vision I noticed a growing gaggle of onlookers. Wonderful.

"Matt, th-this is Charlie. An old friend of mine," I added, as if that might make a difference. "Charlie, Matt."

Charlie wiped his right hand down his shirt then held it out. "Matt." He gave a sombre nod, tripped, steadied himself.

Matt looked at the proffered hand as if it repulsed him. Charlie's hand jerked closer. Matt, after a considerable pause, clasped it in a hand-shake so forceful that Charlie, trapped on the end of it, staggered again.

I took a shaky breath. A handshake. That was good . . . right?

"So." Matt's expression was unreadable. "You two are friends?"

Charlie's arm snaked out and, before I could step out of reach, he pulled me to his side. Splayed his hand possessively over my hip. "Yeah." He grinned. "*Frens.*"

"We went to school together," I hastily inserted, bringing my hand over his and prising it, limpet-like, from me.

Matt's eyes flashed as he watched. He said nothing.

Charlie gave Matt an exaggerated wink. "Frens. Ha ha. Yeah. Used t'go behind th' bike sheds." He swayed on his feet. "But—"

"Charlie," I protested, with a gentle arm-slap, "stop it."

". . . these days," he continued as if I hadn't spoken, "we gedda room. More ci-li-vised."

Oh shut *up*. I should just rip out his tongue and be done with it. "Charlie, I don't think—"

"An' jus' 'tween you'n'me"—he leaned close to Matt, all whiskey breath and confidences—"she's a bloody good shag."

I gasped, felt the blood drain from my face.

Matt's expression froze. A split-second later his fist connected with Charlie's jaw. I felt like I'd been transported to a movie set, but the crunch sounded far too real.

Charlie's head snapped back. Blood appeared at the corner of his mouth and dribbled down his chin. It blotted, ink-like, on his white designer shirt. His feet tap-danced this way and that, arms wind-milling in comic rhythm.

Our audience, with audible delight, moved closer.

Matt pulled his right arm back, fist clenched, muscles bunched, murderous rage all over his face.

I watched with a disturbing mix of pleasure and horror—pleasure that he'd leapt to my defence, horror that he was going about it with such savagery.

Should I stop him? *Could* I stop him? I clutched at my throat, undecided, knowing the next punch would knock Charlie out cold.

And then, as abruptly as the beast had rampaged out of its cage, it was muzzled and back behind bars. Matt's arm dropped to his side. He controlled his fury, steadied his breathing. Flexed his hand once, twice. Took a calculated step back.

He kept his eyes trained on Charlie. His lip curled. "You're not worth it."

Then, turning to me, his voice laden with loathing, "Neither are you."

I flinched as if I'd been struck.

Charlie wiped his mouth on the shoulder of his shirt, leaving a wide smear of red. He staggered a step or two towards Matt. "Fine yer own girlfren'. This one's taken."

Matt looked me up and down, his eyes lifeless. "You're welcome to her," he said, each word a glittery shard of heartbreak.

I reached for him. "Matt—"

"Don't bother." He turned away. "I've met your type before."

My type? After all we'd shared I was just a type? A gulping sob escaped my throat.

"Becky." Charlie started towards me.

No. Not now. Whatever he wanted to say, I didn't want to hear it. I pushed my way through the crowd and raced to the lifts. Punched the 'up' button once, twice, three times. No response. *Come on.* Desperate, I watched the floor indicators. One lift was ambling up past the tenth floor and the other refused to budge off fifth. I gave the button another jab.

A quick glance confirmed Charlie, miraculously upright, was now only ten feet away and closing in fast.

I ran.

"Becky, wait!"

I flung open the stairwell door. "No!" It came out as a strangled cry.

"'S'all right." His voice carried across to me. "He din' hurt me."

Like I cared.

"You just don't get it, do you?" I screamed, and took to the stairs like a marathon runner.

"Wotcha mean?" He reached the base of the stairwell and looked up at me, lolling off the railing. "Y'want me to tell 'im t'f—"

"No!" I flung down at him, sobbing openly now. "You've said plenty. Just leave me alone."

I soon discovered it was quite a challenge to cry, run up stairs, and breathe. By the time I emerged at the seventh floor my lungs were on fire and my legs were buckling with exhaustion. I staggered to my room, fumbled for the key, and fell inside. Leaned against the door until it clicked closed. Slumped there, defeated, trying to rein in my breathing. My heart, out of control, hammered against my ribcage. My head was a jumbled mess of thoughts and feelings. My throat felt swollen and constricted.

Matt.

A high-pitched wail filled the room and I clamped a quick hand over my mouth. The last thing I needed was security showing up.

The lift pinged and a voice—no, two—drew nearer. I pressed my hand more tightly to my mouth, breathing erratically as I stifled my sobs. Gentle murmurs, a masculine chuckle . . . closer . . .

Please keep moving, just keep moving. The sobs built up, dam-like, in my throat.

More laughter, gradually fading as they headed down the corridor.

I sank to the carpet and stared into the darkness of the room. What now?

Minutes passed. Long minutes of nothingness.

Matt. Why?

My tears fell, and the red dots of the bedside clock flashed in my peripheral vision, blink, blink. Precisely separating the hours from the minutes. Blink, blink.

How could he? I'd let him into my *soul*. I loved him. And he damn-well knew it. Just like he knew there was nothing between Charlie and me.

I sat up straighter. Wiped my eyes. Forced my tears back and watched the dots sharpen into focus. Blink, blink.

I should find Matt. Explain. Set the story straight.

And say what? That Charlie meant nothing to me? That I'd only slept with him the once? That I'd wished it were Matt? It sounded trite. Too trite. I flinched as I remembered Matt's granite-hard eyes, his contempt.

I stared at the dots until they turned fuzzy. He was right. I didn't deserve his love.

I dragged off my *Miu Mius*, stood and felt my way over to the curtained windows. Stubbed a toe on a bed-end, checked momentarily, continued. Pain was good. My brain understood pain. I pulled back a curtain and looked out over the grounds, so well-lit it could've been a carnival. A joyful sodding carnival.

What had I expected? That Matt would accept Charlie with good grace? Hardly. Action and reaction, Becs.

The garden lights winked up at me. I pressed my forehead against the window, barely breathing, barely existing. People came and went, some in twos, some in threes. Pantomiming good times. Laughing, happy, smiles all round.

Numbness descended. Time passed. I pushed harder against the window. How much pressure could it withstand before it shattered? I stared down at the ground, tried to gauge the distance. Fifty metres? One hundred?

Enough. With a brisk, back-to-my-senses face-rub I pushed away from the window and closed the curtain. Fumbled for the light switch then, head bowed against the glare, went to the bathroom in search of tissues.

I caught sight of myself in the mirror. So much for looking my best. Clown-like mascara tracks, puffy red-rimmed eyes, smeared lipstick, messed-up hair. How many times would I have to look like this before I accepted the truth? Happy-ever-afters only existed in fairy tales. Reality involved heartache, loneliness and Charlie-ish screw-ups. Big, unpredictable screw-ups that tended to ruin your life.

And now I'd lost Matt. Beautiful, perfect Matt.

I blew my nose, then grabbed another tissue and scrubbed angrily at my mess of a face.

Dammit, this wasn't working. I scowled at my reflection. How could I remove make-up armed with only a tissue and self-hatred? Where were my god-damn cleansing wipes? Fuck it. It was all too hard. I tossed the tissue at the bin and slapped the light switch off. Unclasped my *stupid* dress and stepped out of it, leaving it where it fell.

I crawled into bed and lay there, staring into darkness.

What next?

Matt would be downstairs, whooping it up with Alyssa and congratulating himself on a narrow escape. Charlie would be passed out on a couch somewhere, sleeping it off. And I was up here. Faced with a whole pile of fall-out. Too many people had witnessed our little show-stopper. I'd be the talk of T&T, if not the conference.

My stomach churned. Would I ever live it down? And if, somehow, I did—would I ever be able to face Matt again? Panicky tension rippled through me as I relived his derision, his frosty *'You're welcome to her'*. He didn't want me. In his eyes I was tarnished beyond redemption.

I jammed a fist against my mouth. I couldn't bear to have him look at me with such cold contempt. But, equally, I couldn't bear to lose him.

Too late. I already had. His love for me was gone, dissolved, forgotten the moment he saw Charlie.

I curled up in a tiny ball and cried myself to sleep. I dozed fitfully, feeling like I wasn't sleeping at all. But I must have managed a few minutes, because I woke to the sound of Amanda singing, "Wakey, wakey!" as she prodded my shoulder.

"Go away." I pulled my pillow over my head.

"You'll miss breakfast if you don't hurry up." She tried to lift the pillow.

I held on for grim death. "I'm not hungry."

"You will be," she chirped. "Come on, I'll wait for you."

"Fuck. Off."

Silence.

I felt guilty, but not guilty enough to remove the pillow. "Go down to breakfast, Amanda. I'll get up soon."

"Fine." The door clicked shut behind her.

I leapt out of bed and raced around, feverishly doing what needed to be done while she was at breakfast.

Because, as far as I was concerned, breakfast wasn't on my agenda. In fact, Day Four wasn't on my agenda. Conference Week, far from being the year's social high, had grown horns and evolved into the worst week of my life.

CHAPTER TWENTY-SEVEN

I needed to leave—now, before someone saw me. I grabbed my suitcase, ran for the lift, jiggled impatiently as it lumbered down to the foyer, and almost sent a porter flying as I tore out of the hotel.

I emerged into driving rain. Perfect. No time to dig my umbrella out of my bag, though: here came a cab and, dammit, I was going to have it. I clattered my bag down the steps, stood in the downpour, and hailed the cab.

"Excuse me, that's my taxi," said a snooty-voiced woman.

No way. I was closer. I sprinted over, flung open the door, threw in my suitcase and threw myself in after it.

"Dublin airport, please," I said, slamming the door on the woman's indignation.

The driver gave a cursory nod and pulled away from the kerb.

Good. I didn't feel like talking, either.

Rain ran off me in little rivulets, gathering in a puddle on the floor. My nervous energy ran with it, leaving me empty, a husk.

I gazed out the window. What a waste. I'd always wanted to visit Dublin—now I just wanted to forget it.

The airport came into view and I relaxed, as if I'd been expecting to be caught and cuffed before I could execute a getaway. I took a deep, rallying breath. Okay. All I had to do was get on the plane and this whole miserable mess would be over, *finito*, in the past.

Had it really been only three days?

I thanked the cabbie, handed him some notes, then hauled my reluctant suitcase up the kerb and into the breakfast-flight chaos. Joined the check-in queue with downcast eyes. Kept myself to myself, my head way too full of my own issues to cope with anyone else's.

The queue moved at a snail's pace. Oh, come *on*.

Irritation transmuted into uncertainty. Was this the cosmos telling me I shouldn't be leaving?

I glanced anxiously at my watch then looked around for the nearest exit. I could be back in time for the first workshop . . .

Which Matt would also be attending.

No! I gave myself a mental shake. Don't be *stupid*. Of *course* I should be leaving. Why did a slow queue signify anything more than 'it's a full plane'? Why did one night of passion with Matt signify anything more than convenient sex?

It didn't. As Dani would be quick to point out.

"So you had two men in the same month," she'd summarise. *"So what? You're all adults. It's sex. It's not a crime."*

But Matt didn't see it like that. In his eyes I'd committed a huge crime. And, somehow, I felt like a cheap criminal.

"You both need to get over yourselves," she'd retort.

Perhaps. But how? How could I get over that look he'd given me, as if I'd just thrust a knife hilt-deep in his heart? How could I get over his final words—cold, conclusive, more cutting than any blade?

"Stop thinking and get on with it. Have more sex." Typical Dani advice. She'd be dismissive. *"He's high maintenance. You can do better, Sis."*

No, I couldn't. I loved him. He was The One. But I wasn't good enough for him; he'd already made that crystal clear.

Stalemate.

"Doesn't taste stale to me."

I shot the guy a startled look.

He looked from me to his half-eaten sandwich and back to me. Rats. Had I just spoken aloud? His eloquent are-you-all-there? expression confirmed it.

I muttered, "Sorry," then, unable to put any space between us, looked away and hummed a few notes. Realised I looked even more like a lunatic and went studiously mute, busying myself with the small-print on my ticket.

My mind boomeranged back to Matt and the words blurred. I dashed away a tear. Oh, stop it. As Dani would say, forget him. Move on.

Forget Dani, more like. Why would I even mention any of this to her? She had plenty to say but the empathy of a gnat. She wouldn't get it. Nobody would. I wasn't even sure *I* got it.

The woman at the check-in counter certainly didn't get it. Her disdainful look screamed that I'd dived off the end of the stupid scale. Anyone with half a brain knew you couldn't just swan in and demand a seat to London two days earlier than your ticketed booking. She was downright unfriendly—rude, even—and certainly didn't rate my chances of squeezing onto the next flight.

Neither did I, given her attitude. She left me no option but to tell her about the tragic return of my cancer. Her face, at once stricken, told me my story had hit its mark. Maybe she had a heart, after all.

"I'm sure we can squeeze you in," she assured me in conciliatory tones. "We do, of course, keep a few seats reserved for just these types of emergencies."

And there I'd been, thinking my excuse was original.

"Thank you so much," I whimpered.

She nodded and smiled, her fingers flying over the keyboard as she magicked up a seat for me.

"Right, that should do it." She printed my boarding pass. "I will personally see to it that you're well looked after on the flight."

I wasn't sure whether her direct line was with God or merely the pilot but, either way, it had to be good for me. I snatched up the boarding pass and scuttled off to the departure gate before she changed her mind.

My euphoria at scoring a seat disintegrated as I waited in the departure lounge.

I stared at my ticket, my cabin bag, my coat. How had it come to this? Yesterday I'd been walking on air, bursting with happiness, the luckiest girl alive. And now—now I didn't want to even be alive. A swollen lump of grief rose in my throat, threatening to burst from my mouth and land with a splodge on the floor.

I sent Liz a quick text message. *Cumn hm. Life sux. Mt me @ LHR?*

Her reply—*Sory, out of town. U ok? xx*—set off an unstoppable stream of tears. I huddled in my seat, trying not to cry and trying not to sniff and failing miserably on both counts.

"Here." A hand offered me a tissue.

I took it, avoiding eye contact with the hand's owner, and cleared my throat. "Thanks." Blew my nose, took a shuddery breath, wiped away the tears.

The hand approached once more and rested briefly on my arm in a comforting gesture. A friendly, older hand. A strong, enduring, I've-seen-worse-than-this hand. A hand that spoke of scones and cosy fireside chats and Grandma's unconditional love.

More blasted tears.

"Don't hold back, dear," she said. "Let it all out or you'll make yourself ill."

Just what Grandma would have said. I smiled weakly, still unable to look at her. Screwed my tissue up into a tight little ball. Unscrewed it and blew my nose again. "Sorry."

She patted my arm. "Don't be. Crying shows you have a heart."

Yeah, a stupid, foolish, broken heart.

"It's hard," she said, "when someone close passes away."

I stilled. Passes away? The thought jammed in my brain. Why did she assume someone had died? I could be crying over my power bill! Silly old duck.

Though perhaps not so silly. It had been a death of sorts. After a moment's hesitation I nodded in silent agreement.

"It gets easier with time," she said.

Did it? I couldn't imagine how. I stared sightlessly at the rain battering against the window. The window was me.

Our boarding call came and people began to shepherd themselves into a queue. She gave my arm a gentle squeeze.

"Take care, dear." She stood. "Is someone meeting you?"

"Oh. Um . . ." I looked down at Liz's text message, still displayed on my phone. "No." Then felt her concern and opted for the fib instead. "I mean, yes."

Reassured, she smiled her farewell and joined the queue. I studied the carpet.

Dammit.

Ugly orangey-blue swirls.

Dammit. She was right. I needed someone there for me when I got off the plane. Someone familiar, someone who cared, someone who loved me, fucked-up life and all.

Liz. But she was out of town. Who, then? Jim? No. Much as I adored him, he'd see it all so logically. I couldn't do logical today.

Which left Dani, who'd just poo-poo the whole Matt thing. I definitely couldn't cope with that. Or . . . what if I didn't mention Matt?

What if I pretended I had the flu or something? Yes, that would work.

Sorted. A quick text to Dani—*Mt me @ LHR? Pls?*—and I switched off my mobile. Time to go, I guess.

I looked out the window again, losing myself in the rain's silent rage. The final boarding call came and a few stragglers hurried past.

I blinked, refocused. My fancy new lacy black g-string. Had I packed it? I'd tossed it towards my suitcase, that's right. Seen it land to the left. Thought, "I'll get it later".

Only I hadn't. Fab. Great. Perfect. My chin quivered and my throat ached. I clenched my jaw rigor-mortis-tight. I would *not* cry over a measly scrap of lingerie.

"Er, would you be on this flight, Ma'am?"

I started, then stood, dazed. "Oh. Yes. Sorry."

"No problem, Ma'am. But we do need to hurry. The pilot's waiting for you to board."

And so it was over.

Goodbye, Dublin. Goodbye, Matt.

CHAPTER TWENTY-EIGHT

I emerged at Arrivals and stood for a moment, getting my bearings. Everything looked the same—but it felt so very, very different. Cold. Hard. Unfriendly.

Somebody's trolley bit into my heel. I moved out of the way. "Sorry."

Hang on, why should I apologise? I was the one who'd had a chunk taken out of their heel. I was too nice for my own good. Time to take a leaf from Dani's book.

Dani. Had she replied to my text? I switched on my mobile, but there were no messages, no voicemails, nothing.

What now?

I took a few deep breaths, stretched my lips into a semblance of a smile, and lugged my suitcase towards the underground. Then I spotted Dani striding my way across the glossy tiled floor. Relief surged through me, then gratitude. She'd come when I needed her.

"Dani!" I stopped and, genuinely smiling now, waited for her.

I pulled her gift-wrapped scarf from my bag. Would she like it? I hoped so.

Look at the way she was turning heads. I felt a surge of big-sister pride. She'd been turning heads like that since we were kids.

But something was wrong. My smile faltered. Something was badly wrong. She looked thunderous. Murderous, even. And—crap-a-roony, it looked like I might be her next victim.

She stormed up to me, all avenging-angel-in-stiletto-suede-boots, and came to an abrupt halt only inches from my face, her features so twisted in anger she reminded me of a church gargoyle.

"*You*," she hissed, with such venom my insides wobbled.

Crack! She slapped me, right in the face.

I gasped and took an involuntary step back. Tears stung my eyes.

"You bitch!" she said. "You scheming, self-serving bitch!"

I brought a hand up to my cheek. "What—?"

"How could you?"

"How could I what?"

"You know damn well what I'm talking about," she raged.

"Er—" Would someone tell me what the hell was going on?

"You deserve each other." Her lip curled.

I frowned. Me and who? Matt? But she didn't even know him.

Comprehension dawned like a cold, heavy stone in my belly. I broke out in a cold sweat. "Charlie?"

"Charlie?" she mimicked. "You make me sick."

I felt sick, too. "Charlie's your . . ."—I gulped painfully—"Ex?"

"Thanks to you, yes."

I glanced around. Joy. Another audience. "What do you mean, thanks to me?"

"What do you think I mean? You stole my man."

I frowned, trying to work it all out. "But Dani, I had no idea. You never told me you were involved with Charlie. How was I to know?"

"Oh please. It wasn't rocket science. You knew I was upset with him."

"Well, yes, but I had no idea why. You weren't exactly chatty about it. In fact, you never spoke about him at all." I paused. How could I have missed something as big as this? "I didn't even know you *knew* Charlie. Anyway, you'd already broken up with him. You told me loads of times it was over."

"Because he had a cute little wife at home, remember?"

That's what she'd thought, but she'd been wrong. Charlie's wife was long gone, and ditto the Estepona villa. I opened my mouth to speak, but she barrelled on over the top of me.

"And then I have you holding my hand, telling me there-there, I'm better off without him, and all along you're sitting there smug as fuck 'cause hey-ho, you're sleeping with him too."

"No! I wasn't."

"That's not what I heard." Hands on hips, she glared at me.

Bingo. Fred Tyler. I'd so known that would come back to bite me.

The beginnings of anger stirred in my chest. How was I supposed to have known Charlie was in Dani's life? Not once had she mentioned him. Ever. And I wasn't telepathic.

Anyway, she didn't have a monopoly on the man—they'd broken up, for crying out loud.

"Is that how much you really think of me?" I didn't wait for her to answer. "Give me some credit, Dani. As if I'd jump into bed with any boyfriend of yours."

She barked a harsh laugh. "No? What would you do, then? Take him to a seedy hotel and dance in his lap? Suck him off 'til he begs you to stop?"

Her crass words hit their mark. I flinched.

God, she was right. I'd slept with her man. Okay, her Ex, but that was just semantics to her.

My self-respect shrivelled. If only I'd listened to my gut that Friday, refused Charlie's invitation, and gone to work. I didn't even *do* one-night stands. And look: a one-off fling, and this was the result. My lover hated me, my sister hated me . . . Come to think of it, I didn't think much of me, either.

Fuck. I'd slept with him. *Slept* with *Charlie*. How could I ever make it up to her?

"Dani, I'm—"

"I know, I know." She looked me up and down, contempt all over her face. "You're jealous of me."

"No. That's—"

"Yes you are. Don't deny it. You want my man, you want my body, you want my life. Yeah." She nodded, getting into her stride. "That's what it is. You want to be me. Well, news flash." She shoved her face close. "You're not me. And Charlie's just using you to get back at me. He doesn't want you. What's there to want?"

"Hey," I flared, "that's a bit unfair."

"Why? You're fat, frumpy and boring. Fuck!" She crowed triumphantly. "Your idea of excitement is a trip to Tesco's."

"Is that right?"

All my childhood resentment roared to the surface. It was always *me* who'd given my favourite toys and clothes to Dani, *me* who'd covered for her when she climbed out the window at night, *me* who'd stayed in the wings while Dani took centre-stage in bloody everything.

"I may not be a high-powered pencil-thin rich bitch like you," I blazed, "but I haven't slept my way round Greater London, either."

"At least I don't sleep with my sister's man," she screamed.

I heard murmurs, the odd raised comment, laughter. Add a commercial break and we'd be the next episode of *Days Of Our Lives*.

"If he's your man, why's it such a secret?"

"You hate him. Why would I let you loose on him? And look what happened. We weren't finished 'til you took off with him on a dirty weekend." She lunged at me, hands clawing at my throat.

I quickly backed up, holding her at arm's length when she kept coming at me.

"How could you?" she yelled at point-blank range, more frightening than any gargoyle. "You're meant to be my sister. Not some sex-mad, self-centred bitch on heat."

She drew her arm back to slap me again but this time I was ready. As her hand swung at me I grabbed her wrist and flung it downwards.

"Fuck you!" she shrieked.

I sighed. "Whatever." I belatedly remembered her gift, still clutched in my hand. "Here. I bought you this."

She flung it on the ground at my feet.

"As if I'd accept anything from you. You're no sister of mine. You slept with my man. You're nothing but a cheap, second-grade slut!" Dani about-faced and stalked off through the crowd.

I watched her go and felt suddenly jelly-like, as if a ramrod had been removed from my spine. My head, too heavy for my body, was a pressure-cooker of grief.

Huddles of people still loitered nearby, propped against their trolleys, all focused on me, not one of them meeting my eyes. Someone's video camera blinked red at me. Excellent. My fast-track to fame. *YouTube* footage of my sister disowning me.

Vultures, the lot of them. What were they waiting for? A nervous breakdown? An end-of-scene bow?

I stood stone still, her gift at my feet, my pride in tatters, our lives blown apart. I had never felt so alone.

CHAPTER TWENTY-NINE

I let myself into the flat and stood in the doorway, listening. No off-key whistling, no loud burps reverberating down the stairs, no annoying grasshopper's click of fingers on keyboard. Good. Jim must be at work.

I shut the door and slumped on the bottom stair. Gave myself permission to cry, then found I couldn't. Stared dry-eyed at my suitcase, absorbing the grim reality of my life. Perhaps if I didn't move a muscle, didn't so much as breathe, it would all just go away.

But none of it would, would it? I'd ruined everything and now I had to live with the consequences. A sigh shook itself loose, but still there were no tears. Maybe my tear-ducts had clogged from over-use. Pity my heart wouldn't do the same.

Hmm. I could take the easy way out and down a bottle of pills.

Except I struggled to swallow even a couple of paracetamol.

Did I have it in me to slash my wrists?

It would hurt. Who was I kidding? I can't stand pain. And the thought of all that blood . . . I shuddered.

Sleep, then. I crawled into bed and cocooned myself in the duvet. So what if it was daytime? There was nothing worth staying conscious for. I'd sleep for a decade, wake up and start over.

I dozed, dreaming Matt and Charlie were both in my bed, taking turns with me in a twisted parody of my fucked-up life. Both badgering me to hurry up, but how could I, with Jim in the background systematically tearing the flat apart? Just when it became clear I'd never be sexually fulfilled, dammit, I woke up in a sweaty tangle of duvet and realised someone really was clattering around downstairs.

Typical. I wanted to wallow in self-pity, plot my suicide, that kind of thing, but no. I had to fend off a clumsy intruder instead.

Armed with a can of hairspray, I crept downstairs towards the noise.

It seemed to be coming from the kitchen.

Jim looked up from his culinary efforts, jumped with surprise, and dropped his spoon on the floor. "Shit."

"Oh." I sagged. "It's you."

"So it is." He picked up the spoon, licked it, and shoved it back in the pot.

Eeeuww.

"What are you doing home?" He smirked at my choice of weapon, raised his arms. "Don't shoot!"

"Ha fucking ha." I put the hairspray on the bench and rubbed a weary hand over my eyes.

"Jeez, Becs, am I really that scary?"

"What? Hardly."

"You look like death."

I shot him an I-hate-you look.

"No, really, you do. You're white. *Zombie* white." He cocked his head to one side. "About the colour my gran was when she'd been dead two days."

Insensitive ass. I couldn't decide who should be more affronted, me or Gran. It didn't matter. I wouldn't give him the satisfaction. I did a slow, silent count to ten.

He peered closer. "Are you contagious?"

I abandoned the count. "No, I'm not contagious. Or dead." I elbowed past him and opened the fridge. At a pinch I could probably stuff him in.

"Why aren't you in Dublin?"

"Oh, for Pete's sake." I slammed the fridge door. "It wasn't my scene, okay?"

I noticed a nasty mess of something-or-other on the bench, grabbed the cloth and set to with ferocious energy.

"It wasn't your scene?" he parroted. "Wasn't your scene? Hello!" He thumped his forehead. "Free booze, free food, paid to do nothing. What's not-your-scene about that?"

True. But he hadn't mentioned the free boss and free humiliation.

"Guess I just missed your Jamie Olliver skills." Sarcasm, the lowest form of wit, usually worked a treat with Jim.

"Ah." He gave a sage nod. "Here's my latest lesson. Take can opener.

Extract beans, of baked variety. Place pot on stove. Add beans. Turn knob. Take spoon. Stir. The beans," he clarified. "Eat."

He slurped a demonstrative spoonful into his mouth, then shoved the pot under my nose. "Want some?"

I repressed a shudder and backed out of the kitchen. "No. I've got to go to work."

"What's that got to do with—oh, I get it. The baked beans'll super-size your farts." He cupped his hand to his mouth, megaphone-style. "Building evacuated. Police on hunt for killer sphincter muscle." He cackled, then lifted his leg and let rip a hearty fart.

It hung between us with an almost physical presence. I gagged.

He sniffed, his smile beatific. "Roses. Hang on." He reached into a cupboard and extracted a paper bag. "Take this."

I regarded it suspiciously. He wanted me to *bag* the smell?

"Oh. Sorry." He gouged a couple of holes in the side and handed it to me again. "For your head. Otherwise your boss'll take one look and whip you down to the embalmer's." He fell about laughing, like some demented madman.

For a moment I watched my house-mate. Everything was one big joke to him. Me included. I hated him. "Just fuck off. Fuck. Off."

"That'd be necrophilia. Thanks, but no thanks." He laughed so hard his face turned crimson.

Did he not get it at all? That this was truly, utterly, the worst day of my life? That I couldn't stomach talking to him, or anyone, let alone having a cosy chat about god-damn necrophilia? Suddenly my tear-ducts were working again with a vengeance.

I dived out of the kitchen before he could see me in such a mess, and hurled myself up the stairs into my room. Slammed the door shut and leaned against it. Intermittent *necrophilias* drifted up the stairs, followed by fresh bouts of laughter. Bastard.

I dashed away my tears and took a few deep breaths. Now what? Well . . . Work, like I'd said. Why not? I sat on the bed and stared at the floor. Work. It had just been an excuse to avoid Jim's food, of course. I didn't really need to go in. As far as Gary Silverton knew I was still in Dublin enjoying Conference Week.

But if I stayed home I'd have Jim to contend with.

Fine. Work, then. I stood and opened my wardrobe. Stared blankly at the contents. What to wear? I felt swamped, disoriented, as if someone had disconnected the wires in my brain.

Who was I kidding? If I couldn't even scrape together an outfit, there was no way I'd cope at work. I flopped back down on my bed but couldn't settle. I watched the door nervously, expecting Jim to burst in any second.

I needed to escape. But where?

Immediately I thought of Mum and Dad. Whatever else I might think of their funny old ways, their door was always open and their love unconditional. I could catch the train to Reading and be there in no time at all.

But then I'd have to face their questions. I'd have to give them some answers. And then they'd want to sit me down and talk it over. All of it. As if I were still fifteen. What I'd done, said, thought, wished . . . Every last detail. I'd get the 'you silly girl' comments, the 'back in my day' stuff, and loads of unwelcome puritanical advice.

I couldn't face it.

Why, oh why, had Liz chosen today, of all the god-damn days, to work out of town? I just wanted to hear her voice.

Which was why mobile phones had been invented.

"Liz? Hi, it's me."

"Becs." Her affection warmed me. "How are you? You're home, then?"

"Yes." I hesitated. "When are you back?"

"Tomorrow. Why?"

"Oh, nothing." I chewed on a fingernail. "It'll be good to see you, that's all."

"You're not okay."

A ball of emotion clogged up my throat. I couldn't speak.

"I can come back tonight if you need me. Or—hey, why don't you come down here? I'm in Brighton. It's only a couple of hours by train. We can drive back together."

"Thanks, but no. You're working. I'd just be in the way."

"You wouldn't be."

She'd said that to make me feel better, of course. What a pal.

"Thanks, Liz. No, it can wait. Are you there for the restructure?"

"Yes. Just preliminary data collection for now."

Thank goodness. It was too close to Christmas for redundancies. Or heartbreak.

"See you tomorrow," she said. "Hang in there. I'll call you as soon as I'm back."

I sat on the edge of my bed. A whole day to kill until she came back. How would I cope? What would I do? Twenty. Four. Hours. An eternity.

But what could she do or say that would make one iota's difference? Nothing. Nothing that had happened would un-happen once we'd talked about it. Nothing she said would make it any less awful. It sucked. Matt, Dani, Charlie, work, life. All of it sucked.

Jules wandered in and brushed against my legs. I looked down at him. He waited there until I reached down and stroked him.

"Yeah, okay," I conceded. "You don't suck."

* * *

I arrived at Richmond station with no idea how I'd got there. Scary. Was I having a nervous breakdown?

Maybe. Then again, if I really was, I wouldn't know it, would I?

Or—would I? Cripes, maybe I really was seriously unbalanced. Maybe my whole life was turning pear-shaped because I needed help. What sort of help, though? Drugs? Meditation? Therapy? It all sounded hellish expensive. Would alcohol do?

But then I'd have to sit next to Jim at AA meetings. It seemed easier to just have the breakdown.

Just ahead of me three deer ambled past, all dignity and grace. A rabbit sat up on its haunches to watch me, nose twitching, ears like antennae. It was a scene straight out of a fairy tale—minus the Prince.

I walked into the park. An icy wind ripped through my jacket and I buried my chin deep in the collar—a futile move because my whole body was already snap-frozen. Not that I minded. Perhaps if I stayed cold enough long enough it would numb my heart as well.

An elderly couple passed by, well-wrapped against the weather, arm-in-arm, heads close, happy. They epitomised everything Matt and I would never have and I hated them for it. But I hated me more. How could I have slept with anyone else when all I really wanted was Matt?

222

How could I have thought, even for a moment, Charlie might be a better option?

Workmate, schmurkmate. I *so* needed to get over my stupid past.

You're welcome to her.

I stopped, stared straight ahead, saw nothing. My heart twisted.

Matt didn't love me. I'd been a one-night stand for him, nothing more.

But it had felt like more. So much more.

It still felt like so much more.

My eyes burned. How could he? He'd used me for his freaking one-night stand and put my whole *career* on the line. He knew how much this job meant to me. And now—how could I ever return? How could I face Matt? His scorn? Worse, his pity? And my colleagues. How could I face their sniggers and snide looks, their whispers?

But if I didn't go back I'd never see him again. He was the man I loved; the man who'd saved my life, in more ways than one. How could I just walk away from that?

I about-turned and trudged back the way I'd come. When had it started to rain? I pulled up my hood, but it was too late: I was already wet. And dumped.

Seriously, how could Matt think, after what we'd just shared, I'd leap straight into another man's arms?

Bitter fury balled in my gut. What kind of woman did he think I was?

Well, if that's how little he thought of me I was well shot of him. I kicked at a frozen sod of earth. The sod won. My toe throbbed.

Asshole.

I couldn't hold the tears in any longer and, actually, why try? Matt had caused me enough pain. I didn't need a stomach ulcer as well.

And Dani. How dare she be so . . . so *Dani*-ish? Everything always had to be about her. She never bloody changed.

But she was my sister. I loved her. And now I'd lost her, just like I'd lost Matt. All for a one-night stand with Charlie. I didn't even *do* one-night stands.

Drizzle thickened into downpour, cold against my face. My teeth began to chatter.

Pneumonia. That might work. Would Matt visit me in hospital, tell me it was all a big mistake? Plead with me to pull through so we could start over?

You're welcome to her. Not exactly a happy-ever-after.

It never was, for me.

I'd said I was over men, I'd promised Liz I meant it . . . but we both knew I craved that fairy tale ending. My brain knew the whole in-love-forever thing was make-believe, but my heart still pined for it.

I needed a new dream. A *me* dream. A career / life / whatever dream that didn't depend on Mister Perfect showing up. No more fantasies; I needed a dream I could believe in.

It was as I left the park I heard the *hwooh-hwooh* of wings above me, unusually close.

I ducked as a pigeon cruised past, way too low. Gaped. *Look out!* I waved my arms wildly, started running, but it was too late. Heart in throat, I watched as the pigeon flew arrow-straight and splattered itself head-first into a sign just ahead. My stomach heaved. The bird landed with a thud at my feet.

Oops. I looked down at the bird. Gave it a prod with my right foot. There it lay, limp and lifeless, one beady little eye staring up at me. I shuddered. Poor little sucker. Dead as a dodo . . . er, pigeon. Hysterical laughter bubbled up.

I gingerly scooped it up in my hands. And I thought *I'd* had a grim day. At least I was still alive.

Yeah, but was I really living the life I wanted? Who was I? Who did I want to be?

Little wonder I was miserable. Did I even know myself?

I carried kamikaze pigeon to a sheltered hollow and covered it with leaves and dirt. Rubbed my hands down my jeans. Decided I needed to take control of my life.

Forget Matt, forget Dani, forget it all. Real happiness came from within. And at thirty-one years of age it was high time I got to know the one person I had to live with forever—me.

CHAPTER THIRTY

It didn't take as long as I'd expected. When I'd finished, I looked around at what had been my room, my sanctuary, my own living space for the past three years and felt immensely sad it had come to this. Two packed bags, a laundry hamper, and a bunch of random trinkets bundled up in a sheet. My ex-bedroom looked skeletal, tatty. Every movement echoed. The room felt unloved.

Just like me.

Jules *mrowl*ed from the hallway, but it wasn't a happy *mrowl*. I beckoned him in for a reassuring cuddle, but he stayed right where he was. I'd ruined his sanctuary as well, and he wasn't impressed.

I rang Liz. "I need a favour. Can I stay at your place a couple of nights?"

"Sure. Why? Have you finally seen the light over Jim?"

"No. I'm leaving London."

Silence.

Then, "That's nuts. Whatever's happened, Becs, leaving is not the answer."

"It's bad, Liz." My voice dropped to a whisper. "Real bad."

"Fine. Come and stay. You know you're welcome. And we'll work something out, something less extreme than leaving."

"I've made up my mind, Liz."

"Then un-make it."

She paused. Her voice softened. "He's not worth it, Becs."

My insides went all quivery.

"What time will you be home?" I warbled.

"I'll finish up early. Is five-ish okay?"

"Just work your normal hours, Liz. I'll hang out in the café at the end of the street."

"What, and leave you waiting until nine? Hardly. I'll finish early."

She really was the best friend ever.

"I'll come and get you," she added.

"No, you're doing enough already." And I didn't want her to see my empty room. "I'll taxi over. See you soon."

Through the wall Jim was singing off-key as he tap-tap-tapped at his computer. I'd better not interrupt him. He might try to convince me to stay, and he always put such a logical case. I didn't want to change my mind. And what if he said he'd miss me? No—far easier to write what I had to say.

I bent to pick Jules up for a final hug but he wasn't having a bar of it. With an agitated tail-flick he stalked away from me and into Jim's room. Traitorous—but clever. He knew I wouldn't follow him there.

I left my goodbye note on the top stair. What I didn't expect was that Jim would emerge and find it before I'd even left.

"You've got a hard neck, Becky Jordan."

Adrenalin shot all the way down to my toes, leaving me shaky and short of breath. I stopped, hesitated, turned. He stood halfway down the stairs, the note clamped in one hand and a grim look on his face.

"What do you mean?" I couldn't take any more nasty scenes this week, and his tone had a distinct Nasty Scene ring to it.

"Nine years—*nine years*—we've been house-mates. And what? Not even a fucking goodbye?"

I looked guiltily at the scrap of paper. "My note says goodbye."

"Your note," he enunciated, "is a cop-out. A fucking cop-out. The least you could've done is told me to my face."

"But I was . . . I just thought . . ." I trailed off, belatedly wondering what on earth I *had* been thinking.

"What? That it was easier not to?" He advanced down the stairs.

"I just didn't want a scene," I muttered, my eyes skittering towards the door.

"Well, you've got one now, haven't you?" He stood in front of me, feet apart, arms folded. "Since when did I become the asshole?"

"What? You didn't. I—"

"Then would someone tell me what the fuck is going on?"

I looked at him mutely. He looked mega-angry. I'd never seen him so angry.

"Fuck's sake, Becky. Nine years is longer than some people are married. And now you're gonna—what?" He flung out an arm. "Just up and leave? No discussion, no notice, no thanks-for-the-good-times?" His face reddened. "Who do you think you are? The god-damn freaking Queen?"

I felt chastened and ashamed.

He crumpled the note and threw it at the bin. "Go on, then. Tell me to my face."

I gulped. "There's nothing much to say."

"Nothing to say? Fuck! There's plenty. For starters, what's fucked you up so much you can't even tell me you're fucking leaving? I might not like it, but at least give me a fucking chance to say so." I started to count the fucks. "And so what if you don't want to hear it? After nine years you fucking owe it to me to listen."

"I—"

"And what's got into you," he didn't even pause for breath, "that you fuck off and go AWOL when you're meant to be at the junket of the fucking year? Are you fucked in the head or what? And what's with the fifty fucking phone calls from some Charlie fucker? Good job you're leaving 'cause I'm sick of being your fucking secretary."

Eleven fucks. That was bad.

"Jim, I'm sorry." And I was. Sorry the bloody taxi hadn't turned up. "I should've told you I was leaving."

He scowled at me. "Fu—"

"You deserved better."

He *humpf*ed. But no more fucks.

"Look, I've been in a really bad space this past week. And when I came back from Dublin . . . well, you just turned everything into a joke, and—"

"Hey, if you'd bothered to share . . ."

I looked longingly at the door. Pinched my eyes shut for a second. "Yes, okay, point taken. I—I didn't know where to start."

He rolled his eyes. "Yeah, whatever."

"Hey," I snapped, "a lot happened, okay? I already felt revolting, and then you went all necrophilia on me."

His hackles stood to attention. "That was a joke and you know it. Take a feckin' chill pill."

"It's hard to chill when you've just been bitch-slapped by your sister the minute you step off the plane."

"Yeah?" His hackles settled as curiosity took over. "What did you do to deserve that?"

"That's right." My jaw, rock-hard with tension, began to ache. "Take Dani's side, why don't you?"

"I'm not taking anyone's side."

"You just did."

"I—"

"Hey," I interrupted, "nobody deserves to be attacked, okay? Just 'cause she's my sister doesn't make it okay. And it's not okay for you to think it's okay. Okay?"

"Er—"

"I don't care how much you want to get in her pants. She's a witch. A manipulative, conniving witch. And how dare she call me frumpy? Or fat? My body may not be a perfect ten, but I have feelings, too, you know." I fixed him with an accusing stare. "And you took her side, just like that. Just because you think she's hot."

"I—"

"How could you take her side? It's not like she'll ever sleep with you."

I regretted the words as soon as I saw his expression, but the 'sorry' stuck in my throat.

"Cheers for that." He hunched on the bottom stair.

Then he shook his head as if to clear his mind of rubbish. "Christ! This is exactly why women do my head in." Gangly arms flapped. "Everything's such a drama. You make it all so complicated." He exhaled, scratched at his scalp, collapsed full-length against the stairs then, agitated, leaned forward again. "What's the big deal, here? So your sister's drop-dead gorgeous. So I want to shag her into next week."

I opened my mouth then closed it again.

"So what? I'm a bloke. What do you expect?"

I squirmed uncomfortably. "Do we really need to have this conversation?"

He shot me a wild-eyed look. "Apparently, yes. God knows why."

I looked at my watch. Where was that blasted cab?

"Look, Becky, let's get something straight. Dani is Dani and you are you. Believe it or not, I get that. Dani's sex on a stick, and you're . . ."

He faltered—clearly I wasn't sex on a stick. "You're . . ."

He blew out his cheeks, avoiding my eyes. ". . . my house-mate."

"Ex," I said tightly. "Ex-house-mate."

His features twisted. "And what the hell is that all about?" More arm-flapping.

"Long story. You'd be bored."

"Try me."

I looked away.

His face fell. "Or not." He got to his feet and started up the stairs.

"Jim, don't." I reached out and tugged on his arm. "I'm a bitch."

He looked down at me, his eyes dull.

"I'm sorry," I said. "This isn't really about you."

"Then why leave?" he asked, and I felt his hurt as if it were my own.

"Because I'm leaving London."

His jaw dropped. "You're what?"

"I'm leaving London. Going up north."

"What? Why? That's crazy!"

"Probably," I agreed, "but that's what I'm doing."

"Fuck." He blinked. Stared at me. Stuck a finger in one ear and vigorously scratched. "Fuck."

"I've only just decided or I'd have told you earlier."

He sank back down onto the stair, his goggly eyes even more goggly than usual. "What—just like that?"

I nodded. "I'm leaving in a couple of days. I'll stay with Liz until I finish up at work."

"But—"

"Jim, please don't try and change my mind," I pleaded. "You'll just make it harder than it already is."

"If it's that hard, why do it?"

Then, when I didn't answer, "Come on, Becs, you've got to give me something, here, 'cause I just don't understand."

I sat on the bottom stair next to him and rested my head on his shoulder. "Guess that makes two of us," I said on a sigh.

And with his head touching mine I told him about Matt. The sleeps-with-boss-then-gets-heart-broken version.

"This sounds a bit too Mickey for my liking," he muttered.

So I told him the rest of the story. The original, un-edited, includes-previously-deleted-scenes-with-Charlie-and-Dani version.

"Okay, you're right," he said. "It's not Mickey. It's worse."

I sighed. "Yeah. Much worse."

"Becs, you're like a broken fucking record. Why do you keep doing this?"

I hugged my knees, staring at the carpet. "You can't help who you fall in love with."

After a pause he said a quiet, "I know."

Two words, two unassuming little words. But something in his tone made me glance up sharply. His eyes flickered away from mine. For the first time I could remember, the silence between us felt awkward.

The silence lengthened. Great. Just when I'd thought things couldn't get any worse.

I made to stand and he spoke again. "You know the difference between you and me? I'm recovering from my addiction. You don't even see yours."

"Hey, eight units a week is hardly addicted."

"See what I mean? You don't even know what I'm talking about. It's not alcohol with you. It's men. Men who make you feel inferior."

I stood abruptly. "Don't be ridiculous."

"It's true. You're always telling me it's your fault it didn't work out. You did something or said something or were too much of one thing or not enough of another or—"

"No I—"

"This time it was Matt." He tallied it up on his fingers. "Before him there was Lord What's-his-name who used you as paparazzi fodder while he—"

"Yeah, okay, I remember."

"And Mickey. And before him, that dude who gambled your bank account dry. And what about that crackhead lecturer you shagged back in College?" He shook his head at me. "You're addicted, man."

I climbed the stairs, just to put some distance between us.

"What, to sex?" I tried for frivolous. "Ha! It's just good fun."

"Yeah, alcoholism was just good fun for a while, too."

"Jeez, Jim." I leaned over the banister. "You want me to join a nunnery?"

He studied me, head to one side. "Nah. You wouldn't look good in a habit. Stay here."

I gave him a flat-lining smile, one that didn't even register on the Happy Scale. "Sorry."

"How am I supposed to stick to the programme if you're not here, bullying me every step of the way?"

"You will. Remember what we used to say? *You can lead a drunk to water . . .*"

He joined in, ". . . *but you can't make him drink it.*"

This time my smile was genuine. I came back down the stairs, sat beside him and gave him a gentle shoulder-nudge. "Hey, I'm not the person who stops you drinking. You are."

"And I'm not the person who stops you hating yourself."

Would he give it a rest? "I don't hate myself. I—"

"Then look after Number One for a change. Stay in London. Your friends are here . . ."

"I'll make new ones."

". . . Your job is here . . ."

"I can't go back there."

". . . Your home is here . . ."

"Stop trying to change my mind, Jim."

"Stop running away, Becs."

I ground my teeth. "I'm not running away. I'm making a fresh start."

"Fresh start my ass." He pointed at his backside, then at me. "You're. Running. Away."

A horn blared outside. Thank God. I stood. "That's my cab."

"What—so you take off to fuck knows where, leaving all this Dani-Charlie-Matt shite to fester, all woe is me and doing sod-all about it?"

"That's not fair, Jim."

"Hey," he fired, "I just call it as I see it."

"Don't you just."

We glared at each other. My chin did its tell-tale quiver, and I quickly turned away.

"Can you look after Jules for a bit? Until I get myself sorted?"

"Whatever."

I took a deep breath, and another.

"Sorry I haven't given any notice." I picked up my bags. "I'll keep paying rent until you find someone else."

After a pause he said a grudging, "Thanks."

He scrubbed at his crotch, then reached for my bags. "Here." His voice was gruff. "Give me those. I'll help you out."

"Ta."

"Since you're so determined to go."

I stashed my sheetful of trinkets, so significant to me and worthless to anyone else, in my hamper. Together we hauled the remnants of my life out onto the street and the cab driver stowed it all in the boot.

I turned, gave Jim a quick hug and a whispered 'sorry', then got in the cab and departed without a backward glance.

CHAPTER THIRTY-ONE

The lift doors opened. I poked my head out. Any signs of tall blond Matts? No.

I emerged, wearing my best everything's-hunky-dory smile, and made a beeline for my office. I hadn't thought to check for signs of distinguished grey Garys, though, and dammit, there he was, coming straight towards me. I needed to speak to him, but not here. Not where others might hear.

He glanced at his watch and I silently groaned. Just what I didn't need: the late lecture.

I tried to look business-like.

"That Northern line," I grumbled, bustling past. Not that Liz lived on the Northern line, but Gary didn't know I'd moved in with her.

"Feeling better, Becky?"

My heart raced. Shit. Worse than the late lecture: he knew I'd gone AWOL. I was about to get my pay docked.

I turned slowly to face him, clammy-palmed. Please, not that. I'd done my sums and I needed every miserly penny I could save between now and leaving London.

"I heard you had to come home early," he said. "Bad luck."

Sarcastic or genuine? I watched his expression carefully. "Rotten luck," I agreed.

"You must have been really ill."

Genuine. Phew. I resumed breathing. "Yes. It came out of nowhere."

He shook his head sympathetically. "Ah well, so long as you're over it now."

If only. I forced a smile. "Much better, thanks. I'd better dash; I'm late for my lecture."

As I passed Sal's desk she tut-tutted and looked pointedly at her watch. "Whatever the reason," she sparkled, "I hope it was good."

I couldn't find the energy to respond.

"You can't fool me!" Her voice followed me. "I'm hot on your trail, Becky Jordan."

Was she, indeed? Speculations already, and it was only Monday morning. Which just proved leaving was absolutely the best option.

Might as well get this day over with. Lecture first, then Gary. Sal could wait.

* * *

I placed the envelope on the desk between us, took a step back.

Gary looked at the envelope, then up at me. "What's this?"

I said nothing.

He leaned forward and picked it up. Took a letter opener from his top drawer and slit the seal.

"Have a seat." He indicated a chair.

I perched on the edge of it, hands clamped in my lap. He unfolded my letter and flattened it on the desk in front of him. Glanced my way again, then read the contents. It didn't take long.

His expression hardened. "You want to resign?"

I nodded. A *don't ask why, don't ask why* mantra repeated in my brain.

He steepled his hands. "Why?"

Gary may well be the most understanding boss in the universe, but that didn't mean I was about to bare all about my one-night-stand-gone-wrong. I inhaled, exhaled, said nothing.

"Isn't this a little—premature?" he asked. "You've barely been here six months."

"I know. It's just . . .." My eyes darted left and right as I cast about for a palatable excuse.

"Give it more time, Becky."

"I can't. I need—"

"A break?" He nodded. "It's a stressful job, granted." A pause, then a conclusive nod. "Yes, a couple of weeks' stress leave might be a good idea."

"No! I mean—thank you, that's very kind, but it's not stress. Well, it is, in a manner of speaking. But not . . ." I stopped, pulled myself together, tried again. "It's more . . . personal reasons." I felt myself blush.

His eyebrows shot up. "Oh?"

"Yes."

His gaze dropped to my stomach.

"Oh! I'm not pregnant. I'm . . ." I started to chew on a fingernail then stopped, returned the hand to my lap. "It's my grandmother."

My *grandmother?*

"She's eighty-seven. She—er—needs my help."

He frowned. "Oh?"

Actually, she was way beyond my kind of help, having been dead these past five years.

"Yes," I said, "she's just . . . broken her hip." Then, warming to my theme, "And she really can't manage on her own anymore. She lives in . . . um . . . a remote village, yes, very remote, completely cut off from the world, up in . . . in Yorkshire."

"I see."

"And I'm her *only family*"—I emphasised the words—"so it's up to me to take care of her."

"I'm sorry. I didn't realise your parents had passed away."

I gulped. Lies and me just didn't mix.

"Um—yes, well, I don't remember it." That, at least, was the truth. "It all happened years ago, when I was just a kid, a little kid, barely talking, and I was taken in by some wonderful people who brought me up as their own. They even changed *their* surname to mine, to minimise the trauma for me."

What? *What?*

His eyebrows prepared to launch into orbit.

"Anyway, my parents—that's what they are to me—aren't related to my grandmother. At least, not that I know of. But they don't look anything like her, so I'm sure they're not. And they don't want to interfere—it wouldn't be right—so, you see, I need to go up to Yorkshire for the time being."

"Ah." He blinked. "Of course. Family is family." He paused. "Becky, have you spoken to Matt about this? He is your line manager, after all."

The blood drained away from my head so fast I felt dizzy. No! Not a fainting attack. Not now, please.

"Becky?"

I refocused on his face. "Sorry." Deep breaths, deep breaths. "No, I haven't told Matt." I shook my head. "No."

"I think you should talk to him about this. It'll be easier to finalise details, your finish date and so on, with him."

"Oh. But . . . er . . . that's why I needed to talk to you." Come again? Why was that? I tried to come up with a plausible explanation. "It's just . . . you see, I needed to come straight to you because I . . . I couldn't find Matt. No, I don't know where he is. That's right. He wasn't in his office, or anywhere, and this is so urgent that I need to get it sorted straight away." I nodded emphatically. "Straight away. Like, now."

"He'll be around. Matt's always here early. In fact, I saw him just a few minutes ago."

"Oh. Well, anyway," I said brightly, "I've told you, so that'll do, won't it? I'll tell Matt when I see him," I added, crossing all my fingers as I said it because, if I had my way, I wouldn't be seeing him again. Ever.

"That's fine. I'll leave you to confirm your finishing date with him."

"No!" My heart thudded loud enough for the whole building to hear. "I mean, can't we just do that now? I—well, you know, I might not see him for hours and *hours*, and I was hoping to finish today."

"Today?" Gary looked startled.

I nodded vigorously. "Yes. Gran's desperate. She won't last the week if I'm not there. I mean, she could fall, or take the wrong pills, or starve to death, or—well, anything could happen, she's so unwell, and I really don't want her death on my conscience."

"Becky." He wiped a weary hand down his face. "I'm not sure we can do this at such short notice. Even the end of the week would be more manageable."

"The end of the *week*?" I squeaked. "No! It's got to be today. I have to leave today. Even that's hard enough, knowing I could bump into"— I stopped myself just in time—"er . . . a wall or a desk or something and hurt myself really badly and end up in hospital where I'd be no help whatsoever to my poor old Gran just when she needs me most. A broken ankle at her age is a disaster."

He shot me a sharp look. "Ankle? I thought it was her hip."

"Oh, y-yes, she did break her hip. But, well, you see, she fell really

236

awkwardly and broke her ankle, too. She's far more worried about her hip, but I can see she'll have trouble for months with that ankle." Crap, crap, *crap*.

"She's in a really bad way," I added. In case there was any doubt.

"I see." He placed both palms on the desk and took a deep breath. "Well. In light of your"—he frowned—"determination, I suppose I have no choice but to support your decision."

"*Thank* you," I breathed. "And today's my last day?"

He checked his calendar, then leaned back in his chair and regarded me intently. I shifted from foot to foot, found an interesting patch of carpet to study. Finally, when I thought I'd pass out from the tension, he nodded.

"Fine. Today's your last day. Sick leave for the rest of the week, resignation effective thereafter."

"Thank you," I repeated.

"I'll let payroll know." He shook his head. "I have to say, Becky, I'm very disappointed. You were doing so well here."

"Oh. Yes. Well. I suppose. But, you know, *que sera sera*, whatever will be will be." Oh, shut *up*. I stood and moved towards the door. "Well. Best I be off, then. There's lots to do before I leave. Like . . . packing my office and . . . things."

He nodded, a frown creasing his brow.

I quietly closed his door behind me, avoiding Sal's curious stare, and dashed to the loo for a few moments of privacy. Deep breaths, steady hands. Well, then. That could've been worse. I headed back to reception. Next on the Nasty Task list: Sal. Time to tell her I was leaving. And now I'd fed Gary all that grandmother cock-and-bull I'd better stick to my story.

"Hi, Sal." I leaned over the counter.

"Hey!" She put down her work and clapped her hands with glee. "Gossip time! I've heard the rumours. Are they true?"

"Which ones?"

"You and—"

I held up a stop-sign hand. "Forget it, I don't want to know." I glanced left and right then lowered my voice. "Sal, there's something I need to tell you."

"I knew it." She leaned forward, chin resting on her hands. "Go on, then, I'm all ears." She lifted her hands briefly and waggled her ears, then grinned at me.

"Well, this may come as a surpr—"

"Oh," she interrupted, swivelling away from me with a smug smile. "Hi, Matt."

I saw stars. My mouth went dry. I swallowed convulsively. Followed her gaze.

Sure enough, Matt was approaching the counter. A gamut of emotions clustered in my chest: desire, hurt, anger, sorrow, love.

Love.

And just like that, in less than a second, my hard-won resolve crumbled. How could I possibly leave? How could I just walk away?

Matt stopped in front of Sal and my eyes met his, cold and aloof and totally unyielding.

I looked away, nauseous. Anguish squeezed my heart. I *had* to leave. It was the only way. But first—first I would say goodbye.

I turned back to him and opened my mouth to speak, but nothing came out. Come on, Becs. My chin wobbled. Damn. I flung away from Sal, away from him, and made a run for it, scattering papers from the counter as I went.

"Don't worry about the fliers," she called after me. "I'll pick them up."

* * *

After that, it all happened with frightening speed.

Returning to give Sal the grandmother-and-hip explanation. Her dismay. My guilt: I should have told her my real reason for leaving. Quickly replaced by relief when I saw how fast the news spread. Sal—a good friend but an even better gossip. Telling her the truth would have been suicide.

Packing up my office. Personal effects in one box, lecture notes and texts in another. Fragments of me, all carefully boxed away. Wondering if I'd ever feel whole again. One last glance into my lecture theatre. One last walk down the corridor, past his office. One last trip in the lift, reliving our first kiss.

Desolation.

Knocking at the door, a visitor to my own flat. Standing on the doorstep, handing Jim three weeks' rent and my e-mail address. Telling him I'd send for my bedroom furniture; he could keep the rest if he wanted. Begging him to look after Jules until I found a new place. Jim starting to refuse, then changing his mind and nodding. His 'Sure you're doing the right thing?' echoing in my ears as I left.

The end of an era.

The phone call to my parents, carefully timed when I knew they'd be at Church. Telling them I was going away for a while and wouldn't be home for Christmas. Gulping back tears. My postscript that I would call them on Christmas Day.

The realisation that, with the festive season upon us, I would be celebrating Christmas alone.

Loneliness.

Not ringing Dani. Dani not ringing me. The huge void left where our love-hate relationship had previously been. Realising there was nothing I could do or say to put things right. Allowing my departure to speak for itself.

CHAPTER THIRTY-TWO

"Views of Edinburgh Castle", the advertisement had boasted. I scanned the skyline. Random rooftops, more like.

I sighed, turned back to the tiny attic room. "I'll take it." But only because I couldn't find anything else. Hazardously-low sloping ceilings, and that hideous candlewick bedspread didn't really do it for me.

"First three weeks in advance." The proprietor watched me from the doorway, an eagle honing in on his prey.

"In advance?" *Eek.* That would put a dent my savings.

"Christmas."

Yeah? Thanks for the Christmas spirit, pal.

"Okay," I said. "I've got to collect my bags from Waverley Station so I'll stop for cash on the way."

"No pets, no alcohol, no friends."

No friends? I stifled a laugh. No problem.

"You'll get the key when I get the money." He turned his back on me and headed down the stairs, leaving a pall of stale smoke in my room.

I switched on the oil heater. It gurgled ominously. Oh, *please* work. With snow on the ground and more forecast overnight, a broken heater would be the last straw. I left it running while I tramped downstairs and back to the train station.

I wound my scarf around my neck and pulled up my coat collar, walking as fast as the thickening snow would allow. Collected my luggage and clattered my weary way out of the station, thanking my lucky stars both suitcases had wheels.

"Any spare—"

I jumped and shrieked as the beggar materialised at my side.

He paused momentarily, then continued. ". . . change, Miss?"

"I really hope so," I snapped, "because I need a good strong coffee and I'm seriously thinking I should take up smoking."

Stupid ass. Heart pounding and hands shaking, I stalked off down the street, my suitcases swerving wildly in my wake. Passers-by took a wide berth. A biting wind, direct from the North Pole, cut through my coat. My teeth started to chatter. It really couldn't get any worse, could it?

Behind me, my bags collided. With a warning *krrrritsch*, the zip on my smaller bag gave way and I turned around in time to see the contents burst forth like an overstuffed chicken. Bras and panties spewed out onto the footpath. The snow continued to fall. It looked like Santa meets *Ann Summers*. I made a sound halfway between giggle and sob.

Fine. Things *could* get worse. I quickly stuffed my clothes back in any old how and jammed the bag closed with my knee. How to keep the cursed thing shut? I glanced around but nobody stopped to offer string, nothing useful dropped out of the sky, and if I stayed in this position much longer I'd be frozen to the spot until spring.

Blast. It would have to be my scarf. At least if I got hypothermia I'd be in hospital with a roof over my head.

I'd just finished tying my bag shut when I felt a tap on my shoulder. I turned and came nose-to-fabric with a sodden black, lacy bra.

"This yours?" the beggar asked, all leering grin.

Mortification rose in me. I stared helplessly at my bra. Should I pretend it wasn't mine? But then this slobbery old mutt of a man would keep it like some kind of trophy, I just knew. And it was my favourite one, dammit.

Fiery-cheeked, I glanced around. Nobody seemed to be watching, so I snatched back the bra and stuffed it in my coat pocket.

"Thanks," I muttered.

Miserable with embarrassment, I hoisted my broken suitcase up under one arm. Then, dragging the other behind me, I traipsed back through the slush and snow. God-damn tiny suitcase wheels. They just didn't work on cobbled streets. I had a good mind to write to the manufacturer.

I found a cash machine and withdrew the maximum allowance, then reinserted my card to take out the rest. It took a second read for me to take in the displayed message. *You have reached your daily limit. Please try again later.*

Horror trickled through my already-frozen limbs. Now what? I sat on my larger suitcase.

Jinxed. That's what I was: jinxed.

I took a great big shuddery breath, and another.

I'd have to beg. The proprietor wouldn't be impressed, but what could I do? It wasn't my fault the banks were closed.

I forced myself on and eventually hauled myself and my sodden baggage up the steps of Bellevue B&B. Handed over my cash to the sour-faced landlord.

"Sorry. That's all the cash machine would give me."

He licked his finger and counted out the notes, *humpf*ed as he finished, then looked me in the eye.

"Okay. You look honest." His hard stare dared me to be anything less. "I need the balance in the morning, mind, or you'll be back up to full rate." He handed me the key.

I nodded, feeling like a piece of scum under his boot, and headed for the stairs. He pointedly didn't offer to help. I started the climb to my room. At the first landing I abandoned my intact suitcase; I'd have to come back for it.

Five flights later I reached my own floor and sagged against the wall. How many weeks was I locked in to this place for? Three? I'd be fit as a fiddle. Either that or dead.

And judging by that awful racket, 'dead' might come sooner than expected.

I unlocked my door and opened it with trepidation. The volume increased. I flicked on the light. Nothing happened so I stepped inside. Great. That hideous noise was coming from the heater. Now I had to choose between frostbite or deafness.

Ten seconds later I turned off the heater. I'd take my chances with frostbite.

I stood and surveyed the tiny room, waiting for the claustrophobic gremlins to hit. Phew. Nothing—yet.

I sat on the bed and tried it for bounce. Not much bounce, plenty of sag. I picked at the candlewick. Flicked the fluff into the air and watched it fall to the ground. Picked some more, flicked it.

It was just a nervous habit, but it annoyed me. I folded my arms so I wouldn't be tempted to pick, then unfolded them and reached for my wallet. Pulled out the latest withdrawal slip and checked my bank balance, subtracting what I still owed on the room.

What?

I double-checked my maths. Rent money to Jim, the train ticket up here, three weeks in a B&B . . . I thought I'd been careful but, feck-it-all, half my savings were already committed; savings I'd earmarked for furniture. I crumpled the receipt into a ball and threw it at the bin. Then reconsidered, retrieved it, un-crumpled it and carefully replaced it in my wallet.

My stomach grumbled. If my maths was correct I shouldn't even be buying takeaways, let alone pub meals. I glanced at my only cooking facility: a kettle. Two minute noodles? Cup-a-soups? I could barely wait. At least they wouldn't take much preparation.

I bit a fingernail, then whipped my hand away. Dammit, I'd have no nails left if I wasn't careful. Maybe I should take up smoking instead. No. Too smelly, too poisonous, too expensive.

I went over to the window and looked down at the street. Darkness had fully descended, and I felt a big wave of little-girl-alone. Edinburgh really was a whole different world.

My stomach grumbled again.

Okay, okay. Takeaways. Just for tonight. And tomorrow—tomorrow I needed to find work.

My spirits plummeted as I thought about the job I'd had; the job I'd walked away from.

Matt.

Devastation and loss hit me all over again. I drew the curtains then curled on my saggy bed and cried. Would I ever get through a day without feeling the sorrow?

I pulled back the covers, crawled into bed fully-clothed and, hunger forgotten, escaped into sleep.

* * *

A new day dawned, dammit, and with it came Matt. Not in the flesh, of course, but back in my thoughts, reminding me all over again how much I'd lost, how much I'd never really had.

I pulled the covers over my head and hid. But it didn't work. Everything stayed exactly the same. Daylight, life, Matt.

My body ached with grief. Like a bad dose of flu, I felt it in every muscle. It was a heavy weight in my chest, a painful swelling in my throat, a relentless throbbing in my head. Matt. Matt. Matt. Tears burned my eyes.

Matt at the pool, saving my life.

Matt at work, scrambling my brain, stealing my heart.

Matt at conference, claiming my body, sharing my joy, fulfilling my dreams.

A band of steel tightened around my chest, squeezing, squeezing, until I was sure my next breath would be impossible.

Matt in the foyer, rejecting my love, crippling my soul.

I lay motionless, absorbing the pain, knowing I deserved it. Waited for oblivion or death to take me. Wished it would just hurry up.

Eventually, mentally exhausted, I slept.

I woke much later when some miserable bastard repeatedly revved his motorbike outside my window. Across the way, someone belted out *Here Comes The Sun*. A hoard of over-cocky teens walked by, bins clattering and bottles smashing in their wake. A guy yelled obscenities at them. They yelled better ones back.

My phone rang, over-loud in the confines of my room. I groaned, and heaved myself into a sitting position. Why couldn't everyone shut up and let me sleep, dammit?

The phone shrilled again. I rubbed my eyes. Swung my feet out of bed. Fan-bleeding-tastic. I was awake, okay? Was everyone satisfied?

I reached for the phone.

"Hello stranger," said a way too cheery voice.

My brain ricocheted into full wakefulness. Of all the people to ring, it had to be Charlie.

"How's it going?" he asked.

Where did I even begin?

I decided not to. "Fine. You?"

"Well, it would be better if you were lying next to me, but—"

Quickfire rage rocketed through my veins.

"Stop it, Charlie." My voice rose an octave. "Just stop."

My hands shook. My chest tightened. "Do you have any idea what you've done?"

"I . . . woke you up?"

I forced myself to take a measured breath. And another. "You don't remember a thing, do you? You visited me in Dublin? Made a scene at the hotel? Got into a fight? Ringing any bells?"

"I did drink rather a lot that night," he admitted.

"How about Buxom Becky?"

"Buxom . . ." He cleared his throat. "I think I might owe you an apology."

I wanted to let rip with a good old yelling match. I wanted to say screw him. I wanted to tell him just how badly he'd ruined my life. But I couldn't. Somewhere in the deep dark recesses of my mind, I knew I couldn't blame my crappy life on Charlie.

The blame lay squarely with me.

So, instead of berating him, I told him goodbye—something I should've done ages ago. I explained I'd left London, wished him well with his life, and we parted on reasonable terms. See? I'd learned something in the past seventeen years.

And now, in the absence of a decent life, I at least needed a decent coffee. But the only way I'd get that was if I pulled on my clothes and headed downstairs. All five flights of them.

Down at reception the landlord was sucking on his cigarette as if nicotine was the secret to immortality. A smoky cloud hung around him.

I stayed well back. "Excuse me."

He didn't look up.

I held my breath and stepped closer. "Excuse me."

His eyes continued to pore over—oh, lovely, porn.

Rude bastard. I banged the desk-bell, coughing as smoke attacked my lungs. "Oi. Is it too late for breakfast?"

He turned his head a couple of degrees, checked his watch, then went back to his covergirls. "It's too late for *lunch*."

"Oh. Sorry." Yeah, sorry for bothering him in his excruciatingly important work. "Is there a supermarket nearby?"

"On the corner, four blocks that way." He pointed without lifting his eyes from the magazine.

I stopped at a café for a muffin and coffee, then made my way to the supermarket. Basket in hand, I meandered down the aisles. What did I need?

My old life, that's what. And it wasn't on any of these shelves so looking was pointless. Everything was just pointless.

"Stop it," I muttered. "*Stop* it."

A toddler regarded me with solemn eyes. "Dop it," she mimicked.

"What are you looking at?" I snapped.

Her eyes filled with big gloopy tears and she began to wail.

I looked down at her, stricken. What kind of monster was I? I dropped to my knees in front of the wee girl. "I'm sorry, honey. I didn't mean to scare you."

But when I reached out to hug her, she shrank back, crying louder.

A woman raced up and, giving me a look that would've shrivelled Darth Vader, whisked the toddler away.

I stared down at the linoleum tiles, ridden with self-loathing. That wee girl was scared of me, her mother thought I was some kind of kiddie predator, and as for me, I now felt like a freak. An over-emotional, out-of-control, gotta-take-a-chill-pill freak.

Maybe I really was going mad. I'd had better days, certainly. But did wanting to cry for a week make me mad? If I could just let rip and have a good old losing-it moment, I might be able to get it all out of my system—but only a madwoman would *want* to lose it. Only a complete nutter would consider the pros and cons before they *had* their moment. The more I considered it, the glummer I grew. It was true: I'd gone to the dark side. The mad side.

I straightened, staring sightlessly at the shelves. Maybe I really was mad. I felt perfectly normal—but that's probably what all the crazies said. Well, I didn't want to be whipped away by any men in white coats, so I'd better make like normal.

I took a rallying breath and pasted a shopping-and-loving-it expression on my face. Then focused properly on my surroundings and saw I was in the confectionary aisle. My eyes locked on a familiar red packet. Maltezers. I felt a pang of homesickness. What I'd give for a Maltezer-tossing competition with Jim right now. We could be mad together.

I picked up a pack and jiggled it wistfully, dropped it in my basket. Kept walking. Then turned back and grabbed two more packs. I'd send them to Jim for Christmas. They were personal and funny; he'd love them. But I'd better post them today or he wouldn't get them in time.

I emerged from the shop some twenty minutes later with two bulging supermarket bags. Looked down at my hands, surprised. How strange. Had I bought that much?

"Hey! That's shoplifting, lady!"

I turned for a glimpse of the thief and screamed as a burly guy in uniform grabbed my arm, twisting it painfully behind my back. I dropped a bag. The contents splattered on the footpath.

"Don't even think about it," he snarled.

I blinked. Think about what? Thinking wasn't my strong-point today.

"Either you pay or we prosecute. Let's go." He frog-marched me back inside.

"But—my groceries," I wailed, struggling. They'd be gone in five seconds if I left them out there.

"You mean *our* groceries."

Panic gurgled in my gut. "I—"

Realisation, a heavy gavel-strike, left me winded. He was right. I hadn't paid.

I started to speak, to apologise, to sort out the misunderstanding, but the security guard wasn't programmed to listen.

Into the shop we went, watched avidly by a crowd of shoppers. I hung my head, mortified. The guard marched me up a rickety set of stairs to the manager's office, knocked on the door and shoved me in.

"Shoplifter," he barked then shut the door and stood behind me, his very presence threatening.

The manager looked up at me across his desk and narrowed his eyes.

My lip trembled. "I'm not a shoplifter."

"Did you pay?"

"Well, no. But . . ." I stammered to a halt under the manager's steely gaze. Shifted uncomfortably.

"I didn't *intend* to not pay," I said miserably.

"Do you know how many times I've heard that excuse, Miss?"

Tears banked up, ready to spill. My chin trembled. "I'm not a criminal. Please. It was a simple mistake. Just let me pay and let me go."

His eyes bored into mine. "We are within our rights to prosecute, you know."

Prosecution? I broke out in a sweat. My pulse accelerated. Prison? Suddenly I needed to pee.

"W-why? I've said I'll pay. I'm happy to pay. I want to pay." My voice rose. "My life's bad enough without you adding your ten p' into the mix."

I turned to go and banged into Burly Boy. Tears burst forth.

"Let me pay!" I shrieked, feeling like I was drowning.

Oh God. Here it came. The full-throttled, freaking-madwoman psychotic moment, and now it was here I really, really, really didn't want to have it. I blundered past him and shot down the stairs, sobbing loudly. Returned to my checkout counter, pushed in front of the other shoppers, gesticulated wildly in front of the operator. "How much do I owe?"

She looked nervous. "I'll just check."

I took fifty quid out of my wallet and threw it on the counter.

White-faced and trembling, she took the notes, rang up the transaction and gave me my change. "Have a nice day," she whispered.

I stared at her, stupefied. Have a nice *day*?

I rearranged my features into a quasi-dignified expression, did the walk of shame out of the shop, retrieved my miraculously untouched shopping bags and escaped the scene of my crime.

CHAPTER THIRTY-THREE

Christmas Day.

I woke in a foul mood. For a while I tossed and turned, but sleep eluded me. So I lay there, scowling at the ceiling and resenting the day, my mood, life.

I'd lost my man, my career, and my dignity. And, as if that wasn't enough, now I had to face Christmas alone.

I didn't want to be missing my family, but I did. Mum, Dad, even Dani. This would be the first Christmas I'd spent without them.

Not that I'd ever enjoyed our Christmas Day Eating-fests. Stuffing our faces as if we hadn't eaten in a month. Eating like we had no off-switch, here's to Santa, have another chocolate; eat-eat-eating until I felt like a big blubbery ball of misappropriated gastro-waste.

But Christmas was *Christmas*. Somehow, it just didn't seem right to spend it alone. Perhaps if I just heard their voices . . .

I sat up, reached for my mobile and dialled home.

"Mer-ry Christmas! Ho ho ho!" The voice chimed.

My knees went weak. I sat abruptly on the bed. Maybe not *that* voice. "Dani. Hi."

There was an audible sucking-in of breath.

"Um . . ." I floundered. "Merry Christmas."

Why had I rung? *Why?*

Dani hesitated one, two, three long seconds before saying, "I'll get Mum."

Which was about the shortest sentence she'd ever said to me since coming out of the womb. Clearly my popularity hadn't increased.

"Darling?"

"Hi Mum," I said, trying to sound jolly. "Merry Christmas."

"Merry Christmas to you, too, darling." She blew a kiss down the phone. "What a shame you're not here. You should see the tree. It's our best ever."

I smiled in spite of myself. She said that every year.

"But I think I over-fed the Christmas cake." Then, "No, George, not that plate. Use the *good* one, with the gilt edging." She tut-tutted. "Your father doesn't have a clue. Honestly, if I died he would be at a complete loss."

She said that every year, too. I felt suddenly tearful.

"If only you were here, darling. *You* know which plates to use. Oh dear." She raised her voice. "Not that one, George. The other one. For goodness sake." She exhaled. "Here, talk to your father while I sort out the plates."

Dad's voice came down the line. "Hello, love."

"Hi, Dad. Merry Christmas." I choked on the last word.

"Is it?" He chuckled. "I'm just keeping out of everyone's way. You know me. Now, what's this nonsense with you and your sister?"

"Um . . ." A bad liar at the best of times, I couldn't even attempt it with Dad.

"B, a word of advice. This too will blow over."

I wiped away a tear.

"Your sister's very . . . dramatic."

In the background Mum shrilled, "George! The meat needs carving."

Suddenly desperate for the call to be over, I said, "You'd better go. I love you."

"Love you, too, dear. Here's your mother."

"No, Dad, I—"

"Rebecca, we so miss not having you here at Christmas. Why don't you catch a pla—"

"Mum," I interrupted. "I've got to go. Sorry. My phone's about to die." I rushed my words. "Love you. 'Bye."

I ended the call and ran a weary hand over my face.

For a moment I stood statue-still, taking in my room. My silent, cheerless room. No presents, no tree, no tinsel and baubles, no cute little Santas.

A thread of icy air whistled through a gap in the window, catching my solitary Christmas card. It fluttered from the sill and landed face-down on the floor. I went and picked it up, re-read it.

To Becky, Love from Becky, xx

And how pathetic was that? I carefully set it back on the windowsill, then furiously snatched it up and shoved it in the bin.

I powered off the phone. Forget Christmas. Forget the bloody Christmas calls. Let the world celebrate without me. I was over it.

* * *

As dusk fell I roused myself from bed and went out, walking randomly through the back streets of Edinburgh.

My mobile weighed heavily in my pocket, a constant reminder of everything—everyone—that wasn't in my life. I finally gave in and turned it on. Several voicemails immediately announced themselves.

First message: Jim's voice, gruff but friendly, hoping I was having a good day, thanking me for the maltezers, challenging me to a toss-off in the New Year, and cackling at his creative vulgarity.

Second message: what *was* that racket? A yowling cat? I listened to the message again. It *was* a yowling cat. Jules. Oh no! What was Jim doing to my cat? Bastard.

Third message: Jim again, this time in cat falsetto, wishing me a Purry Christmas and hoping I was having a *meow* of a time because he sure wasn't and he couldn't believe I'd abandoned him with that psycho cat-killer Jim.

I smiled. Jim's offbeat humour hadn't changed. I'd routinely cursed his anti-social manner and slovenly habits for years, yet now I missed it. Our friendship, our daily companionship, our fun.

Fourth message: a tone-deaf rendition of *We Wish You A Merry Christmas*, unmistakeably Liz. I leaned against a brick wall and returned her call. "Liz?"

"Hey, Becs. Merry Christmas."

"Yeah, you too." I could barely hear her. "Where are you? Sounds like you're partying in the underground."

"Similar," she bellowed. "It's a basement party."

Liz at a party? "That's so not your thing."

"Tell me about it. I'll escape soon. If I can find the exit," she added. "It's swarming with people, standing room only. You'd love it."

"Yeah, until I got claustrophobic."

She laughed. "True. Here's Sal."

"Hi, Sal."

"Hi Luv." I imagined her leaning in to Liz, best friends sharing the call. "Had a good day?"

"Quiet." A fresh pang of homesickness hit me. "I wish I was down there with you guys. It's pretty sad up here."

"What did you expect?" Liz yelled.

I *humpf*ed.

Liz shut a door, muffling the background din. "Becs, shifting cities is hard. I did warn you."

And she thought I wanted an I-told-you-so lecture? I bit back my snarl. "I couldn't stay in London, Liz. Not with things the way they were."

"We'll never agree on that. But you're in Edinburgh now, so best you find a way to make it work."

"Gee, thanks for the sympathy."

It was okay for her: she was still in London doing a job she loved, and surrounded by friends and family and total familiarity. She had no idea what it was like up here, living out of a suitcase, eating cold meals and takeaways, spending Christmas alone, and not a single friend to my name.

"You know what?" Her voice sharpened. "You can't have it both ways. Make the move and mean it, or come back home. Either way, stop whining and sort yourself out."

Fuck.

I stared blindly ahead.

Fuck.

I blinked. Took a great shuddering breath and tried to make sense of what she'd said and how I felt. Couldn't get past the fact that Liz, my greatest advocate, my rock, had just told me off like I was a pesky little kid.

"Fine," I said into the silence. "I didn't mean to bore you."

"You didn't bore me. I just—"

"Merry Christmas, then," I said in a small voice.

"Stop it, Becs!"

"I've got to go, now." And I meant it. If I didn't hang up right now she'd hear me crying or vomiting or choking or whatever it was my body was about to do.

"I'll ring you tomorrow. I miss you."

Yeah, whatever.

Then my phone played its godforsaken over-cheerful you've-got-a-message music and a text from Charlie appeared on-screen. *Xmas shag outa qestn?* With a god-damn wide-mouthed smiley face.

As if. I should never have turned on my bloody phone. Everyone was so full of festive freaking cheer. And the one person I really wanted to hear from hadn't even bothered to ring.

Not that I'd really expected him to.

Well, he could get fucked, too. I hurled my phone with venom. It flew across the street, hit a fence and dropped into the snow.

Good-*bye*.

CHAPTER THIRTY-FOUR

"Stop whining and sort out your life."

Fine. I'd sort it. No problem, Liz. I'd just been through a major life crisis *and* spent the festive season alone *and* shifted to a completely new *country*—but not to worry, I had the message loud and clear. Loud and crystal clear. No holidays allowed. No R&R. No taking time out to mend an aching heart. Just get a job, fast.

Honestly, the way she went on, anyone would think I was an emotional wreck.

I'd show her.

I hauled on my coat and strode out. Internet access, that's what I needed. And a new friend. I marched grimly along, watch-out-world-here-I-come, searching for an internet café.

Aha. Found one. I looked in through the steamed-up window. Excellent. A free table. I dived inside and sat down before anyone else could take it. Mmm. Those pancakes at the next table looked good. I ordered a stack and wolfed them down, defiant then greedy and, eventually, sick. Why, why, why did I always over-eat when I felt down?

I waddled to a computer, typed 'Edinburgh jobs' and waited for *Google* to do its thing. Stared wide-eyed as about thirty pages of results popped up. Gosh. Now what? I clicked on the first result and a fill-the-blanks page appeared. Oh dear. So many questions. What kind of work? What city? What suburb? Full-time or part-time? Permanent or temporary? Keywords to narrow my search? Other options?

I bit my lip. What did I want? Another lecturing job? No. Never again. It would be a constant reminder of how much I'd messed up back home. Everything I'd had, everything I'd lost. My great career . . . Matt . . .

Stop it! I stared at the screen, gritted my teeth and keyed in 'immediate start'. Scrolled through the results.

Postie? No—needed to know Edinburgh.

Hairstylist? No—needed hairdressing qualifications.

Legal advisor? No—needed degree, qual's, experience, and a fancy car, too, I bet.

Apprentice Baker? Hmm. But did I really want to be a) a baker, b) on apprenticeship wages, and c) starting that early each day? No, no and no.

I leaned back in my chair and fumed. I wasn't fussy. I just wanted a job. Fast. Before Liz had another go at me.

Ooh! How about a Recruitment Agency? Let *them* find a job for me.

I headed back out into the chill, found a payphone and flicked through the Yellow Pages. There. Recruitment Agencies. With a furtive look left and right I ripped out the pages and pocketed them.

See? I really was a low-down criminal.

* * *

The woman, fifty-something and terrifyingly professional in her black no-nonsense suit, looked at me over the top of her black no-nonsense glasses. "Well. You've had a"—she coughed gently—"varied career path."

Was that a compliment or an insult? I made do with a faint smile. "I took a few . . . interim jobs while I waited for the right opening."

"Hmm."

She wasn't buying it. I tried again. "When I was travelling I picked up work where and when I could. But my travels were critical training for the roles I took in travel and then lecturing. Without those short-term jobs funding my training, I couldn't have achieved what I have in my career."

And what had I achieved, exactly? I brushed the thought aside and gave her a confident smile.

This time she rewarded me with a slight inclination of her head. "I expect we'll be able to place you. If you could fill in this form"—she passed it across the desk—"we'll carry out our checks."

"Fine."

I glanced down at it. Date of birth. Current address. Prior address. Qualifications. Work references. Personal references. Drivers licence.

Next of kin. Marital status. Number of dependents. Gosh, everything except the colour of my panties.

"You should hear from us by . . ." She paused to consult a desktop calendar. ". . . early in the New Year."

"In the New *Year*?" By then I'd be down to my last quid.

"Yes. Processing takes longer over Christmas."

"Can't you just, you know, take me on spec?"

Her eyebrows shot up into her black no-nonsense fringe. "Oh dear me, no. Our clients rely on us to vet all personnel *very* carefully." She cleared her throat. "Firstline Solutions prides itself on maintaining excellent standards at all times."

My spirits plummeted.

"Oh. Of course." I stood. "Well, I'll look forward to hearing from you. Eventually."

She compressed her lips at me, then dismissed me with a downward glance. "Indeed."

Frosty bitch. I took the tiny lift downstairs, regretting it as soon as the doors closed. Lift. Claustrophobia. Matt. No! Think about something else. Um . . .

Jobs. One thing was sure: if I wanted a job through Firstline Solutions I'd be waiting a very long time.

Well, they weren't the only agency in town. The lift doors opened and I escaped out into fresh air. There, see? I was fine. No claustrophobia. Nothing major, anyway. I pulled the torn pages from my pocket, chose three other agencies at random, then started another payphone search. If only I'd just switched my mobile off instead of throwing it away. Talk about stupid.

Eventually I found a payphone and five minutes later had three appointments lined up. Stick that up your hoity-toity backside, Dragon Lady.

That called for a celebration. I headed back to the café and, cappuccino ordered, sat down to read one of their newspapers. Death, destruction and economic misery monopolised the front page. I opted for the horoscopes.

A waitress stopped at the next table. "Hey, Scott. What's up?"

"The usual." I liked the way his eyes crinkled at the corners as he smiled. "Caffeine fix while I try to sort my life."

Ditto at my table. I listened in, pretending to be absorbed in my horoscope.

"Poor you," she said. "What is it this time?"

"Work. One of the girls has left us in the lurch. Gone. No notice. Not even so much as a phone call." He ran his hands through his hair. "Today, of all days. How on earth do I find a replacement at such short notice?"

I straightened in my chair. Quickly re-read my horoscope in case I shouldn't be tempted. Because this was fate at its best. All I had to do was speak up.

"Ring a temping agency?" she suggested.

He shrugged. "In our line of work we don't get too many volunteers."

What line of work was that? How bad could it be?

She grinned. "Yeah. Hardly surprising. And don't look at me, Scott, 'cause the answer's a big fat 'No'."

Okay, it must be bad. Exterminating rats? Unblocking sewerage pipes? Infiltrating drug rings?

He laughed. "Damn. You were my last shot."

She moved to the next table. "Get to work. You're late, you're the boss, and you're a man down."

My heart beat faster. I'd watched *Fear Factor* countless times. I could kill rats. I could stick my arm in raw sewerage. Drug rings might be a bit intense but, hey, if the money was good . . .

Suddenly nervous, I stood and walked over to Scott's table. "Er— excuse me."

Then, when he looked up, "I'm looking for work. I'll fill in for you."

He opened his mobile phone, dialled a number, held it to his ear. "I don't think so."

What exactly was that supposed to mean? Cheeky bastard!

"Come on." I disguised my irritation with a winning smile. "You need a worker, I need work. Everybody wins."

He regarded me steadily, then closed his phone and looked out the window, rat-a-tatting his fingers on the table.

Long seconds went by.

Just as I decided I'd made a big enough fool of myself, his fingers stilled. "You'll do anything?"

I shrugged. "If you pay me."

Careful, Becs. What if he ran a massage parlour?

Abruptly he stood. "Fine, then. As of now you're a window cleaner." He took one last gulp of his coffee and stood. "Let's go."

He strode out of the café.

I scrambled for my things and followed him. Was that all he'd been stressing about? An AWOL window cleaner? Anyone could do windows. They were a doss compared with the Jim-ified bathroom and kitchen horrors I'd dealt with over the years.

Actually, I had a trick or two up my sleeve. Vinegar. And newspaper. Tips from Grandma. I'd show him. I'd be the best damn window cleaner he'd ever clapped eyes on.

Until I found another job, of course.

I trotted to keep up. "Should I go home and get changed?"

He shook his head. "We've got protective gear."

"Protective gear?" It sounded like he was about to throw me down a mine shaft.

He saw my expression. "Get wet in this weather," he clarified, "and you'll freeze to death."

Oh. True.

A few minutes later we stopped in front of a building.

Shops! Fantastic! To our left, a designer clothing store and, to our right, a jewellery shop. Both reeked of exclusive. I grinned. He wanted me to clean *these* shop windows? No problem-o. I could check out the latest catwalk creations. Maybe even spot someone famous.

"Right," he said. "It's this building. We'll go out back and get organised while the boys set up the equipment."

Equipment? Oh, right. Like buckets and hoses and stuff.

He unlocked the store-room and rifled through a filing cabinet. "Have you done window cleaning before?"

"Yes."

"The full range?"

Range? Grandma's windows had been the bane of my life. Leadlights, fanlights, louver windows . . . even that awful, impossible-to-clean, bubbly bathroom glass. Yep, I'd cleaned the full range, all right. I nodded.

He pulled out a form. "Low-rise and high-rise?"

Oh. Different range. He meant technique. Side-to-side versus up-and-down. Thank goodness for Grandma and her housekeeping lessons.

I smiled. "Yes. Been there, done that."

He raised both eyebrows. "Really? Guess it's my lucky day. You'll need to sign this." He handed me the form.

I scanned the pages. Gosh. A full-on questionnaire. High blood pressure? Seizures? Dizziness? I ticked all the 'no' boxes, signed at the bottom and gave it back to him.

He took his time checking over my responses then nodded. Grinned at me then tossed a pair of waterproof overalls my way. Glanced at my high street boots then selected some wellies.

"Get those on," he said.

A moment later a pair of gloves landed at my feet. Then protective glasses. "Some of the lads use them, some won't touch them. Up to you."

Overalls half on, I gaped at the glasses. Laughter bubbled up inside me. Did he think we were on a sci-fi movie set? A giggle escaped.

Scott eyeballed me and I quickly looked down, stifling my mirth. Zipped up my overalls.

"Come on." He marched out.

I grabbed the gloves and hurried after him, leaving the glasses on the ground. No way was I wearing them, especially in front of those high-end window displays.

As we reached the street an Arctic blast sliced at me, so cold it brought tears to my eyes. I shivered, glad of the overalls. He turned to face the gorgeous windows. I did the same.

"So," I said, business-like. "Inside and out?"

"Yep. Inside and out. Eighty windows."

Eighty? *Eighty?*

"O-kaaay. Where are the oth—"

He looked skywards and I stopped. Followed his gaze. Felt the colour drain from my cheeks. Oh crap. Crappety crappety *crap.*

Suspended in mid-air, hanging by a couple of lengths of string, swung a rectangular bucket-type arrangement. In the bucket stood an overalled figure, scrubbing at the window as if it were at ground level.

At Scott's yell the figure turned, looked down at us, waved. The bucket swayed.

My stomach turned. *This* was my window cleaning job?

Eighty windows, and only four of them could be cleaned with my feet on the ground.

CHAPTER THIRTY-FIVE

Scott waved back and beckoned him down, then turned to me with a knowing grin, a grin that knew precisely what sort of window cleaning I'd done, a grin that dared me to do my usual and run away.

I gulped and tried to steady my breathing. The bucket slowly descended until it reached the ground beside us.

Scott stepped forward. "Danny, great news. I've found us a replacement. This is . . ." He checked my form. ". . . Becky."

Danny took off a glove and held out his hand. "Hi, Becky. Gid tae hae ye wi' us."

Huh? It sounded like another language. I shook his hand and smiled weakly. "Hi. I'm just filling in."

"Yes," said Scott. "We're grateful. Danny will show you the ropes. So to speak." His lips twitched. Mine trembled. "Still keen?"

"Of course." I *refused* to be scared. This was like a theme park ride, only I didn't have to pay and I got to ride all day. Thousands of people would leap at the chance.

Though probably not until mid-summer.

And probably not dressed like a circus sideshow.

I clambered into the bucket and Danny steadied me. "Ready?"

Whatever. I nodded. If we plummeted to the earth in a bone-shattering mess, at least it'd be quick.

This probably counted as a good alternative to that high-wire activity at the Kinetix Centre. From where I stood, the high-wires suddenly seemed rather appealing.

We started gliding upwards. Would Matt attend my funeral? Would he grieve over my mushed-beyond-recognition body? Would he wonder 'what if' for the rest of his life?

I suddenly realised Danny was speaking. "Sorry?"

He repeated something in gobbledegook and I squinted at him, frowning. "Could you say that again please, slowly?"

He chuckled. "Sorry, hen. I'm from Dundee," he said in perfect English. "Up the road a ways. How long have you been doing high-rises?"

I swallowed. "Actually, this is my first."

"Eh?" His eyes threatened to pop out of their sockets. "You're joking."

I shook my head.

"You've had training, though, right?"

I shook my head.

His face reddened. "You *haven't?*"

I shook my head.

"None? Not even the safety stuff?"

I bit my lip, shook my head yet again.

He pushed a button and brought the bucket to a swinging halt. "And Scott kens it?"

"He, um, might have guessed." I knew full well he'd guessed. I'd seen the expression on his face. I'd heard the challenge in his words. He'd guessed, all right, the bastard.

"Then what the hell's he daein'?" he demanded, his accent rapidly thickening. "Christ! If ye die up here, it's *my* ba's on the line."

Seriously, if I died up here I had more than his ba's, whatever they were, to worry about.

"I think he was playing a joke on me," I offered.

"On me, mair like," he muttered. He leaned over the edge of the bucket and roared, "Scott!"

Scott turned and waved.

"What ye givin' me a fuckin' virgin for?" he yelled.

Sadly, I understood that too darn well. As did half of Edinburgh, who now thought I was a thirty-something sexual novice. Just kill me now.

Scott grinned. "Is she?"

Danny shook his fist at Scott. Then, wiping a hand over his face, he turned back to me. Hesitated.

I waited.

He chuckled. "Guess you're doing the inside windows, then."

We began our descent.

"Guess I am," I said, more relieved than disappointed.

"Nice trip?" Scott asked as we reached the ground.

I felt played. "Short and sweet."

"Sorry, Dan." Scott gave him a playful punch. "Couldn't resist it."

Danny shook his head. "I bet. Give me a bit of warning next time, eh?"

"Not likely!" Scott turned to me. "Why did you tell me you'd done high-rises?"

"I thought you meant . . ." I trailed off. Looked down at my feet; the feet of the most stupid person on the planet. I couldn't tell him what I'd thought: he'd laugh himself into next week.

"Don't worry." He waved a dismissive hand. "I worked it out from the form."

I looked up at him sharply. "Why'd you send me up there, then?"

He shrugged. "Pay-back." With a grin for Dan, he expanded with, "Dan's a bit of a practical joker. He deserved a fright."

"Hey, no problem. Any time you want to play a joke on someone, just feel free to dress me up like a clown and parade me around in mid-air." I folded my arms and glared at him. "I hope I'm getting paid for this, pal."

He winked. "I'll do better than that. I'll give you a full day's work, plus a bonus for the mid-air thing. Sound fair?"

More than fair, actually. I unfolded my arms and smiled.

"We really are short-staffed, as you know. But I can't have you doing high-rise work. Health and safety. You'll have to stay inside." Then, to Dan, "Paulie can run the inside team. I'll join you on the high-rise stuff."

Danny nodded, clamping a cigarette between his lips.

I shot Danny a smile. "Thanks for the joyride."

He lit his cigarette, inhaled deeply. "Nae problem, hen," he said through a smoky exhalation, his accent back to full strength. "Next time, don't wait 'til the fourth floor to give me heart failure."

* * *

"Thanks." I pocketed the cash Scott proffered. "I enjoyed today."

Surprisingly, I had. Grandma would be amazed.

"That's good," said Scott. "You were a great help."

He saw my scepticism. "No, really. I mean it."

I acknowledged his words with a shy smile. "Do you need me tomorrow?"

"If you're available, yes. I've advertised for a high-rise worker but it'll take a couple of weeks to get a replacement."

"Okay. I don't have anything else yet, so I'm happy to help out." I shrugged on my coat.

Scott pulled a bag of sweets out of his pocket.

I stared at it, mesmerised. Jim's maltezers.

"You want some?" He jangled the bag my way.

"Thanks."

I took a couple and, before I'd even thought about it, tossed one up in the air. My heart rate cranked up, as if it were Jim beside me instead of Scott. Come on. This time, please. Just let me catch the stupid thing in my mouth and prove I wasn't a complete waste of genetics.

Down it came, closer, closer. I was right underneath it, watching, waiting, ready for it, all lined up . . .

It ricocheted off my lip. I blushed. "Rats."

I should just ring Jim and be done with it. Less embarrassing.

"Unlucky," said Scott.

Yeah, that was me all over.

"Want another one?" he asked.

I shook my head. Pulled on my hat and gloves. Changed the subject. "Is it hard to find high-rise workers?"

"Sometimes. Mid-winter's always tough."

"And if you don't find anyone?"

"Well, then I guess we look at training someone."

"Oh." I shoved my hands in my pockets. Thought about it. "Is it hard?"

He grinned. "Not if you're a rock climber."

My heart tripped. Matt was a rock climber. Which didn't make much sense, given his fear of heights. Except, knowing him, the fear was probably exactly why he did it. To test himself, force himself outside his comfort zone.

Pity he hadn't done that with me.

Scott was still speaking. "You've got to be pretty confident with heights, of course. Are you offering?"

Who, me? Make like Spiderman? My laugh sounded brittle. "No. Fat chance."

* * *

I craned my neck and watched the climbing instructor scale the wall. He made it look so easy, but I wasn't fooled. That was high.

Not that the height bothered me. What bothered me was my weight. How could I possibly hang on to that sheer face by my fingertips, supporting my entire body?

He abseiled down and landed gracefully beside me. "Your turn."

I hitched at my safety harness. It felt awkward and uncomfortable and I just *knew* it turned my legs and butt into squashed-up sausage-meat. Maybe this wasn't such a good idea.

"You'll be fine," he said.

Would I? Climbing a sheer face for the simple joy of touching a circle of paint at the top, entrusting my life to a flimsy scrap of rope? Madness.

About as mad as getting sucked in by Scott's *'Are you offering?'*.

But one thing was certain: I shouldn't even consider high-rise window cleaning if I couldn't attempt this piddly little wall.

I looked up again. What on earth possessed people to do this stuff?

"We'll take it real slow," he reassured me. "One hold at a time."

I looked at him, harnessed up and every bit the rugged hot male, and felt a fresh wave of embarrassment. What must he think when he saw the likes of me, all squidgy untoned thigh, squeezing into a harness and throwing myself at a wall?

I knew what I thought: I'd done it the wrong way round. I needed to get fit first, *then* try climbing. Maybe I should start swimming again.

Only then I'd have to get back in the water.

"Okay," he said, aiming for Instructor Of The Year, "watch carefully. You're going to do this"—he demonstrated—"then this, then this . . ." His hands and feet moved in total synch, and within a micro-second his whole body was higher than my head.

I stared up at him, amazed.

He grinned then leapt down from the wall, landing with feline grace beside me. "Ready?"

No. "Sure."

I attempted a smile, wiped clammy hands down my T-shirt, then experimentally grasped a jutting bit of rock.

"Nice. Now, where are you going to put your foot? And think about your other hand, too."

Cripes. Move *and* think? I bit my lip.

He pointed to a couple of handhold options. "Try those."

I did.

"Great work!"

What, with one foot still grounded? Imagine his excitement if I actually gained height.

I took a deep breath and held on tight. Lifted the other foot and toe-tapped the wall until I found purchase.

"Awesome! Don't look down. Look up and find your next holds."

Don't look down, don't look down.

I looked up, found a hold, whipped my left hand out. My body slipped. Heart pounding, I grabbed the rock and clung there, limpet-like.

Don't look down, don't look down.

"You're doing just fine."

He reminded me so much of Matt. Matt used just this tone, just this manner, with his College and Kinetix students. Matt had a gift for getting the best out of people. This guy wasn't bad, either.

"Now move your foot."

I found another foothold. Then realised what I'd done: I'd *found* another *foothold*. Far out! I was climbing the wall!

I wanted to shriek and yell and leap around, but then I'd land in a very un-cool heap at my hot instructor's feet so I focused on the task. Hand, foot, hand, foot, don't look down.

"Keep close to the wall. Your backside, too."

Charming. His butt was taut, toned, and rather deliciously Matt-like. Mine was rather more . . . sticky-out-y.

"I've got a sway back," I called out.

"Doesn't make any difference."

He would say that.

If only Matt could see me now. We could've gone rock climbing together. Travelled to exotic rock climbing destinations. Had rock climbing babies.

My arms began to shake with the strain. "Okay, tired now."

"Let go, then. I'll lower you down."

Let go? I broke out in a sweat. "Are you sure it's safe?"

I glanced down and immediately regretted it.

He grinned. "Guess you'll find out." Then, "Yes, it's safe. Lean backwards, the way I taught you. I'll do the rest."

I let go of the rock, transferring my grip to the rope. Then, with a silent prayer, I leaned backwards.

Panic ripped through me, every nerve in my body screaming that this was all wrong, pain was imminent, death was certain—and as he gently lowered me groundwards it took a couple of seconds to register that, actually, this felt great. I was weightless, free, a bird on a downdraft.

"Well done," he said. "Want another go?"

"Sure. Just let me catch my breath."

I clenched and unclenched my hands a few times to get the blood flowing, then we did it all again. The downward trip was just as exciting second time round.

Maybe high-rise windows were an option, after all. Spiderwoman meets Sadie The Cleaning Lady. Yes. Why not?

The instructor looked at his watch. "Time's up. I've got another booking, but I'll pair you up with someone if you want to keep going."

"Not today, thanks." I grimaced. "I'm not as fit as I used to be."

"Sure. Best not to overdo it." He unclipped my harness from the rope. "You're a natural, you know. Have you done this before?"

Oh *please*. Who was he kidding?

"No. The closest I've got is listening to my"—How should I describe Matt?—"er, workmate talk about it. He's a big rock climber."

"Yeah?"

I nodded. "He lectures Recreational Tourism. Runs a weekend confidence course for disadvantaged kids." Matt's pride and joy. I'd wanted to show him I could conquer that high-wire challenge. No chance of that now.

"Really? Where's that?"

"Down in Surrey."

He drew his brows together. "You mean the Kinetix Centre?"

"Yes." I looked at him, surprised.

One side of his mouth tugged up. "I know Matt Frobisher."

CHAPTER THIRTY-SIX

My heart thudded hard and fast. "You do?"

My climbing instructor nodded. "I worked down south for a while. Helped him set up the Kinetix Centre. Small world, eh?"

"Yes." Too small. We headed back to reception.

"How's Matt doing these days? He had it pretty rough for a while there."

Fresh adrenalin kicked through my body. What was he about to say?

"Mmm," I said, *über*-casual.

"What kind of mother does that? I couldn't believe it."

"Me neither." My mind raced. What exactly had his mother done?

"Sure, Matt had left home, but what about his little brother? The kid was totally dependent on her and she just took off."

"Cerebral palsy," I murmured. Cripes. Had Matt's mother *abandoned* Stef?

He shot me a speculative look. "Matt doesn't tell many people about Stef. You must know him well."

I didn't answer. Did I know Matt well? I'd thought so—until Dublin. Then I'd changed my mind. And now—now I was just plain confused.

We reached the front desk.

"Back when I knew him," the instructor continued, "he held down a full-time job and cared for his brother. Wouldn't have been my choice." He shrugged. "I was too busy screwing everything that moved, but that was the last thing on Matt's mind."

"His father had died." My throat constricted. "It was down to Matt."

"Yeah. At least, that's how he saw it. He got guardianship in the end, but he had to really fight for it. You've got to respect a guy who puts family first like that."

The R-word ricocheted around my brain. How did I feel about

respect and Matt? I watched the instructor slip out of his harness.

He looked up at me. "Did he ever get together with anyone?"

My heart staccatoed in my chest. I ducked my flaming face, ignored the question and busied myself with my own harness.

"Matt deserves a good woman."

I yanked desperately at the harness straps. God-damn boa constrictor.

"Here. You need to loosen it here"—he reached around me and showed me how—"and here."

"Thanks." Avoiding his eyes, I stepped out of the harness. "I'd better go. I'm late."

* * *

I sat in the cab, jaw clenched. He could've told me he didn't do trust, didn't do love. He could've told me I'd have to fight his demons as well as my own.

But he hadn't. Matt had strung me along then cut me loose when there was a bit of work involved.

Hell, if he'd valued what we had the least he could've done was stop to ask a few questions.

Maybe that was the point. Maybe he hadn't valued what we had. Maybe, deep down, he hadn't really believed in us. If he'd really believed in us he would've made more of an effort, right?

Well, screw him. I had the rest of my life to live and I was better off without Matt and all his baggage.

"Baggage?" bleated a pesky little voice in my head. *"Look who's talking, Sunshine."*

I told the voice to shut up, but it kept taunting me.

"Think you're any better? How much of an effort did you make?"

"He couldn't trust his mum. Why would he trust you more?"

I chewed on a nail. Forced myself to stop. Looked out the window, saw nothing but Matt's cold, cold eyes.

"Are you just going to sit there and sulk, or are you going to sort it out?"

I looked down at my hands, thought about my miserable new life up here.

Had I tried hard enough with Matt? Really?

"What street is it, again?" The cabbie eyed me in the rear-vision mirror.

"Here." I handed him the scrap of paper. "I'm looking at them all. You choose."

He glanced at the list, nodded. "Right."

Flats to view: three. Likelihood of success: nil. They'd probably all be awful—but what if I liked one? I folded the address list into the tiniest square, unfolded it, did it all again. Should I sign up? Commit to a long-term lease?

But that sounded . . . permanent. Did I really want to settle in Edinburgh? What about Matt?

Number one was nightmarish. I took in the ripped curtains, holes in walls, ancient stove. Politely declined.

Number two reeked of—what? Urine? Something chemical? Maybe living out of a suitcase wasn't so bad.

Number three had potential. It was big enough that I wouldn't feel cramped, small enough that I wouldn't feel lost, and cheap enough that I wouldn't feel bankrupt. I bit my lip. Tried to imagine myself living there. Could. I bit my lip harder.

"Well?" the agent prompted. "What do you think?"

On the downside, it looked grubby. Worse-than-Jim grubby. Nothing a good scrub wouldn't fix, though.

"I like it, but . . ."

Was I scrubbing Matt out of my life too soon?

"It will, of course, be professionally cleaned when the current tenants leave."

"Ah." I eyed up the kitchen. Shuddered. Would a professional clean be enough? And, cleaned or not, would this ever be home?

The agent must have sensed my indecision. "If you're interested, I suggest you sign up now. I have five more clients viewing today and, as you know, flats of this quality are extremely hard to find. Oh." She glanced out the window. "There's the next couple."

My shoulders sagged. "Fine. I'll take it."

* * *

"Hi—Scott? Hi, it's Becky Jordan here. I'd like to apply for your high-rise job."

Silence.

I suppressed a nervous giggle. I'd expected surprise, yes; but not speechlessness.

He cleared his throat. "You would?"

"Well, I'd like to do the training, at least, and see how I go. You don't have to pay me until I prove myself."

"Well. We'd love to have you." He hesitated. "I have to warn you, though. Physically, it's fairly demanding."

"Yeah, I figured that. My fitness regime starts tomorrow."

"Listen, if you're serious about this—"

"Oh, I am." More than he knew, because this was me taking a stand, restarting my life, truly meaning it.

"Well, we can probably arrange part-time work for you until your training's complete. No high-rise stuff, obviously, but there's plenty of other work."

"Really? Brilliant!"

"The pay's not great, but it'll keep you fed. And no more practical jokes," he added. "I promise."

* * *

I pulled my swimming bag out of the wardrobe and the familiar chlorine smell wafted up. A knot of fear twisted in my gut. The choking, the drowning, the panic—I could feel it all, as if it were yesterday. A peaceful way to go? No way. Not for me.

Come on. It would be fine. It'd be a swim, not a death sentence. Millions of people swam every day without getting killed. I could, too.

But . . .

No buts. Time to flick the finger at this ridiculous fear.

I drew back the curtains. Fresh snow had blanketed the ground overnight. And—no. *Not* a good excuse, Becs. Get on with it. Go swimming.

Right. I wrapped up warm, tramped down my five flights of stairs— which, thankfully, I wouldn't have to suffer much longer—and through the snow to the local leisure centre. Made it as far as the changing rooms and sat on a bench, shaking so hard I couldn't even unzip my bag.

271

Okay, then. Not today. Maybe tomorrow.

The next morning I woke feeling nauseous. Not today either, then. Funny how the nausea disappeared as soon as I let myself off the hook.

Okay, maybe swimming wasn't a great idea. I'd never really enjoyed it, anyway. I *definitely* didn't enjoy the early mornings, and there were plenty of other ways to get fit. Jogging wouldn't cost a penny. And I could join a gym, or take Pilates. Yes. Pilates and jogging. Good idea.

I pulled on leggings and a big curve-covering t-shirt, then dusted off my trainers. Enough procrastinating. Time to get fit, fast.

* * *

I let myself into my new flat and paused at the threshold, smiling. Home. Finally. Then I stepped inside and my smile dissolved.

Something wasn't right.

They couldn't call this fully furnished. Surely.

Had they switched the furniture on me? It hadn't looked like this when I'd viewed the place. Look at those living room chairs! Rickety hard-backed things straight out of Tom Brown's schooldays. Functional, but I bet they fell well short on comfort.

I walked through to the bedroom. Joy. Saggy bed syndrome. Eyes peeled now for every inadequacy, I stalked around the flat with increasing anger. Carpet: stained. Curtains: didn't meet in the middle. Kitchenette: filthy sink, cupboards to match. I picked up a random glass and stared, dismayed, at the crusty red wine dregs. Even Jim had better standards than this.

I squared my shoulders. Fine. Whatever. My flat was grim. It matched my life.

Come on, was it really that bad? Uninhabited houses always looked grim. Remember how bad my room back home had looked when it was empty. I just needed to move in.

And spend a week or two cleaning.

Or maybe I should give up, go back to London, and try to work it out with Matt. Because that's what I kept imagining myself doing.

No. This was nuts. I'd done the hard stuff. No more looking back. Time to look forward. Time to clean.

Cleaning was good for the soul, right?

I wasn't convinced. Maybe a relaxing cup of coffee would help. I fossicked through kitchen cupboards until I found a mug.

Dirty.

So was the next one, and the next.

Okay, I'd wash the dishes—every last one—and *then* I'd have a coffee. I ran the hot water.

Hot water?

No hot water.

I ran the tap a bit longer. Really? No hot water? I turned to the stove-top and frantically fiddled with switches.

Please, no. No gas? No blasted gas? I raced through to the hall and turned the heater on. *Aarrgh!* No blasted *fucking* gas. My chin wobbled. Pig-useless bloody gasman. I'd given them plenty of notice. Plenty.

I bit down on my lip until pain stifled the chin-wobble, then lifted the phone. Thank God. A dial tone. At least British Telecom had done their bit. I punched in the number and asked the stupid, *useless* gas company when they were planning on connecting my gas.

"I'm sorry, Ma'am," said the sales rep, not half as sorry as me. "I'll just bring up your details."

Piped music shrilled in my ear. By the time she'd found my details I had a headache.

"I'm sorry, Ma'am," she repeated. "It seems there's been a misunderstanding."

My headache strengthened.

"Misunderstanding?" My voice rose an octave. "How can 'please connect my gas' be misunderstood?"

"I'm sorry, Ma'am. It'll be seen to within the next twenty-four hours. I'm afraid that's the best we can do."

Perfect. A whole day without heating. In January. I slammed the phone into the cradle. A piece of plastic pinged out onto the floor.

I stared at it, aghast. If my phone no longer worked, so help me, I'd . . .

I'd what? Ring BT and complain? Return to London?

* * *

An icy-cold shower the next morning clinched it. I couldn't hurry the gas company but there were other things about my new home I could change. The bed, for starters. I needed one that wouldn't give me backache or bites—both of which I'd acquired overnight. I also needed a heater. Not to mention comfy chairs.

And that was just the start of my shopping list because, dammit, if I was going to make this my home I wanted a few creature comforts around me.

I took a trip to the *Ikea* store, strode around as if I owned the place, and drew up a long list of must-haves. Tossed in a few what-the-hell extras. Then marched up to a counter and slapped the list down.

"I need all of these," I informed the startled shop assistant, and whipped out my credit card. "Put it all on this. Oh, and I'll take same-day delivery, thanks."

"Um." He ran his eyes down the list. "I'm not sure we'll manage a delivery of this size today. Will tomorrow do?"

First the gas, and now my furniture?

My shoulders sagged. "I suppose so. But if you can manage it today"—I fluttered my eyelashes at him—"I'd be ever so grateful. I'm trying to transform a hovel into a home."

Truthfully, I wasn't sure my flat would ever feel like home, but I had to try. It was the only home I had.

CHAPTER THIRTY-SEVEN

I woke with a start. What was wrong? I lay there, heart pounding, every sense alert.

Rap-a-rap.

I glanced at the bedside clock—eight o'clock—then staggered out of bed to answer the door.

"Who is it?" I opened the door a smidgeon, put an eye to the gap. "Liz?"

I flung the door wide, grinning like an idiot. "Liz! What are you doing here?"

"Waiting for you to invite me in." She stamped her feet, shivering. "It's arctic out here."

"Oh! Sorry." I stepped aside so she could enter.

She thrust a box at me then made a beeline for the nearest heater.

"Thanks. What's this?" The weight shifted in my hands and I looked at her, eyes shining, heart full, knowing exactly what was inside.

"It's a peace offering," she said, twisting her hands together. "I was a bitch. Sorry."

"Don't be. You said what I needed to hear." Only as I said it did I realise it was true. "I didn't like it, but you were being a good friend. An honest one."

She smiled. Her hands relaxed. "Go on, then, open it."

I peeked inside the box. "Jules!"

One very miffed cat emitted a how-could-you-incarcerate-me-like-that meow and climbed out. With a disdainful glance my way, he stalked off towards my bedroom, stopping every few feet to sniff warily.

I grabbed Liz in a bear hug. "Thanks so much."

She hugged me back. We stepped apart and stood looking at each other a moment. I wiped away a tear, reached out for another quick hug,

275

then went and busied myself in the kitchenette. "Coffee?"

"Please. Strong. That overnighter's a killer."

I poured some milk into a saucer. "Jules! Puss-puss-puss."

He was instantly at my side, all grievances forgotten.

We took our steaming mugs and settled in the living room.

"How's your restructure going?" I asked.

Liz took her time answering, her hand smoothing the arm of her chair, up and down, up and down. She finally met my eyes. "It's tough. That's the other reason I'm here. I needed a break."

I studied her face, the tension in her mouth, the smudges beneath her eyes. Poor thing. The sooner this restructure was done and dusted, the better.

"I don't know how you do it," I said, and I meant it. I could never hand people their redundancy notices, offering a tissue and a back pat as their world crumbled. No wonder Liz looked stressed. "Is your own job safe?"

She sighed, leaned her head against the back of the chair. "I think so. Head office isn't affected as much as the branches. Jim says hi," she added, with the most unsubtle subject change ever.

I played along. "How is he?"

"Painful. Turns every conversation into something about sex."

No change there, then.

"And the house should be condemned." She shook her head, disgusted. "The way he lives? It's just not healthy."

I smiled. He sounded just fine.

"He needs a house-mate. Someone to keep him human."

"He hasn't got one yet?"

"No. But your bed and drawers are still there. And that chair by the window. And your computer desk."

Rats. I'd put them out of my mind. It was probably my fault he didn't have a new house-mate. "I'd better ring him."

"And you've left a bunch of things at my place, too, remember?" She watched me closely. "When were you planning on moving it all up here, anyway?"

Remnants from my old life? I hesitated. Shrugged. "I don't know. Maybe I'll give it to Jim."

"Jim?" She snorted. "He'll just let it rot. I can sort through it all for you if you want."

"No," I said, too quickly.

Her eyebrows shot up.

"I'll do it soon." I felt defensive. "Maybe in spring."

"Spring's almost here."

"Summer, then."

She gave me a look full of pity, and a sudden blast of anger surged through me.

"Stop it!" I wanted to scream. *"Stop analysing me!"*

I knew it was nuts and I needed to just toughen up and get on with it—but it was hard, okay? What I didn't need was her or anyone else putting pressure on me. And if she told me to see a counsellor . . . I braced myself.

"Any news on the job front?" she asked.

I breathed again. This I could cope with. "Actually, yes."

"That's brilliant. What are you doing?"

"I still can't believe it's happening, but . . . well, I've just signed on as a window cleaner."

Her jaw dropped. Her eyes bulged. I giggled.

"You what?"

I nodded, keeping my face straight. "First I've got to do the training. No guarantees I'll pass, either. It's really tough."

Her eyes narrowed. "You're having a laugh, right?"

"No. God's truth. I'm training to be a window cleaner." A grin burst onto my face.

"A window cleaner."

"A *high-rise* window cleaner."

"High-rise?" she repeated faintly.

I shrugged. "New life, new job."

"Right . . ."

Silence. Then, "Is it dangerous?"

"Is driving dangerous?"

"You don't hang in mid-air when you're driving."

"You don't share the road with drunks and psychos when you're cleaning high-rises."

"I guess." She didn't sound convinced. "Won't you miss lecturing?"

"The people, maybe." One in particular. A lump burned my throat.

"Sal really misses you," she said.

Wrong person.

I chewed at a fingernail. Caught myself and stopped. "You didn't tell her the real reason I left, did you?"

"No, but I should've." Liz's eyes were accusing. "She was really upset when she asked after your gran."

"You didn't say Gran was . . ." I trailed off, shredded the nail.

"Dead and buried? Yes."

I groaned.

"What was I meant to say, Becs? Sal asked how she was. I didn't know you'd fed her a pack of lies."

"Why else do you think she'd be asking after my dead grandmother?"

"Don't worry, I didn't blow your cover. She thinks you've been organising funerals and stuff."

"Thank you," I breathed.

She took her empty cup out to the kitchenette. "Becs, why make it so complicated? Why not just tell her the truth?"

"I couldn't. Imagine if everyone knew I'd been sleeping with the boss." I drained my coffee. "Think of the shame. I'd die."

"Why? You've left. It doesn't matter."

It mattered to me.

"What else is new, then?" I kept my voice light. "Any gossip?"

For a moment she said nothing, regarding me steadily. I blinked to break the contact.

"No gossip," she said. "The restructure continues. People hate me. Ooh!" Her face lit up. "Sal was telling me about—what's her name? Melissa? . . . you worked with her at Beacon Travel."

"Alyssa?"

"That's it. She turned up at T&T a couple of times."

"Why? Oh." I nodded, recalling our conversation in Dublin. "She fancies her chances as a Rec. Tourism lecturer. Can't see it, myself."

"Actually, she was after your old job." Liz sat down, gave me a quizzical look. "I thought you knew that. You were one of her referees."

I frowned. "That's news to me."

"Oh? Sal says Alyssa says you two are like that." She crossed her fingers.

"As if I'd referee for her. They'd be mad to employ her."

Liz chuckled. "I gather Sal wasn't impressed."

"Can you believe that? Alyssa spoke to me at Conference. You'd think she'd ask before she used me as a referee."

"Alyssa went to Conference, did she? That'll be where she met him, then."

"Who?"

Realisation dawned. My face blanched.

"Who do you think?"

My hearing went haywire. Her voice zoomed in and out, loud, louder, *louder*, until she was booming the words out at earsplitting level; then, just as quickly, back through mid-volume towards mouse-quiet, until she was barely discernible.

"Come on, have a guess," she said, the volume increasing again so that *'guess'* resounded in my skull with rock concert power.

No. This was so wrong. How could he have chosen Alyssa, of all people?

Liz waited expectantly.

I couldn't say his name. *Please* don't make me say his name. I gulped for air, feeling breathless, sick, trapped.

She opened her mouth to speak, and I tensed for the bullet-thump of his name into my heart.

"Charlie Hollingworth."

The air whooshed out of me. My jaw sagged. I slumped into the back of the chair.

"Charlie?"

Liz clapped her hands, delighted. "Yes! Small world. He knows you, apparently."

My thoughts were drowning in syrupy goo. "Um, yes. He does."

"Sal says Alyssa was like the cat that got the cream. Told Sal way too much about Charlie's bedroom technique."

My lips stretched into a slow smile, a smile that grew, widening and widening until it threatened to leap off my face and dance around the room. Then a giggle escaped. Just a tiny giggle; barely audible. But the one that followed was definitely audible. And the one after that was actually quite loud. Giggles became guffaws and I gave in to a long-overdue belly laugh, flailing around like a madwoman in my chair, almost hysterical with it all and totally unable to stop. Liz's bewildered expression just made things worse.

Eventually I subsided into relative silence.

"Was it something I said?" Liz asked.

"Yes." I clamped down hard on another giggle. Massaged my aching cheeks.

"What's so funny about his bedroom technique?"

I grinned. "Nothing. His bedroom technique's just fine."

She raised her eyebrows and I shrugged. "We had a wee fling. He's good fun. Just . . ."

". . . not for you?" she finished.

I smiled. "No."

Then stopped, surprised. Was that *affection* I felt for Charlie? After so many years loathing him liked chopped liver, to suddenly catch myself thinking of him in more . . . *steak pie* terms was disconcerting. Yet refreshing. See? Big-girl panties moment: I'd finally moved on.

"Alyssa's probably perfect for him, though," I said.

"Then what's so funny?"

"Nothing." I giggled again. "I just thought, when you talked about Alyssa hooking up with some guy—"

I stopped. Suddenly it wasn't the slightest bit funny. I gulped. Took a breath and tried again.

"I wasn't expecting it to be Charlie. I thought you meant she and . . ." My throat closed around his name.

"Matt."

I bit my lip, nodded.

"Becs," she said, her voice gentle, "why don't you just pick up the phone and ring him?"

She watched me. I felt like a frog about to be dissected.

"It'll be Valentines Day in a couple of weeks," she added.

As if I needed her reminding me of that.

I shook my head vigorously. "No. No way. I can't. It has to be a clean break or—"

"Or what? You'll still miss him?"

"I don't," I flared. "Not one bit. I'm better off without him and his god-damn baggage."

One of her eyebrows tweaked upwards. "Except you don't think that."

For long moments neither of us spoke.

"We all have baggage, Becs."

I inspected my coffee mug. "I met someone who knows him. Said Matt brought up his little brother when their mum took off."

"Yeah? That's pretty amazing."

I met her gaze. "Why couldn't he tell me that? It's important."

"Is it?" She shrugged. "Maybe he didn't want you pigeonholing him."

"I didn't. But that's exactly what he did to me."

"And if you talk to him you'll be able to sort that out. Ring him."

She made it sound so easy. I felt nauseous.

"No." I leapt to my feet. "I've been the fool too many times, Liz. I'm not going to do it again. If he'd wanted to sort anything out with me, he'd have done it long ago." My voice broke on the last word.

"Okay." Liz got out of her chair and gave me a hug. "You have to do it your way. But I think you're nuts."

CHAPTER THIRTY-EIGHT

I made my way to the end of the pool, dead woman walking.

Hands to my neck in a self-protective gesture, I stood and stared down at the water. My throat felt dry. I sipped at my water bottle but it made no difference.

Come on. I needed to stop overthinking this. It was all in my head. This was just water. This was just a swim. Everything would be okay. I needed to face my demon head-on if I was going to conquer the fear.

Today. Now. This minute.

All I had to do was get in.

A corset of fear constricted my chest. I tried to breathe deep and slow. Failed. Fear churned in my belly.

I should've let Liz come with me.

I approached the ladder and took a hold of the rails. My teeth chattered. My breathing came in tight little pants. I inched my way down, clinging to the ladder, and eventually stood waist-deep in the tepid water.

There. That wasn't so bad, was it?

I backed myself against the end of the pool and looked down the lane. Oh God. What if I'd forgotten how to swim? What if I collided with—

No. Stop it. I knew how to swim and I wouldn't collide with anything. There was only one other swimmer in my lane, and they weren't doing butterfly.

I waited until my lane-mate touched the far end of the pool. Then, with a deep breath and quick prayer, I pushed off. My body protested but soon remembered what it was supposed to do. Rhythmic arms, rhythmic legs, easy did it. And before I knew it I'd reached the familiar halfway mark. No panic attack, no collision, not even a misjudged inhalation.

But where was that other swimmer? I lifted my head briefly, couldn't see them, glanced behind me and saw they'd already passed by. Excellent. I had the rest of the lane to myself. I relaxed, and my in-breaths immediately became less forced.

I reached the other end and hugged the wall. Thank God. After several gasping breaths I turned and scanned the leisure centre. Nobody was watching, nobody stared. I was just another goggled swimmer doing a routine swim. I grinned to myself. I'd done it!

I couldn't wait to share my news with Liz. If only I'd let her swim with me, we could be sharing my victory. But—no. It had been important for me to do this on my own.

As with a few other demons I needed to face.

I forced myself through ten laps then leapt out, full of euphoric energy. Sauntered back to the changing rooms, then jumped up and down like a maniac.

"Yes!" I punched the air. "Yes, yes, *yes!*" I laughed as it echoed around the deserted room.

An elderly woman tottered out of a toilet cubicle and eyed me with interest. "Was it a Lottery win, dear?"

"It feels like it," I said with a sheepish smile. Then dressed in double-quick time and fast-walked out to the café, looking for Liz.

There she was, over by the window. She turned and waited, a pensive expression on her face. I gave her a thumbs-up and the biggest grin. She stood, threw her arms in the air, and whooped as if her football team had just won the decider.

Still grinning, I dodged chairs and kids and coffees to reach her. *"I DID IT!"*

"Becs, I'm so proud of you."

She hugged me, and I squeezed her tight. "I'm proud of me, too. It was hell-scary, though."

"I bet. But you know what? It'll never be that scary again."

We ordered our usual—trim decaf for Liz and full-fat caffeine-maxed for me—then sat and watched people coming and going. My sense of satisfaction lingered.

I met Liz's eye and grinned again. "It's funny. Swimming's been such a bogey for me and suddenly it's a big nothing. Already I feel like 'why did I avoid swimming so long?'"

"I guess you had to do it in your own time." She paused. Sipped at her coffee. Made a show of placing the cup on its saucer with just-so precision. "Anything else you might be rethinking?"

"Like?"

She shrugged, made a moue, gazed off around the café.

I narrowed my eyes at her. "You mean Matt."

"Don't you think it's time?"

"No I d—" I stopped. If I could face my fear of death, for crying out loud, surely I could face Matt as well.

Couldn't I?

I inhaled. Thought about it. Exhaled.

"Go on," said Liz. "Ring him. You know you want to."

No. I couldn't do something that big over the phone. What if he simply hung up, didn't let me get past 'hello'?

"I think I'd have to speak to him face to face."

"So come down and visit. Speak to him face-to-face. Then you'll know."

My pulse fluttered in my throat. Was I ready to know?

But even if I wasn't, I'd wasted too many tears over Matt. Liz was right. This nagging feeling of unfinished business wasn't helping me get on with my life. I needed it finished.

A lifetime with Matt at my side would have been heavenly, but I could cope without him. I'd shown myself that. And now I'd beaten the swimming pool. I wouldn't let fear cripple me again.

No more running away. It was time to face up to Matt. And while I was at it, I may as well face up to my sister, too.

* * *

"It's been terrific seeing you again." I gave Liz one last hug. "Say hi to Sal for me."

"Will do. Take care. And get a new phone, for goodness sake. You have my numbers?"

I patted my pocket. "Yes, Mum."

She grinned. "Ring Matt."

I rolled my eyes at her. "Uh-nuh."

She got on the bus. "Or find another man," she called.

Yeah, and look where that had got me. I was still dealing with Charlie fall-out.

"Find one yourself," I said. Like that would happen. She was so into her work she'd never find time for a man.

Liz settled in her seat.

"Book a holiday," I yelled through the window at her.

We blew kisses at each other, the bus blew a black cloud of fumes at me, and then it was just me and a couple of homeless guys hunkering down for the night.

I walked on to my own bus-stop, feeling very lonely. Which was crazy; she'd only been here four days.

The N26 pulled up as I approached the bus-stop. With a wave and yell, I ran the last few metres and onto the bus. "Thanks."

The driver grunted, hefted the steering wheel, and we pulled away from the kerb.

I paid and staggered into a seat, staring out into darkness. The rocking motion of the bus soon lulled me into a half-doze and I closed my eyes, leaning against the window. I couldn't wait to be tucked up in bed with Jules warming my feet.

My head jarred against the glass as we pulled into another stop. I opened my eyes, watching a couple disembark. Not long until my stop.

We merged back into the traffic and brakes shrieked close behind us. I idly wondered who had been at fault. At the next stop the bus braked with such force I had to brace my arm against the seat in front. Behind me a guy swore. The bus sped up then abruptly decelerated. I pitched forward again. Idiot driver. What was he playing at?

We flew along Roseburn Terrace, faster and faster, our headlights slashing left and right. A pedestrian dived out of the way.

Unbelievable. I'd so be making a complaint.

We took the bend and the bus swerved wildly left and right. Upstairs, people screamed. Left, right, left, and we went into a sideways skid. My heart pounded. The brakes hollered like constipated geese. The wheels thumped against a kerb. My body tensed. Up and down the bus people bounced like pins in a bowling alley. I clung to the seat railing with a white-knuckled grip.

For a moment all was still. Then, like a great tree felled, the bus began to topple.

Everything slowed. I lost my footing . . . screamed . . . scrabbled for purchase . . . landed heavily on my side. Pain in my arm. Blood in my mouth. Twenty degrees, thirty. More screams.

I cowered in the foetal position, crammed between a seat and a window. *Fuck.* This was it. I was going to die. No closure with Matt. No forgiveness from Dani. I'd made such a mess of my life, and now it was too late.

Forty degrees, fifty, sixty. I braced against the seat. This would hurt. Please let me be brave. Here it came . . . any second now . . .

A hard, sharp jolt as we hit the ground. My head walloped against the window. On its side, the bus slewed across the icy road. My senses went into overdrive. The chilling graunch of metal against asphalt. The god-awful stench of burning rubber. The crack and tinkle of breaking glass. Shrieking brakes, blaring horns. Bile in my throat.

Every bump in the road jarred against my spine until, finally, we shuddered to a stop.

Silence.

Interior lights flickered.

My heart beat like a jackhammer in my chest. What next? I waited, but—nothing.

Someone moaned. Glass tinkled.

Everything hurt: my side, my arm, my neck, my back.

A baby wailed.

I moved my head a fraction, looked around. God, what a mess. I lay in a maze of crumpled metal. Above me, the window had crazed into a giant cobweb, refracting the light from the streetlamp in, gosh, quite a beautiful way.

But what if all that glass shattered on top of me? And that seat, just hanging there, directly above my head—what if that fell?

I didn't want to die. Not like this.

As people began to move, other noises filtered through. Grunts, groans, the odd shout. I eased myself to my knees. Gasped. Lifted one knee and brushed away a fragment of glass.

Good grief, so much glass. Glass at my feet. Glass on my clothes. Glass on the seats. I touched a hand to my hair. Even in my hair. Glass bloody everywhere.

What was that smell? Diesel. Oh *fuck*. I had to get out of here. *Now.*

286

Before the bus exploded. I moved into a crouching position, my breath coming in short gasps. Something brushed against my face and I ducked back, horrified. Reached out a tentative hand and realised it was dangling wires. Whipped my hand back, heart racing. Were they live?

Did it matter? I might survive an electric shock, but if I didn't get out of here I'd spend next Christmas in a burns unit. Or a box.

Breathe. I needed to breathe. But my chest felt tight, too tight. So deathly tight it was the lift all over again.

"Relax," said my brain. "Breathe in-two-three, out-two-three."

"SCREW relaxed!" shrieked my body. "You're trapped in a mushed-up bus!"

The urge to take triple in-breaths was too strong. I gave in, then immediately regretted it as I began to hyperventilate.

Stop it! Stop. It.

Further down the bus a woman wailed in a high-pitched monotone. "No . . . no . . . no . . . no . . ."

Shite, what was she no-ing at? What could she see, hear, feel? I gasped for air, increasingly dizzy.

I had to fight it. I had to stay conscious, or I'd never make it out of here. What would Matt tell me to do?

Okay, breathe slowly in, breathe slowly out, very slowly in, very slowly out . . .

"No . . . no . . ."

Inhale, exhale . . . I found myself breathing in time to her cries and that flimsy thread of human connection helped me regain control. Gradually my breathing became more measured.

Up and down the bus, people were making an ever-increasing racket as they lumbered around. Groaning, crying, shouting. Behind me a woman swore at top volume. A few rows up, a man sobbed for his mum. Outside, in the street, more yelling. Every sound reverberated in my ears. I couldn't think. Would everyone just shut up?

Out. I needed out. Which way? I cast my eyes left and right, disoriented. Tried to quell the panic as it rose. Where were the doors?

Oh. Above me. I looked up at the nearest one. Closed. But some of the windows had lost their glass; their frames would be plenty big enough for me to get through.

But—too high. I'd never reach them up there.

"Where's the emergency exit?" someone yelled.

"Here," came the reply. "Top deck."

"The stairs!" a guy shouted. "Quick!"

People pushed and shoved, stampeding towards the stairwell. I joined the flow, until someone jostled me and I lost my footing, landing on my backside in a heap of broken glass. Uncaring, they trampled over my legs. I crab-shuffled out of the way, slicing my hands in glass.

Blood oozed. I looked down at it, then quickly away. I would *not* faint. I would *not* get hysterical—or even upset. It wasn't bad. Little nicks, that's all. Nothing serious.

Passengers blundered past me like panicked sheep. I looked back down at my hands. Crap. More blood. Maybe it *was* serious. And what about that pain in my elbow? It seemed to be getting worse. Fear blocked my throat. I gulped it down.

Could I move my fingers? Yes? Okay. I breathed in, then released it super-slowly through my mouth. Everything was under control. I was fine. We were fine. Everything was fine, fine, fine.

Fucked-up, insecure, neurotic, emotional. F.I.N.E.

In the background the bus continued to idle. Wasn't that dangerous? Shouldn't the driver turn off the engine, in case it caught fire?

God, no, please don't let me burn to death. Searing my finger against a pan was bad enough—but over every inch of my body? And prolonged, excruciatingly intense? I retched at the thought. It would be undiluted agony.

I carefully stood and, trying to hurry without hurrying, moved towards the stairs. Ducked to avoid a low-hanging sheet of ragged metal. Why had I chosen *this* bus, with *this* driver?

Where was he, anyway? Selfish prick. I bet he'd snuck out through some secret little driver exit and left us all to fend for ourselves.

Just wait until I got out of here. I'd make sure he got the sack.

If I got out of here.

I made it to the stairwell, glanced behind me and realised I was lucky last. Joy. If we went up in fireworks it'd be my limbs they found plastered all over the lower deck.

I was about to climb through to the top when I heard it. A sound. Something animal. Long and low, halfway between a zombie groan and a toddler gagging on their greens.

Was it human? Or—my stomach dropped. Maybe it was rats, sniffing out the blood and coming to eat me alive.

"Hello?" I wobbled.

There it went again. That couldn't be rats. It had to be human. I cocked my head, listening. "Are you okay?"

Stupid question. They'd be talking if they were okay.

"*Grr-hkkk . . .*"

I swung round, all senses trained towards the front of the bus. Nothing, nobody. Where were they? It wasn't my imagination. Someone was definitely there. Yet, with the driver's cab dominating the space, I could see every nook.

Every nook except the cab itself.

The driver. It must be the driver.

And if he thought I was going to wait around for him when he'd caused this mess . . .

I turned towards the stairs, away from the sound. Then stopped. How would I feel if it were me trapped in there? If he died could I live with myself, knowing I walked away? I closed my eyes, wishing I was a cold-hearted bitch with no compassion and even less conscience.

But I wasn't, dammit. I opened my eyes, looked forward. A quick check, then. It would take seconds, and then I'd leave. I'd leave and find help.

CHAPTER THIRTY-NINE

With the bus on its side, the only way I'd get a closer view of the cab would be to shimmy along the stairwell wall. I heaved myself up onto the wall, cursing my restricted movement in skinny jeans, then crawled along until I was looking down through the bandit screen.

There he was. My breath hitched in my throat. He lay in a mess of broken window, his head accentuated by a halo of blood. Thin grey stubble stood out in stark relief against the blue-white pallor of his skin. Was he still breathing? I couldn't tell.

Grief, the *blood*. My head felt tight with sudden pressure. My eyes swam.

Do not faint. Do *not* faint. I looked away and concentrated on breathing. Waited for my eyes to return to normal then refocused on him.

"Hey," I called, "are you alive?"

His eyes opened and he stared up at me. I jumped, squeaked with fright, then felt a surge of relief. He wasn't dead.

"How do I get in?" I asked.

With one arm he reached laboriously skywards, towards the screen. There must be a latch in there but I couldn't even see it, let alone reach it. He'd have to do it for me.

"That's it, you can do it."

His outstretched fingers approached the unseen latch. I waited, heart in mouth. He winced in sudden pain and his arm dropped to his chest. I winced in sympathy, my mind racing with a myriad of possible medical conditions, none of which I knew a thing about and all of which scared the bejeezus out of me.

After some heavy breathing he looked up at me and shook his head. "Aunt."

Aunt?

Oh—*can't*. So I'd have to break in. But how? The screen must be reinforced; it was taking my full weight. I shuffled onto my backside and kicked at it with my heels. No joy; my heels just bounced.

"Don't worry," I said. "Help is coming."

Which seemed pretty inadequate for a guy lying in a pool of his own blood. Especially since I didn't know if it was true.

His eyes fluttered closed and my pulse raced. Now what? Was he dying? Catching a quick nap? Praying?

I looked longingly at the stairs. Maybe I should go. There wasn't much I could do here. The fact was, I was a claustrophobe who didn't much like dealing with blood, looking down on a bleeding man in a crushed bus that might explode into flames any second. It didn't get much worse.

I glanced back at him and his eyes were open, watching me. They looked sad, like he knew I would leave.

Well? Was I going or staying? I looked up at the night sky and knew the answer.

Why couldn't someone else have stopped for him? Why did it have to be me?

I took a deep breath and yelled loud enough to wake the neighbourhood. "Driver's hurt! We need help, fast."

Then, to him, "Hang in there, okay? I'll stay with you."

I couldn't hold his hand so I placed my hand palm-down, fingers spread, on the glass.

He gave a barely perceptible nod, mouthed, "Thanks." His hand splayed at his side, mimicking mine.

I smiled down at him but his eyes had already lost focus.

No! He needed to stay conscious. Um . . . Didn't he?

Well, sure. That's what happened in the movies.

And was I really so retarded I had to draw on what I'd seen in the bloody movies?

Apparently, yes. Nothing else sprang to mind.

I bit my lip, not liking this one bit. "Is someone waiting at home for you?"

He blinked, frowned, blinked again, as if to clear his head.

"Your wife?" Come on, Mister, concentrate.

He gave a slow nod.

"Well, you just keep thinking about her. You'll be out of here soon." I bloody hoped so, because I wasn't sure how long I could keep up this cup-half-full talk.

I closed my eyes and said a quick prayer. It couldn't hurt. When I looked back down at the driver, he was straining to reach a black control panel near the steering wheel.

"What are you doing?"

He didn't reply. His face turned puce with effort as he closed his fingers around a raised switch. Pain cut deep grooves in his face as he ponderously turned the switch anti-clockwise. The bus shuddered and the engine cut.

An eery silence filled the space.

"Well done," I said. As if he needed a cheerleader.

The driver didn't respond. He lay there, still—too still—his hand on the switch.

Panic tore at my gut.

"Hey!" I thumped the screen. "Don't you die! Don't you dare die!"

His fingers twitched.

I released the breath I'd been holding. Thank you, God.

Inch by laborious inch, he felt his way along the panel towards another switch.

Abruptly, the lights cut.

My pulse skittered along like a frightened rabbit. What had he done?

Now our only light came from a nearby lamp-post. I could barely make him out. Down the bus, the obstacle course of twisted metal had become a maze of ghostly shapes and long, foreign shadows. I felt like an extra in a Stephen King movie. Fear would probably kill me if nothing else did.

"I can hardly see you," I said, trying to keep it conversational but desperate to keep him talking, for me as much as him.

No reply.

"Hello? Are you awake?"

Still nothing. If only my arm were long enough to reach through the coin window and shake him. "I need you to talk to me. Please. Come on, open your eyes. Look at me. Say something."

He mumbled.

"Good. Hang in there. They'll be here soon."

They'd better be.

"My . . . wife. Tell . . ." He struggled to keep his eyes open.

"Tell her what?"

"Love . . ." His eyelids fell over his eyes, like a curtain falling at the end of a show.

"Tell her yourself." Then, louder, "Hey! You're going to be fine."

He didn't respond.

My hands felt clammy. I didn't want to watch him die. It was bad enough watching him hurt. Anyway, wasn't someone meant to read him his last rites if he was dying? I had no idea how they went, and I sure didn't want to ruin his death for him, so he couldn't die now and that was that.

Wasn't hearing the last sense to go? What could I say that would bring him back?

"The paramedics are here." A lie, but only a tiny one, said with the best of intentions.

And then I really did hear sirens approaching. I didn't know whether to laugh or cry, but for once I was really, *really* happy the cosmos had turned my lie into a truth.

Several heavy, truck-sized vehicles pulled up, followed by lighter ones—cars? Ambulances? Doors slammed. People shouted.

"They're here," I repeated, then stood and waved wildly through the windscreen. "In here! Help!"

Weighty objects met the ground with hard thuds, metal clanged on metal, something was winched, *prrcht-prrcht-prrcht*, then more shouted instructions, a throbbing pulse of hammering . . . What was happening? I felt disoriented.

Light blazed on me. I blinked, shielded my eyes, then looked up as footsteps sounded on the vehicle above me. A man stood looking down on me, framed in the window, every bit the mad scientist. All he needed was the spaceship and evil laugh.

"Are you okay?" he asked through his heavy-duty face-mask. Why was he wearing that? Was the air contaminated? Was *I* contaminated?

"Yes, I'm okay. But the driver—he's in the cab. I can't get to him." I swallowed a sob. "I hope he's still alive."

He lowered a ladder through the window and a moment later was standing beside me. "Let's get you out of here. Up you go." He pointed. "My pal's waiting for you at the top."

Another man waved down at me.

"Go on. We'll sort out the driver."

"Will he be okay?" I asked.

"We'll know more once we get to him. Best you climb out now. You're doing great," he added, as if encouraging a child.

He moved off through the wreckage, checking for people. I grasped a rung, my tremors shaking the whole ladder. I looked skyward. How would I ever make it up?

The guy at the top must have seen my expression. "Here, I'll help you," he said and scooted down.

"Thanks." I swiped away tears. What I'd give for a familiar face right now.

"You go first. I'll follow behind. Hold the ladder, that's it. Start climbing. Don't worry, I'm right here. You won't fall. A few more steps . . ."

And then we were there.

A third rescuer helped me off the ladder.

"Thanks," I whispered, feeling like the only kid in class who couldn't remember the alphabet.

She guided me down a second ladder and finally my feet were on solid ground. A blanket appeared around my shoulders.

I gazed about, bewildered and frightened. It looked like I'd climbed into an episode of CSI. Flashing lights, red and blue; loads of uniformed, stern-faced people shouting at each other; walky-talky radios and vehicle radios, all going at once; stretchers and medical supplies; limping, bloodied people; traffic banking up. And, underpinning it all, the constant bass thrum of the fire-fighters' emergency vehicle.

Tape neatly cordoned off the scene from the inevitable crowd of rubberneckers, who strained for a view of—what? Blood? Injuries? Death?

But this was no TV show. This was real. This was my bus trip home. I looked back at it, and my teeth started chattering.

A policewoman approached me, notebook in hand. "Can you tell me your name, Ma'am?"

"R-Rebecca Jordan. I'm t-tired. Could someone t-take me home, please?"

I really didn't want to be here. I wanted to ring my parents, hug Liz, laugh with Jim, put things right with Dani . . . but most of all, I wanted to see Matt. My heart ached. I didn't just want to see him. I wanted to touch him, speak to him, hold him.

Love him.

I swallowed back a burning ball of heartbreak.

"Are you feeling any pain?" the policewoman asked.

Yes. Everywhere. It hadn't eased in months.

I shook my head.

"Is there anyone we can call for you?"

Hope flared in my chest. "To come and collect me?"

She smiled. "No. So they know you've been in an accident."

"Oh." My parents!

No, they'd be desperate to help, and powerless to do anything from down in Reading. Liz was stuck on a bus heading south. Jim? Dani? Matt?

I hugged the blanket tighter around me. "No, thanks."

The policewoman wrote briefly on a little pad then signalled to another woman, who came closer. "If you'll just come with me, we need to assess your injuries."

A giant-liquidiser noise erupted into the night air. I started, whirled around. My throat tightened. The windscreen.

"I don't need help," I said. "It's the driver you should be worrying about."

Abrupt silence. I strained to see if they'd reached him. *Please* let him live.

The paramedic gently turned me towards an ambulance. "He'll be fine. This won't take long, Ma'am."

She bathed my cut hands, using tweezers to pick out miniscule pebbles of glass. I tried not to watch. She bandaged my sprained elbow and advised me to R.I.C.E. it.

"You'll be transported to hospital soon," she said.

"Hospital? Why?"

"Standard procedure. We need to check for internal injuries."

Internal . . . ?

"And we've probably missed some of the glass. We need to make sure every last piece is removed, to avoid any complications later on."

Hurry up, then. I'd had enough complications for one lifetime.

I walked out of the ambulance and back into all that frenzied activity. Stopped. Stared around me. It all felt too over-the-top to be true. Any minute now someone would yell, "Cut."

Then some medics hurried past with a body, limp and pale, on a stretcher. Real people in a real emergency. Shockwaves rippled through my body. No actors here.

We could have died. We all could have died.

Died.

A police officer approached. "Excuse me, are you all right?"

I swallowed, breathed, nodded. I was alive. That was enough. "What about the bus driver?"

The policeman cleared his throat. "Ma'am, I'm not at liber—"

"I waited. In there." I pointed to the wreckage. "With him. *With* him. I'm claustrophobic, but I did it. So I need to know—will he live?"

He inspected his feet. Then, with an infinitesimal nod, met my eye. "It's a suspected heart attack, but yes, they think he'll live."

A heart attack? I'd been cursing him for being a lousy, inconsiderate driver, and all along he'd been having a heart attack? That poor, poor man.

"Thank you."

"Ma'am, you need to wait over here." He guided me to the area where passengers awaited transfer to hospital. "I think you should sit down for a while."

Good idea. I collapsed into a plastic chair, leaned back and closed my eyes, weary to my soul. Numb.

"Don't worry," he said. "You'll be safely home soon."

Safe, maybe—but not home. Home was all about family and friends and happiness and togetherness. Truth pierced my heart with to-the-hilt certainty: home was London, not Edinburgh.

My eyes flew open. Beautiful as Edinburgh was, this move had always been a temporary measure; a quick escape, nothing more.

I'd escaped, all right. But up here in Edinburgh I'd found me. I'd found self-belief, and the confidence to live my life for me. I finally knew what mattered. And now—I needed to go. I had bridges to build, rifts to mend, a life to live.

CHAPTER FORTY

I nervously paced the living room, listening as the phone pealed on in my ear. Three times . . . four . . . five . . . Blast! I'd stewed about this call for hours. And now I'd finally found the courage to ring, she wasn't going to even pick up?

"Hello," she said, and I jumped. "Dani Jordan speaking."

My body *zing*ed with a fresh rush of nerves. "Hi—Dani? It's Becky."

"Finally!" she exclaimed. "Where have you *been* all this time? We *so* need to talk."

"I know. That's why I'm ringing." I steeled myself. "Dan, I owe you an apology. A big one."

"Tell me about it. I've left loads of messages for you and you've ignored them all."

"What?" I tried to realign my thinking with Dani's. "Um . . . on my mobile?"

"Of course. You haven't told me your landline yet." She sounded surprised—but what had she expected, after practically disowning me?

"Oh. Sorry. I . . . I lost it. My mobile, I mean."

"Ooh, nightmare. That'd kill me. I'd have to replace it strai—"

"Dani," I interrupted.

"Remember that time my phone was on 'silent' and I couldn't find it? It drove me nuts and in the end I—"

"*Dani!*" Oops, too loud. I lowered my voice. "Sorry, but this is hard for me to do, and I just need you to be quiet for a minute so I can get this out because it's been on my mind for ages and if I don't say it now I might never manage to say it and I just can't live with this any longer, okay?"

"Er . . . okay." She sounded stunned.

"Okay. You know that Edinburgh bus crash that's been in the

297

news?"

"Ooh, yes. Wasn't it horrific? I couldn't believe—"

"I was in it."

She gasped. "Are you okay? You're not in hospital, are you? Have you told Mum and Dad? Where—"

"I'm fine. I'm resting up at home. But look. What I'm trying to say is that the accident gave me a bit of a wake-up call. Life is short. So . . ." I took a deep breath. "There are some things I need to say."

"Are you dying?"

"No." But it might be easier than this. Shut *up*, Dani!

"Dani, I don't want us to be enemies. I'm sorry I made you hate me, but you must know I'd never do anything to hurt you." I tracked up and down my living room floor. "So I'm sorry. Really, really sorry."

"What—"

"No, Dan, let me finish. You're a great sister. The best. And I love you to bits. You're my little sis and I'll always be there for you. And as for sleeping with your man, believe me, I just wouldn't go there. Ever. Surely you know that? It was an honest mistake."

I didn't give her time to respond, but ploughed on, desperate to get it all said. "But, mistake or not, I let you down and sisters aren't supposed to do that. They're supposed to be there for each other. So I'm sorry. And I understand why you said the things you said, but honestly, Dan, I'm not the person you accused me of being."

I stopped, took a deep breath in, blew out my cheeks. "So. Do you think you could meet me halfway, maybe? Agree to let bygones be bygones? 'Cause I really miss you."

She was silent a moment. "Can I speak now?"

"Sure. Your turn. Thanks for listening."

"What on *earth* are you talking about?"

"What am I—?" I pulled the phone away from my ear and looked at it, incredulous. Put it back to my ear. "Charlie, you ditz!"

"Charlie? Oh! Grief, Becky, you don't need to apologise for that. You did me a favour. I should be thanking *you*."

"Sorry?" I felt like my brain needed rewiring.

"Hell, if it hadn't been for you I might've married him. And that would've been a fast track to misery. Charlie thinks it's all about him, but he's wrong. It's all about me." She giggled. "Everyone knows that. We'd have killed each other."

I laughed. I hadn't thought of it before but, actually, she was right. "Well, I'm glad something good came out of it. But I know I hurt you, and I'm sorry."

"Sure. Great. Can we talk about me, now?"

"I thought we were."

"No, Becs. I've got news. Big news. Can you guess?"

"Um . . ." She couldn't be pregnant; she'd be crying. New man? No, that would be news, but not 'big' news. "It's something really exciting. I can hear it in your voice."

"Yep." She sounded like she might burst.

"You've got a new job. A major promotion. Partner or director or something?"

"Nope. Not even close." Her voice climbed an octave.

"Not even . . . You must be kidding. You've won the Lottery?" I ended on a shout. "*Really?*"

"No-o," she scoffed. "Way better than that."

What could be better for my I-Want-It-So-I'll-Damn-Well-Have-It sister than a multi-million-pound Lottery win? Nothing. "I give up. What's your news?"

"I'm getting married!"

"You're getting—"

"To the most gorgeous man on the planet," she squealed.

My throat closed over. My grip on the phone loosened. Matt? She was marrying *Matt*? Oh, fuck, no. Not now. Not when I'd just got my head together. Not my *sister* and *Matt*. My heart squeezed tighter and tighter. Blackness descended.

"His name's Sebastian Gauthier and I can't wait for you to meet him."

The blackness lifted, my heart released, and air surged into my lungs. I felt light-headed and floppy, like a raggedy-Ann doll.

"Married? You? I thought you thought marriage was pointless and old-fa—"

"Yes, but I hadn't met Sebi then. Becs, he's divine. I couldn't say no. Wait 'til you meet him; you'll see."

"Wow. What can I say? That's . . . fantastic, Dani," I managed. "The best news ever. Wow."

I rubbed my eyes.

"I'm thrilled for you," I added, trying to sound enthusiastic because that was what she wanted to hear. But, actually, I wasn't thrilled at all. I was big-time, big-sister worried.

How long had she known this guy? Not long; I'd only been gone four months. And she reckoned she knew him well enough to marry him? Legally link herself to him for life? This was nuts. He'd probably checked out her pay packet, sized up her apartment, and decided he was onto a good thing.

She may be hearing wedding bells, but I could see them and they were big red warning ones.

Dani let out another squeal. "You have to come home, because I want you to be my Chief Bridesmaid."

"Really?"

I felt as if I'd followed Alice down the rabbit-hole. A few minutes ago I'd been stressing about how to keep Dani on the phone long enough to finish my apology. And now she was engaged to a virtual stranger and I was Chief Bridesmaid?

"Thanks, Dan. I . . . well, I'd be honoured."

"You need to come down as soon as poss. This weekend, even, so we can organise your dress." She spoke so fast her words ran together. "Jump on a plane. I'll pay. Just do it." More squealing. "Can you believe it?"

"No. Not really."

"Love you! Thanks for ringing. Gotta go. Sebi's here. *Ciao.*"

"*Ciao,*" I said, but she'd already gone. I flicked my mobile closed and collapsed in a chair.

What?

I felt like laughing and crying all at once. I'd spent months stressing about Charlie, knowing I'd made my own sister hate me. Months consumed by guilt, wishing I could undo what I'd done. And now—*poof!* Gone. As if it never happened. The wrong—righted. The guilt—wiped.

But in its place: disquiet.

In Dani's head it was as if our rift had never been. She'd moved on. Fast. Crazy fast.

My relief and joy at having my sister back was overshadowed by concern. Dani didn't know what she was doing. This Sebi scumbag must

300

be running some kind of con. I needed to protect her.

But in one shameful, dark little corner of my mind, I wasn't sure I wanted to protect her, because I also felt a bit peeved. Peeved at the months of guilt, and soul-searching, and self-imposed exile. Peeved at all the emotional energy I'd expended, none of which had apparently been necessary. Dani, after venting her anger at me so venomously, had gone home, slept like a baby, and got on with life as if none of it had happened.

Which was just so Dani.

And just so me to pull it apart, analyse it, and put it back together all wrong.

I shoved my petty annoyance back in the cave it had come from. Enough of the self-pity. Yes, it had been a hard few months, but they hadn't killed me, and I'd learned a few lessons that would stand me in good stead.

I wiped my hands down my face. Back to the bigger issue. Dani. I needed to respect her decision to get married if that was what she really wanted.

But was it what she really wanted?

Only one way to find out. I had nothing else planned for the weekend. Guess I should pay my sister a visit.

CHAPTER FORTY-ONE

"Ladies and gentleman, we will shortly be landing at London Heathrow. Please ensure your seatbacks . . ."

I tuned out, watching the murky pall part to reveal rooftops and roads and cars and greenery. A band of tightness formed in my chest. Was I ready for this? I wiped clammy hands down my jeans.

The wheels touched, bounced, and we were on the ground, hurtling towards the end of the runway. The brakes screamed, the overhead lockers shook so hard they threatened to spew luggage all over us, then we sedately approached the terminal.

I took a rallying breath. This was it. My first weekend in London since . . .

Since Dublin. That awful, hideous, never-to-be-forgotten week.

Christmas, New Year, Valentines Day, a new home and a career change later, yet that week still caused me pain.

But here I was, for better or worse.

The 'fasten seatbelts' sign finally *ping*ed off, the doors opened, and we herded ourselves off the aircraft. People peeled off towards baggage claim. I kept walking and emerged into the Arrivals lounge.

I stood for a moment and looked around. Over there. That was where Dani had publicly disowned me. I took a couple of deep breaths to ease the pressure in my chest.

Smoggy, festering London.

Home.

"Becky!"

I turned and there was Liz, waving and grinning, pushing through the crowd towards me. She enveloped me in a hug. "You're here."

"I am. It feels a bit weird. Thanks for meeting me."

Her eyebrows spiked. "My best friend finally comes home and I'm

302

not there to meet her? Fat chance."

A wave of emotion stole my words and I had to make do with a hand-squeeze. Good old Liz. I'd always been able to count on her, and here she was, making me feel like I belonged all over again.

She took my overnight bag from me and headed us towards the car park.

"You're travelling light," she said. "Not back for long, huh?"

"Not this time. I leave on Sunday."

"But . . . maybe next time?"

I chuckled. "Or the time after."

She stopped and searched my face. "Really?"

"Yes." I grinned.

Her eyes shone. "Brilliant! When?"

"Soon. I've got to pack, give notice at work, that sort of thing."

"Can't you just cut and run?"

"No. I'm sick of doing that."

She raised an eyebrow, nodded, smiled. "Good for you."

We continued on to the car, and joined the traffic queue.

"What brings you down?" she asked. "Flat-hunting?"

"Catching up with Dani. She's asked me to be bridesmaid."

Liz gaped at me. *"Bridesmaid?"* The car pig-jumped and stalled.

I laughed. She looked every bit as astounded as I'd felt.

Liz hastily restarted the engine. "She's getting married?" Then, "Hang on. She's even speaking to you?"

"Amazing, eh?"

She blinked, frowned. "Miraculous. How did that happen?"

"I rang her. Very weird. She made like nothing had happened and suddenly I'm her bridesmaid and coming down for a fitting. But I think I'd like to check out her man while I'm here; make sure she's doing the right thing. It all seems very sudden."

"Knowing Dani, she won't be taken for a ride."

I raised an eyebrow at Liz.

She met my eye and grimaced. "Okay. You're right. You'd better check him out."

"Tomorrow. There's someone else I'd like to see today."

* * *

I stood at my front gate. Correction: *Jim's* front gate. Anxiety washed over me. Would he even give me the time of day?

I hoped so. When all was said and done, he'd been throwing smelly socks and verbal abuse my way for close to a decade and, oddball beast that he was, I missed him.

But it wasn't just a matter of getting past an argument. The day I'd left, he'd all but said he was in love with me, and now here I was, back on his doorstep. Not for love: for friendship. Would we be able to bridge that?

I walked up the path and knocked on the door. It swung open a little, so I poked my head through the gap. "Hello?"

Silence.

I pushed the door fully open. "Anyone home? Jim?"

I looked towards the kitchen, took in the piles of dirty dishes littering every surface, the frozen meal cartons, the empty bottles. Man, he'd really outdone himself on the hygiene front. I wandered through to the lounge.

He lay full-length on the couch, earphones in, one hand beating time to whatever-it-was. A half-empty maltezer bag lay in his crotch, his free hand ferreting for the chocolate balls one by one and lobbing them up to his waiting mouth.

For a moment I watched, smiling. Then I leaned into his field of vision. "Hey."

His head jerked back. The maltezer missed his mouth and rolled down his cheek. He grunted, pulled out an earphone, fumbled for the lost chocolate. "You put me off."

"Hi to you, too." I came around the couch and stole a few maltezers.

He brought his knees up in reflexive self-defence. "Hey!"

"Hey, nothing. It's not like I was after *your* balls."

"You know you want to." He gave a Jim-ish hip thrust.

Thank God. He was still weird, but normal-weird rather than can't-talk-to-you-weird.

"You wish." I lay on the floor next to the couch and arced a maltezer. It sailed through the air towards my open mouth with Serena Williams precision. Here it came . . . I snapped my lips closed and almost choked the ball down whole. *Eureka!*

Jubilant, I nevertheless repressed my natural leap-and-shriek response and made do with a demure, "Mmm, yum."

Jim turned to watch. I repeated my performance then waggled my eyebrows at him.

"You've been practising," he accused me.

"No. Sheer talent." I did it again.

He sat up, catching the bag of maltezers just as it upended, and stuffed a handful of chocolates in his mouth.

"What's for lunch, BJ?" He chewed as he spoke, his mouth Mississippi-wide.

I smiled. The nickname didn't annoy me anymore. In fact, I quite liked it. "Whatever you make."

"Maltezers, then." He tipped his head and opened his mouth, like a baby bird demanding food, then emptied the bag into his mouth.

"Got a room for rent?"

"Who'th ngookin'?" he mumbled as he chewed.

"Me. I'm shifting back to London."

He waved a vague hand. "Room'th upthtairth. Firtht on the right."

"You didn't rent my room, then?"

He burped and shrugged. "Too much like hard work. Besides . . ." He paused to pick his teeth. "I knew you'd be back. You miss me."

"Yeah, right." I grinned, tossed a maltezer at him.

He caught it in his mouth. "See? You gave me your last maltezer. That's love."

* * *

Liz dusted off the bottle. "I knew there was another one in here somewhere." She popped the cork and sniffed. "Mmm, shiraz."

She leaned over and refilled my wine-glass.

"Stop!" I cried, too late. "That was white."

"Oh." She looked at the bottle in her hand, then at my glass. Shrugged. "Guess it's rosé now."

I giggled. "I like rosé."

"You like wine." She flopped back down at the other end of the couch. "I still can't believe Jim never rented your room."

"Me neither. Lucky, eh."

"Or unlucky. Depends which way you look at it." She leaned

forward. "Cheers."

We clinked glasses.

"He's not that bad," I said. "You just don't understand him."

"I bet he turned your room into a shrine. Lit candles, sprayed your perfume, pinned up your panties. Did you look in the wardrobe? That's where they usually do it."

I wrinkled my nose at her. "He's weird, but he's not psycho. I'll have you know all my panties are accounted for."

"Okay, maybe not the panties. But he definitely couldn't bear renting your room out."

"Couldn't be bothered, more like."

She held up her glass, inspecting the wine as if she'd spotted a dead bug in there. "No. He loves you."

"Only 'cause I do his dishes."

She sipped her wine, looked smug.

"Liz, this is Jim we're talking about. He's about as in love with me as . . . as . . ."

"As Matt?"

I glared at her. "Actually, yes."

I shifted my gaze to the couch fabric. Stared at it, in all its threadbare 70's glory. Drank some wine. Shot her a festering look. She pretended not to notice.

"You just couldn't help yourself, could you?" I grumbled.

"Guess not. Did you call him?"

I twisted my lips, shook my head.

"You're such an idiot, Becs."

"Probably. But I've been waiting until I was back in town. I can't just ring him. I need to see him for this."

"So you're going to visit him this weekend?"

"I won't have time."

"You'll never have time." She exhaled. "Whatever. Don't call him. It's your life."

"Ooh, the old reverse psychology trick."

She grinned. "Too obvious?"

"Mm-hmm."

"Worth a shot."

I stretched out, wiggling my toes, "I'm over him, Liz. Time you did

306

the same."

She looked sceptical.

"No, really. I've done heaps of thinking these past few months. Yes, I want to talk to him, and I will, but only so I can move on." I sipped at my faux-rosé, grimaced. "I've worked out what I want, and Matt's not it. Sorry. I'm not chasing a guy who doesn't want me enough to make an effort. Life's too short."

"You've said that before."

"I know. But it's different now. I've worked out I'm an okay person."

Liz looked at me with affection. "Very okay."

"And you know what? I'd rather be happy on my own than unhappy with a jerk."

Her expression changed. "You really mean it, don't you?"

"Yep, I do." Because this time it was my life, my decisions, my terms. Look out, London, I was back. Standing tall, feeling strong.

CHAPTER FORTY-TWO

I rang Dani's doorbell then stepped back to wait.

This felt so wrong. In the past I'd have just walked in, or used my key. I couldn't remember ever standing on her doorstep, waiting like a stranger.

I shuffled my feet, nervous. It was one thing to have a quick phone conversation, quite another to meet face-to-face. Still, she'd asked me to be chief bridesmaid, so hopefully she wouldn't toss me out on my ear.

The door opened and there stood Hugh Jackman's twin, wearing nothing but a hand towel.

I blinked, blushed. "Oh, I, uh . . ."

His eyes crinkled at the corners. "You must be Becky."

Ooh! Hugh Jackman with a foreign accent!

"Dani told me all about you," he added.

"Oh, I . . ." What had she told him? That I'd slept with her lover? That he should keep a firm grip on the hand towel? I kept my gaze strictly above-waist. "You're Sebi, right?"

"I am." He inclined his head, then stepped back. "Please. *Entrez.* Dani's in the bedroom."

No doubt. I glanced at his towel. "Is she decent?"

"Maybe." He grinned, shrugged. "No matter. She's very happy to see you."

I stepped into the hallway, taking care not to brush against him. Heaven only knew what was holding that towel in place, and I didn't want to be the reason it fell.

"Danielle," he called. She hated her full name, hadn't used it for years, but Sebi made it sound so god-damn sexy I suddenly had name envy. 'Rebecca' sounded prudish, and as for 'Becky' . . . whatever the accent, it was just plain old 'Becky'.

I followed him into the living room.

"Can I get you a drink?" His accent made it sound as if he'd just suggested a hot tub experience. "Coffee, tea, something stronger?"

"I'd love a coffee, thanks." Although I might have to resort to something stronger if he didn't hurry up and get dressed.

I dragged my eyes away and made a beeline for the photos on the sideboard, giving them my full attention. Best I remember I was here to check Sebi's credentials—and not just the ones beneath that towel.

"Becs!"

I turned and there was Dani, framed in the doorway, looking all sultry and Playgirl-of-the-week in a skimpy white silk kimono.

She skipped across the room and hugged me.

"You're here! Perfect." She grabbed my hand and pulled me towards the door. "I need your help." And, to Sebi, "Espresso for me, cappuccino for Becs. Be a love and bring them upstairs?"

He gave her a low, exaggerated bow and I watched, fascinated, as the hand towel somehow stayed there.

"Anything for you, *Chérie*."

She blew him a kiss. "Make sure you knock first."

We climbed the wide, marbled staircase and I marvelled, as always, at the contrast between my slovenly flat and my sister's white-walled, white-floored, minimalist upper-class apartment. How did she afford it?

"You didn't tell me he was *French*," I stage-whispered.

"Oh, yes, he's *all* French." Her voice was dreamy. "And everything you've heard about Frenchmen in bed? It's true."

"I thought you said Italians were the best lovers."

She flashed me the dirtiest grin. "I changed my mind." Then, as we reached her room, "Quick, shut the door."

I closed it behind me. "Why so secret squirrel?"

She flung open the doors to her walk-in, careful-or-you-might-get-lost-in-here robe.

"It's my wedding dress." She sighed. "I think it's all wrong."

"Why?"

"I thought it looked good in the shop, but now . . ." She disappeared and started rustling around. "I'm pretty sure it makes me look like a giant puffball." She reappeared, holding the dress against her. "What do you think?"

"No idea. Try it on and I'll tell you."

"Promise you'll be honest?"

"Brutal." I bared my teeth at her.

She bit her lip, looking so miserable with uncertainty I felt like a bitch.

"Aw, come on, Dan. You know I don't mean it." I crossed the room and hugged her. "I'll tell you the truth, okay? That's what you want, isn't it?"

She nodded.

"Go on, then." I gave her a gentle nudge. "Try it on."

"Okay. Back in a sec." She returned to the wardrobe.

I lay on her king-sized, four-poster, over-pillowed bed and watched shadows flicker across the ceiling. "Tell me about Sebi. Where did you meet him?"

"At the pub. Rossco introduced us."

"Really?" I leaned up on my elbows. Rossco, the hot young bartender, had been chatting Dani up for months. "What did Rossco think about you and Sebi getting together?"

She poked her head out. "I didn't ask. Why would I?"

I laughed. "Oh, come *on*, Dan!"

She disappeared back amongst her clothes. "Rossco's a bit of fun, that's all. But Sebi? He's a keeper. He's delicious. I couldn't let him get away, could I?"

Hell, no. Dani never let a man get away. She just discarded them when it suited. Charlie had been her notable exception.

And the less I thought about that the better. Apparently we'd all moved on from there.

"How long have you known him?" I asked, hoping I didn't sound too interrogator-ish.

"A couple of months. The best two months ever," she added.

Given what I'd seen of him so far, I didn't doubt it. But anyone could be Prince Charming for a couple of months.

"Dan, isn't this all happening very, very fast?"

"Whirlwind," she agreed from the depths of her wardrobe. "But it feels so right."

"You're sure?"

"Absolutely."

"You're sure you're sure?" Everything else aside, she was still my kid sister.

Dani re-emerged and took both my hands in hers. Gave me a gentle, unhurried, at-peace smile. A smile that had me thinking maybe she'd been cloned, except they'd wired in someone else's personality.

"Becs, I have never been so sure about anything in my life. I promise. Two months or two years, it wouldn't make any difference. I know him inside out. He's the one."

Hearing these words coming from Dani's mouth seemed all wrong. It was unnerving. But if she was so utterly sure, then that was that. I'd asked the question and it was all I could do.

Besides, maybe she was right. Maybe he really was absolutely perfect for her. And if looks were anything to go by . . .

"What does he do?" I asked.

She giggled. "Plays golf, mostly."

"Quite rich, then?"

"Stinking. His grandfather set up the *Empire* hotel chain."

"Nice."

How did Dani do it? She was about to marry the gorgeous Frenchman with the sexy accent, have mindblowing sex all day, wine and dine at the best restaurants all night, and live happily ever after. While I . . . I was going back to my grotty wee flat, with nothing to look forward to except Old Maid-dom, Friday night curries, and a close relationship with my cat.

She emerged from the wardrobe wearing her wedding gown. My breath caught.

"Dan, it's gorgeous," I breathed.

She stood before me in a floor-length figure-hugging raw silk creation, stunning in its simplicity. No big frills, no wads of fabric, no heavy embroidery or sequin clusters or lacy whatevers. But, off-the-shoulder and low-backed, it screamed elegance.

"Really?" She did a slow twirl.

"Absolutely. It's . . . I can't even find the words. Dan, why on earth did you think puff-ball? It's not even close."

She bit her lip. "I don't know. It's white."

"Cream."

"And bride-y."

"You're a bride!"

She looked at herself in the mirror. "I—I'm just not sure."

"What do you want? You're not a frills girl. Lace, maybe? A different colour?"

"I don't know." More lip biting.

"Dan, this is so unlike you." I came to stand beside her. "Where's your confidence? Look, hon, it's made now, so how about you just go with it? Personally, I think you've chosen brilliantly. It's gorgeous. Classy and sexy and unique and absolutely showstoppingly perfect."

She turned and looked over her shoulder at herself, then turned back to the front and met my eyes in the mirror. "You think?"

I smiled, nodded. "Yes."

She grabbed my hands, squeezing them tight. "Becs, can you believe it? I'm getting *married*!"

I returned the squeeze and grinned. "Yeah. My little sister, married."

"Here. Try this on." She returned to the wardrobe and came back holding a wide, flat cardboard box. "I think it'll look good on you."

"My dress?"

She nodded. I took the box from her, peeled back the layers of tissue and lifted out my dress. "Wow. Gorgeous colour."

"Champagne. Subtle but sexy."

I held it against me. "Well?"

Head to one side, she nodded and smiled. "The colour's perfect for you. Brings out the highlights in your hair. I guessed the size but you've lost a few pounds, I think." She waved a dismissive hand. "No matter. They can alter it. Come on! Try it on."

I stripped down to my underwear, then carefully stepped into the dress. I loved the feel of the raw silk against my skin. But this would never suit me. It was a knee-length version of the wedding dress, and I had way more meat on my bones than Dani.

"Who are you bringing to the wedding?" she asked.

"Oh—uh, not sure."

"Are you seeing anyone?" She zipped me up then stepped back, waiting for me to turn around.

I shook my head, pretending to fuss with the neckline.

"You could bring Charlie."

I swung round, face flaming. Then saw the laughter in her eyes.

"Jeez," I muttered. "For a minute I thought you meant it."

"Anyway, you'll have to let me know so I can finalise the table settings."

What about Jim? Yes. He'd partner me.

But then he'd stand up in the middle of the service and announce why she shouldn't be getting married. Or he'd sing slash-your-wrists heartbreak songs all night until I took to him with a dessert spoon and pummelled him to death.

"Maybe I'll just come on my own," I said.

She hustled me towards the mirror. "Did I choose well?"

I approached with trepidation. Got ready to smile. However ugly this dress was, however much I hated it, I would hide my disappointment. This wasn't about me. It was Dani's wedding. I'd been playing Ugly Older Sister for years; I could play Ugly Bridesmaid, too.

"Hang on. Don't look yet." Dani fishtailed over to me as fast as her dress allowed. "It's too loose. I'll get it taken in, like this." Standing behind me, she hauled on the back of the dress.

I *eek*ed in surprise, stumbling backwards. She steadied me, her knuckles pushing into my spine, and I looked at my reflection.

My eyes widened. Was that me?

I turned this way and that, not quite believing what I saw. When had my hair gotten so glossy and long? When had my body become so slim, so toned? When had I become the person I'd always wished I could be?

I looked from me to Dani then back again, and began to smile. We looked so alike. Such different colouring, so unmistakeably sisters.

My throat constricted.

"Do you like it?" she asked.

"Oh, Dan, I love it."

She smiled, looking relieved.

"Great." She hesitated. "Becs, thanks so much for being here. I don't know what I'd have done if I couldn't have you as my bridesmaid."

"Who are the others?" I unzipped the dress and let it drop to the floor at my feet.

"Other bridesmaids?" She shook her head. "You're it."

I stared at her. "Really?"

She shrugged.

I couldn't hold back my tears.

"I'm honoured," I whispered, and reached out to give her a hug.

"Me too," she whispered back, then batted me away. "Watch my dress! You'll crease it."

CHAPTER FORTY-THREE

Dad looked at his watch. "Thirty minutes and counting, ladies. Are we ready?"

"No!" Dani wailed. "Not even close!"

She tugged at her dress, stamped her foot. "This isn't sitting right. It doesn't fit."

"It does," I soothed. "Here, let me help." I unzipped her, realigned the side seams, and zipped her back up. "See? Perfect."

She looked at it with suspicion, then sighed. "Thanks."

"George!" Mum honed in on his tie and started fussing. "You can't go out like that."

"What?" He compressed his lips. "It's fine."

"Well, then, I'm embarrassed." She shook her head. "To think I've let you tie your own ties for years and you've been doing *this* to them." She tutted again.

He shot me a long-suffering look.

Dani let out a high-pitched scream.

I swore. Mum shrieked. Dad reared up as if he'd touched electrical wires.

"What?" I demanded.

"What happened?" Mum shrilled, almost as hysterical as Dani.

Dani pointed to her left shoulder. "*That,*" she sobbed. "*That's* what happened."

Mum and I peered at the fabric.

"What?" I asked.

"I don't see anything, darling," said Mum.

"Then look harder," snapped Dani. "It's dirty. *Dirty. Now* what will I do?"

"Lord, give me strength," Dad muttered, running a hand over his face. "I need a drink."

He edged out of the room.

I moved closer and spotted a slight blemish, no larger than a pinhead.

"I think I see it. Just here." I showed Mum.

Mum put on her glasses. "Oh, yes. I see it now." She patted Dani's unblemished shoulder. "Don't worry, dear, nobody will notice. And if they do, they're just being rude. They shouldn't be looking."

"Mum, I'm the bloody bride. Of *course* they'll be looking."

"It's only a spot of make-up," I said. "I'll sponge it out."

"No!" Dani screeched. "Not on raw silk! You'll leave a water-stain."

"O-kaaay," I said, my voice measured. "I'll just blow on it, then, ever so gently. And if that doesn't work—hell, you can always wear jeans."

For a moment she looked outraged. Then worked out I was kidding and giggled. I smiled back at her, gave her arm a squeeze.

"Ten minutes," Dad yelled from the lounge.

"Sorry," she said.

I blew on the blemish. "No worries, Bridezilla."

"Rebecca!" Mum looked horrified.

Dani and I grinned at each other.

"How's that?" I asked, stepping back to check her shoulder.

"Better," she admitted. "Much better. Thanks."

We trooped through to the lounge, and Dad's eyes locked on Dani. He stepped forward with such a look of pride on his face I felt suddenly tearful, overcome with a strange mix of gladness that Dani had given him this moment and wistfulness that I couldn't give it to him.

"Dani. Beautiful girl," he said. "And I'm about to give you away." His eyes narrowed. "He'd better treat you right or he'll have me to answer to."

"And me," added Mum.

We all laughed. Mum was by far the scarier prospect.

"Let's go, then." Dad held the front door open.

I lifted Dani's whisper of a train.

"Mind the step, ladies. That's it." Dad locked the door.

"Stop!" Dani squeaked.

We all stopped.

"What now?" I asked.

Dani swivelled from Mum to Dad to me. Her eyes locked on mine.

"What am I . . ." Her hand went to her face. "I don't think I can do this."

She was just doing this for effect, right?

But imagine if I read her wrong. She'd never speak to me again— *again*.

I played it safe. "Of course you can, Dan." I set down her train and caught her hands in mine. "If you want to, that is. Do you want to marry Sebi?"

She hesitated. Her hands trembled. Oh heck. She really was scared, poor thing. And who wouldn't be? I totally empathised. Marriage was a big step. A huge step. I wasn't sure I could do it.

Yeah, and who was I kidding? If it had been Matt . . .

Stop it! I focused on Dani. "Okay. Different question. Do you want to be with Sebi?"

She nodded emphatically.

"Forever?"

Another nod.

"And you're sure he loves you back?"

A nod, and a glimmer of a smile.

"Have his kids and cook his meals?"

She cocked her head to one side and raised an eyebrow.

I grinned. "Brain working again?"

"Yeah." She exhaled slowly. "Thanks."

"Ready, then?"

"As I'll ever be." She adjusted her dress. "Right, let's do this."

Dad came forward and put an arm around her shoulders. "If it makes you feel any better, love, I'm still not sure I should've married your mother." He smiled.

Dani caught my eye and we both laughed.

I picked up her train. "Um, no, Dad, I don't think that helps her one little bit."

* * *

It felt like a dream. Disjointed fragments that seemingly meant little. Fragments that, by the end of day, would add up to something far more meaningful. Something momentous. My sister would be married.

Fragment one: a short journey by limo. All of us smiling and excited. Yet, hovering between us, a certain tension. Our family unit for the past thirty-odd years about to change forever.

Fragment two: a short walk down the aisle. Me, the not-too-ugly sister, following a few steps behind model-gorgeous Dani, terrified I would ruin her day by tripping and falling face-first in front of their many guests.

Fragment three: a short ceremony. Everything progressing smoothly. No wild interruptions from jilted lovers, no forgotten vows, no missing rings.

Fragment four: "You may kiss the bride." Sebi grinning, stepping closer to Dani. Tilting her chin up with his forefinger, then bringing his lips down to graze hers ever so gently, as if she might crumble at his touch.

Dani made a small sound and reached out for him. He pulled her into his arms and, with serious fan-your-face French lover flair, kissed her. And kissed her. The church erupted in whoops and cheers, and still he kissed her. The priest *ahem*'d. Sebi's left hand wandered down Dani's spine to cup one perfect buttock. I began to feel embarrassed as it all turned mildly pornographic.

Fragment five: a short photo shoot. Champagne flowing, spirits high. Look this way, a little to the left, smile, wonderful, next shot please.

Fragment six: a short series of speeches. Dad, tugging at his collar, out of his comfort zone but determined to do this for his daughter. Sebi, confident and smooth-talking, bringing a blush to Dani's face as he declared his love all over again. Dani, relaxed and happy, thanking guests for attending, her hand never far from Sebi's.

I couldn't take my eyes off my sister. She looked beautiful. No, not beautiful—she'd always been that. Today she was more than beautiful. It was as if she'd finally found herself and, with that discovery, every worry she'd ever had simply disappeared. She looked radiant.

The M.C. announced the wedding dance, and Sebi stood, offering Dani his hand. She took it with a smile and they walked onto the dance floor. The opening bars of Joe Cocker's *You Are So Beautiful* played and Sebi turned, pulling Dani close. She reached up to whisper in his ear. He smiled at whatever she'd said then kissed her nose. She rested her head against his chest and for a moment they just stood there, motionless. A contented smile played around her lips. She seemed different around him. Softer. More feminine. It suited her.

They danced as one, so engrossed in each other the rest of us may as well not have existed. They looked perfect together, complete.

This hasty, hasty marriage was built on rock-solid love.

I dabbed at my eyes. To think I'd almost missed being a part of this ultra-important day in her life. And over a man, for goodness sake. No man should ever come between sisters.

Or perfectly happy couples.

My throat felt raw. What I would've given to have had all this with Matt.

And enough already. His loss.

But mine, too. Which was why I would ring him. Soon.

I moved to the Best Man's side. "Come on. Our turn, now," I said, and dragged him onto the dance floor.

* * *

". . . And don't forget to water the yukka," said Dani.

"The yukka? Dan, hang up. Have sex. Have a honeymoon. Fuck the yukka."

She laughed. "Okay, I'm gone. Thanks, Becs. Wish you were here."

"No you don't."

"*Au revoir.*" She ended the call and I smiled. How long before Dani's every other word was French?

A fresh flurry of nerves stole my breath and I gazed around the bustling café, hand to throat. Was he here yet?

No. Good. I wasn't ready. I needed to breathe. Feel calm. Be strong.

I wiped clammy hands down my jeans. Inhaled long. Exhaled hard.

Oh, come on. Pull yourself together, girl.

I watched a couple loving it up a few tables away. What if he didn't show? What if he still thought I wasn't worth it?

I bit my lip, fiddled with a loose thread on my jacket.

Well, he might. And in the end, if that was his choice, then that was his right. Yes, it would hurt to know he couldn't even be bothered talking to me, but at least I'd know.

I'd rung him, and I was here, and that was the important thing.

My phone rang and my heart shunted downwards. I checked the caller. Liz. My heart limped back to its rightful place.

"Hi, Becs. What are you up to?"

"Nothing much."

I'd tell her later. I didn't want her *there-there*-ing me right now. She'd have me in tears and no way would I let Matt see me like that. "You?"

"I'm flying to the States. My aunt's died."

"Oh, hon, I'm so sorry."

"It's okay." Liz's tone was brusque. "I haven't seen her in years. We weren't that close."

"Is this the one you stayed with for a bit?"

"Yes. I wouldn't bother making the trip, but her lawyer rang and . . ." She paused, sighed. "Apparently Elsie left me her entire estate."

I sat up straighter. "Really?"

"Yeah." She sounded as excited as Eeyore. "From what I remember, it's mostly landfill. She's basically picked me as her cleaning lady."

"Oh."

It didn't sound exactly happy families, but whose ever was? Liz didn't really speak about hers. She obviously had her reasons so I'd never pushed her on it. Now I wished I knew more.

"Are you sure you want to fly all that way, then?" I checked my watch. Still no Matt. He must've got cold feet. Fine. Coffee for one, then. I stood and made my way to the counter.

"Well," she said, "I need a couple of weeks off now I've got through the restructure work, so it may as well be there as anywhere."

Cleaning lady for a dead person, or soaking up the sun in the Mediterranean? It was a no-brainer—unless Liz wasn't telling me everything. Which, knowing Liz, was highly likely.

"It doesn't sound like much of a holiday." I joined the back of the queue, shivering as, behind me, the café door opened.

"Duty calls and all that."

Duty? She didn't even like the woman but still felt a duty to her? Now I *really* wanted to know more.

I shivered again, turned to close the door. "Liz, there's nothing wrong with telling the lawyer to—"

The air whooshed out of my lungs. The world rocked beneath my feet. There, in the doorway, stood Matt.

CHAPTER FORTY-FOUR

Our eyes collided, jarred, held.

The sounds of the café receded until it was just the two of us.

Time slowed. The silence yawned between us. Palpable. Deafening.

Small details caught my attention. The stitching on his jeans . . . a miniscule rip in his bag . . . the grey-black smudges under his eyes . . . the two-day stubble, several shades darker than his hair.

"Becs," Liz prompted. "Are you there?"

I started, realised I still held the phone to my ear.

"Hello? Becs?"

I blinked, forced myself to turn away.

"I'll call you back," I said. Flicked the phone closed.

Like iron filings to a magnet, my gaze swung back to Matt. He stepped forward and the door swung to behind him. His eyes, dark and brooding, held mine. I felt naked. Vulnerable.

I tried to speak but no words emerged. Something to do with my heart relocating up near my tonsils. I swallowed, cleared my throat, tried again. "Matt."

"Becky."

The sound of my name on his lips turned my knees to jelly.

"Hi." I felt light-headed.

"You're back." His tone sounded—different. Un-Matt-like.

"Yes. My sister just got married."

"Ah." He paused, looked past me. "It's busy here."

At his words, the café returned to life. I looked around and all I could see was people, people everywhere. It felt noisy and crowded and far too intrusive for our first post-Us meeting.

"Yes. Too busy. I was just leaving," I said, then felt like a complete idiot. I wasn't leaving. I'd arranged to meet him here. My bag and jacket were still at the table.

He cleared his throat. "Sorry I'm late. My meeting went over time."

I nodded.

"Shall we go somewhere quieter?" he asked.

"Sure." I scooted back, collected my things, and met him at the door.

He held it open for me and I walked through, careful not to touch him on the way.

We loitered on the path outside.

"Are you in town long?" he asked.

"I've just moved back."

He nodded.

Silence.

I shuffled my feet. "Where do you want to go?"

He watched me intently. Frog-watching-a-fly intently.

Finally, when the silence threatened to kill, he said, "You're a hard woman to track down, Becky."

I hugged my jacket to my chest. "Am I?"

I guess that was what happened when you left everything behind, threw away your mobile and started over.

He'd tried to track me down?

Quickly, before I could chicken out, said, "Let's go back to my place."

His eyebrow quirked up just the way I remembered it. Humorous. Sexy.

Fuck.

"It's close, that's all. Handy. In Clapham. Well, it's my sister's place, actually. I'm house-sitting while she's away. It won't take long to get there." Was I prattling? It sounded like prattling to me.

His mouth twisted. "Well . . ."

He glanced at his watch, and my stomach clenched. Don't leave, don't slot me back into your past. Not yet. I needed to truly move on, and I could only do that if we talked.

"Coffee and a cooked breakfast?" I suggested. "Brunch? Whatever?"

What was I doing? Offering to cook for Matt? The very man I'd abandoned my whole life to avoid? Oh God, commit me now. I opened my mouth to un-invite him, but he'd already started speaking.

"I guess I could manage a couple of hours. My next lecture's at midday."

Damn. Now I couldn't even renege.

"Great." I arranged my face into a smile, doing a quick mental calculation. He'd only be able to stay an hour-and-a-half, tops. I could manage that. Hell, if *he* didn't leave *I* could leave. "How does bacon and eggs sound?"

"Sounds a lot better than my packed lunch." He grinned. "I'd do anything for a good fry-up."

And best I didn't go there.

"Your hair's longer." His eyes lingered and my scalp tingled as if it had been his fingers.

"Yeah? I—I guess I haven't had it cut for a while." Or coloured. Or straightened.

"I like it."

I felt hot. Heatwave hot. Not that I cared what he thought about my hair. *I* liked it, and that was what mattered.

Side by side we headed for the underground.

"Did you have a good Christmas?" he asked.

"Oh, it was fab! I'd just arrived in Edinburgh so it was really exciting," I gabbled, "catching up with friends and family and eating all that yummy food and—well, you know. Busy busy. I love Christmas." I felt deflated, like a used, abandoned balloon. "How was yours?"

"Pretty quiet. It was just Stef and me." He shrugged. "Truthfully, I wasn't in the mood."

"Oh." I fell silent, wishing I hadn't lied. Then, "How's Stef doing?"

"Okay. He's still frustrated, but a bit less angry these days. He's getting on with it."

Matt glanced down at me. "How's your grandmother? I heard she was unwell."

Crap. "Oh, she—uh, she's not so good. Actually . . . she passed away." Double crap.

"I'm sorry. I didn't realise. You were looking after her, weren't you?"

I didn't want to lie. I *so* didn't want to lie. Especially not to Matt. But what could I say? He waited. I felt myself redden. It started at my neck and crept all the way up my face and into my scalp until I was one big head-and-shoulders blush. Hook me up and I'd light up London.

"Um." I cleared my throat. "Look, I'm not quite sure how to say this, so I'm just going to say it." I ducked my head and muttered, "Grandma died five years ago. I used her as an excuse to leave."

Matt said nothing. I shot him a quick glance and, dammit, his lips were twitching. He thought it was *funny*, the bastard.

Which, I suppose, it was—if you weren't me. I took a deep breath. "So now you know my dirty little secret. And you're allowed to cancel breakfast if you want. Here's the train." I moved closer, waited for the doors to open, and got on.

He stood in the doorway. We eyed each other like territorial cats. The doors started to close, touched him, reopened. Warning bells sounded. I bit my lip. Come on, *move*!

"Are your bacon and eggs real?" he asked.

I hesitated, nodded.

"Then I'm not cancelling anything." His smile was the full, I-really-mean-it variety, and my heart flip-flopped, a landed fish in its death throes.

I returned his smile and, damn-and-blast, it felt so good standing next to him and just *being*.

We didn't try to talk over the clattering din of wheels on tracks, but every time we rounded a bend, every time our bodies brushed, every time our eyes met, my pulse leapt. By the time we reached Clapham Common I was in such a state of heightened awareness I could barely breathe.

"This is our stop." I bolted off the train as soon as the doors opened.

Matt followed at a more leisurely pace and we made our way back up to daylight.

"Have you found work?" he asked. "I can probably get you some casual lecturing if you want."

"Thanks, but no. I've got a job."

"Oh? Where are you?"

"All over. I'm a window cleaner."

He blinked. "Oh. That's . . . different."

I smiled. "Actually, I love it. I do the high-rise work."

His eyebrows shot up. "What—as in mid-air?"

My smile broadened. "Yep."

"Rather you than me. Though I suppose claustrophobia wouldn't be a problem up there." He gave a lopsided grin, then shook his head.

"How'd you get into that?"

I laughed. "By mistake, but it's a lot of fun. And now I'm back in London I've found work really quickly, thanks to Scott."

"Good for you." He hesitated. "Scott?"

"My boss in Edinburgh."

"Ah."

We turned into Dani's street.

"Almost there," I said.

As if on signal, our conversation dried up. Nothing had changed, but everything had changed. We didn't look at each other. The silence became awkward. I felt nervous. Oh, please-please-*please* let this go well. I needed my heart back.

"This is it." I unlocked the door and ushered him in. "Make yourself at home."

CHAPTER FORTY-FIVE

Matt's gaze flickered over Dani's artfully-placed coffee table reading, her gold-crested chaise longue, the six-foot yukka in the corner. "Nice place."

I walked through to the kitchen. "Yeah. Not that she's ever home to enjoy it." I pulled out the bacon and started removing excess fat. "Maybe that'll change now she's married. How do you have your eggs?"

He stood in the doorway, watching. "Sunny side up, thanks."

"Two?"

"Great." He came into the kitchen. "I'll put the kettle on."

"Cups are in the far cupboard." I pointed. "Tea, coffee, sugar over here. Coffee for me, please. White—"

"No sugar," he finished. "I remember."

He remembered? I smiled to myself. He remembered.

Not that I was reading anything into that. He simply had a good memory. Just like I could remember he took his coffee black, strong, and really, really hot. "Want some music? Help yourself. Sound system's in the living room."

My mobile phone pealed. I reached for it. "Hello?"

With my other hand I threw hash browns on a tray and put them in the oven.

"Hi," said Liz. "Why'd you hang up in such a hurry?"

I turned away from Matt, lowered my voice. "Someone turned up. I had to go."

"Who? Must've been important."

"Um . . ." I glanced over my shoulder at Matt, who caught my eye and smiled, then held up a CD, eyebrows raised in query. I shrugged—whatever. Turned away. "Just, er, you know . . ."

"No way. Not Matt?"

"Yes," I said faintly.

She screamed.

I held the phone closer to my ear. "Sssh!"

"He's still there?"

"Er . . . yes."

Another scream.

"We're just chatting, Liz. No big deal."

Behind me, Matt came into the kitchen. I turned and mouthed 'Sorry' to him. "Hey, I'll call you later, okay?"

"You'd better. I want to know *everything*."

"Bye."

"Love you!" she sang.

"Love you too." I ended the call.

He looked up from his coffee-making with a fading-to-zero smile. Oh dear. And what should I take that to mean? He wished he'd never come round? He remembered everything he despised about me?

I tried to smile back but it felt like my skin might split with the strain. After all these months I finally had Matt right here, close enough to touch, reminding me of us, of not-us, of everything I'd lost. And, somehow, I had to get past the look he'd just sent me and find a way to broach the Charlie/Dublin disaster with him. Because, although we weren't destined to be together, Matt not hating me would be a not-bad consolation prize.

He handed me a mug. "White, no sugar."

I took it, careful our fingers didn't touch. "Thanks."

He leaned back against the bench. The silence lengthened. I glanced his way. He scowled into his coffee. What? Were the coffee beans old? I picked up my mug and took an experimental sip. No, hot as hell but tasted fine.

Unsure what to do with his mood-swing, I ignored it. "How many slices of bacon do you want?"

I pulled out a frying pan, turned on the gas.

He took his time answering. So long, in fact, that I began to repeat the question.

"As many as I'm allowed," he said. Then, "Who was that?"

"The CD?" I frowned. "I'm not—"

His scowl deepened. "I mean the bloody phone and you know it."

I took a deep, staying-calm breath. Exactly who did he think I'd— Oh, for crying out loud, was he still festering over Dublin? Did he think I'd been speaking to Charlie?

Stupid ass. Well, if that's what he still believed, he could wallow in it a bit longer.

"Just a friend." I kept my tone light, offloading all the bacon into the pan. It spat at me and I leapt back, swearing under my breath.

"Just a friend," he repeated. The air bristled with tension.

I narrowed my eyes. "Yes, that's right. A friend. I do have a couple, you know."

"Anyone I know?"

"How do you like your bacon?"

He frowned, then pushed himself upright and folded his arms. "Crispy. And honest."

What the hell? Here I was, cooking breakfast for the man who'd dumped me, made a public laughing stock of me, and broken my heart. And—what? He was accusing me of lying? I eyed the rubbish bin.

No, I'd invited him here for a reason, and binning his food wouldn't help. It'd do the opposite: he'd be gone. Like Elvis. And I'd be left alone singing *Heartbreak Hotel*.

Fine. I'd give him his sodding breakfast. Then I'd take my god-damn hell-fired heart and head for the freaking hills. Possessive bastard. I cracked the eggs with venom and threw them in the pan.

Matt turned and took two plates from the cupboard, placing them on the bench beside me.

"Another *old school friend?*" he asked, his voice cool.

"College, actually. Not that it's any business of yours." I flipped the bacon, checked the hash browns, watched the eggs. Grand finale'd it all onto the plates and shoved one his way.

"Thanks." He picked up his plate and stood looking down at me. "Why all the secrecy?"

"Why all the third degree?" I fired back.

A nerve staccatoed at his jawline. "Just making conversation."

I grabbed my plate and marched out of the kitchen. "The hell you were."

He followed me. "I take it you're still with . . ." He paused. "What's-his-name?"

I rounded on him. "What—you want a blow-by-blow of my life since you ditched me?"

"No! I want—" He stopped. "Becky, we need to talk."

"We needed to talk months ago."

"Then why," he ground out, "did you disappear and go

incommunicado?"

Oh, right. This was my fault. I dropped my plate abruptly onto the table. The bacon bounced. Steady, Becs, steady.

Fuck steady. He needed a damn good slapping.

I faced him, hands on hips. "What did you expect, Matt? You'd just dumped me, remember?"

He slammed his own plate down on the breakfast bar. Swung back to me. If he'd been a lion he would've roared.

"And what did you expect of me?" His face reddened. "Goddammit, Becky, some prick had just told me you were sleeping with him."

Four months of hurt mutated into raw anger. And yes, it was childish and wrong and made me look like a whining emotional wreck of a woman, but I couldn't hold it in one second longer.

"How could you? You bastard. You took the word of a complete stranger—a complete stranger so drunk he could barely stand—and you didn't even question it."

My chin trembled but I carried on, because I'd never get another chance to say this. "How do you think that made me feel?"

"I—"

"Do you have any idea? I was in love with you, dammit." Tears fell and I angrily dashed them away. "And then you tell me, in front of a hundred-odd witnesses, that I'm 'not worth it'." I air-scribed vicious little speech marks. "Really, Matt? Really? I'm so 'not worth it' that you wouldn't even ask a question or two? You thought that little of me?"

"No, I just—"

"You just assumed. You assumed I'd been unfaithful because that's what a half-cut stranger told you and, hey, that's just the kind of woman I am, right?" I stalked over to the window, just to put some distance between us, then swung round and glared at him. "Why didn't I stick around? 'Cause you're an asshole, that's why." I turned back to the window. "It just took me a while to work it out."

"You don't mean that."

"Try me." I gazed out at nothing.

"Fine, then. I'm an asshole. Now can I speak?"

I faced him, arms folded. "You said your piece four months ago."

"Oh, for fuck's sake. Are we going to be stuck back there forever? Help me out here, Becs."

"Why should I?"

"Because this is what you wanted!" My sub-conscious screamed. *"Didn't*

329

"Because it's important!" Matt steamed. "Bloody hell! For the past four months I've done nothing but think about what happened that night."

"And I've done nothing but try to forget it."

I looked down at the floor, Dani's perfect white-tiled minimalist fucking floor. She'd be in Barbados by now, gorging herself on sun and sex and Sebi. How had she ended up with such a perfect life?

I raised my head and met his gaze. "You ruined my life that night."

He walked towards me. "I ruined my own as well."

My stomach plummeted. I stared at him. He held my gaze. Dizziness threatened. He stopped in front of me, so close our bodies almost touched. My heart tripped and hurried. I couldn't breathe.

"I fucked up," he said, his eyes searching mine, "and I'm sorry. Really sorry."

My heart may not have understood the danger, but my head sure did. I gave him a stony stare. Found my breath and said, tough as flint, "It's a bit late for sorry," my heart shattering all the while into millions of tiny pieces.

"Jesus Christ, woman, can't you see I'm trying to—" He broke off and raked a hand through his hair.

My breath hitched. "What?"

He swore. And then his arms came around me, crushing me to him, his lips on mine, his hands tangling in my hair.

Even as my lips softened under his, my body moulding against him, my head warned, *Don't let it happen. This mustn't happen.* Because if it happened like it seemed to be happening I might never recover. I pushed against him, but I could feel myself slipping, sinking, drowning in his nearness. Matt. I couldn't fight this. It felt too right.

And, just like that, I was lost all over again.

His smell, his taste, his touch. Lost.

"I love you, Becs."

I stilled. Pulled back slightly so I could see his eyes.

He returned my gaze and the truth blazed between us.

I frowned, trying to make sense of it all. "Then why . . . ? How could you just . . . push me away? Give all that up?"

"I was a fool." He kissed my forehead. "I thought you were playing me, like—"

"But I—"

"Sssh." He touched a finger to my lips. "I need to explain."

He hesitated. "Remember I told you I'd been engaged?"

I nodded.

"Well, it didn't last long. I fell in love, thought she felt the same way, then found her in bed with someone else. I swore I'd never let myself get played like that again. Ever." His face twisted. "So when I saw you with that drunk idiot in Dublin—"

"We weren't—"

"I know." He caressed my face, his fingers tangling in my hair. "I knee-jerked. Sorry."

"Me too."

"I lost you once. I am not"—his grip tightened—"losing you again. I love you."

My world tilted, shifted, settled. I clung to him. We kissed. Heaven on earth. If I died now I'd die happy.

I rested my head on his chest, feeling the strong, solid beat of his heart against my cheek. "I love you, too."

He kissed the top of my head. "I've missed you, Becs. Like air."

I looked up at him. "Matt . . ."

As if I might take flight, his arm tightened around my waist. "Mm-hmm?"

I flattened my hands against his chest. Took a deep breath, drawing strength from him. "I wasn't unfaithful."

"I know." He trailed one finger along my neckline.

"You know that too? Then why the hell did you—"

His finger stilled. "I know *now*. I was too angry back then. Some guy was with my girl; that's all I saw. I wanted to kill the bastard."

"So you dumped me instead." I shook my head. "Nice work, cowboy."

He lowered his head. "Shows how much you addled my brain." His lips found mine and he kissed me slowly, thoroughly, as if it were our first.

I felt a wave of heat. "Mmm, nice work, cowboy."

His hands felt their way inside my top, lifting the fabric with them. Our kiss deepened. He dispensed with my top, gave a satisfied growl. He trailed hot kisses down my neck and, bending his head, moved lower. His tongue licked and probed the edge of my bra, lifting the lace, promising more, sending hot arrows of lust shooting down to my core. I shivered. My hands roamed beneath his T-shirt. God, he was beautiful. I wanted him. Right now.

He whipped off his T-shirt and pulled me close again, his breathing as ragged as mine. Skin whispered against skin. Hands explored. My bra disappeared. Flashpoint.

"Don't forget your lecture," I murmured.

His lips grazed my ear. "Fuck the lecture."

Connect with Maggie

www.maggielepage.com
www.facebook.com/MaggieLePage

Sign up for Maggie's (Infrequent) Newsletters

http://eepurl.com/xNOu5

Also by Maggie Le Page

The Trouble With Dying

When Faith Carson wakes up on a hospital ceiling looking down on her body in a coma, it's a bad start to the week. A very bad start. She has no idea who she is or how she got there or why, and the biggest mystery of all is why she married the schmuck who wants her ventilator switched off.

As if that's not enough Faith has a dead gran haunting her, a young daughter missing her, and one devilishly delicious man making her wish she could have a second chance at life. And maybe she can, if she finds a way back into her body and wakes up by Friday. But if she doesn't, this will be her last bad week—ever.

Nate Sutherland decided long ago he'd settle for friendship if he couldn't have Faith's heart. But now, as she nears death, he's going to have to listen to his feelings in a whole new way—and act. Because if he doesn't, this week will be the worst damn week of his life. He'll lose everything he's ever loved.

Read an excerpt at:
www.maggielepage.com/TTWDexcerpt.html

Connect with Maggie

www.maggielepage.com
www.facebook.com/MaggieLePage